AFTER WINTER, THE SPRING....

Letha parted the curtains and looked out at the lake. Blue-grey ice. The white folds of the slopes around the water. At the far end of the lake, a coil of chimney smoke spoke of the Hunt Ranch house. Her breath frosted on the window. Cold out. Too cold, and high-time there was help for it.

She went to her room and pulled her pajamas off, pulled on the robe, and stepped barefoot out onto the porch. It was darn cold, and it shouldn't be. A coil of smoke down the lake shore told of her neighbor also up, but she ignored it. The Lake held her attention. The raven croaked from the willow tree.

She crossed the gravel to the shore, where clear water overlapped the ice, then looked up at the sky. "Precious Spring," she began, and inhaled the cold air, dropped her robe onto the earth, and stepped forward, naked, so her toes were bathed in cold water.

"Precious Spring, time of life borning. Time of new grass, new calf, new foal of the morning. Time of raven birth and catkin, new growth of hay, time of bonding and mating, new light warms the day." She held still, eyes closed, poised at the lake edge, focused inside herself to feel the answering heat of Spring flow up from the earth, from the lake water hidden under ice. It came, flooding up through her toes, her legs to her hidden core, igniting life, hope, a new year that would lead to fall harvest.

Her body trembled with the heat. Sweat beaded her brow, even as the cold wind surrounded her, even as she knelt to plunge her hands, fingers spread wide, into the water.

Spring, she thought, as the power surged through her, ran out through her fingertips. She opened her eyes and saw the power crackle through the lake ice, heard the grind of deep cracks forming, of ice giving way before the Spring's warmth.

Books By the Author

Romance
Ashes and Light
Shades of Moonlight
Judas Kiss
Second Spring
A Different Nightmusic
Shadow Play
Mutable Things
Surviving Safe Harbor
Coming Down Christmas

Fantasy
***The Cartographer Universe* series:**
The Cartographer's Daughter

Afterburn
Aftershock
Aftermath
Afterimage

Terra Incognita
Terra Infirma
Terra Nueva

SECOND SPRING

KAREN L. ABRAHAMSON

*Dedicated to the wonderful people of Williams Lake, B.C.
and to the real Shelter Lake that will
forever live in my heart.*

Prologue

Shelter Lake, British Columbia
April 12, 1994

Before the sun rose, the pickup trucks rumbled through last year's hay stubble to stop by the unlit bonfire. Shadow figures climbed out of the trucks and the people came together quietly in the dim light amid the frosted Queen Anne's lace of the lake shore.

Once each generation they came to witness the choice of a gift bound to Spring — a sacrifice to bring new life and new sap in the leaves, through the breaking of ice.

In the cold of the lake, Letha resented the fact she was here, shivering, with Kristienne, Sylvia, and five other girls.

"How long will it take, do you think?" Kristienne, one of Letha's best friends, shifted in the knee-deep water so that the lake's surface shattered the reflection of her eleven-year-old face, glazed by dawn's first glow.

"As long as it takes, Mom says." Letha crossed her arms over her body, hating the fact that her mother and Valley tradition had forced her here. It wasn't a choice she would have made, but when had anyone ever listened to her preferences? No one ever listened to what you wanted when you were eleven. So she gave in like always. What she wanted didn't matter. Besides, doing what she was told made life easier for everyone.

But since her granny died, an unspeakable dread had kept her awake at nights with bad dreams of the lake that left her queasy. Standing like this made it worse. She looked at the other girls around her.

Let it be one of them. Don't let her be chosen.

All of her granny's old stories shivered in her, sending nervous energy coursing through her blood and making her stomach churn. The uncertainty of her future chilled her more. Brushing red hair back, she looked defiantly at those on shore, but her teeth were chattering too hard, and they were too far off for her defiance to show.

"It's freezing out here. Your lips are blue as Mom's Saskatoon-berry jam." Kristienne whispered, as she rubbed her palm briskly down Letha's thin, goose-pimpled arm. The blue cotton shifts they all wore were no guard against the chill wind.

They both looked at Sylvia, their third. Grandma Meyers said they were like a three-legged stool, always propping each other up, but Letha wasn't so sure. Her mom was always upset that they got in trouble a lot in school. Mom said she thought Sylvia might be a bad influence. Her granny had just laughed and told her mother they'd get their growth and common sense soon enough. Letha missed Granny.

Sylvia, on the other hand, waited reverent and calm. Her eyes held a firm acceptance, knowledge this was her place and time, even though her skin had gooseflesh, too. All their short lives, Sylvia had waited for the time of the choosing.

"We all knew it would be cold this morning. It's all part of the test. Spring wants to know we're strong enough to be married to him." She smiled a look of knowing.

"*I'm* not marrying anyone." Kristienne's emphatic words sent the water shivering again, and that was just like her. Kristienne got away with saying things like that because her family was 'from away'. Letha sighed, wishing she had the same right. But if she'd said that, her mother would have washed her mouth out with soap — if she'd heard.

"Good. *I* want to be chosen."

"Aren't you special enough? I mean, come on Sylvia, I'd love to be able to talk to my filly or that old barn cat, like you. I'll bet they'd have stories," Kristienne said.

"It's not like that." Sylvia snapped. Then she stopped herself, biting her lip. Sylvia was always the quickest of them to anger and the quickest to smooth it away. Of course, that didn't mean it didn't simmer below the surface. "Sorry. It's just — I've — I've always known that something was out there for me. You know that. Shelter Lake is important, and since Letha's Granny died it's like I feel something waiting out here in the lake — for me."

"It's like — darkness." Letha spoke dreamily and caught her friends' hands, suddenly afraid they'd let her fall into a nightmare. Or they'd vanish.

The dread had been like that — as if she'd be left all alone. Or like one of those horrible dreams where you're standing naked in a crowd and everyone sees. "Grandma always talked about sacrifice and being in prison. I don't want to live my life like that."

The thought of it made her heart pound faster. She thought she might be sick. Kristienne's fingers tightened comfortingly on hers.

"It's not darkness. Or prison," Sylvia lectured. "The lake is good. Can't you feel it? Besides, the animals all depend on this choosing. Just like the people."

Sylvia scanned the shore, the groups of waiting Valley people. "Uncle Joseph says they need our sacrifice for harvest. Without the chosen one, the land can't renew."

Her words sounded like she'd memorized them, but then Sylvia was always studying and always at the top of their class at Shelter Valley's one-room school.

"Then I hope the lake chooses you." Letha felt the lake's darkness stir slowly. "Not me." Not me. Please, not me.

"How can you fear something so beautiful?" Sylvia demanded, motioning around them. The water glistened darkly along the shore, but just beyond where they stood, a thick white layer of ice waited for Spring to come. Overhead the night sky faded toward dawn's pale blue. The morning star glittered at the horizon's edge.

Letha shivered at a sense of pending doom.

"Uncle Joseph says it can't be wrong for the chosen one to bring Spring. Someone has to maintain the Valley's balance. Is *that* wrong?"

Letha rolled her eyes and Sylvia reacted. Her gaze flashed with resentment, quickly hidden. As if Letha had everything — well, at least she had a mom and dad.

"You take belonging for granted. You don't understand how important this is."Sylvia's grimace smoothed away. "Now stop saying things against the ceremony. I don't want to be angry. Letha's Granny said you can't feel anything bad."

She dragged in deep breaths and lifted her chin at the shore.

"The boys are all waiting. There's Tyler. They act cool, and like they don't care what happens to their younger sisters."

"Ty cares about us," Letha said, peering into the predawn to where Ty hunkered next to the unlit bonfire with his friends. She could always pick him out because he was so much taller than the rest. And because, even though he was five years older, he looked at her instead of ignoring her like the other boys always did. Like now. She caught his glance out to the group of girls huddled in the water, and it warmed her a little. Ty was — well — special. A special friend.

"Ty cares about *you*, Letha." Kristienne tightened her hold on Letha's fingers.

"And you. Us."

Kristienne snorted. "He has to care about me. I'm his sister."

"So." Sylvia looked at Letha, pale in the predawn, and fervently hoped to be chosen. It would mean so much to really be part of something great and wonderful like Spring. "They just want to know who's chosen. The boys always like the Consort of Spring. She's the most popular girl. Marry her, and you're almost as important as she is."

"Ty doesn't care about that."

"Maybe." Trying to rid herself of jealousy, Sylvia squeezed Letha's cold hand in hers. "Don't be afraid of the lake, Leth. It's part of us. Part of a plan, and if we're chosen we keep this place whole."

"It might be your plan, but I want out of Shelter Valley. I want to see all those places in the magazine pictures."

Sylvia rolled her eyes. Letha and her darn plans and pictures. She was never happy, even with everything she had. Everyone liked Letha, even the boys, and Ty Hunt especially. Why would she ever want to leave? Sylvia wouldn't.

"It's not my plan. It's something bigger. Can't you feel it? Something wonderful?" Sylvia could. A tremor of energy, like excitement, that ran up her legs from the soft lake mud.

As the sun lifted a burnt edge over the horizon, Letha felt the lake stir — the girls faced each other and joined hands. Wind rippled across the ice-burdened water, and on shore the bonfire flames leapt skyward in ancient greeting.

The eight girls formed a huddled circle, eyes closed.

Dread rising, Letha heard the wind hum.

"I just want to be myself, not the Valley's chosen. I want to be able to choose where I live," she muttered.

"You won't be chosen saying things like that, Letha. Me, Kristienne, the others — the lake will chose one of us. It wants reverence, not distrust and fear."

"Hey! I'm only here because Mom made me come," Kristienne said. "She said we're part of the Valley now." She shrugged. "'sides, you guys were here — and there's hot chocolate after."

Her disbelief in the power of the lake showed in her face. Then water sparked around Kristienne's knees and she jerked and frowned.

"What the heck? The water's glittering. It's circling Sylvia. Look, Letha, see? Around your feet."

Letha opened her tightly clenched eyes. The water glowed, the wind warmed. A tingling power rose through hers legs. It held questions, found answers. She clenched her eyes closed again.

"I want to leave Shelter Lake. Not this, not this, not me." Letha pleaded. "Take Sylvia. She already hears animal thoughts, she's the one who's ready to serve you. I could never serve you properly or bravely like Granny did. It's not me, can never be me."

The power rose like a river flooding her, a wind in her head, a green-gold lightening in her flesh. There was the ache of her father's diabetes. There was awareness of the new-born kit foxes on the shore. She heard Sylvia scream betrayal as the Valley folk sang the sun up into the sky, as the power lifted Letha's hair, became her life blood.

All the Valley's life swelled in her.

And Letha's thin legs gave at the burden she bore.

Chapter 1

Shelter Lake, British Columbia
April, 2007

The Valley, Tyler Hunt mused, was a lot like the Tennessee back-woods. At least, that was what you saw when you first drove in. Small, ramshackle homesteads suggested people minded their own business. And didn't talk. 'Course that hadn't been true when he'd tried hiding in a Tennessee valley.

But this would be different. Here in this place where light glowed distinctively golden, he knew the people kept secrets across generations. Or had.

And it was home, or had been. Question was whether they'd remember Tyler Hunt, the young man who'd left for school and never returned. Ten years away left changes and deep wounds. And anger. He wondered if it were possible to return.

Once he had been part of this landscape as he rode his Quarter Horse through lodgepole pine, along streams, and across beaver dams, up into the folded hills chasing his father's roan cattle. He'd spent hot, dusty days training Hunt Ranch's prized reining and cutting horses.

He rubbed the numb patch on his right leg and the throb in his back, resenting the wound the bullet had left near his spine. At least he was walking and riding again — regardless of the doctor's concerns.

And seeing the Valley before him, with its poplar-edged ice-bound lake, reminded him he was damned lucky he'd survived the hit, and that the FBI had hidden that fact.

Coming here allowed for new beginnings, even a healing. He touched his truck brakes, checking his horse trailer in the side mirrors. He'd stayed in William's Lake last night, even though it was only a two-hour drive and his friend Matt Kelly had readied everything in the Valley. Avoiding the inevitable, Tyler supposed. A coward's avoidance, and he was never a coward. His father, dead now, would have homed in on anything like that as a sign of weakness.

That was one reunion he wasn't sad he'd miss. But then, he'd proved he wasn't weak anymore. All those Bureau years, all those undercover investigations and living on the edge had earned him respect. He'd been looking for the daily rush. 'The game' he had called it, until the last one. Disaster, total disaster, when a stupid phone call had betrayed him to the Russian mob. He'd gone to ground in Tennessee, until they'd somehow tracked him. The hit had almost succeeded and he'd lain hospitalized and dreaming of a golden lit lake. Dreaming of peace…

Abort that thought. Time at the lake was time to heal, and that was all; agents had no peaceful times. His Bureau buddies would clean up the situation and then he'd have his life as an agent back.

The truck neared the lake, which filled the landscape to his right, and he turned onto gravel that fronted the last cabin. The truck rocked, with impatient movements transferred from the oversize horse trailer. Hauberk — demanding to be noticed. Ty grinned. Stallions were up-front about their feelings. He supposed that was why he still rode. Horses were honest. Horses were something to be part of; when you rode, you could be something greater.

He backed the trailer up next to the cabin and stepped out into chill morning wind. Inhaling the sweet scent of ice-melt, Ty realized he'd missed this place.

§

In the light wind off Shelter Lake Kristienne brushed her dark hair back from her eyes as she held the ranch's first colt for Sylvia's examination. The motion, Sylvia knew, was Kristienne's way of hiding her emotion. Given how she clenched her callused hands, how her shoulders stiffened her plaid cowgirl shirt, and how her full lips held a disgusted downturn, she wasn't exactly successful in her attempts.

"I can't believe you'd do that."

"I provided an opportunity. It'll help her, and in the long run she'll only thank me," Sylvia said.

"You trapped her. Letha finally works up the courage, takes a huge chance, tries to finally leave, and you use it to entangle her more. That's some friendship, Sylvia, buying a store and then having her sign papers as co-owner. Knowing you, you guilted her into it, too. You know how responsible she is. She makes a commitment and she always follows through. But then you were counting on that, weren't you? Some friend. How're you goin' t'deal, when she realizes what you've really done?"

Sylvia thought of the visit into town. Letha *had* been excited at her first trip to town since she was eleven — and trusting. In fact, Kristienne had been pretty accurate in her assessment of what Sylvia had done, but darn it all, after all these years Letha was getting too close to working up the courage to leave. Someone had to do *something* to hold on to her. The Valley couldn't chance the alternative. And so she'd done what she had: bought a cabin to transform into a store, and made Letha cosign — responsible for Sylvia's money. Letha wouldn't let her down. Not Letha. It was like overcompensation for her refusal to embrace her Consort duties.

"You've always taken her side in this."

Kristienne scowled, the frown placing hardness around her eyes that made even cowboys wince. "Someone bloody-well has to in this crazy Valley."

Sylvia smoothed her hand down the handsome colt's leg and lifted the dainty hoof. "Letha has to accept her larger responsibility for her place. She might be responsible in other things, but not that. She wants to leave — for good, this time. Surely to goodness you know what that'd bring. The Valley almost died before."

"So the stories say. I don't choose to believe it. Besides, it's still her decision."

"One that's always terrified her. I just took away the terror." Releasing the colt's leg, Sylvia collected her vet gear and turned toward her white "Shelter Valley Veterinary Services" truck. It took all her control not to tell Kristienne what she really thought. Her brown-haired friend could so easily undo Sylvia's resolve to stop swearing. "Your colt's got a bold spirit to nurture. He'll make a good cutting horse. He already hates cattle."

"Don't change the subject, you know this's wrong."

"Letha's not trapped here, it's her place. She needs it. It's different for her," Sylvia said as she hefted her tools into the truck. "You'll see it's all for the best."

"Let her be herself."

Sylvia turned around as a chestnut horse and rider came through the trees.

"Looks like she is. Herself. Don't make this harder, Kristienne." Sylvia pleaded as she glanced at her stubborn friend. "Just let her try it. It'll make her happy, having something of her own to do." Then, raising her voice as Letha approached, "Hey, fine morning, stranger. We were just talking about you and the store."

"Fine morning." Her face flushed by wind, Letha reined in. "I couldn't resist a morning ride. I'll open the store later, okay Sylvia?"

"Whatever you think. You're co-owner. How's it coming?"

"Well, fine, I think. I moved my things in last night."

"Whoa, you're parents are okay? They take the change well?"

"As well as expected, Syl. I came over to borrow your cell phone."

"Help yourself." Sylvia waited until Letha had climbed in the vet truck and turned triumphant to Kristienne. "Real unhappy, I'd say."

Kristienne's glare could peel paint. "She's used to pretending."

After about fifteen minutes, Letha returned. Her eyes shone as she waved a paper at them. A hint of mischief showed in her half-swallowed grin. "That was easier than I thought it'd be. The co-op had some of the supplies, but I'm going to have to get catalogues."

"But the order list, I showed it to you. Right?"

"Yeah… but woman cannot live by bread alone, so I've expanded. Maybe you can come over to the store later. Come see…" She swung up on her mare, smile flashing as she gathered her reins. "Come. Okay?"

"She seems happy," Sylvia drawled as she and Kristienne watched Letha leave for the trail by the lake. "Happy to plan. Yup, she's definitely been trapped. Written all over her."

"She's expanded." Kristienne tried to hide her satisfaction. With Letha, there was no telling what expanded might mean.

Late that morning, excited and feeling proprietary pleasure and fear, Letha greeted their trucks. The cabin-cum-store stood by itself at one end of the lake. Grey-weathered logs had settled comfortably onto an earthen foundation. It had a pleasant porch that faced the lake and a red-painted door beckoned welcome. Behind the cabin stood a falling-down corral and small barn. A pair of chairs and small table stood on the porch.

"So what do you think?" Letha asked. "I happened to see Johnny Warner when I was home collecting my stuff. Um, what's your opinion, Kristienne? I know you have different taste than Sylvia, so you'd know if it'll suit the summer people's tastes."

"Sure." Slowly Kristienne did a 360 scan of the yard. "Not what you'd expect." She returned Letha's gaze, then stepped onto the newly-swept porch.

The cabin's yard was populated with strange metal sculptures and statues, rattling whirligigs, and delicate carvings of wind-weathered wood. A four-foot wide, spider-fine spirit catcher that Letha'd had in her room for years hung at one side of the front porch, and held twists of sweet grass and eagle feather tassels. Chunky blue pottery and blue glass bottles lined the porch and window ledges in casual display.

By the door, etched into a slab of wood, were 'Letha's Store and Artwork'. A huge black raven Letha had always called Roscoe sat on the eaves, tugging at the leather cord that held the spirit catcher.

"Darn it, Roscoe, would you quit that!" Letha waved at the bird that just croaked and hopped back. She turned back to Sylvia. "You know, I still don't feel comfortable calling it my store. It should be "Sylvia's Store and Artwork.""

Sylvia pursed her lips. Her gaze was tight as it swung around the yard, but she smiled as she looked back at Letha. "We agreed the store was yours to run. You run it; your name goes on the sign."

The interior wood floors gleamed under a small braided rug, strong coffee scent wafted outside, and a comfortable chair had been positioned near a small display of paperback books. Behind a small counter waited the single bedroom and bathroom of the place.

Sylvia slowly turned, taking in the room as if she couldn't believe her eyes, as Letha stood hands clasped and swallowing a smile.

"I started thinking about who I wanted to serve here. I know the Valley people buy supplies weekly in town, but the newcomers never think of the distance to stores. So they'll need milk and butter, but there's more. The newcomers and tourists have money, right? And they're looking for something unique, like a trophy to remember this place by. Then I ran into Johnny and remembered his carving. Then I asked if he wanted to help, 'cause some of his art styles go back generations, but he has never had the chance to show it. It might even bring more people to the Valley—"

Letha's excitement faded when Sylvia's face stiffened. "You're trying to bring more people here."

"Sure. Business. A business succeeds on planning how to grow." She looked at her partner, then at Kristienne's face, and all the blood seemed to depart Letha's head.

Lips taut, Sylvia scanned the room, picked up a book. As she scanned the title, her frown deepened. "*Backpacking in Central Asia*, Letha?" she questioned, then put the book down. "If this was what I'd envisioned, I'd have arranged for an artist to manage the store. The locals won't like it, and they're the economic base here. I'm really not sure, Letha."

"What d'you think?" Letha, straining not to appear stubborn, turned to Kristienne. "I really thought I'd done this right. I worked all night," she said as she clenched her fists at her sides. "If I can't leave, I want the world to come here."

"*I* like it, but my opinion doesn't count. But if Sylvia's got her knickers in a roper's twist about your store, think how the Valley folk'll react."

§

Letha didn't rightly care what the Valley folk thought, but silence ticked around her when she was alone again. When the delivery hadn't arrived by two o'clock, she was going stir-crazy waiting. Every time a truck slowed outside, she ran to the door. When she went outside barefoot for a walk, figuring that even time by the lake was better than her anxiousness, she let the land and water's soothing convince her Kristienne erred.

Power whispered in the soil, revealing it was almost time for this year's ceremony, for breaking ice, for spring. Her fingertips tingled slightly, her body ached deeply as she scanned the poplar and the willow shoots along the lake for hints of the coming that would satisfy what she felt. Hints of change ran through the air. Something was coming, bringing ill-ease, like crows in storm. It had troubled her dreams.

Nothing was there, as usual. Power existed only in the lake. No matter that Sylvia had said Letha's freedom could only be bought if she found an alternative way to consecrate the Spring. The lake knew she'd tried.

She stopped in a cool patch of snow under the eaves of a poplar grove, leaves still furled tightly closed, and listened to the wind. Not Spring, not yet. She wasn't going to allow it to come, any more than she was going to do Sylvia's bidding about the store.

"Right. I'm right." Rebelliously, she turned back to the cabin and stopped dead.

'Wild' was Ty's first thought of her. Wild red curls around a porcelain, heart-shaped face, and a shirt-jacket that kept slipping off her shoulder. Her dark eyes made him think of taming fearful horses, and his hand half-rose in gentling response.

"Sorry about startling you, but I was just exploring the lake shore."

"Exploring's allowed. And I don't startle."

"A nice talent. Good. All the whirring oddities drew me here. I'm Ty. Tyler Hunt."

"I know. Letha." She looked past him, fighting to calm herself. She knew Ty Hunt's regular features from her dreams. He'd been the one teen-aged boy she'd been drawn to back then. And the one who'd refused the sexual advances of a confused thirteen-year-old who'd been trying to gain her freedom.

Older now, a slight hint of old pain edged his firm lips. Lines, collected during ten years away, radiated from calm brown eyes. The nose, not quite straight, from a boyhood brawl that, Letha recalled, ruined a long-time friendship. Brown hair, a little curly, that hung a little too long for Valley folk's taste. Something to like about him. And a steady gaze with a calm, deeply-intent focus and a smile that seemed to urge quiet and trust.

She remembered Kristienne's brother as forthright. Patient, kind. But the tremble that surged through her, said this man was the source of the darkness she'd been dreading.

His broad shoulders carried a rider's strength. He wore low-riding, well-worn jeans that hung loose and a plaid flannel shirt-jacket. But the strength of his arms and his callused hands made her take a step away from where he stood. The fear she'd felt—was it for her or the Valley?

"Just visiting?" she asked as she avoided his shadow.

"Guess you could say that. I'm setting up in the cabin down the way."

"Thought you'd go home." She started toward the store, aware she was being rude but afraid to stay.

"Not the best place, and besides, here I can visit your art collection." He raised his chin at the cabin. "The inside as interesting?"

"No."

Ty frowned at her. "That's not very neighborly. Poor for business, too," he added when she glanced back at him.

"No." She climbed the steps to the porch, white-knuckling the rail and shook her head. "I'm sorry. I guess you did surprise me — I was thinking. A new business requires it." Her voice was stiff and her gaze wouldn't quite meet his straight on. "I suppose that's why I'm not showing that Valley hospitality right this moment."

"Must be."

"Howdy, stranger."

Ty turned as a rider arrived, and he grinned at his old friend and ranch hand, Matt Kelly. "Howdy, yourself Matt."

"You gone around home to see your mom and that sister of yours?"

"Held off so far."

"Your mother's really been havin' a time of it lately. The winter's been lastin' a little long this year, ya know. Your mom's been a little down that spring ain't come. Pardon me for sayin' what's true, Ma'am." Matt, ever the tradition-bound buckaroo, tipped his broad-brimmed cowboy hat in Letha's direction, his smile buried in his handlebar moustache, then turned back to Ty.

"Trouble?" Ty asked.

"Yer sister's gotta keep an eye sharp all the time."

Not what Ty wanted to hear. "Then I'll try to make it over sometime today. Seems your Letha here's attempting to beautify the lake, Matt."

"Looks like ya got all th' kid's art." Matt scanned the yard's whirling display, shifting his batwing-chaps-covered legs in the saddle. "That's Johnny Warner's work, ain't it? Heard Sylvia bought you a store."

"Yes." Letha's resentment rose in her chest. The Valley folk were all just humoring her. "The art. You think the tourists'll like it?"

"A simple man like me don't pay much attention to what city folk like or dislike. Got a feeling, though, that yer parents might not approve. Not too sure o' the old folk, either. They're the one's as matter. You get yerself over to visit your ma and your sister, Ty," he tipped his hat. "Before your ma does something else."

"Sure, Matt." Ty fought down the disquiet Matt's words brought, but then he'd known things weren't good with his mom for a while. He watched Matt turn his horse, then purposely looked back at Letha, somehow wanting to comfort the brief vulnerability he'd seen bloom in her eyes at Matt's comments. "The artwork's good, Letha."

She tossed her head prettily. Fussed with the blue-bottle display, the pottery, waiting for him to leave.

Letha Rivers, he thought, he'd have never predicted the carrot-topped kid would've grown into this ethereal woman. Of course, he remembered as he limped home, she'd always been like a pretty filly, all legs and timid curiosity.

His age-grayed log cabin sat back from the lake shore at the far side of the copse of white-barked poplar and willow that separated his place from Letha's. His horse trailer and truck were parked around back near the four-stall, hip-roof barn and broken down corral. At the cabin's front porch a white truck sat parked, a familiar petite blonde leaning against the driver's door. Wouldn't hurt, Ty thought, to know a little more about his lovely neighbor. He walked up to the driver.

"Long time, Sylvia."

"Long time."

"What brings you here?"

"Letha." Sylvia straightened and stretched her arms behind her back.

Still proving herself strong. Still plagued by those childhood insecurities he'd noticed so long ago.

"Matt told me 'bout your conversation. She's breaking tradition, and this valley is about as hide-bound in tradition as any," Sylvia said.

"She's selling Valley art. And that means she's breaking covenant?"

"God's truth."

"You honestly think that's true, Sylvia?"

"Might be, Ty." Sylvia wouldn't meet his gaze, instead studying his horse trailer. Her brow furrowed prettily and he remembered Sylvia's odd so-called talent, as she got a far-away look in her eyes. "I hoped the store would settle her. She's been hell-bent on leaving, so I was always afraid she would run. But with all this art rigmarole, she hasn't even brought in the Spring. You saw the ice on the lake."

"Yeah, I'm just suggesting maybe the Valley's being pretty hard on her for doing something creative."

Sylvia snorted, then lifted her chin back toward the cabin down at the lake. "Creation sits in the lake, Ty. Selling art, now… Spring's never operated a store." She shook her head. "I must have been nuts."

"There's nothing in the covenant that forbids selling art."

"Ty, maybe you've been away long enough to forget."

"I would never forget," he denied.

"So maybe you remember. Maybe it's Letha, maybe she's caught your sympathy."

"My sympathy? Maybe you should question why you're bothering me when you got business to attend." He held back his smile, knowing she'd wonder if she had him upset — and that not knowing would bother her. Miss Sylvia always was just a little too sure of herself.

She stayed silent a moment, then, "Ty Hunt, always a taskmaster." She motioned to the barn. "You still picking up strays, or have you actually bought yourself a horse? Stallion, huh?"

"Jokes, now. I'd ask if you're still making like Dr. Doolittle, but the truck and your question, it kinda answers me."

"You got a problem with that?" Sylvia's fists closed white-knuckled at her sides, and with that Ty knew he'd gotten under her skin

— not that hard to do. Hell, he'd always been good at it even when not intending to, but right now her not-too-subtle warnings just plain pissed him off.

"Subtlety, Ty, a quality you're missing."

"I'm just guessing, but maybe your heart wasn't in exactly the right place when you bought Letha a store."

Sylvia's derisive laughter rang loud, as she climbed into her truck Ty looked down the lake shore, recalled Letha's eyes, and felt compelled to see her again.

After Sylvia left, he checked Hauberk where he'd left him in the barn, fed the stallion, and unpacked his gear. Then he headed toward the store. The afternoon wind rattled the whirligigs and sighed in the willow, counterpoint to soft singing from inside. Tire tracks, Ty noted, fresh in the soil, and the clatter and humming from inside spoke of new merchandise and a life newly begun.

"You busy in here?" he asked, ducking his head to peer in the door.

"Yup. Town truck finally came with my order." Letha looked up from unloading condensed milk onto shelves. "Supplies for Valley folk. Old 'uns like sweetened milk, but it's the art that'll make the money."

"You're preaching to the converted," Ty said, smiling. "And I'll take on anyone who disputes it, unless it happens to be some big time New York art critic."

Across from her, Ty hefted himself onto the counter, considered the view. "You should come by my place after. I've got some beer cooling."

"Right. And I've got nothing better to do."

"We can fix that, too. Give us a chance to get reacquainted and all that?"

"I already remember you." But she did straighten, and look him right in the eye. "My place is here."

"You're saying you're happy in the Valley?"

"Never said that. But this store is supposed to earn me money, money I'll save. It's something that's mine, something I can do my way — no matter what Sylvia says. When I save enough, I can leave. I make the rules here. You think I give a damn about complaints? No way."

"The folk's feelings don't matter, then. But I was just being neighborly. Thought you could update me on the Valley's news." He grabbed a box on the counter and saw Letha start when he began passing her boxes of matches. "So Sylvia Hill bought the store."

"So what?" Letha intently finished stacking a shelf, then surveyed the results. "Yeah. She did. An investment, she said. Her, and the bank, secretly, but there're no secrets in-Valley."

"And Sylvia's not exactly a confidence-keeper, is she? But her heart's always been in the right place. Caring," Ty murmured casually. "Weird gal — at least you could say that about her hearing animal emotions."

Letha looked up at his calm regard, somehow needing to come to her friend's defense.

"You've got her…" Saying he'd got Sylvia "all wrong" seemed inappropriate when he seemed pretty astute otherwise. "You don't know her anymore."

"No? I don't," Ty agreed, "But I'm generally a good judge of people. It's sort of a hobby I've developed and honed over my years outside the Valley. Sylvia now, she hasn't changed that much. Her needs still drive her."

"Sylvia's always been my friend."

"Good, then. So that's why you're working here? As friends?"

Letha avoided him, so Ty decided to bow out. "Letha, I remember as a kid you planned to leave. Given I've been around in the world a couple of times, I'd be happy to talk."

"You don't remember much if you think that'd help. Now I need to tidy this store." Like that, she shut him down. He placed the emptied box on the counter.

"I'll leave." Whirligigs whined outside, the wind having picked up across the lake. "But, my cabin's there," Ty looked back at her and saw how fear filled her eyes. "The Valley doesn't hold me the same. I don't hold the same views, either, Letha Rivers. If you want to talk about it, I'm there."

Trembling inside, Letha watched his shadowed form. Late afternoon sunlight on the cabin's porch placed his silhouette across her gingham curtained windows. The whirligigs' howled in a wind that chilled her. She swayed, and felt the cabin walls press in, press lungs, check her breath. She couldn't breathe. Caught and imprisoned. Trapped and dying.

How had she let Sylvia do this to her, when everything inside her throbbed and demanded something more? But it was so typical of her life, wasn't it? Always doing what made others happy. She'd been like that as a kid and as a young woman. It was just that now she wanted more — even if she wasn't sure how to get it. Tyler Hunt had suggested as much in his not so veiled words. She remembered him as a horse-crazy teenager, with intense green eyes. That detail came easily, why did she remember? Tyler Hunt was nothing. He meant nothing.

And she was only biding her time in the Valley. She would leave. He was wrong about Sylvia trapping her.

Leaving the half-emptied boxes, she stepped onto the porch as Ty studied the lake. The cold wind across the frozen water picked up more force, tearing branches and rocking the whirligigs.

It blasted into her and sent her stumbling, so that she fell against Ty's left side. A bright flash across her vision, a sense of heat and long unanswered desire. Hers or his — the feelings were all mixed up and as dangerously confused as a rattler nest newly awakened in spring. She yanked away, inhaling old-ice and man-scent.

She couldn't slow her heart, couldn't quiet its pounding in her ears, as loud as horse herd hooves. She pushed her hair from her eyes and found herself caught in Ty's serious green gaze.

"What'd you do? Shock me?" But she knew that wasn't it, saw an answering awareness form deep in Ty Hunt's eyes. Warm gaze, surprised, knowing, denying.

"I can't... I won't..."

"Yeah, bloody strange." Ty's voice had a strangled edge, as if he choked back emotions he'd never wanted to find. "Shit, I don't need this."

"Don't need what?" Hesitating, Letha brushed Ty's shoulder. Another spike of need and darkness sent her reeling back.

"Nothing you need to know. Nothing. It's just the Spring wind." But it wasn't Spring, he thought. Letha, the Spring, she hadn't brought it yet. "Tourist season soon. Better ready the store, Letha," he said softly, and left her.

§

Holy-shit-mother-of-god-damn-it, he didn't like this feeling. The sensation that had rammed through him when the wind had thrown her against him, its intensity, had almost overwhelmed. Being overwhelmed was bad. It could get you killed. For all the Valley's remoteness and distance, he knew he had to guard against people wanting him dead. Letha Rivers was a danger to him because of his reaction to her.

He strode down the path along the lake shore that linked his log cabin to Letha's store. Shit, there was no such thing as the human embodiment of the marriage of Spring. That was an old wife's tale. He was an FBI agent, his buddies would laugh.

What the hell drug had he been on when he decided to hide in *this* tradition-bound community, in the very place he'd spent his early years, fighting his father's iron-bound rules and the hide-bound beliefs of a community he'd always planned to escape?

He passed his cabin for the barn, entered. Horses had always taught him calm. When everything else was going to hell, the animal's need for calm consistency salved him. Most of the time — but there were exceptions, like today.

A snort, coming from the stall with the open window, told him he was right. A stallion was a good judge of character, better than any FBI agent. Better than Sylvia Hill, regardless of his memories of her talents.

He entered the dim-lit stall, and feeling the stallion's unease, stopped and exhaled his pique.

"Sorry to leave you like this, friend. But the corral here needs mending, and I don't need you breaking loose. I promise you'll have more space soon. But for now, I need your help."

The dim lighting gradually receded. Stallion movements. Hay scent, snuffed breath on his hand, a brown eye, uncertain, awaiting calm. Hauberk formed like darkness birthed from the darkness, his deep brown coat glowing. His bloodlines were of the famous Hanoverian breed, bred for greatness if his spirit agreed, but just as likely to be uncontrolled when aroused.

Just like Ty was aroused by certain events by the lake. They raised a devastating wave of desire.

He wouldn't respond. He'd no need to interact, no need to see her. Hauberk snorted his displeasure, and a kick slammed the stall wall. The Valley wasn't Ty's place anymore; he belonged outside, but when he closed his eyes all he could see was the Valley fading to nothing, a blackened road forever before him, if he failed to answer the call.

He stroked Hauberk, the stallion's coat smooth under his hands. "You think you can control me?" he said to the air. "I'm not yours anymore. You'll see, I can leave again." He rested his forehead on Hauberk's neck. "Or stay if I want."

§

Letha, tired from the emotional roller-coaster of the day, was on the porch in her heavy jacket checking lists and watching the sunset, when Sylvia's truck wheeled into the gravel lot. "Still at it," Sylvia said as she climbed out of the truck. "Always knew you had work ethic. Thought

I'd come see how you managed today." She grabbed the other chair and slumped down, pulling her fleece collar close around her neck. "You got your stock. How's the shelving and pricing going?"

"Good enough," Letha sighed. It was good to see the shop really come together. Cleaned, shelves all stocked, prices in place. She'd accomplished it all with only minor interruptions. And not quite so minor. "Ty Hunt dropped by. He's different than I remember."

"Yummy." Sylvia glanced at her amber-haired friend, caught in the failing sunlight, a worried look niggled the edges of Letha's eyes. "He hassle you? Probably just worried about his mom's drinking."

"Not again?"

"Yeah, poor Kristienne. Sad… but ya can't heal those as don't want ta be." She gazed across the lake ice to the distant Hunt house. "So, was this good, Letha?"

"As good as honest work, Pa would say. But I need to re-rail the corral."

"You should take some time to relax and do what comes natural, maybe go down among the mint sinks. The weather's fine and the wind even has hints Spring might come." She said it hopefully, and Letha stiffened.

"And I'll just bet the Valley elders put you up to that comment."

Sylvia's lips bowed. "You seem kind of tense right now. It couldn't be the change of season now, 'cause that would mean you have duties to attend. What happened today that's got you so on edge?"

"Nothing."

"Well nothing doesn't leave you sitting on the porch in a cold wind. You should be inside, snug and warm and satisfied at your work."

"All right, something did happen today. With Ty."

"What'd he do? He's always been good people."

"I stumbled and fell against him, that's what. There was a flash, and then darkness. Like an… explosion inside me."

She was being stupid and she knew it, but she kept going. "He felt it, too. His eyes showed he did. But he wouldn't admit it and he left."

"Probably got angry at you; never much for imagination, our Ty."

"If that was imagination, then it's verging too close to real." Shivering, Letha stood and pushed past. "Either way it startled me — and likely chased away my closest neighbor."

Sylvia studied her and chewed her lip. "Might have. But I'll bet he comes back."

"Comes back."

"Spring draws people," Sylvia frowned. "My assessment? Probably not anything more than two people attracting each other. He's not hard on the eyes and you could do worse than to follow your attraction."

The wind tugged Letha's hair and she held it back. Held her emotions back, too. "That's not what I felt."

"Might be true. Might even be fun to find out. He likes you, you like him. What more's required?"

Letha shivered and felt the darkness swell over her again, but this time it was an old darkness. "I couldn't possibly be like that."

"You tried it once, didn't you?" Sylvia reminded her of things best forgotten. "Didn't hurt. You had a bit of fun then, sowed some oats with some young men. It doesn't matter what you do, Letha. As long as you don't leave."

Letha couldn't find breath. The pain, it choked, and Sylvia didn't understand how trapped she was, how she died inside. The only time she'd felt something different was in the sensation from Ty. And that frightening desire wasn't to be repeated. Frantically she sought for something to say.

"I'm going over to Johnny Warner's tomorrow to see some different stuff, paintings, and talk prices. All that and I'll be too busy to leave."

"One way to do it, I guess, but I really think you should focus on the store — not this crazy arts and crafts notion." Sylvia paused as she stepped down the stairs. "Letha? You could still have some fun, you know."

"When has my life been fun?" Letha snapped. She turned and closed the red door, shutting the world behind her.

Chapter 2

Up with the sunrise, Letha had gone on horseback to visit Johnny Warner — a slim-fingered seventeen-year-old who made art between schoolwork and ranch chores. Letha had spent time in his tarpaper shed, looking at delicate watercolor paintings of leaves and flowers, and helping him set prices.

She left feeling happy. Even if she wasn't leaving the Valley, she was doing something for herself and helping others while doing it. She was helping Johnny step out in the world when everyone else in the Valley thought his artwork was silly.

It was a matter of purpose. Johnny'd been born to a ranch family, so he was expected to ranch. Just like when she'd been chosen by Spring, everyone just assumed that was her only purpose in life. Well, people had choice, too. They weren't like a tree, held in place by roots that would never let go.

Once she'd been chosen, her mother hadn't even wanted Letha to go to school, but the law had been on Letha's side. She'd gone to school, had even brought home one of Kristienne's cast-off computers, and had begun her own explorations of the world outside. Yes, the Valley was her home, her birthright, and her responsibility — and she'd been glad of that — but there was *so much more.*

That knowledge had grown into a longing that ached like a missing part of her.

The problem was, Spring must have chosen wrongly when it selected her, and no one understood how that could be. It should have chosen Sylvia.

If she left it could have Sylvia — or someone else.

And she *would* leave. All she needed was money, a ride, and to deal with the darned sickness that took her every time she passed Jed Hartley's cabin. Then Sylvia could have her rightful place. Next time Letha left she wouldn't be coming back. There were pills for motion sickness. With money, she could buy them. It was as simple as that. They had to work.

Had to.

Still, Sylvia hadn't set up the store to help Letha's escape. And even though Sylvia's empathy worked mainly with animals, she could sense human emotion a little. That meant Letha had to be careful. She had to hold her plans close. If need be, she'd just take the money and run.

Staying wasn't an option.

She reined in her chestnut mare by the Spring Lake Ranch house and studied the old building. Frost still lay in the shadow of the old peaked structure. Last year's Queen Anne's Lace stood brittle and laced with crystals. But just a light nudge would bring Spring. It hovered in the air, waiting. She urged her mare forward, knowing she was being bitchy with her denial of the Spring rite, but it was her right to choose when Spring came. The only important choice she'd been allowed to keep.

One day soon, she thought, as her mare forded Brewster Stream toward the store, she would have so many choices. It would be fascinating to see what she did with them.

Would she become a woman like Sylvia, who had left the Valley for a time to go to school, but who had chosen to return? To be so confident this was your place. To be so sure about who you were, what you wanted, and how to get it. That must be what the outside world did, build certainty about who you were, because you could do and be anyone at all.

The thought made her hands tremble.

Yes, and while Sylvia had her own unique talents, anyone could learn to make choices, to become their own person. Sylvia was teaching her that, though she might not realize it, nor agree with Letha's choices. The store had taught her that she could stand her ground — at least on little things. And that was a surprise.

Ahead lay Ty Hunt's cabin and she urged the mare into a trot. She didn't want to deal with him on such a fine morning. Instead, she'd fix the mare's corral, so her horse could enjoy more freedom just as Letha was doing. Maybe she'd even plan a website for the store's artwork to bring in outside customers.

And that was her choice.

§

She finished hand-painting a sign and put it up next to the turnoff from the main Valley road to the two lake cabins. It was a fine bit of artwork, if she did say so herself. A spirit catcher drawn as an outside frame, 'Letha's Store and Artwork' woven into the web. She'd even found a few of Roscoe's feathers to hang from the sign so they dangled and fluttered in the wind. It should attract attention — even from the Valley folk.

Maybe even gain her respect for herself — beyond that which came with her position as Spring Consort. Let them see her as something other than that. Let them learn about Letha the entrepreneur and shopkeeper. Letha the person.

Setting her toolbox down beside the two-stall shed that served as home to her mare, Inca, she inhaled the sweet scent of new hay from the stall and studied the corral. Putting up rail fences wasn't her favorite thing, but she'd be darned if the mare was going to have less fun than Letha was out of all this change. From the stall window, Inca turned a dark eye on Letha and snorted.

"No, I haven't forgotten you; you and your need to kick up your heels." Work gloves on, she grabbed one of the cut poles Sylvia had arranged to be delivered and dragged it to a spot where one of the old fence rails had rotted, then leaned down to grab her hammer.

Dangerous curves ahead, Ty thought as he paused in his traipse along the lake. He really had just been headed out for a walk. The store just happened to be along the way, along with its attractive proprietor. Somehow Letha Rivers brought a whole new perspective to a man's work shirt and old jeans — one that deserved to be appreciated.

The wind shushed cool through the willows, but Letha didn't seem to notice as she used the hammer to haul down the broken rail and wrestled the new one into place.

"Looking good."

Startled, she almost dropped the end of the rail, and swore soft cowgirl epithets against the son-o-gun piece of wood. It made him smile, the gentle remonstrations of the Valley, as did her quick glance at him and the way she turned and finished the rail. He sauntered across the yard, straightening a metal statue that had settled askew in yesterday's wind.

"Easier with two sets of hands." He strolled over to grab another rail, but she caught it from him, careful not to touch him, he noted.

"I'm fine, thanks. I can manage."

"You've got a heap of rails here. Something of a job." He reached down and grabbed a few more rails, hefting them between himself and Letha. "So where do you want them?"

She looked him in the eye and he shrugged.

"I figure the top rail needs replacing all round. There're a few others. But I really don't need —"

He was already dragging the poles into position, checking the strength of the others in each panel. The horse in the stall caught his eye. "Nice horse. Mare?"

He climbed through the fence at a break and went over to the stall to hold out his hand. The horse snuffled his fingers, snorted, and he rubbed the spot behind its ears. With a sense borne of years of undercover work, he felt Letha come up behind him.

"Her name's Inca, 'cause every time she gets scared she sacrifices her rider. Couldn't tell you how many times I've been dumped." Why the heck was she telling him this? The best way to get rid of him was to focus on the fence. She turned back to the rail she'd been nailing and hefted the other end into place. "I've gotta get a place for her to exercise or she'll eat me alive. She's not getting enough riding."

"A bored horse is nothing but trouble, my trainer used to say."

"Trainer?"

"Outside I used to ride horses competitively. Here, I'll hold this end in place while you nail yours."

A quick bang-bang, and the long spike was in place. She was good with a hammer. They continued on to the next rail and the next until she paused and wiped sweat from her eyes. "Thank you, neighbor."

"Nothing to it. Works up a thirst though, even in this weather. You got drinks in that store?"

"Yeah."

"You figure out which other rails need replacing and I'll get the drinks." He grinned casually and she knew he'd spotted her hesitation.

"Fine. Thanks." Damn him, he'd done that on purpose. Too neighborly for his own good. Or hers. Or the Valley's.

He covered the ground to the cabin in a sure, easy stroll that carried a slight limp. She didn't want him here, taking her choices away, pushing her to hurry.

She fumed as she used the hammer to haul other rotten rails loose. At least the hammering used up some of her anger.

He returned juggling two bottles of Coke and two of uncarbonated spring water, making soft oaths at how cold the bottles were. She smiled.

"Guess I should turn the fridge down." She took a bottle of water from him, careful not meet his fingers, watched as he kept the other and set the Cokes down beside her tool box. Very precise. Nice he preferred the water. But that could just be because she chose it. She turned back to the fence. "I was just worried things would go off if I didn't keep 'em cold."

"Well, cold they are. Here." He held out a five dollar bill. "Let me pay for these. I'll take the Cokes, too."

"Ty," she said and shifted to look at him. She wanted to ask him why he was here, why he was helping. Instead she said, "You're helping. The least I can do is offer cold drinks. Keep your money."

"Well now, that's mighty neighborly."

He stuffed the bill back in his pocket and took a long pull on the bottle of water as she rolled her eyes at his affected drawl. He hadn't lived in the Valley for friggin' ten years. But there was something about the way he leaned back against the new rail, the way he studied the landscape — masculine, appraising — part of the landscape itself and yet… not. It lit a small tingle in her body.

She remembered the feeling she'd had when she was thirteen. Her pre-teen crush turned aside by the much older and wiser Ty. He was eighteen then, and this was like that crush only more so. A woman's feelings for a man she was attracted to.

Not to this man. No way in heck.

"I gotta thank you for your help. Would have taken me all afternoon."

"No problemo." He looked back at the mare, then at her with a slow casual glance that sent another jolt through her, reminiscent of the flash she'd felt the night before. She had to fight the small moan in her throat.

He took another swig of water, then, "This a red-headed league or something?" He lifted his chin, his brown hair gleaming in the sunlight. "You. The mare. You got something against blondes or brunettes, 'cause I might feel unwelcome."

She rolled her eyes again. "Jeeze, Ty. Chestnut mares're a dime a dozen and every one as ornery as the last."

"Yeah, but chestnut women, now…"

She froze, wanting him to stop, wanting him to leave, Ty saw, but not knowing how to tell him. Well, he could respect some of that, but — he hefted another rail and pulled it into position, took the hammer from her, and with a single blow, nailed the end in place. Repeated the action at the other end. "Hmm, still haven't lost the touch." He handed the hammer back to her.

She'd wanted to finish this herself, she thought. She wanted to keep busy until customers came. She wanted the time to plan. Otherwise this could be just more waiting — just like all her twenty three years. But it just wasn't to be.

Helplessly, she watched as Ty brought another load of rails. They started nailing them up.

"So, you been to see your mom and Kristienne yet?"

"My mom," he said, but it came out with a sigh. "I stopped in yesterday evening. Got forced into staying for dinner, and Kristienne can't cook to save her life." He blew his hair up over his forehead. "Yeah, I saw my mom."

There was grief in his tone, in the way he picked up his water bottle, saw it was empty, and carefully set it down. He looked up at her and smiled, and the sad curve of his lips made her heart go out to this man. It was never easy seeing a parent fail, and Elizabeth Hunt had fallen far from the graceful opera singer who had come from New York with her husband. No wonder Ty'd left and never come back.

"You must have seen a lot out in the big world. A lot to keep you busy."

"There's a lot, all right." She had such steady eyes, he thought as he looked back at her. Steady and not really grey, just a blue as deep as denim that seemed to catch everything around her and just… be. When she looked away it was like suddenly being alone and empty. She didn't look away for long. Curiosity, he thought. Like a hunger. "A lot of people. A lot of crime. A lot of shit going down, pardon my language."

"You were a cop?"

"Could say that. Law enforcement. My dad was a cop before he decided to come to Canada and take up ranching. His dad was a cop, too. Hard to believe we're still considered newcomers to the Valley. I feel like I've lived here my whole life. You know, this is going to make a pretty solid loafing corral for that mare of yours."

"You think so?" She pulled back on a new-hung rail, testing its strength. Even a horse leaning into it was going to have to work to get it loose. Another choice: of a job, and the job well done. She nodded her pleasure. "Good work."

"I'd say you've got one hell of an arm on you. Good with a hammer, can set up a home pretty well, too, from what I saw in your shop. Going to make some Valley beau one happy fella."

"I'm not." Her body went stiff as the rail she stood beside. "Not ever."

"Never's a pretty long, lonely time," he said softly.

"It's not going to happen. And it's none of your business." She turned toward him, eyes flashing.

"Hold on there. I was just making a joke, okay. I just — know what it's like alone."

"I'm sorry," she said archly.

"So am I."

"So how long are you planning on staying in our fair Valley?"

"Long enough." He climbed through the fence and looked back, daring her. Letha's flares of temper were something to be watched, something that spoke of too much pressure inside. How does Letha Rivers let off pressure, he wondered. "Fence's fixed. How 'bout we set that mare of yours loose and see how big a fool she can make of herself?"

"Big as her owner," Letha grumbled, joining him inside the fence. "Pretty big."

"Let me be the judge of that. I've met some pretty big fools in my day." And you're making one of yourself right now.

"All right. Just you wait." For some reason she didn't want to annoy him — perhaps it was fear of the darkness she felt associated with him, or perhaps it was that tingling sensation that still jangled in her belly. She went to the stall and undid the slide, the mare lipping her fingers. "Stand back. She can explode outta here. It's a bad habit I've been trying to break her of since I got her."

She stepped back and swung the stall door wide, the mare slamming out the door in a single wild leap. She squealed, tucked her head, and bucked her way around the corral, before collapsing into the dirt for a good solid roll, legs raking the sky as she ground her back into the earth. Letha's delighted laughter rang across the corral.

"Damn foolish," he said, grinning. "Right up there, I'd say. And after that display, I better head home put some time into my own corral. Pleasure seeing you, Letha." He nodded.

"Thanks for the help, Ty."

He headed back to his cabin following the path on the lake shore, thinking about Letha Rivers. Something about her… Strong, capable to be sure, good with animals, fiercely independent, and just a tad scared of something. The way she avoided his touch, it could almost be him.

He paused as he stepped over a loose patch of ice between the willows and pulled the collar of his fleece jacket up. The ice edge of the lake had gone clear, rotten, but it wasn't receding. It should be Spring, so the melts would come. Around William's Lake, loggers were off work due to the thaws. And that lake was half ice-free. But not here. The Valley might be higher in elevation than William's Lake, but it should still be seeing new green grass. Something wasn't right.

He glanced back at the store and knew the thing that wasn't right was Letha. Something in her was worryingly wrong.

§

Letha rang up the cash register and made small talk with old Mrs. Zigheld. Mrs. Zigheld had had her son Harry, the local Postman, drive her to the store just to see what all the fuss was about, and probably to report to the other Valley elders. After fussing about the store and sniffing at the 'new-fangled ideas of young people' however, she'd bought a pound of butter because, she'd said, she had a hankering for shortbread cookies, and a tiny wooden rabbit ornament carved by Tessa Rogers, another of the Valley kids. A little triumph.

Letha watched Harry help the old woman in her sturdy black boots and heavy coat to his truck that doubled as mail delivery vehicle, but before she climbed in the old woman stopped. She stuck her wizened face up at Letha. "'bout time fer ya to be thinkin' about Spring, girl. Been a long winter." She climbed in, shaking her head as the truck crunched out of the yard.

At least she'd shopped. She'd been impressed enough with Letha's goods, she'd probably be back. She might even give a good report to the others.

The lake lay like a white disc, the ice cold blue under the sun. She shivered at the cold, and the lonely sound of the wind through the willows, and the distant caws of crows. A thump and nearby croak brought her to the spirit catcher at the end of porch. Roscoe sat on the rail, tugging at the fluttering feathers.

"Git! Git away!" She shushed the darn bird with a sweep of her hand, but the raven only fluttered up to the peak of the roof. "You do that again, I'll get a gun," she warned, even though it was an empty threat.

The raven croaked a retort and she grinned, turned, and smacked right into a solid chest. A bright flash, and her knees wobbled. Ty. He tried to steady her, caught her arm, but she yanked away.

Shock and something else — panic? — filled her. "Ty! Sorry. I didn't see you. God, I really should watch where I'm going."

She tried to duck past him.

"Whoa there. I'm fine. I realized I didn't buy any jam or peanut butter in town for my lunch, thought maybe the store…" He let her pass and followed her into the store, taking care to keep his distance. "Nice and warm in here. Unseasonably cool morning, though."

"The fire." She nodded at the wood heater radiating warmth in the corner, and hurried to a set of shelves near the window where the jars of jam waited. Being surprised wasn't something she was used to. Usually she felt people's presence before they arrived. But not Ty. Except for the darkness. His presence now — it brought a fluttering sense of panic to her stomach.

"Peanut butter and jam. What kind of jam, 'cause I've got strawberry and raspberry and marmalade, but then you didn't say marmalade, did you?"

"Calm down, Letha."

"Pardon me?"

"Calm down." He smiled kindly as he stepped up beside her to examine the jam labels. "I didn't come to assault you or anything."

"Sure. Fine." Frustration flared at herself and at this man who always seemed to insert himself into her space. "There's the jam."

She ducked behind the counter and he had a tough time holding back the smile. "So what'd you figure goes best with peanut butter? I've never fancied marmalade, but strawberry can be kind of boring after a while."

"Raspberry, then." Just get the selection over with and leave. She didn't need him here, with his capable hands and his touch that made her go weak in the knees. His gaze on her was like a too-hot towel right out of her mom's dryer.

"Thought maybe you could make use of this. I found it in my barn." He came up to the counter and placed the jam jar and a bundle beside her hand.

Letha just looked at the bundle, wrapped in what looked like an old t-shirt. "What is it?"

"Something for the store."

She rang up the jam and peanut butter and accepted the money he put on the counter. Put his change there, as well, beside the bundle.

"Go on. Open it."

She didn't want his gifts, but curiosity got the better of her. She unfolded the three folds of cloth that protected the gift. A brass bell on a chain, newly shone to amber brilliance. She picked it up, and a single clear note seemed to fill the store and a hollow place inside her.

"It's beautiful."

"Great sound. It was buried in some old manure. I figured it needed a better home than that. Thought you could hang it by your door, so customers can call you if you're outside."

She was shaking her head. "No. This is an antique. It's worth something."

"And so it's worth giving as a gift." He looked around the store and grinned sheepishly. "Got any bread? I forgot that, too."

She packed the loaf of bread, the jam, and the peanut butter into a bag and watched him out the door. He waved back at her as she shut the door and stepped back to the counter. The bell lay, glistening. She picked it up and it rang again. The sound made her smile.

§

Kristienne Hunt looked up from the ugly truth of the account books at the sound of a horse in the yard. It was too late for Matt and the other ranch hands to be leaving — she'd heard them hours ago — and it was too early for them to be back. A small chill of concern ran up her neck.

God, what was it now? After the way her mother had taken a turn for the worse six months ago, Kristienne was always on edge. The coffee she seemed to consume in ever-increasing amounts wasn't helping, either. She pushed her mug away.

Of course she could manage it. She always managed everything, had learned how at her father's knee and had taken over when he passed so suddenly. Good thing she liked the ranch and the way the work and the finances ebbed and flowed like the seasons and harvest. Or the way the seasons were supposed to flow.

She glanced toward the front window of the log house. It sat on sheltered bottom-land overlooking the frozen lake. Her mother's crocuses should be pushing up through the last snows at this time of year, but this April the snow was still heaped around the house. Well, everyone deserved to have a tantrum once in a while, and Letha was no exception.

She, Kristienne, had had her tantrum the other night when Ty had dropped in outta the blue. Ten years with only the occasional phone call, and then he arrives and his whole presence said he expected to be the man of the house. After she'd held things together, there was no way she was going to put up with that.

Ty's voice reached her from outside — talking to his horse, she supposed. He'd said he'd brought one with him. Always was horse crazy. As if he preferred the animals to the people who owned them, even though people always seemed attracted to the old Ty.

As if living things — animals and people — were drawn to him. Unlike her. That was how he'd been as a kid before he went away to school. Always popular. Even when he came back for his brief visits he'd fit right in, been an open book for people to read.

But the Ty that had come back this time was different, Kristienne thought. He was still caring and concerned, but this time there was a wall blocking some of those qualities away. This time there was an aura of secrets about him, as if he wouldn't let you in. Their mom had felt it, too, and she'd been more difficult the past two days.

He should never have come back.

Hearing his booted footfall on the rear porch, she stood to pour him a cup of slightly-burned coffee, and handed it to him as he came in wiping his hands. His appearance stopped her dead, but Ty still accepted the coffee. What the hell was he wearing? High black boots and thigh-tight britches. Nothing any self-respecting cattle-man would wear.

"Damn cold out there. Gotta get some stuff from the barn to fix the flue in my chimney. Damn near suffocated myself on smoke. Then I opened the windows and nearly froze my ass off."

Wearing his well-worn working boots and comfortable English breeches, he settled into their father's old blood-red leather wingback, and Kristienne frowned and sat back at the ranch's business desk in the corner. She was doing books, he saw. He really should be asking her how the business was doing, but he supposed if she'd run the place the past two years she didn't need him checking over her shoulder.

"So how's Mom?"

"Fine. Sleeping," Kristienne told him. "Your little surprise visit really threw her for a loop. She spent yesterday in your old room, making sure everything was as she remembered, then she wanted Matt and the boys to go get you and your stuff. She thinks you should be here, Ty. In your old room, and we'd be a family again." She held out a piece of paper. "And someone named Samuels called and asked if you were here. I told him 'no', but that I'd see you got his message. I'm not your messenger service, hear?"

"Yeah…" he said slowly as he scanned the note. He looked up at her. "Not going to happen — moving in, I mean." He stood up and shifted around the room. Samuels, his partner, didn't know he was here. No one but the Assistant Director Buckley, did, and Buckley knew better than to contact him unless it was an emergency. What the hell was going on? "You shouldn't take messages for me. Anyone calls, I'm not here."

Kristienne noted the distraction in his voice. He'd got like that when he was a kid, too. Mostly when he was busy chasing some girl or other, and too busy to entertain his younger sister and her friends. When he wasn't distracted, he'd been a good companion and sometimes a champion. Hmm. "So how's it going at your end of the lake? Met your neighbor?"

He glanced at her as she looked up at him. "Letha? She's grown up."

Kristienne sniffed. "A matter of years. We all do. So you saw her, spoke to her."

"Yeah. I'm kinda…" he stopped himself and cocked his head, his longish hair reminding her of when they were much younger together. "You're still her friend, right? Have you seen her lately? Checked up on her?"

Kristienne looked heavenward. The last thing Letha Rivers needed was another person checking on her. "Sure, we're still friends. But I'm a friend who believes everyone deserves space, and that's something not too common around these parts — the belief, I mean. Not the space. I saw the artwork, if that's what you're asking."

"It's not the artwork. It's just… hell, I don't know. I just get the sense that something's wrong — I mean, where the hell's Spring?"

His question sent a little shiver down her back. She'd put it down to Letha's orneriness, but maybe there was something more. "Tell you what. I'll go see how she's doing if you'll hang with Mom for a while. But first let's go look at this horseflesh that has you dressing like a pansy fool."

He looked down at himself, realized how strangely he was dressed for folk who preferred old jeans and shit-kicking boots, then grinned and shrugged. "Sounds like a deal."

The Hunt Ranch was her pride, the operations efficient. In Kristienne's world, a well-run ranch was one where the cattle were fat and happy, the horses were cattle-eating Quarter Horses, and the men were focused on keeping them that way. She didn't mind the long winters that came with Central British Columbia, nor the fact that the only men she met were cowboys and rich folk looking to buy a horse as a toy.

Hunt Ranch was well known for cutting and reining horses that carried the bloodlines of past world champions in both fields. A cattle-eating horse would get you to your cow and keep you there, and the prize money was big. Her horses were solid in body and mind — the product of good breeding practices and real-life work — not some trainer in Las Vegas or New York.

She hauled on her riding boots and her worn fleece jacket, and paused outside to inhale the healthy smells of fresh manure and spread hay from the paddocks by the main barn that stood beyond the house. Neat rail fences quartered the land satisfyingly into gardens, paddocks, and loafing sheds for cattle. A hay barn and the main horse barn lay beyond, for mares delivering in winter and horses that were in training. Activity near the covered riding ring told of two-year-olds being broke to saddle. All as it should be.

It wouldn't upset her if the rest of the world disappeared — except she needed outsiders as customers. The 150 acres of poplar and lodgepole pine forest, the meadow and hay fields their father had bought, and the range rights to a half section of Crown Land were a small, self-contained world, and all the world she needed right now.

She stepped off the back porch and stopped. Closer, in a small corral next to the house that she usually used for mares with new foals, waited Ty's horse. "Holy shit, is that a moose?"

The horse stood in the corral like a mountain — must have weighed close to 1400 pounds — not like the tidy 900-pound reining or cutting horses she rode — not even like the big old plodding ranch horses a lot of the Valley people owned. Black mane and tail, body a brown so dark it was like shadows in deep water. Muscled and well-made, but snorting and way too hellishly high off the ground to make a decent cattle horse.

And every horse worth owning had to be a decent cattle horse to earn its keep.

Not that she didn't enjoy leggier horses. There was something to be said for a horse that could run. Every morning before the ranch's demands took over her day, she'd take her gelding, Strata, out for a good ride and they always enjoyed a run together. She'd even toyed with the notion of jockeying before she got her growth, but this horse — he was too heavy for racing, too.

"Must be over sixteen hands tall." She stood at the corral gate and looked up — way up — and at 5-feet-seven she wasn't short. She tossed her long brown hair back and rested her cowboy boot on the bottom rail.

"What the hell do you do with a horse like that? You couldn't even ride in the hills because you'd get caught in all the branches."

"Hey, he's my horse — Hauberk's his name — European Warm-blood, Hanoverian, and great bloodlines — that's why he's a stud. He's a dressage horse, Kris, takes the reining horse athleticism and raises it to art — like in the Olympics — or those Lipizzaner stallions. I'll show you some time."

She heard the pride in his voice and knew her face showed her doubts. She scanned the horse, noting the silly-looking English saddle that went with her brother's embarrassing get-up, and searched for something to compliment. She knew her face showed just how hard she was working at it. She never had been able to smooth away her emotions like Ty — even though their features were similar in their wide-set eyes and full mouths. "Got a good hip on him, I guess. Good legs. Good bone."

"And hooves like steel, and movement like a dancer. Just you wait, you'll see."

She nodded, wondering what had happened to her brother to make him go all prissy like this.

"Guess I'll head over to Letha's." She shook her head and lifted her chin at the horse. "Matt sees him and he's never going to forgive you."

"Maybe."

She ducked away to the truck and started the engine, sitting back in the seat while she fought to compose herself. Giggles demanded release and she slammed the truck in gear, laughing and hoping Ty wouldn't see. Her big brother — a damned, pansy, flat-saddle rider.

She was still laughing when she pulled into the packed snow and gravel lot in front of the store. Sylvia's white truck sat out front, and that choked out her mirth. What was the woman doing to Letha this time?

Sylvia was seated in the lone inside chair, but even at rest she didn't look relaxed. She held a sheaf of invoices in her hand, her eyes scanning their contents in quick, bird-like glances, her forefingers tapping a light dance on the paper. Letha hovered nearby, trying to look casual while her whole body radiated nerves.

Sylvia could do that to most people, which didn't make a lot of sense given how good she was with animals. She needed to stop doing it to Letha.

Kristienne pushed through the door and nodded at Letha. "Thought I'd see how you were making out, but I guess I know, given Sylvia's here."

"Kristienne." Sylvia rattled her papers as if to reprimand Kristienne for interrupting. "I thought the ranch brought in its own supplies from down south so it wouldn't have to deal locally?"

She ignored the jab and turned to Letha. "She been bitchy like this with you? 'Cause I can take her."

"Like hell. You might be taller, but I've wrestled a damn-sight more horses and cattle than you. I've got muscles. You — you've got spindly little rider arms."

"I'd tell you where to take your muscles, but you might need them the next time I've got a breach-birth foal. Letha, I really did come just to see how you were doing. How's business?"

"Fine. A few customers. Mrs. Zigheld and Harry came by."

Kristienne wrinkled her nose. "Harry say anything about Ty being back? I swear that guy still harbors a grudge."

Letha shook her head. "I got some of Johnny Warner's paintings that I think are going to sell real well. I'll show you." She ducked into the back bedroom.

"You putting more pressure on her, Syl?"

"Just minding the store, so to speak." She looked back at the papers. "Don't go putting ideas in her head."

"You should talk."

"What the hell's that supposed to mean?"

"She's got her own ideas, Syl. You notice anything about the seasons?"

"No."

"I never thought you were a liar before," Kristienne said as Letha returned with an armful of stretched canvases.

"You've got to see these. He had them stuffed in a corner in his shed at home and no one except his teacher has seen them."

She laid the wood-framed canvases on the counter, and leaving Sylvia to her papers and her disapproval, displayed the first one.

"You studied some art when you were away at school, and didn't your mom take you to galleries in New York? What d'you think?"

It was a watercolor of poplar leaves in water. They were caught at the edge of rounded stream stones, and the work was so fine Kristienne could see the veining of the gold-green colored leaves and could almost hear the burble of water. "Wow. This is great. Johnny Warner did this?"

"And all these others. I want to help him; get people to know about his work."

"That'll take some effort."

"Hey, it's what this is all about, isn't it? And when his stuff starts to sell, I'll start taking a bit of commission and earn money that way."

"What? Sylvia not paying you enough to run this operation?"

"It's Sylvia's store. She financed the whole thing. I get a cut of everything when we start making money, but right now we're not even break-even."

Kristienne heard wistfulness in Letha's voice, but also the enduring faith of a long-time friend. The friendship was something she admired Letha for, but the wistfulness was as if there was something pining inside.

Kristienne studied her friend as she lifted another canvas, this one of a heron in early morning mist. The kid had talent, that was for sure. But Letha, there were shadows in and under her eyes. Well, starting a new business could do that, Kristienne decided.

Letha seemed to have a good mind for it too, judging by the neatly stacked shelves and the tidy displays of charming, wood-carved ornaments hung on a tree branch she'd positioned by the window.

Kristienne looked through the other canvases, then went back to the first canvas Letha had shown her. She glanced over her shoulder at Sylvia, knowing what she was about to do would piss Syl off.

"I shouldn't be doing this."

Letha paused. She frowned. "You can come in here whenever you like. It's a store, for goodness sake."

"I mean I'm going to have to buy this painting, because if I don't, someone else will. These paintings — and the ornaments and the carvings out front — they're all unique and wonderful. They'll put this store on the map. You just wait — you'll have customers coming from all over."

A radiant smile bloomed on Letha's face.

"We don't need to bring in more people. We just need a general store," Sylvia said from her chair. "It'll disrupt things."

"You open a store and you need business. The Valley'll deal, just you wait and see. And all the local artists are going to be thanking you for the extra income. You'll be a hero, Syl. Just like you always wanted. So what do

I owe you, Letha?"

Apologizing, she named a price that was on the low side for a piece of quality art — even if it was by an unknown artist.

"Okay. I'll have to come back with my wallet, but hold the painting for me, all right? I'd love to get something different for the house."

Pleased at Kristienne's reaction to her efforts, Letha wrote up the bill, a little song humming in her head.

Kristienne looked at the numbers and shook her head. "Cheap at twice the price. But Ty is going to laugh his butt off when he sees this."

Letha froze. "Ty?"

"Yeah, my long lost bro came for a visit this morning. Said I should look in on you."

Letha's eyes turned darker grey, like a gathering storm. She gathered up the canvases and hurried out of the room as a gust of cold wind suddenly rattled the store windows and seemed to rush through the room.

Kristienne looked after her, glanced at Sylvia, who still had her nose buried in invoices, and turned thoughtfully to go. Something *was* happening here. Something more than a delay of Spring.

§

Darkness and cold, the night sky hidden with clouds, and the air laden with ice and snow. A harsh wind blew through the benighted Valley, drifting the snow, smothering everything and everyone there — including Letha.

The lake lay glistening, the water hissing as the snow hit the water, and ice crackled at its edges. Along the shoreline, the pale green willow catkins shriveled and blackened. Birds huddled amid naked branches. A chickadee shivered and fell, its taupe and grey feathers lost in the drifts. Through the blizzard a figure rode through the snow, then toppled off the horse to lay still.

Creatures — people — were dying of the darkness, and it waited for her.

Letha shifted in sleep, contesting the vision. No. Spring would come, just as it always came. The valley could not be like this. There was too much she held dear.

She walked naked through the snow. Her skin was pale as lake ice, her eyes dark as the snowy sky. Wind caught in her hair, dragged it wild around her face and head.

The lake, if she could only reach the lake she could save things —

the man, the bird, so many others. But something hunted in the snow. Something human and dark.

He was a figure just glimpsed. A sound of hooves at the edge of hearing. Wanting her. Wanting to help her.

No! Wanting to end life. Hers and all others.

Darkness, it followed him and it masked his face when he came to her on a dark steed. Her own heat filled her with need and sent her to him. Snow melted on her skin, trickled through her curls. She looked up for his face but saw only darkness, felt only his wanting and the ravenous darkness that followed behind him.

Darkness that tore her up, tore her, crying, out of the Valley, and spoke to her in a wind-swept voice. She felt hands on her waist. "The Valley's gone. You're free of it."

She stood in a place she had never been — a city of glass, broad concrete streets, the sound of engines and steam. The smell of diesel and urine. Cold. So cold. Still naked, she walked through the crowds and the people did nothing. Said nothing. Walked through her.

"I'm Letha," she said. No one responded.

Was she wrong? Who-what was Letha? She was, wasn't she? And the cold crept inside and froze her heat. She was coming apart, falling apart, forgetting herself except for the darkness's hold on her. She needed to get away. Needed the Valley.

She yanked away, fell away.

Fell, and landed in snow. The man, he would help her.

The wind and voice laughed cold as ice, colder than her heat, froze the man before her, his steed. Ice formed on his brow, on the horse's eyes. Tree limbs cracked and fell to the earth. The forest crumbled into darkness.

The lake. She had to get to the lake. To Spring. She ran through the snow, darkness at her heels. A wolf howled and died. A deer screamed. Another. Fire in the darkness. The old Lake Stage Coach house aflame. Human voices, afraid. Afraid like she was. Darkness pulsed as she ran, as her fear sent her on.

Black surface before her. She stumbled and fell, tumbling down a slope through frozen thistle and ice, coming up against a willow that had cracks through its trunk.

She scrambled to her feet, dry grass and snow caught at her ankles, held her back from the lake, the water, the Spring, and darkness had almost caught her, was almost upon her.

Crying, she looked over her shoulder; it came on black wings, slamming her back against the tree. Get free. Get to the lake and save them all.

She stumbled around the tree, hobbled the last few feet to the water on frozen feet — "*Oh, Precious Spring,*" she began the rite — stepped out…

…onto ice, and slipped to her knees.

The whole lake was frozen. She pounded at the ice with her fists, pleading with Spring to come, ramming her knuckles into the hard surface until bones broke, until her spirit broke, and all she could hear was darkness laughing. All she could feel were her tears and the unending pain as she kept on pounding.

Chapter 3

The sound of pounding brought Letha awake in the log bedroom in the morning. She lay dazed and tired under the thick warmth of the blue and white quilt and did not remember why. Except there was something she had to do and the first thing was see what the pounding was.

It was just past seven thirty as she threw her chenille robe over her flannel pajamas and went outside to find Roscoe once again pecking at the feathers on the spirit catcher. The wooden ring of the catcher thumped against the cabin wall each time the Raven tried to pull the feather loose, as if the darn bird was doing it on purpose.

She shushed the Raven away and went inside, adding wood to the heater to take the chill off the room. The scent and crackle of pine sap filled the cabin. It was Monday and she'd decided the store was closed. A choice she had made.

She started to make coffee, then stopped herself. Something she must do. She felt it in her heart — an urgency, like birds trapped in a room. As if Roscoe's work had typed her a message.

She parted the curtains and looked out at the lake. Blue-grey ice. The white folds of the slopes around the water. The high, peaked roof of the old Lake Stage Road House seen just beyond the slope of the snow-covered hay field that rolled down to the lake. Gray haze of naked poplar following Brewster Stream, and the creases in the landscape where the spring runoff ran. At the far end of the lake, a coil of chimney smoke spoke of the Hunt Ranch house. Her breath frosted on the window. Cold out. Too cold, and high-time there was help for it.

She went to her room and pulled her pajamas off, pulled on the robe, and stepped barefoot out onto the porch. It was darn cold, and it shouldn't be. A coil of smoke down the lake shore told of her neighbor also up, but she ignored it. The Lake held her attention. Roscoe croaked from the willow tree.

She crossed the gravel to the shore, where clear water overlapped the ice, then looked up at the sky. "Precious Spring," she began, and inhaled the cold air, dropped her robe onto the earth, and stepped forward, naked, so her toes were bathed in cold water.

"Precious Spring, time of life borning. Time of new grass, new calf, new foal of the morning. Time of raven birth and catkin, new growth of hay, time of bonding and mating, new light warms the day." She held still, eyes closed, poised at the lake edge, focused inside herself to feel the answering heat of Spring flow up from the earth, from the lake water hidden under ice. It came, flooding up through her toes, her legs to her hidden core, igniting life, hope, a new year that would lead to fall harvest.

Her body trembled with the heat. Sweat beaded her brow, even as the cold wind surrounded her, even as she knelt to plunge her hands, fingers spread wide, into the water.

Spring, she thought, as the power surged through her, ran out through her fingertips. She opened her eyes and saw the power crackle through the lake ice, heard the grind of deep cracks forming, of ice giving way before the Spring's warmth.

She stepped into the water and the ice receded in front of her. Water up to her knees, her thighs, her groin. She submerged herself and felt the tiny kisses of hundreds of minnows that were drawn to her heat. Their bodies glowed in the dark water, took up her heat, and threaded away into the water. The lake's ice cracked into a million pieces when she came up for air and slicked back her hair, before a warm wind blew across the water catching her in its arms, drying and lifting her curls around her shoulders.

"Here is life. Here I am — and Spring." It was like a small bell tolled across the opening water, followed by the sound of sparrows singing a Spring song, snow-melt gurgling through the folds of the hills, and Roscoe's chortle. It broke her heart and lifted it at the same time. Something of her would always be joined to the Valley, but her mind and heart were forever drawn somewhere else.

She was leaving, and there was no help for it. If she didn't, the bright spark that made her Letha would die. For now, though, she would treasure this link with the lake. She wondered how she would feel when the link was broken, and a sudden vision of cold concrete filled her head and then was gone.

She swam toward shore, a simple breast stroke with the cool water on her skin, then waded, dripping, from the lake and pulled her blue robe on.

A sense of presence chased her peace away and she jerked around, already knowing who she would find. A rider, his face hidden in the sun, sat astride a huge, dark, foam-flecked horse, with an antler-like, two-prong brand on its hip. She fell back a pace, the hem of her robe trailing in the water.

"Letha. Thought it was you."

Ty's voice. "Good morning," she said hearing the tremor in the words. It *had* been, the Spring rite always left her with a sense of euphoria and arousal. She wanted to enjoy the pleasure in her own way. Welcome the catkins to full bloom, the sparrows to their nests. Help the Valley dust itself free of winter. Ty Hunt's presence raised a little tremor of fear.

"Seems Spring's finally come." He leaned on the pommel of his flat saddle, the huge stallion sidling under him. "Nice day for a ride. Hauberk and I been out for a while. Nice day for a swim, too, I guess."

He'd spied her in the water, been on the far side of the lake when the lake ice suddenly groaned and a lightening flash of cracks appeared in its surface. He'd looked out, then, and seen a slim white form like a deer sink into the water and swim out into the lake. Driven, he'd turned Hauberk back, galloping to get here, to greet her as she came glowing and glorious from the water. Too bad her face had become guarded now.

"It was time." She pulled her robe up under her chin even though the wind had turned warm from the south. "I should go get dried off."

"I've got a thermos of hot coffee waiting back home and a kettle that's just aching to make tea, if that's your preference," he said simply. "Why don't you throw on some clothes and come over. You can be my first guest."

"Well…"

"Come on, help me christen the place."

"But… the store…."

"I thought there was a 'Closed Mondays' sign in the window."

"There is, but there're still things to be done."

"Letha, is it just me, or is it all men that you resent?"

"I don't resent men. I've just got things to do."

"Then let me buy you a cup of coffee on your day off. To warm you up." He nodded toward her place, and turned his horse. "Go on. I'll expect you in fifteen."

He didn't seem to move in the saddle, but suddenly that great horse wheeled and leapt forward into a canter down the lake shore, leaving her to reflect on how his voice seemed to catch at the lake-warmth in her belly, how he and his mount moved like one great beast, and how her own choice had just seemed to evaporate in his presence and leave her breathless. She went up to the store, dressed in her jeans, flannel shirt, and boots, fed her mare, and then plucked a small, carved horse and rider ornament from her display to take as a housewarming gift. It was her choice to be neighborly.

"So what made today the first day of Spring?" he asked as he met her at the door with an old blue mug, filled with fragrant coffee.

She accepted the cup, careful of his touch. "I don't know. It just was." He stood so close, her heart yammered in her chest. Her breath seemed to stutter. "Winter's been long this year."

He didn't give her that recriminating look of a Valley person, she'd grown so used to since she held off with the rite this year. Instead he simply nodded. Dressed in the high black boots and form-fitting dark brown breeches and tan rugby shirt, he looked masculine, moved like a predator.

As a cop, she thought, he would.

"You were out early to ride," she said, searching for conversation.

"Yeah, Hauberk needs it. You want to meet him? He's just in the barn until he finishes cooling out."

She heard the anxious pride in his voice. "Sure," she said amiably. After his help with the fence, the least she could do was admire his horse.

A snort and the sound of pawing hooves met then at the barn door. Letha hesitated at the darkness inside and the sense of wildness and power she sensed from the horse. There was a low whinny and stomping.

"You okay with stallions? He can be a bit pushy, but he's okay. I don't let him get away with much."

She nodded and followed him into the dim-lit, log-sidec barn, inhaling the scents of expensive mixed grain, alfalfa, and oiled leather. When her eyes adjusted she saw the order in the place. A pole was set like a saw horse, holding his English saddle. A bridle — cleaned — hung on a peg on the wall. A plastic bin held grain. Bales of hay were stacked neatly in the corner. Cross-ties were set up above a newly swept, wood plank floor.

Hauberk hung his head over his stall door, more massive-seeming in the confines of the small barn. The deep brown of his coat made her think of good soil, covering the bones of the land. In Hauberk's case, it was well-developed muscles. But it was his liquid eyes that caught her. Aware, intelligent, and a little pissed off at being left in his stall.

Letha held her hand out for the horse to sniff. He plunked his muzzle into her hand, looking for treats she supposed, and warm moist breath filled her palm. When she had nothing to give him he nudged her chest with his nose.

"Sorry. I haven't quite taught him manners yet. But for a stud he's pretty good."

Letha laughed and slid her hand up along the soft coat of his face to his ears. Hauberk lowered his head for her and nudged her again when her fingers stopped rubbing.

"He's four," Ty explained as he came back from the plastic bin with a couple of lumps of feed. He gave one to Letha and fed the other to the horse himself. Hauberk gently took the offerings and let his head hang relaxed as he crunched the food. "Still pretty young, but totally trainable and with a hell of a lot of talent. I've been looking a long time for a horse like this."

"He's gorgeous. Biggest horse I ever saw, though, next to Murphy's Belgians. He part draft horse?"

Ty chuckled. "Well, if you go way, way back, yeah. The Europeans bred knight's horses from draft horses. Then those were refined more to pull coaches, and then, when the Europeans wanted horses for sport like fox hunting and military use, they bred horses like Hauberk here. He's a little more refined, from Thoroughbred blood, but still pretty much what they call a Warmblood."

"So you do a lot of fox hunting and military field work, do you?"

Ty heard the jest in her voice as she ran her hands down Hauberk's neck, and he grinned. "Not so much. These days they're used for dressage and jumping. In Hauberk's case, dressage. That's French for 'training' and it's like…"

"… it's like the white stallions of Vienna. I know, I hope to go see them some day." She glanced up at him and stopped rubbing Hauberk's ears until the horse nudged her again.

"Hauberk, that's enough. She's worshipped at your greatness, already."

"It's okay. When you're as magnificent as him, you can demand worship."

The stallion lowered his head and gave Letha one great head butt that caught her off guard and sent her onto her rear before Ty could react. She managed to hold onto her cup, but the coffee sprayed everywhere.

"Hauberk! Back! Letha, I'm sorry. He knows better than that." Ty grabbed her arm and lifted her to her feet in one smooth motion. "You okay?"

"Fine. I'm fine." But all the breath had left her lungs, at her fall and his touch. Heat and the frightening darkness roared into her as he brushed dust from her jeans. He wasn't hurting her, though. Instead, his gaze spoke of concern for her and pique that his horse had done this.

She pulled loose and shook her head.

"You didn't hit your tailbone or anything, did you? Horse doesn't know his own strength. God, I'm so sorry." Then he realized she was actually smiling at him.

"What? What's the matter?"

"It's just that no one's ever been that concerned about me when I did something stupid. My fault, really. I let him get away with the nudges the first couple of times. I wouldn't have let my mare do it." She looked down at herself. "So much for clean clothes."

"Did sort of make a mess of things. Come on to the cabin."

She looked up at him, realized how tall he was — six-feet-two, at least — and how close he stood, so close he could kiss her if he wanted to, so close she could feel his body heat as a reflection of her own. She nodded.

His hands had told him there were strong muscles under those form-fitting jeans. Strength in that willow-like body he'd seen. Even the heavy shirt-jacket couldn't hide her gentle curves. Limping, he led her to the door, then turned. "Hauberk, we're going to have to talk about your manners."

The horse snorted and shook his head, then ducked back into his stall as if ignoring Ty. "Shows you how much respect I get," he laughed.

On the cabin porch he hauled off his boots with a bootjack and she followed suit. He went inside, and Letha, curious, followed as he padded around the small, crowded space.

Everything in its place, just like the barn. The old brown overstuffed chairs sat facing the old river-stone fireplace along one wall, even though a wood heater in the corner was clearly what heated the place. A couple of Hudson Bay blankets had been thrown over the chair backs, the red and green stripes brightening up the wood-walled room. A neat table and chairs, with salt and pepper shakers shaped like cowboy boots. Clear counters in a small corner kitchen and clean stove. An open door revealed the one bedroom, with a rust-red and tan quilt-covered bed and a sturdy, wood rocking chair.

He padded over to a coffee maker. "Small space like this, took me a bit to get used to it. You learn pretty quick that to keep it livable, everything has to be kept in its place." He looked back at her. "You want to wash up, the bathroom's in the back."

She looked down at herself, not wanting the intimacy that came from walking through a man's bedroom and the use of his bathroom. Most of the coffee was on her flannel shirt-jacket. "Kitchen sink'll do."

She stripped off the jacket and stood in her thermal undershirt, washing out the coffee and washing horse off her hands. "Nice, handy kitchen. Well laid out."

He smiled at her and considered the place, with its granite counter and stainless steel sink and miniature propane range, a copper-bottomed sauté pan and sauce pot hung above the stove. To him it was a big step down from his place just outside D.C., but to her it was probably pretty nice, given that most of the long-time Valley folk lived pretty basic lives. "Owners had it renovated. It'll do. Doesn't get much use, though. Commitments down south."

"Too bad." To Letha, it looked snug enough to take someone through the winter. The log walls were in good repair and the windows looking out onto the lake were large and triple paned. Inside, all the cupboards and counters shone, like whoever owned this place had taken the time to put in good quality — as if they intended to spend time here. A place you could love coming to or living in.

"Who're the owners? I heard the Murphy's had sold, but no one knew who bought the place." She finished her shirt and hung it on the back of a kitchen chair near the heater.

He grinned. "Okay, I'll come clean. We did."

She raised a brow and glanced at him. We? Kristienne hadn't said a thing about her brother getting married. There was no ring on his finger. And there was that thing she felt whenever her touched her...

But *we*?

"Yeah, me and Matt. I told him I needed a place to come home to, but could still be on my own. He bought the place with my financing."

Why was he telling her this? When he came to the Valley he wasn't planning on letting anyone in, just coast along, depending on the fact everyone already knew him.

"Matt. Of course."

He stopped fussing over putting cream and sugar on the table and pouring the coffee, and turned to her. His grin broadened. "You were wondering if I'd gotten married? Nah, nobody'd have me."

He plunked over-full coffee mugs on the table and added a bit of sugar to his, motioned her to help herself, then took his cup over to the fireplace. It was laid and ready. One match, and a merry little fire licked at the kindling. "Some skills you just don't lose," he said, nodding her to the other chair.

"I really should be getting back."

"Come on. It's your day off. Anything you have to do, will wait."

She sighed and accepted the chair, pulling the tissue-wrapped ornament out of her pocket. "Almost forgot. Housewarming present."

Ty's moss-green gaze met hers a moment as he accepted the gift. The fire was warm on her face, seemed almost too warm as he held her gaze while he unwrapped the gift. He lifted the delicate horse carving out of the wrapping and she suddenly felt dull and foolish for giving him this. He was a man, and men generally weren't equipped to appreciate the charm of delicate artwork. She'd have done better to bring him another pot of jam.

A low whistle through his teeth. "Wow, this is great. It's an Indian hunter, isn't it?"

"That's what it looked like to me. A tracker maybe, but the way he and the horse are one — it made me think of you and Hauberk."

"Great." He stood and placed the carving on the tree-slab that functioned as a mantle. "I'll hang it there later. Place of honor for my first gift."

He sat down and looked at her, and his gaze made her pulse jump. She stood and went to the window. "Nice view from here. The windows really let you see the lake."

From where he sat, the better view was of Letha. Without her heavy jacket, the curve of her breast, the lean strength of her hips and legs showed through the mask of her clothes. He could see hints of the white form in the lake, the glimpse he'd had of her through the willow as she slipped into her robe.

"The view's important," he said, and she caught the way he looked at her — slow and appraising — as if they both knew that there was something between them — something that happened whenever their bodies touched. He stood and moved beside her to look out at the lake, felt her shift away.

"Well, it's nice to watch the seasons change, I guess. I'd like bigger windows in the store, but that would subtract shelf space, and Sylvia won't be having any of that."

"I saw you in the lake this morning. I was on the far side of the lake and just heading out on my ride, but when I saw you I turned Hauberk back. I wanted to see if you were feeling neighborly today." He glanced at the ornament. "Guess you were." He wanted to touch her, his hand almost raised of its own accord to see if the feeling she raised in him was real. He held his mug with both hands. "Maybe we could go for a ride together."

"I couldn't. I… I have to work on the webpage for the store so when I get my phone line I'm ready." She took a long gulp of coffee and he knew she was about to rush off.

"All right. We'll have to plan on another day. Something to look forward to. And for now we'll sit and have a pleasant conversation."

He plunked down in his chair and slowly she followed. Like a fine, untamed horse, he thought as he admired her athletic way of moving. Step in, step away. That was how you played it. Get them comfortable, comfortable enough to follow you on their own. That was how he was going to play it. It was how he'd played his last undercover gig, too.

He hoped this time things didn't go quite so wrong.

§

He seemed to need supplies from Letha's store almost daily. Fresh cream when he didn't take cream in his coffee, a box of Band-Aids in case he cut himself, a bottle of dishwashing soap when he already had one under the sink. Each time he came limping in, the brass bell she had rigged as a warning just outside the door rang, and he saw Letha look at him with one brow raised. But it got her used to him being around, got them both used to eye contact and that strange sensation that happened whenever they happened to touch.

'Course, others happened to pick up the fact he was visiting a fair amount. Sylvia caught him a fair few times, and Matt happened to comment that whenever he came by Ty wasn't home. That meant the rest of the Valley probably knew.

"Couldn't happen to have something ta do with Spring and a certain neighbor, now could it?" Matt asked from on horseback as Ty strolled up through the willow and aspen to his cabin, his limp slowly disappearing with all his exercise, a container of copper cleaner he'd had Letha special order for him in his pocket.

Karen L. Abrahamson

He looked up at his old friend. Matt was dressed in all his buckaroo finery, heavy batwing chaps, silver spurs, and broad-brimmed, silver-banded, cowboy hat shadowing his upper face all the way down to his dark brown handlebar moustache. His saddle had silver florets on the plain leather skirts and a well-worn lariat hung by the pommel. With some men it was an affectation, but for Matt it spoke of his commitment to an older way of life, where living in balance with horses and cattle was an art-form in and of itself.

"Might have. Been better since Spring came, don'tcha think?"

"Might be. Nice day to take a youngster out for a spin." He motioned at his mount. "Cattle are startin' ta fatten on new grass, but you got that cat-that-ate-the-canary look if I ever seen it. You be careful, Ty. No one wants you stealin' our girl away."

"Right." He shook his head. Matt was right. He was here for a time, that was all. He glanced back in the direction of the store. "You ride over here to warn me off?"

"Hey, I'm not one to warn Ty Hunt off've anything, and you know it. Letha Rivers is her own woman, more or less, and quite a woman, t'boot. Nope, I mind my own business where women are concerned, but there's a problem at the ranch, and Kristienne — she's gone inta town. I called her, and she said call you. It's yer Ma, Ty. She's been inta the bottle again and she's out wanderin' the road. I tried to lasso her inta goin' home, but she wouldn't have none of it. Thought maybe you could handle it."

" 'Course I'll handle it. Shit. Thanks." He grabbed his truck keys from the cabin and headed out, watching in the rearview mirror as Matt half-spun his young mount toward home along the lake trail. Good horseman, Matt. Kind handed, thoughtful, and gentle if firm. A dying breed. Ty'd always hoped he could be as good a rider. Shame the man hadn't found a wife yet.

He headed his truck down the road to where the pavement ran out and the side road turned toward the Hunt Ranch. Gravel pinged the underbelly of the truck as he steered through an area marked with For Sale signs on lots along the road. He hadn't known the ranch was selling some of its bottom land.

He frowned, and then saw a horse-drawn wagon up ahead with two figures on board. One was clearly his mother, with her fair hair billowing grey-gold around her slim shoulders. The other....

"Shit." Harry Zigheld. Had Matt known? Probably not, because there's no way Matt would want to put Ty and Harry in front of each other — not since they'd near beaten each other to a pulp over a horse Harry had bought from the Hunts. When the horse had died looking poorly, he'd refused to pay, saying the Hunts didn't raise good horseflesh. Looking at the scars on the colt's mouth and flanks, Ty had been convinced that the horse had been abused. And if there was one thing he couldn't countenance, it was an abusive owner. The two boys had grown into men, but the years hadn't changed Ty's opinions any.

He passed the wagon and pulled over onto the shoulder of the road by a gully filled with rushes and young poplar that rattled in the comfortably warm breeze. Run-off followed the gully bottom toward the lake and glittered through the tall grass as he climbed out to wait for the team and wagon to pull even.

It was a poor wagon and poorer team. Grey geldings, both with ribs showing through rough winter coats. The stench that came with the wagon said it was hauling manure, and that was where his mother perched instead of sitting with Harry on the seat. Ty felt himself stiffen.

"Morning, Harry." He fought to keep his voice country-pleasant.

"Well, Lord a'mighty. Look what the cat's dragged home. Ty Hunt in all his glory." Wearing faded jeans and a patched flannel shirt, Harry hauled back on the lines so the team of horses stopped dead. He peered down at Ty through glazed eyes that if anything looked closer-set than they had as a kid. His mop of blonde hair was cut short at the back, but the top hung forward over his eyes, and his mouth had taken a downturn as soon as he recognized Ty.

"So where you headed this fine day?" It *was* a fine day — blue sky, and Spring taking over the fields, and a pleasant conversation with Letha — until now.

"What's it to ya? Bought me a piece of Hunt Ranch bottom land and I'm haulin' some manure over to build me a garden. Man can't stay livin' with his folks ferever." He glanced back at his stinking load. "Found me a passenger, too." He grinned.

Ty walked past Harry on his buckboard seat to look up at his mother, seated on top of the half-rotted manure. Elizabeth Hunt had been a beautiful woman in her day — the yellowing photos on the wall of the Hunt Ranch house showed her in her performances in La Boheme, Lucia de Lammermoor, and Carmen on the stage of The Met and other Opera houses around America and Europe. Tall and blonde, with high cheekbones and vivid green eyes she'd given to her son, and a grace and culture that never fit into the Valley she'd come to after marrying a New York detective she'd met during a police investigation.

She looked down at him now, her green gaze as cloudy as absinthe, but then she recognized her son and her mouth bowed into the dazzling smile Ty had always loved as a child. "Ty! I was just coming to see you! I've got your room all fixed up spiffy so you can move in."

"Mom, what're you doing up there?" he said gently, and caught her hand as it fluttered up to his cheek. Her fingers trembled from drink, and the reek of alcohol hung in the air. Damn it, how long had she been drinking like this? She'd been tippling a little when he left — it had always been hard for her, being trapped on the ranch. His mother was a creature of cities. Why hadn't he been told?

Because you haven't shown a damn bit of interest, have you.

"Mom?" She turned distracted eyes back to him after following a flight of geese down to the lake.

"Aren't they fine looking birds? Yes, well, I saw Harry and his fine team and he offered me a ride. He said he'd take me by your place on his way home." She smiled at Harry. He tipped his hat with a smirk and nodded.

"Well, let's get you down from there and I can give you a ride in my truck, Ma. We can go see my place and have lunch together and go for a walk, and then I can take you home when Kristienne gets back."

She chewed the inside of her cheek for a moment, giving him a look that was nothing short of petulant, and Ty's stomach clenched with a deep sorrow and anger. She shouldn't be like this. Who had let her get like this?

He pulled gently on her hand. "Come on, Ma. I'll lift you down. You shouldn't be riding in a load of manure."

"Manure?" She looked around her, the breeze catching in her pale, loose hair, lifting the long skirt she wore over faded jeans as she stood. "I haven't had a wagon ride in so long. Remember when you used to hitch up that black team of ours in winter and we'd take the bobsled out? That darn team never was much good, was it? We spent more time digging ourselves out of snowdrifts than getting anywhere, but your father did love that team."

"They were a couple of retired reining horses, Ma. Never had any sense for driving, but Dad wanted them to earn their keep." And Dad always got what he wanted, Ty thought grimly. Lifting her down from the manure, he realized just how light his mother had become. Flesh had melted from her bones, her face, leaving her a shadow of the mother he remembered, who used to sing Puccini whenever Spring came back to the Valley.

He put his arm around her, frowning at the apple-alcohol scent as he guided her toward the truck and got her seated in the cab. Then he went back to Harry. "You could have at least had the decency to put her beside you on the seat," he said through gritted teeth.

Harry shrugged, all flamboyant innocence. Just like with the horse. "Hell, ya should be thankin' me, Ty. She was out staggerin' down the road, like she was about to pass out somewheres. I was thinkin' o' your sister — she don't want the neighbors talkin' more. Thing like this — it's a family thing." Smirking again.

He started to gather the reins and Ty grabbed them. He leaned in close enough he could smell the apple-scent on Harry's breath. "You listen to me, Harry Zigheld. I know this gave you a hell of rush — putting a Hunt in manure." His hand reached under the wagon seat and he hauled out a bottle of home-made hooch. "But if you ever — I mean ever — come near my mother again or feed her this rotgut, I'll show you a shining like you never had before. That beating I gave you as a kid — well, it'll take more than a month of bed-rest to get yourself right this time. You got that?"

Harry's gaze narrowed. "You got no right to threaten me, Hunt. You don't live in this Valley no more, and if you cared so damn much about yer ma, then why'd you stay away so fuckin' long?" He yanked the reins out of Ty's hands. "I've a mind to get together a couple o' the boys and come pay you a visit. I owe you one, remember? Git up, ya bastards!"

He slapped the grays' rumps with the reins and the wagon jerked into motion, running past Ty's truck where his mother gave a merry wave goodbye to Harry. Damn it, she thought Harry was her friend!

Ty stood in the road watching the wagon drive away as he fought to contain his anger. He scuffed his boot in the gravel. Nice one, Hunt. Get the locals pissed at you and probably your family. Great way to live quiet and not draw attention to yourself. Hauberk breaking loose was the least of your worries.

It was his own self-control that was the problem.

§

Kristienne stomped her boots on the porch and met Ty at the door of the Hunt Ranch house. "She okay? I got back as soon as I could," she began. "How bad was it?"

"Bad enough. Found her in the back of Harry Zigheld's manure wagon — full."

She closed her eyes at the tightening in her belly. "What happened?"

"What d'you mean, what happened? I got Ma. I left. What's to tell?"

Kristienne pushed past him into the house and down the hall to set her bundle of groceries on the kitchen table. "Like you've ever just dealt with Harry Zigheld with a quick thanks and goodbye." She turned back to him. "Maggie Murphy waved me down on the way back from town. She was just coming from the store. Sylvia's there again, damn it. Word'd already reached her you and Harry got into it."

"Whoa, there, sister. I didn't lay a hand on Harry Zigheld. Not my way anymore."

"So what'd you do?"

Ty peeked into the grocery bag and pulled out a box of cookies, pulled them open, and bit into an oatmeal one as he slid up onto the counter. "Let's just say I warned him to be good to our mother."

Kristienne rolled her eyes. "And I suppose that's as close to the truth as I'm going to get."

"Any closer it'll hurt you. I'm just protecting what's worth protecting."

She put her carton of eggs down, then gave him a peck on the cheek. "You always were a good older brother, but I don't need your protecting anymore."

"Mom does."

"Mom's way past protecting, Ty."

He slid off the counter. "Why didn't you tell me how bad it'd got? She was depressed when I left and she tippled from time to time, but nothing like this. I knew she'd lost weight, but hell, is she living on booze? She was so far in her cups today I thought she was drowning. It's killing her. We've got to do something."

"So you've decided to be the man of the family and rescue our mother when you come for a visit?" She had her hands on her hips and she knew he'd see her anger, and she just didn't bloody well care, did she? "You think I haven't tried? You think I've just stood back and watched? Where the heck were you, Ty? All these years. It got worse after Dad died, and you could have come back. Hell, you didn't even come for the funeral. You know how that hit her? After all those years trying to bring peace between you and Dad, she thought you were mad at her, too."

Ty took the shot in the gut and knew he deserved it. He held up his hands. This was his baby sister. "Whoa. Stop. I don't want to cause trouble, and I know you've done everything you could, and everything right." He held up a framed photo of a lovely, slender woman in a long full evening gown he'd obviously taken down from the hallway wall. "It's just that this is our mother. Not this person, now."

"Damn straight. I got her in treatment — twice — but it didn't take. I don't know what to do. Other than to protect her."

Ty shook his head, then caught her shoulders. "Listen, I was wondering. I know Sylvia's got that talent with the animals. You ever think of asking her to look into Ma, find out what's wrong?"

"You're a big-time FBI agent, and you want to use Valley hooey to find out what's wrong with our mother?"

"Couldn't hurt. You ever asked her?"

"No, I never asked her, and I wouldn't ask her. You might believe in Sylvia's 'talent,' but that doesn't mean I have to. Besides, *if* Sylvia had a talent, she'd use it for her own benefit — just like she does everything."

"But it might help give us some insight into what's wrong with Ma."

"And pigs might fly if they had wings. Come on, Ty. Get real. If you want to ask her, ask her yourself. She's at the store all the time and I hear you're there a lot." She raised her brows at him. "You getting lucky with Ms. Letha? Do I need to thank you for the Spring?"

"Letha's a neighbor, that's all."

"Right. And I'm deaf as well as blind. She's still got you buffaloed, huh?"

"If and when I want a date, I'll ask her. Now quit changing the subject. I think Sylvia might be able to tell us something. I think you might have better luck with her than me."

"Fine. I'll talk to her. Now would you get yourself out of here? I've got business to do." She turned her back on him and waited for his footsteps to recede down the hall, but infuriatingly he stayed where he was. She swung back to him. "Now?"

He nodded and she swore at him, hauled the truck keys from her pocket and strode down the hall. "This better be worth it, Ty Hunt. 'Cause you know how I hate to be in debt, and believe you me, Sylvia always makes you pay."

She slammed the truck in gear, taking deep gulps of diesel-tanged air to stop her anger. It was a damned fool's errand. Sylvia and her talent. Sure, as a kid she'd believed. They'd all believed. Sylvia had a talent to hear animal's feelings, Kristienne had had a talent for weather — at least, she thought she could change the shapes of clouds. Letha hadn't claimed any talent — other than being a gardener — until she was chosen in that woo-woo ceremony of Spring. Kristienne shook her head and shivered at the memory of a green-gold explosion of light.

As she got older, she'd known it was ridiculous. Science explained how clouds changed shape in the winds. Letha, who railed against it, was forced to conduct archaic rites by the darned Valley elders. Only Sylvia really held on to the notion that things were different for her. That she was special.

Of course, it was that Sylvia wasn't quite special enough; and her annoyance when Letha was chosen by Spring, that had always been something Kristienne couldn't countenance. Over the years, Sylvia seemed to want to control Letha — as if she'd hold the power — as if there was any — vicariously. And gentle Letha was left with even less control over her life.

Kristienne geared down for the turn into the lakeside drive, and parked in the gravel lot of the store next to Sylvia's white truck. The lake glimmered with small wavelets, almost cleared of ice. A flock of ducks came in a V formation, settling with a splash to begin dabbling in the reeds along the south shore. Pretty, but not pretty enough to change her mood.

She stomped onto the porch and went inside, the brass bell tolling a welcoming tone. Nice touch. Typical Letha.

The store smelled of coffee, and Sylvia looked around from where she sat at a computer she'd set up on a small table pulled into one corner. She gave Kristienne a cool smile that set her teeth on edge. Letha stood at her shoulder.

"Kris! What a nice surprise. You need anything?" Letha asked. "I got fresh dairy delivered today, and some great croissants. Mrs. Rogers was saying as she remembered them from when she traveled to Paris on her honeymoon, so I found someone who baked them, and bought a dozen. There're still a few left. I'm told they're best fresh."

"I didn't come to shop."

"Your loss." Sylvia looked back at the computer screen. "So what brings you to disturb the peace?"

Kristienne took a deep breath. "I need to talk to you."

"Me?" Sylvia looked at Letha with feigned shock on her face. "My god, pigs finally have learned to fly. Check the skies."

"Sylvia, stop it. She's your friend."

Sylvia looked back at the computer. "Letha, I'm still not convinced a website is a good idea. We're just a little general store." She glanced at Kristienne. "So talk."

Kristienne looked at the ceiling, shuffled her feet, and finally jammed her hands in her pockets. Damn her, she was still busy with the computer. "Ty asked me to ask you a favor."

"Mmm hmm."

"Damn it, look at me."

Sylvia looked away from the computer. "What's got your knickers in a twist?"

"It's Mom, all right. More problems."

Sylvia nodded. "Maggie Rogers mentioned Harry and Ty got into it. Something about your mother, and Harry giving her a ride." She shook her head. "Told her it was none of our business, not that it'll do any good."

At least Sylvia wasn't a rumor mill queen like most of the Valley folk. She *did* mind her own business — most of the time. Okay, then just get it out and said and see what happened. As Ty said, it couldn't hurt.

"Ty thought… I mean, Mom's in a bad way… oh, heck!" She walked over to the window, looked out to try to find calm in the lake. "Syl, we're wondering if you could try that talent of yours out on Mom, to help us find out what her problem is. We'd pay you for your time."

"Pay me?"

Kristienne turned around and froze at Sylvia's grim face. "Yeah. What the heck's the problem?"

"Kristienne, I've had this talent for years. Have you ever seen me ask for payment?"

Don't go there, Kristienne, she thought even as she blurted "When have you ever not?"

"What the hell's that supposed to mean?" Syl pushed back from the table, stood. "Of course I'll try to help. I charge for my veterinary skills, nothing else."

"Yeah, you take it out in kind for your other 'skills'. Like Letha here, you buy a store and let her run it, and that lets you run her life."

"Kris, no! It's not like that." Letha stepped in between the two of them.

"I'm sorry, Letha, but you let her!"

Kristienne spun on her heel and slammed out of the cabin.

Sylvia sighed, then patted Letha's arm. "Our friend seems particularly tense today. Guess it really was bad."

"You two shouldn't fight like that. We're all supposed to be friends. Friends forever."

"Friends fight. So do lovers. It's normal." She caught Letha's hand and pulled her back to the computer. "We can't all be like you, at peace with everything. Kristienne and I, well, we just fight a little more because we're both strong-willed, and our lives drive us in different directions."

"You act like you hate each other."

Sylvia smiled. "Nope. No hate here. Just tired. I'll check out her mom when I get a chance, and if I can read her, which isn't too likely, I will. If there's something there, I'll let Kristienne know." She yawned and ran a hand through her hair. "Tell you what. I'm bagged and I know you've got things to do. Go ahead with the website. What can it hurt? The phone lines'll be coming in the next few days, so we'll just get DHL at the same time. I'll make the call." She patted Letha's hand.

"So you don't mind what I'm doing? 'Cause sometimes I feel like nothing I'm doing, nothing I've got planned, is good enough."

"It's all good. Everything here. But tell you what. How about we take the horses out for a ride tomorrow and you can tell me about your plans for the place. All of them."

Chapter 4

Damn Harry, but it was the sort of juvenile action Ty expected of the man. Harry hadn't grown out of his vindictive nature. As a boy, he'd pulled dirty tricks on his teacher when she failed him on an exam, or on a girl who wouldn't go out with him. Nothing serious, just stupid pranks and spitefulness. Thankfully, his imagination didn't seem to have made his actions any more serious. Just messy.

Ty stood looking at the disaster in his living room. Apparently he'd 'forgotten' to close the cabin door properly when he went over to visit his mom, and wild animals had gotten in to spread the food around and do their business on the floor. Must have been a few of those 'pack dogs' — they were very strategic in where their scat was placed — and they weren't long gone, judging by the flour still sifting through the air. It had Harry Zigheld's marks all over it, including the footprint of a worn boot in flour by the porch stair — left like a calling card, no doubt.

Ty righted a chair that had been powdered with cornflakes, and bundled up the Hudson Bay blanket that would need a lake dousing to rid it of dog feces. Maybe he was giving Harry more credit than he was due about leaving a calling card. The footprint was an accident, most likely.

A sound outside brought his head up, and he stepped out onto the porch into clear evening air. Out on the open lake a loon called under the first stars.

A low whinny. Shit. Harry wasn't stupid enough to hurt Hauberk, was he? That was something Ty wouldn't ignore. Ty's skin chilled at memories and the breeze off the lake. The guy was stupid enough to wreck a promising youngster years ago. From what he'd seen the other day, Harry hadn't gotten any brighter.

Ty leapt off the porch and went around to the paddock he'd built off of Hauberk's stall so the stallion could exercise at will. The big horse stood stock-still in the middle of the paddock in the gathering gloom, but nickered at Ty's approach.

"Hey, there, big guy. You doing okay?"

Hauberk tossed his head, a snort rumbling in his nostrils. Ty dug in his pocket for a piece of the processed grain that he used as treats. He held it out on his palm, but Hauberk didn't move.

Now that was strange. Hauberk was as big a glutton as any horse when it came to this molasses-infused grain. Ty frowned and started forward when a something not-breeze stirred the bushes to one side. Hauberk's snort rolled through the night as Ty went cold.

He straightened, and all the worst thoughts went through his head. He wanted to go to his horse, but Hauberk seemed fine and there was something to take care of first. This was no professional hit. No professional would spread flour in his cabin. "Let's get you in your stall, big guy."

He ducked around to the barn's front door, then, when his movement was screened by the bulk of the door, he crept through the bushes that hedged the cabin's clearing from the road. There. Down the road, as he'd suspected, sat a late model pickup, its paint gleaming dully.

Head down, he jogged along the verge of the road, careful of noise, then paused and crept down toward the brush. Two dark figures stood whispering among the young poplar and cedar. Typical, stupid-assed perps, wanting to enjoy the results of their actions.

Ty had them by the collars of their jean jackets before they knew what hit them. He yanked them backward to the road, dragged them up the slight incline, and when one of them tried to yank loose, Ty released him with a swift boot to the butt. The figure staggered into the road just as another pickup came rumbling down the pavement, its high beams sweeping the tableau of Ty, Harry Zigheld, and his brother Jimmy.

Ty swore under his breath and released Harry as the truck pulled up and the window hummed down.

"We got a problem here, boys?" Murphy Rogers leaned on the sill, his round cheeks rosy even in the dim light. "'Cause I don't countenance fightin' an' you know it." The Rogerses had always been strictly religious members of the community and had a tough time even accepting the Spring rites.

"No, sir," Ty said, feeling like a teenager again. He lifted his chin at Harry and his brother. "Caught these two messing up my cabin. Was just convincing them it wasn't a good idea to repeat."

"That a fact?"

Harry's narrow gaze looked like a storm cloud gathering in a mountain pass, and Jimmy had a sheepish look in eyes that were just as close-set, but nowhere near as vicious as his brother's. Jimmy nodded.

"You don't go messin' with a man's things. You both know that — yer Pa taught ya better and so did yer Ma."

Again the sheepish nod, and Harry's scowl that never left Ty's face. Murphy kept on in his dressing down of the Zigheld boys — just like he'd done when they were fourteen, not edging toward forty.

Finally he turned back to Ty. "How you settlin' in?"

"Fine, Mr. Rogers. Just fine."

Rogers glanced down the lake, a smile fleeting across his lips. "Ya must have brought Spring with ya, I think." The smile became a grin. "Ya got a good neighbor, I hear."

Ty felt himself color slightly. Damn it, where was everyone getting these ideas about him and Letha — not that they were bad ideas, but everything in its own time. "Yeah, I got a neighbor."

"Well, seeing as this is all taken care off, I'm off home. You boys behave, now." He dropped the truck in gear and started away, with a last wave of the hand.

Ty turned back to Harry and Jimmy. "You heard the man, get outta here and don't bother coming back. If anything — I mean anything — happens at my place again, I'll be hunting you, Harry. You got that?"

Harry didn't even bother to hide his fury. His scowl was as dark as the night forming around him. "You got no right coming here and orderin' me around, shooting me down when I help yer ma, embarrassing me in front of folk. You just wait, big city man. Accidents can happen out here in the country — or you ferget that? You and yer big city horse — if ya can even call it a horse." He spat on the ground at Ty's feet and stomped off toward his truck, Jimmy trailing behind.

Ty slowly uncurled his fists and waited for the men to start their truck and drive off. Back in D.C. he'd have run the idiot in just on attitude, but here the police were a long way away. Harry Zigheld had one looong memory, and this was a dressing down he wasn't going to forget. Ty was going to have to watch his back.

§

The truck taillights had disappeared in a red flare down the road before Ty turned back to the cabin and his horse. When he stepped down through the thin spot in the brush where Harry and Jimmy had lurked, he saw the stallion's bulk still in the same spot. He controlled the alarm bells ringing in his head.

Inside the corral the problem was clear, and Ty swore oaths up to the star-filled heavens. In some spate of apparent carelessness, an old loose roll of rusted barbed wire had been left where Hauberk could find it. The big horse had, and now stood with the wire tangled around all four legs. As Ty watched, Hauberk tried to pull loose, snorting his frustration.

Ty swung up and over the newly-installed fence rails and down into the corral. "Hey, big guy," he said using his calming voice, but Hauberk made as if to leap away. "Whoa there, fella. This isn't our usual game of tag. This is serious."

He walked to the horse slowly, knowing Hauberk's habit of leaping away at the last moment. This time the horse stayed still. The big horse was sweating and shaking, damn it. Ty ran his hands over the horse's neck, his head, and Hauberk put his face against Ty's chest blowing a huge, rolling sigh out his nostrils. Ty fed him a treat.

"What they done to you, big guy?" Ty said, inhaling the sweet scent of horse breath as he ran his hands down his horse's damp flank to his legs. His annoyance swelled into real anger.

The wire had obviously been placed for the horse to walk right into. The wire bands were tangled right up to Hauberk's hocks, the metal strands twisted tight from where he'd tried to get free. Now they cut into the fine dark skin. When Ty tried to loosen the loops, his hands came away dark with Hauberk's blood.

Ty knew the horse reacted to his emotions, felt the stallion become restive as Ty fought back his fury. Thank the heavens he was raised a cowboy amongst cowboys and had taught Hauberk about hobbles as a young colt, so he didn't fight too badly when his legs were caught. Any other dressage horse Ty'd owned would have torn his legs beyond repair.

He struggled with the wire, but there was no way he could pull the loops loose with his bare hands and steady Hauberk at the same time. Hell, he couldn't even find the end of the loops in the darkness. He needed light and he needed someone to hold Hauberk while he worked, because if the horse got spooked, he could do himself some serious damage — correction — more serious damage than he'd already done.

"OK, big guy. I'll be back in a couple. You hang tough here and I'll get you fixed up." He stepped away and Hauberk tried to follow him like a little kid afraid of the dark. "No, fella. You stay where you are, stay put. Don't move."

Snorting, Hauberk tossed his head and Ty swiftly climbed the corral rails and jogged down the trail toward the store. Letha would help, and from what he'd seen, she was good with horses.

There were no lights on that he could see, just the blue-green glow of a computer screen. He stomped up the stairs and tried the door. Locked. Surprising for the Valley, but not where he came from. He knocked the brass bell so it jangled and was about to leave, when he saw movement inside and froze when he found himself looking down the barrel of a well-maintained shotgun aimed at him through the door window.

"Letha! It's me, Ty."

The barrel didn't waver. "What do you want?" In the dim light of the cabin he could see her pale face — paler than usual and filled with fear and suspicion.

"I need your help. Hauberk's in a jam. I need a hand with him."

The shotgun barrel bobbled slightly. "Hauberk? What's the matter?"

"He's got himself all tangled in barbed wire. I need someone to hold him while I work. I'm praying his legs are okay. Come on, be a good neighbor."

The gun barrel steadied slightly. "Good neighbors knock on doors. They don't just try to come in."

What the hell was the matter with the woman? He'd thought they'd put their rocky start behind them. He thought they were friends. He rubbed his hands over his face. "Fine then. Can I use your phone? Or can you call Sylvia for me?"

There was a click and the door opened. Letha stood with her gun half-lowered and uncertainty in her eyes. "I was sleeping. Dreaming. I guess I thought…." The shotgun barrel wavered as her gaze searched his. "I guess you surprised me. Of course I'll help. Just let me get dressed. How bad is it?"

He watched her as she set the gun — a rancher's bird-hunting gun, by the look of it — by the fireplace, and then dart to her bedroom. The woman couldn't even look ungraceful in tatty flannel pajamas with her hair tangled around her face. But she'd really been scared when she came to the door. It had been in her eyes and had only increased when she's seen it was him. Maybe it was because she'd been sleeping, but what had he ever done to Letha Rivers?

She came out in jeans and her ubiquitous, shrouding flannel shirt-jacket. "Do I need to get my emergency vet kit?"

Her eyes had cleared. She was Letha now, practical, but still slightly wary of him. She swayed when she came up to him, her breathing still rapid.

"I've got one. Hey, you okay?"

"Fine," she said, but she swayed again and he caught her elbow until she pulled loose and leaned against the doorframe. "You just scared me. I… had a bad dream, and then there was someone yanking at the door, the bell going. I didn't know what was going on."

"So I was in your dreams, huh? Every Valley man's desire." He grinned, and she looked sideways at him and couldn't stop herself from grinning back.

"I don't think you were the good guy, if you must know."

"So I was the mysterious stranger? The messenger out of the storm who might bring good news or bad."

How did he know these things? Along with the strange feelings he raised in her, Ty Hunt had the weird ability to put word to her thoughts before she could. "How…?"

"Blame Joseph Campbell. When I was in school we learned all about archetypes."

She followed him down the porch and along the lake, feeling vulnerable at the darkness, at the fact that, aside from the loon cry across the water, there seemed to be only the two of them in the world. She'd gone to bed early with a book and had fallen asleep into a dark place of dreams. Even now the dream faded so she couldn't recall it, only that there was something dark coming, and it came with Ty Hunt.

"Is Hauberk hurt?"

"He's bleeding, so his legs are cut. I can't tell how bad. I need you to hold his head and a light so I can see what I'm working on."

She went into the barn with him, waited in the darkness as he fumbled around.

"Remind me to put the flashlight by the door in future." He turned around and walked into her, sending a flash of warmth through her body. The flashlight flicked on. "Guess I should use this."

The low light placed deep shadows across his face that brought a shiver down her spine. She swallowed and stepped back, almost falling over the saddle tree. He caught her elbow.

"Guess you should," she said.

"Yeah." But he didn't release her. He stood too close, looking down at her, those green eyes too dark and intense so that her insides shivered.

"Your horse?" she found her voice.

"Hauberk. Yeah." He grabbed a neat red box off the shelf and turned her toward the back of the barn, still holding her elbow as they went through Hauberk's stall to the corral. That strange flow of — something — ran through her and left her weak at the knees.

The horse tossed his head as they came up to him. Sweat blackened his flanks. Letha pulled away from the discomfiting warmth of Ty's hand and went to Hauberk's head. The stallion blew warm breath in her hand, lowered his head, and pressed the hard ridge of his face into her chest. "You're just a big baby wanting comfort, aren't you?" she said, rubbing the bump between his ears.

"He likes you." Ty handed her the flashlight and knelt as she illuminated the mess around the horse's legs. "Damn. It's worse than I thought. Look at this cut."

It was. The flashlight showed wire wrapped in loop after loop around the fine, dark legs from fetlock to hock. An open line of flesh at the back of a knee showed where Hauberk had struggled at the biting barbs and the wire had cut him. How serious it was, was reflected in the lines around Ty's mouth. Barely suppressed anger brought sharp edges to the lines around his eyes. That he cared deeply for this horse was clear, and she liked that in him.

"How'd this happen?" she asked.

"Some fool would have you believe I'd leave barbed wire where my horse could get into it. Just like I'd leave my cabin door open for wolves or bears or dogs to get in."

"You oughta know better, Ty." Softly.

"Right. So after finding my cabin trashed I come out here and find Hauberk, with Harry and Jimmy Zigheld snickering in the brush. We had a little talk. Ah, that's got it." He grunted and unwound a long loop from around and around Hauberk's left foreleg, then ran his hand up and down the flesh. "Cuts, but the tendons all seem okay."

He shifted to the rear leg, leaving her with a view of his strong shoulders and narrow hips, and a brief view of tanned back where his jacket and shirt rode up. Strong. Long muscled. Like his horse. Letha jerked her gaze away.

"So how long have you had him," she asked to try to diffuse the little tingle that had formed in her belly. She used her fingers to untangle Hauberk's forelock.

"Just over three years. Since he was a colt. He's four now. Bought him as a foal because there was no way on earth I could afford something as good him that was riding age."

"These… Warmbloods… are expensive?"

"Think hundreds of thousands of dollars."

She whistled and he glanced up at her with a little-boy grin as he finished untangling the next leg. "I didn't pay that. Not on my salary."

His salary. She still didn't know where he worked — except it had something to do with law enforcement, but friends knew those sorts of things about each other. She was at a distinct disadvantage with Ty, because he knew just about everything of interest in her life. As he worked on the next leg, Hauberk stirred against her, wanting her attention. She ran comforting hands over him, wanting him to calm, wanting him to be whole, be well. She felt the power of the lake and Ty's nearness, filling her, flowing through her as she watched him work.

Confident. Kind. Strong hands that were gentle. She liked his hands and the intent concern on his face. He'd turned that look on her, too, though she'd ignored it. "I'm sorry," she blurted. He glanced up at her. "About the gun-greeting and all. You just surprised me."

He shrugged. "No need. I scared you. I'm sorry for that." The wire on the third leg came free, and Ty stood up and eased his back before coming forward to her, his limp pronounced. His gaze felt warm on her face, but Hauberk, legs no longer tied together, tried to move away. Ty grabbed his head. "Hold on there." He nodded.

The last leg planted on the ground, and Ty knelt again. So near, and Letha's awareness of him mounted. It was like something poured into her, just like the Lake's pour, just like Spring. It left her knees shaking, her hands trembling.

She breathed in, out, closed her eyes and laid her face against the big horse's neck. Don't let Ty worry you. Focus on the horse. Don't let him be injured. She found a calm place inside. Peace and calm and healing. Her body tingled with it. Her hands tingled with it. She opened her eyes, and where she ran her hands down Hauberk's shoulder it was like watching a firefly's trace in the grass — green glow and gone, and then she was staggering with fatigue.

Hauberk stirred as Ty stood and pulled the last loops of wire away from the horse, hauled them across the corral, and tossed them over the rails in disgust. "Man'd do that is more a beast than any animal."

He came back and found her gaze on him, the blue lost in the darkness so there were only shadows of concern in her eyes. Calm seemed to radiate from her slim form. It made his anger, his concern, more bearable. "You've got a good way with horses. Hauberk won't stand for just anybody."

"We're friends, aren't we?" she said, looking in the big horse's eye.

"You and Hauberk, or you and me?" he asked softly, and felt her gaze jerk toward him, that quiver of concern rising like a wave across calm water. He let it go — it shouldn't be so important that this woman like him — and knelt beside Hauberk's legs, hauling his veterinarian kit toward him.

He ran his hands down the foreleg; yes, tendons okay. But there had been so many cuts and puncture wounds. They must sting like heck, and the hair and wire had been sticky with blood.

The sticky blood was still there, dark on Hauberk's coat. Ty ran his hand down the leg seeking the source of the blood, but found nothing. He frowned. The puncture wounds must be too small. He used a rag to rub the blood away, slicked the lower leg with medicated ointment, then moved onto the left foreleg.

Same result, when he was sure there'd been a large gash just behind the knee. He repeated his actions. Repeated them on the hind legs, then stood, distracted by what he'd found. He might be tired and angry, but he was trained to observe and assess. Law enforcement and first aid training made him sure of his observations, so what the heck was going on? That cut on the foreleg had done some real damage.

"Something the matter?"

Letha met his gaze, and there was that predator-thing in his eyes again. Something fierce, yet calm and assessing, was hunting again, and as long as he looked at her it might be *her*. She looked away, but felt his gaze still on her as he came to her side.

"Damndest thing I ever saw," he said softly. He stood beside her, not moving. "His legs are all fine. Not a mark on them, though there's blood where they were bleeding."

"So maybe they weren't serious."

"Maybe."

Karen L. Abrahamson

He was still standing there like a flame in the night, and beyond him stood darkness. It made her nervous and she wasn't sure what it was, his heat or the darkness beyond. "Maybe they healed."

"And maybe there's power enough in Spring to heal them."

"Spring." She looked back at him and instantly wished she hadn't. Too close. He was too close.

He caught her hand on Hauberk's halter and released her fingers from the leather, but held her hand captive. The stallion shook his head and took a tentative step away. Took another. Trotted across the corral, his head and tail up.

"What'd you do, Letha?"

She felt his words like breath on her cheek. "Do? I don't know what you're talking about."

"Sure you do. You affect everything around you, don't you?" His voice was so soft, so deadly, she had to strain to hear.

No, she wanted to say. I don't. But it would have been a lie. That was the problem, wasn't it? She was too tied to this place, where the birds and animals and trees were like her bones and the lake lay at her heart. How do you ever get free of that?

'Never' seemed to echo in her head as she looked up at Ty.

Even through his unreasonable anger, she looked like she was close to tears, her eyes pools of sorrow, and Ty was suddenly ashamed he'd confronted her, even though it was all true — something had to explain the disappearance of Hauberk's wounds, but she looked so damned vulnerable. And defiant, and desirable beyond words.

He pulled her hand to his chest, to his lips, and kissed her palm, pulled her into him, and placed his lips on hers.

She froze as he inhaled her soft, female scent. Froze, and he released her and she stumbled back a step, her eyes frightened as a deer's. Releasing her was like stepping away from heat, warmth, and comfort.

Ty swallowed. The whole world was going nuts — him included. "I didn't mean… I… I'm sorry. That shouldn't have happened."

Her throat tightened as she swallowed at the sensation of his mouth still on hers. His lips were warm, soft — not hard, as she'd imagined.

She felt the heat flush through her. Yes, she had imagined it, hadn't she? And for one brief moment she'd felt herself yield.

God, he hadn't meant to do that, didn't want to place a barrier between them. But this whole evening was friggin' weird, and she was so slim in the night. So fine and fair and ready to spring away in fear. What had her so afraid? Your own clumsy advance, he thought. This is a woman who doesn't want involvements. You know that. She's bonded to Spring. But his hands still ached to touch her, for the feel of her hand. Hell, he didn't want involvements, either.

He stepped away and looked at Hauberk, standing on the far side of the corral, looking at them as if he saw something that bore watching.

"Look." He lifted his chin. "Darn horse is as shocked as we are." Ty strolled over to stand by the horse. "Damndest thing I ever saw, the way he's healed." He looked back at Letha. "Guess I've kept you up too long, haven't I?" He grabbed the horse and led him to his stall. "Time for all of us to be headed for our beds. Hauberk included."

He caught Letha's nod from the corner of his eye as he led Hauberk inside, and hoped she'd forgive him what he'd done. At least if they ended things like this — easy-like and focused on something else — maybe there was still a chance they could be friends.

Or maybe not, he thought when he turned to latch the corral door. His stomach tightened a little.

Letha might need a true friend, but it obviously wasn't him. She was already gone.

§

The morning came far too slowly for Ty. Lack of sleep can do that for you. So can thoughts of a woman, pale in the night, or seen across ice like Spring after a long winter. At dawn he was up and out to check on Hauberk. The stallion greeted him with a whinny and demanded to be let out, but when Ty dug in his pocket for a treat, he found the message his sister had given him from Samuels. Ty supposed he should check in with Buckley, because he should find out what was happening with the case. Later, maybe. Ty let Hauberk roll, then hosed off the horse's legs.

When he still couldn't find any sign of injury he shook his head, brushed Hauberk 'til he shone, and then saddled and headed out for a ride.

He rode past Letha's cabin, hoping to see her, but if she was up, she didn't let him know it. He pushed Hauberk into a canter and headed on around the lake.

The lake-side trail wound through the poplar, gleaming with white bark and new leaves he hadn't realized he missed so much, working down in the lower 48 states. While in the States spring came earlier, here Spring came to the Valley with a vigor that was as if everything worked overtime to jumpstart life. He'd missed the fact you could almost see the plants grow, the yellow pollen forming on the trees.

Hauberk started and jumped sideways as he rounded the far end of the lake toward the small stream that bled water down into the lower Valley. A red fox and three brilliant red kits dashed across a sink-hole filled with clean-smelling mint and into the brush.

Ty reined in. "It's a fox, Hauberk. Not a stallion-eating monster. No monsters at all, buddy." Hauberk blew foam from his nostrils and sidled where he stood.

"Fool," Ty muttered, grinning, and urged the horse into the stream that rose almost to the stallion's belly, loving the feel of the animal's power. Hauberk lunged up the steep bank on the other side and came in sight of the Hunt Ranch. Smoke curled out of the main house chimney, and also from the bunkhouse, set back at the edge of the trees. Calls and whistles came from the covered riding arena.

Kris, like all ranchers, was an early riser — and it was a habit Ty'd never been able to break in the city — but it seemed that he wasn't as early a riser as Matt and the other cowboys. Ty rode up to the open-sided arena and reined in. On Hauberk he could peer in through the open space between the roof and the solid arena sides. Hauberk hung his head over the siding so he could nose the hat of the man standing there.

"Holy Moses! You tryin' ta give a man a heart attack?" Matt Kelly spun around and grabbed his broad-brimmed tan Stetson out of Hauberk's teeth. His eyes widened as he looked up and up at the horse. "Damn, Ty. What the hell you ridin'?"

Beside him stood Kris, a satisfied expression on her face. "Told you he wouldn't be impressed."

Ty looked from face to face and smoothed Hauberk's short mane. He should expect this when no horse he'd ridden on the ranch had ever been over fifteen and a half hands, and they certainly hadn't been anything but a well-bred Quarter Horse. "Don't you recognize good horseflesh when you see it?"

"How c'n I tell, when all I can see is a head the size of a moose? You bring that 'horse' around where I c'n see him."

Ty met them at the gate, feeling his skin prickle at the grin on his sister's face as she stood back and let Matt take in Ty's horse.

"Shit, Ty, — 'scuse my language, Ma'am — any self respectin' calf could run right under that thing. What kind o' cattle man would want to ride a horse like that? An' in a flat saddle…." Matt's disgust showed in the way he slapped his hat against his thigh. "Didn't growing up here teach you anything?"

Ty grinned. The way Matt's gaze went to each part of Hauberk — the long sloping shoulder, the good hip, the solid bone of the legs, the large, clear eye, he knew Matt was judging the horseflesh in front of him, and there wasn't much fault to find. Finally he caught Ty's eye. "Put together okay."

Ty's grin broadened. That was praise indeed coming from Matt, who was a hard judge of horses and people alike.

"Bet he's not a damn bit o' good with a cow."

"Shoot, Matt, what's he going to do with a cow in that saddle? Got no horn — nothing to dally up to and nothing to hold himself on with."

"Hell of a long way to fall, too, I reckon."

Kris stuck her tongue out at her brother, enjoying the look of defensiveness on his face. Her brother wasn't often someone you could get in that position. "Seems to me you've got two choices, Ty — show us why you bought this thing you call a horse instead of something that makes sense, or else get down off your high horse, buy us a cup of coffee, and tell us why you've bothered morning workouts."

Ty glanced at the cutting horse gates and pens in the arena and the low-built colt facing down a calf, to stop it from returning to the other calves in the pen. He slid his leg over Hauberk's neck and down to the ground. No way Matt or Kris would see the different kind of talent Hauberk had — especially not when he was standing right beside a well-bred cutting horse colt. Besides, there were other talents he wanted to talk about.

"So where's the coffee?"

They led him to the horse barn, where Ty put Hauberk in cross ties and accepted the coffee mug Matt offered. He took a sip and coughed at the cowboy coffee — blacker than hell — certainly darker than anything available at the coffee shops that dotted D.C. streets.

"What's the matter? You gone lily-livered as well as weird in yer horse choice?"

"Forgot how good it is," Ty grimaced around another sip.

"So talk, bro. What's got you down-lake this morning?"

Ty sipped the coffee again. It actually was pretty good once you got over the initial shock. A little thicker than usual coffee, given it was just grounds boiled in a pot, but rich and full of chicory flavor. He'd forgotten the taste that filled your mouth like a meal of its own. "Got a visit from Harry Zigheld last night."

Kris closed her eyes. Matt simply waited.

Ty leaned back against a stall door and filled them in. When he got to the part about the barbed wire, Matt swore softly, then glanced at Kris and apologized. That was part of Matt's charm, the old-fashioned etiquette of the true buckaroo cowboy.

"That boy never had an ounce o' sense on him. Barbed wire around horses. Shee-it." He glanced at Kris, colored slightly, and walked away, shaking his head as he strolled down to Hauberk, leaned down to check the stallion's legs and feet.

"You got lucky, Ty. There're no marks. All the tendons look good, too. Must've had horseshoes up yer backside."

"I might have had other help. You tell me."

"What're you talking about?" Kris's hazel eyes had gone dark and she held Ty in her stare.

"Listen…" the words failed to come, how to say this without sounding like an idiot.

"Yeah?"

"I had to get help with Hauberk. He was so tangled and I needed light to see what I was doing, so I got Letha to help." There, keep it light. She *was* just there to help. He didn't have to mention what had happened. Hell, nothing had happened. "Had her hold him and the flashlight while I worked."

"Yeah?"

Matt had finished checking Hauberk and returned shaking his head. "That horse has enough bone for two horses. Solid. Good feet, too. I got to give you that. Amazing there's no marks."

"That's the thing. There were marks. A lot of them. Had a deep cut at the back of his left knee that was going to leave a lot of proud-flesh. I was worried sick. But after I got the wire off and went to doctor them, well, the cuts weren't there anymore." Ty looked at Matt, who was only five years his senior, but who had always been Ty's mentor. He looked at his sister, who had lived in the Valley all her life. "You ever hear of something like that before — like a healing?"

Kris slowly sat down on a hay bale and Matt softly swore, "Well, Shee-it," following it with another apology.

"What? What is it?"

"For someone born and raised in the Valley, ya sure do ferget your history, Ty."

"What're you talking about?"

Matt went to answer, but Kris cast him a look that made him shut his mouth. She stood to face Ty. "It's an old wife's tale, that's all. An old story about the Consort sometimes being able to heal. Hasn't happened for a few generations, as I recall, right, Matt?"

"Best o' my recollection, could be almost a hundred years back."

But the way their gazes slipped away from his, there was something more — he'd seen it in too many suspect's eyes — something Matt would have told him until Kris put a stop to it. He should have separated them. He'd have to make a point of getting Matt alone. "This does have something to do with Letha, then."

Kris eyed her brother, her gaze holding the same cool consideration she used when she watched a colt working. "You got some feelings for her, Ty?"

Ty stiffened. Normally he'd have denied it, but right now he didn't know.

"Shee-it," Matt muttered, leaving Ty to wonder if something was written on his face that even he didn't know.

"I told you. I'm worried about her — that's all. She doesn't seem to have anyone around except Sylvia, and you said yourself, that's hard on Letha. I wanted to ask you — could you make a point of going round to her place more. Be more of a friend?"

"You asked me that before. I said yes. I'm not setting you up with her, Ty."

"I can get my own dates when I want them, thanks-very-much-for-the-vote-of-confidence. Just be a friend. Do girl-stuff."

"And when have I ever been a girl?" She lifted her chin and thrust her shoulders back, which only got an appreciative grin from Matt.

"I'm not asking you to giggle and have pajama parties — just do stuff together. Go for a ride. Talk. Do each other's hair. Whatever. Give her a shoulder, Kris."

"Do each other's hair." The grin on her face told him she was loving this.

"Damn it, don't make this any more difficult than it is. I'm your brother. She's your friend. I'm asking for help, okay?"

She cast a glance at Matt. "He thinks we do hair. Are all you guys so obtuse?"

"'Scuse me Ma'am, just what're you sayin' about us men?"

Kris rolled her eyes. They were just going to gang up on her now if she pushed this any farther. Boys against girls, just like in grade school. She and Letha had been much closer once. They could be again. Besides, she'd seen the look on Ty's face. Maybe something good could come of it, even if he asked her to do stupid things like ask favors of Syl.

§

In the bright light of morning, Letha rode Inca over to the meeting tree to wait for Sylvia. The tree was a spreading poplar the placed cool shade on the greening earth. Letha knew there'd be a wait. There always was. Not because Sylvia wasn't punctual to a fault, but because Letha was always early. She disliked for anyone to have to wait for her, because she didn't like to impose her will on anything or anyone, and being late, in her opinion, was just a form of control.

The spot was different than when she'd waited for her trip to town with Sylvia. That had been her first trip out of the Valley since she was chosen as Spring's consort. The trip with Sylvia had been when Syl sprang the store idea on her and they signed on as co-signatories for the purchase of the store. Letha'd been sick as heck until she got back to the winter-clad valley. Now the new leaves were uncurling and the ground under Inca's hooves had shed its snow. Brewster's Creek rushed along its channel. The air smelled of new green and moist soil, and through the haze of spring green she could see the coil of smoke rising from her parent's home. In the pasture beyond the creek, a rider pushed a herd of heifers and bawling calves toward the hills.

Lucky it was the Spring season. Her folks were busy with ranch business and their minds weren't on her — not that they ever really seemed to focus on her except to tell her of her duties. When they had the time, they'd be by to discourage her store, too.

Her store. It was a surprise she felt that way. It was more of a surprise she felt determined to make it work. But she'd had to get away from there today. She didn't want to see Ty, and she knew he'd be by.

Even the thought of him caused a little tremor inside her. He must think she was weird, the way she'd run off last night. She'd heard his horse's hooves this morning when she was saddling Inca, and had purposely quieted the mare until he carried on. What had happened last night — well, she didn't understand it any more than he did, but she didn't want to talk about it, either. And she knew he would.

And he might want to kiss her again, too.

She touched her lips, wondering if that wasn't a good thing, then slid her hand under Inca's mane to rid herself of the memory with the feel of the mare's soft coat. She loosened her reins so the horse could crop the first new grass. The warmth of the mare was always a comfort.

"That grass is going to muck up her bit."

Letha looked around as she guiltily hauled Inca's head up.

Sylvia sat astride her grey gelding, a gay, blue saddle blanket peeking out from under the heavily tooled western saddle. She caught Letha's glance and grinned. "Seemed like a day to break out the party clothes. Spring!"

She urged her gelding up beside Letha. "So I packed a lunch and thought we'd ride up to Fish Lake if you're up to it." She motioned at the blue sky. "Got the weather."

"All right." But her agreement didn't really matter. Sylvia had made a decision and was already heading her horse down the road. As usual, Letha could follow or not. She urged Inca after, just like always.

They cantered along the side of the road until they came to Jed Hartley's cabin, then followed his fence line westward into the pine, down through the stream, and up into the hills. The trail they used was still clotted with snow in spots, but grouse thrummed happily on the forest floor and they spotted two deer and a fawn close by the beaver dam that spanned an ice-crusted, dark pool in a fold of the hills. The horses splashed through water so high the women had to lift their boots to keep them from getting wet. The air smelled of sap running.

By eleven they'd made it to Fish Lake and the busted-down cabin that sat back in the trees. It had been built years back by a drifter, but the man had drifted on when the Valley didn't exactly welcome him, and left the rickety cabin to fall into ruin. Now it slumped on one side as its foundations slowly rotted into the soil, but Letha smiled at the old structure. This place had always been one of her favorites because Fish Lake showed how nature changed the landscape over time.

The horses threaded through the last of the lodgepole pine and into the clearing that surrounded the lake. Years before, the lake had filled the clearing, but time had built up peat soil at the edges until now the lake was a small pothole in the midst of an open field of wild chives and meadow grass and pale pink lupine that had always been a favorite of Sylvia's.

Sylvia slid off her grey and stomped on the ground. "Not too bad. Dry enough we can have our lunch out here in the sun." She slid her saddle off her horse, left the pad to dry, grabbed her saddle bags, and set the horse loose. Animals always came when Sylvia called.

After setting Inca loose to graze, Letha followed Sylvia out toward the water. A couple of trees had been felled, tethered together, and set up like a small wharf that stretched halfway out into the lake for the Valley boys who came here to fish. At the land end, Sylvia had set up lunch on the wood because the peat nearer the water was still soft and squelchy.

"Come on. Sit down and let's talk." Her white-gold head bobbed as she opened a thermos and poured two cups. The scent of mint filled the clear air. Each summer Letha harvested some of the wild plant, because Sylvia had taken to using it as a comforting tea.

"Did you go see Mrs. Hunt yet?" Letha asked.

Sylvia shook her head. "No chance yet. Maybe tonight or tomorrow." She unwrapped her sandwich and shook her head. "Don't really want to do it. I'm never really sure what I pick up with people. Better to ignore it, you know. Never feels right." She took a huge bite.

"So how's business?" Sylvia asked around the mouthful of corned beef and cheddar and pickle — Letha's favorite sandwich concoction as a kid.

Letha took a bite and chewed slowly, considering. Sylvia never made these sandwiches — she never cared for them that much — which meant this wasn't just a friendly lunch. "If you wanted to look at the accounts, we should have stayed at the store."

"I don't want to look at books, silly. I want to know how it's going."

"Fine, I guess. More Valley folk have been in. Even been a few compliments. And believe it or not, Harry Zigheld brought in some of those little quilted tea cozies his mom always gives as Hope Chest gifts to the teenaged girls. He wanted to know if I'd be willing to try selling them." She shook her head.

"What is it?"

Letha looked out over the water that sat like a calm disc, and felt the comforting thrum of fish presence. "Just that he seems to be dropping by a lot. It kinda makes me uncomfortable after what happened last night."

"Last night?"

Letha told her about the damage to Ty's cabin, the barbed wire in the corral, and Hauberk's legs, but she didn't mention the thing that had been on her mind. Sylvia would just tell the elders.

"Shit. Stupid-assed thing to do. And you didn't call me. That horse's legs must be all cut up. Barbed wire's the worst. Had to stitch up Fred Mather's mare's chest the other day when a coyote spooked her into a fence. Damn worrisome. The mare almost rejected her foal she was so upset. Good looking filly. Glad things worked themselves out, but the ranchers really should go back to rail fences. Kristienne's got that right."

"Hauberk's legs are fine."

"How the hell can that be?" Sylvia looked at her friend. Something closed and thoughtful about Letha. That wasn't like her — at least, not the closed part. "Letha?"

A quick glance at Sylvia, and then back to the lake. "They just were. But the fact Harry did it, well, that just sort of sends a shiver down my back, if you know what I mean."

"Harry's not a bad guy — just hot-headed. You know that."

"And that's why I stopped dating him as a teenager, too."

"But he comes from a good family. Mrs. Z is good people. So's her husband."

Letha slowly turned to look at Sylvia. Long ago, they'd both agreed that Harry Zigheld was something of a creep. "I thought we were talking about the store."

"We are — sort of. Sort of roundabout, but we are. And you brought up Harry — not me. Everything's connected in the Valley, right? We always said that as kids. Like the toe bone connected to the foot bone, connected to the ankle bone, connected to the leg bone, and so on."

"What bones are we talking about?" Sylvia was being too blithe, too casual, and too difficult to understand for someone who was usually such a straight shooter. Something was going on, and suddenly each bite Letha'd had of the sandwich felt leaden in her belly. Sylvia wanted something.

"Leth, you know the history of the Valley as well as I do — settlers coming from northern Europe and England — all people tied to old faiths, old Celtic ways. They came here and found a place they could hold to those ways — Beltane fires, Solstices, Harvest rites. The land answered them here — just like the Native people said it would." Sylvia caught Letha's hand. Looked in her eyes so Letha could see the earnestness there.

A little surge of fear ran through Letha.

"Sure." She fought to keep her voice casual. "So they trap a girl each generation, and I happened to draw the short straw in this one. I'm a friggin' living legend."

"But it's a good legend. A legend that speaks of life and growth and harvest and renewed life each year. Because of you."

Letha stood up. What Sylvia said was true, but… "How many times have we had this conversation, Syl? You think this is a gift and I think it's a curse. Let's just leave it at that." Her hands were shaking, she was so angry. Sylvia — she just didn't get it, couldn't hear anything over her own opinions. They must be real loud in her head.

"Come on, Leth. Sit down and enjoy the lunch. I'm sorry. I didn't mean to get you upset, okay?"

Letha finally nodded and plunked down on the wharf again. "I just don't want to talk about it, okay?" The water stirred in the lake, and they ate in silence. Letha stared out over the glittering ripples and sipped her tea. A hawk soared overhead, rasping its cry into the insect silence around the lake. Among the trees, a woodpecker beat its tattoo on dead wood. Wind hummed in her ears as she eyed the hills and spotted red-blotched trees close by the lake.

She stood.

"Sylvia… is that…?"

"Beetle kill. Yup. Thought you'd spot it."

Letha looked down at her friend. "What d'you mean?"

Sylvia couldn't look at her, because this was where things got hard. This was the thing she'd known it would come to, even if Letha was living in a world of denial, and it hurt like hell to be the one that had to bring this up. She'd begged the elders not to make her, but they'd said she was the best for the task. She should damn well tell them to do their own dirty work — she'd done enough, what with arranging the financing for the store and making sure Letha made it into town and back. She blew her bangs off her face.

"You saw it when we went into town. The hills are covered with beetle-killed trees."

Letha nodded. She was turning now, studying the hills around them. Blotches of red dotted the hills, like acne on a teenager's face. "It shouldn't be here — not here at the edge of the Valley. Not on the Valley slopes."

"They say it's wiping out whole sections of land west of William's Lake. I hear folk talk about the clouds reflecting pink from the dead trees." Sylvia leaned back on her arms and lifted her face to the sky. "Climate change. Global warming. Whatever you want to call it — it's changed the ecology in most of the area, and so the beetle is killing the trees."

"But not here. Here the Valley protects us."

"Does it? Or do we protect the Valley? The legend isn't clear. There's a bond between our people and the land — that's for certain. You're proof of that." She blinked up at Letha, who stood frozen, scanning the hills. "Elders saw it coming the last ten years. Been watching the trees die on the road to town, but they were hoping that having a new, young consort would hold the blight beyond the Valley."

Letha's face was pale in the sunlight. She shivered and hugged herself as if a cold wind came off the hills, when all Sylvia could feel was the comforting warmth of the sun cupped in the clearing. But that warmth was a lie, wasn't it? Well, these things had to be done. It was time for Letha to grow up and do something other than moan about being trapped. They all had purposes in life, and if she'd accept it, maybe she'd find she enjoyed it.

"There's another part of the legend, Letha." She whirled on Sylvia, her eyes wild with fear and — anger? When had Letha ever been forceful enough to show real anger? "I know you've been rejecting Spring all your life. You refused to study the old writings, so maybe I better fill you in."

"So, what good news have you got for me this time?" The snarl on Letha's face made Sylvia cringe. She didn't want to do this.

"When our people first came here, they married a daughter of the Valley to Spring. They've done it every generation since. It brought Spring weather. It brought the fields to fallow for the farmers to plant. But in the early days of their settlement, life was very hard. The land had to be wrestled from wildness. Tamed like a horse. Tamed and made to bring forth life."

Letha had wrapped her arms around herself. She stepped up onto the wharf and looked down at the lake. The water's surface seemed to boil with fish that were trapped there over winter, growing fat and lazy so they were attracted to Letha's shadow. Or to her and the power that ran in her.

Sylvia looked back at her hands, recalling the ceremony and a brief flash of green-gold and a searing sense of burning. It filled her with sudden sympathy. If she were Letha she would be angry, furious even, at what the Valley would do to her. But it had to be done, to protect them all, and it was part of the natural order of things. Birth, life, and procreation. She blew out a long breath and continued, low voiced.

"There was another part of the ceremony back then — one that carried on from the old countries. The Consort of Spring — she bonds with the Lake and represents the land, awaiting the fertility of the horned god."

Letha's head snapped around. "There's no horned god…"

"There was in the old days. According to the old diaries, the girl chosen by Spring was married as soon as she reached menarche. Each spring, part of the ceremony was not just the waking of the Lake, but also the hunt of the horned god. The young men pursued the Consort. The one who caught her — he took her — and that was what made this Valley fertile."

"But we don't do that anymore," Letha said, finally relaxing at the foolish beliefs of her ancestors. This had nothing to do with her. She'd done her part by accepting Spring.

"Besides, it's archaic — breeding eleven- and twelve-year-old girls. Government wouldn't stand for it. Good riddance of that part of the ceremony, if you ask me." She sat down across from Sylvia and smiled until she saw the look of pity in Sylvia's eyes. The wind off the hills seemed to run cold right down Letha's back, and despite herself she was suddenly afraid.

"It's an old legend — a forgotten rite. That's all."

"You can say this when you know you're bound to the Spring?"

Letha just waited. It was all in Sylvia's gaze to be read — it just needed to be spoken for it to be real. Sylvia held out her hand, caught Letha's in a firm warm grip that sent a tingling through her hand, but it didn't stop the cold that had sent Letha's body trembling.

"The elders — they're concerned about the beetle kill entering the Valley. It's actually killed a bunch of the trees on the Rogers' place. They've talked and talked and now they've brought out the old records. They believe they've erred all these years by letting the Consort get married the usual way. They're thinking their error has weakened the Valley's life force and that you being single for so long is just making it worse."

"Are you telling me they want to — to reintroduce the old ways?"

Sylvia nodded. "They might, next time out, but right now they just know they need to save the Valley. The land needs to be replenished. You're twenty-three, and not getting any younger. Most of the appropriate young Valley men are married and have families."

"Except Harry Zigheld," they said together.

§

Kristienne surveyed the Hunt Ranch yard and sighed her satisfaction. At least here, everything was as it should be.

The mares and foals were waiting close by the barn for the ranch hands to bring them in to dinner. The spring green field was empty of cattle — they'd been driven out to range yesterday — and Matt was by the arena just walking out a colt after a bucking match with the youngster, who'd decided saddles were not for him.

Matt saw her and waved, so she lifted her hand in response. Colt looked docile enough now — until tomorrow. She liked this time of day, when things were winding down and settling into the comfortable fatigue of honest work. From the house behind her, Kristienne smelled roast beef for dinner. It was one of her mother's good days – no thanks to Syl and Ty's stupid idea.

It was times like these she could almost feel like she belonged here. But the Valley folk would never accept her and the Hunts as one of their own. She would go to her grave as the 'new girl', even though she'd been born here when Ty was six.

At this stage, the Valley folk's determination to consider the Hunts outsiders had become an amusement to her. She could live here all her life, but would never belong, while just because Letha was born here, she was considered part of the landscape.

She grinned. Served the elders right that the one person they wanted here most, was the most determined to leave. At least *she'd* made her peace with her life — being an outsider here was a darn sight easier than being an outsider in the world beyond the Valley. She had made her place here and it was comfortable, though sometimes, at night, a twinge of loneliness found her in her bed.

Thankfully, a working ranch rarely gave you time to be lonely. She had occasional dalliances with men from town, but hadn't had a serious relationship in years. Who needed one? She had all the men she needed around the ranch — and sex, well, there were things a woman could do for herself.

She climbed into the ranch truck and headed out to Letha's. What with the push to get the cattle out, it had taken a day to get over to talk to her like Ty had asked, but her brother's story, and the look on his face, had never been far from her mind. It brought a little shiver across her shoulders.

She pulled into the store's gravel parking area and stepped out into the whirring of the windmills and the creaking of some of the metal sculptures that also moved in the wind. They moved as slowly as life did around here.

When she spotted Letha through one of the cabin windows, she hesitated. Maybe she should buy something and head back to her roast beef dinner herself, but that would be a cop out. She shook out her hair and stomped up the store steps. There was Ty to worry about — and Letha.

"Howdy, there, stranger," she said, the bell jangling over her shoulder and, by the look on Letha's face, obviously startling her. "Sorry. Thought you saw the truck."

"No. No I didn't. How are you? It's been a bit, hasn't it?"

"Did I catch you at a bad time? You're looking a little distracted."

"No." Not distracted, Letha thought. Downright terrified would be more like it, since her ride with Sylvia. Harry Zigheld. It made sense, now, that Mrs. Zigheld had her son bring her around, that she'd been so darned friendly and — well, complimentary of the store. She was scoping out a potential daughter-in-law. "A little upset, is all. I… got some news. I'll get over it."

"Listen, I realized we haven't seen much of each other, and Mom's cooked this big roast of beef, so I wondered if you'd like to come for dinner."

"Right." She looked around the store as if seeking something, anything, to latch on to, but her gaze wouldn't stick. She turned dazed eyes on Kristienne. "I really have things to do here."

"Mom makes the best roast beef in the Valley. You used to say so, yourself. Now she might not be at the top of her game these days, but a bad day of Mom's cooking is better than you eating whatever you planned to cook." She caught Letha's hand — cold — too cold. "Come on, girlfriend. You need some distraction. Heck, maybe we can solve your problem."

Letha hesitated, not sure what she wanted to do, until Kristienne handed her the flannel shirt off the hook by the door and led her outside. There really was nothing for it but to climb in the truck and get away. Inca was fed. Everything was actually done at the store. Maybe — maybe it would be good to not think about Sylvia's news, to have time with an old friend who wasn't Sylvia. Kristienne always was a bit more understanding of Letha's feelings, and maybe she could help sort this whole thing out.

"Store going well?"

"As well as can be expected. I'm putting a website up to advertise the arts and crafts. I'd like to send notices of our work out to some galleries in Vancouver."

Kristienne glanced at Letha as she guided the truck along the road toward Hunt Ranch. The way she twisted a strand of her hair around a finger, she looked about twelve, not twenty-five. "Not a bad idea. You know, Mom used to have all kinds of connections to galleries in New York and other cities along the east coast — Boston, Washington, Miami. Maybe she could arrange some introductions — get the stuff seen in the big leagues. There's a market for craft art. We'll ask her."

Letha nodded. She needed to get her thoughts in order, stop thinking about Harry Zigheld, when every part of her was revolted at the very thought of his touch. She'd been there once during her embarrassing time of seeking — it wasn't something she would do again. "They can't make me," she muttered.

"Damn straight. The whole Spring thing is a bunch of horse pucky." Kristienne stopped the truck at the front of the low-slung ranch house and turned to look at Letha in the quiet after the pinging of gravel. "Who can't make you do what?"

Letha just shook her head.

Kristienne slid out from behind the wheel, inhaled deeply and waited for Letha to join her on the porch. "Ain't that just the best smell in the world? Roast beef and Yorkshire pudding. Yumm."

Inside, the smells were even more delicious. Pie — apple by the scent of it — and something else sweet. From the kitchen that sat at the rear of the house with huge windows overlooking both the ranch buildings and the lake, came the sound of male voices and the clatter of dishes. "Good timing. Crews in, so we don't have to wait, but they won't have eaten it all yet."

She hauled Letha down the hall and into a room filled with freshly scrubbed male faces and way too much testosterone. The guys stopped their argument over horseflesh — the constant point of conversation on the ranch — and scrambled to their feet. Beyond them, on the wall, gleamed a painting Letha had admired all through her childhood. It was a brightly colored painting of whimsical people walking the streets of a city caught in the rain. They all had bright umbrellas among a shoal of taxis that sent up glittering spray.

"Ma'am," Matt muttered. The others followed his lead.

Kristienne rolled her eyes. Matt was so damned old-fashioned it was enough to drive her mad. "Didn't I tell you my mother is 'Ma'am'? I'm Kris. This is Letha. You've known us since we were kids — or most of you have. Now get outta my way and let us have seats."

She angled around the table, still hauling Letha, motioned her to a chair, then found her own at the head of the table, Matt to her right, her mother to her left.

Elizabeth Hunt looked almost herself tonight. Her fine hair was twisted up in a knot at the top of her head that showed off the fine length of her neck. She wore jeans and a flannel shirt the same as Kristienne and the six men. Only the scent of mouthwash and the palsy of her hands as she raised them for grace hinted that she'd been at the bottle as she cooked the meal.

"It looks great, Mom. My mouth was watering when I left to get Letha."

After the prayer, the room filled with the clanking of plates heaped with sliced roast beef and bowls of mashed potatoes, Yorkshire pudding, and vegetables passed around the table.

"That roan colt getting any better, Matt?" Kristienne asked as she poured gravy on her potatoes.

"Only bogged his head and bucked once today. Took all his piss and vinegar out on the calves. Tell ya — that one, if you can stay on 'im long enough to ride out the cold back, yer goin' to have one heck of a cutting horse. Don't know if he's ever goin' t' get over the buckin', though."

"Kind of hard to ask top dollar if he's going to buck off all those city-slicker cowboys."

"Gee — they might have to learn how t' ride. He's one that's going to need a real horseman."

"An' where ya goin' ta find one of them in New York?" asked Billy Fitsch, who had been only a few years ahead of Kristienne and Letha in school.

"Maybe the same place your brother found that horse o' his."

Loud guffaws circled the table. Kristienne grinned.

Letha watched the laughter, jibes, and conversation swirl around the table. It was so unlike meals on her parent's ranch. Her dad and mom were so — well — dour. A meal was a time to give thanks and gain the sustenance you needed to get back to work. Everything was responsibilities and duties.

Like her duty to marry. The sounds of friendship faded, like voices lost in the trees, until all she heard was Sylvia's voice and Harry Zigheld's name.

He was not the man for her — she'd known that quickly as a teenager, during the short time they slept together. He was a hard youngster who grew into a harder man — even if he did stay at the family ranch. Any wife of his would be burdened not just with his household, but with the little cruelties he was prone to. She rubbed the back of her hand. As a kid, he'd pinched her if she didn't do things as he'd wanted. What would he do now?

She couldn't think about it — wouldn't think about it because she wasn't going to marry him. They couldn't make her — she hoped.

"You don't like Mrs. H.'s cooking?" The voice of Dwight Peters cut through her thoughts. He was the youngest of the ranch hands — a smooth-faced Native kid out from Williams Lake that Kristienne had taken a fancy to — she said for his talent with horses. "You're not eating."

She looked at her plate — untouched — before her. "N…no." She picked up her knife and fork and began to saw through the meat, her stomach so tight she doubted it would ever feel relaxed again.

"It's real good, Mrs. H. I haven't had Yorkshire pudding this good — since the last time I was here."

Elizabeth Hunt smiled and surveyed the table, but her face then turned troubled, Letha thought, trying to pull away from her own troubles.

"Ty should be here for this. He always loved my roast beef. Why isn't he here, Kristienne?"

Matt and a couple of the older hands sat back and looked at Mrs. H. Kristienne caught her mother's hand with a gentleness people reserved for the very ill. "Mom, Ty had other stuff to do."

The mention of Ty sent a shiver down Letha's back. The store, the feeling of darkness coming — they'd all happened at the same time — when Ty Hunt arrived. And now this new threat to her leaving. No wonder she was scared of him. No wonder she didn't like the feeling he raised when she was around him, even though she still felt his kiss.

"He's at that cabin. Why is he there — he should be here, in his home, with his mother!" The men at the table excused themselves, chairs scraping back, and took their dessert — two types of cake and apple pie — out onto the porch to watch the sun down. A few stalked away to the bunk house, but Matt stuck around — just like Matt always would where the Hunts were concerned. He'd been around a long time — long enough he'd watched Kristienne and her friends grow from gangly fillies to the women they were today.

"Mom, I wanted to ask you about something. Letha wants to do a website for the store and advertise the craft art she's got for sale. I thought maybe you could help her — refer her to some east coast dealers. What'd you think?"

"Don't try to change the subject, Kristienne. You know how I hate that. I want my son here — where he should be."

"Mom. Stop it. You know he needs his space. He's always needed his space."

Elizabeth Hunt slammed her chair back from the table, yanked her hand loose, and stood swaying. Her cheeks bore bright spots and her eyes were glazed and trained on her daughter.

"You just don't want him here. *You* keep him away from here. It's you! You're just like your father!" She turned and fled the room, leaving Kristienne to slump in her chair like some defeated thing. She sat there silently until Letha shifted down the table to comfort her friend. Their eyes met, and Kristienne smiled ruefully and shook her head. "Sorry about that."

"You all right?" Letha's words seemed to echo in the silence of the room. From upstairs came the banging of a door. Outside, men's boots clumped on the porch as they left the house.

"I was supposed to be helping you. Getting you away from your cabin and with people."

"Well… you did that."

"Jeeze, Letha — what am I going to do? I'm not trying to keep Ty away, but she's convinced of it, now, just like she's sure Dad kept him away all those years. I just don't want him strolling in here and getting her all worked up that he's come home, only to have him leave again. I don't think she could take it, and I don't think I could take the aftermath. We went through enough when he left the first time."

She rubbed her face — a sure sign of her fatigue — and Letha sat back in her chair. "You know, I always thought Kristienne Hunt had it all together. You're like Sylvia, you know what you want in life."

"Funny. I'd say the same about you."

"Yeah, but you stand a chance of getting it."

"And you would too, if you'd stand up for yourself. Face down those old people. Look at what you're doing with the store."

Letha sighed. "They let the store go because it doesn't matter to them. I'm still here. It's like they trained me to obey or something, all these years. Trained me to believe I have to do things their way. It's like I've got this invisible tether, and I'm just now realizing it, and I don't know how to get rid of it. Remember in school there was that lesson on learned helplessness. It has got to be something like that. The thing that's hard is that Sylvia's in on it. Today she told me they're concerned the beetle kill is going to destroy the Valley forests. If it does that, it's going to change the range land and leave the forest unlivable for most animals. There'll be less rain — hell, the whole place could be more desert. And the elders — they think the reason it's happening is Spring's power is fading."

"Letha, you and I both know that this Spring thing is archaic and way overblown by the people here. It's a myth — a legend they cling to, and you don't."

"Yes, but — maybe…"

"No maybes. You've spent all these years doing what they want — playing the good girl — the priestess of the Valley. It's high time you do what you want — or are you going to live your life like this? 'Cause if you are, don't come crying to me when you're old and still here. So, are you and Ty enjoying each other's company?"

Taken aback by the vehemence of the lecture and surprised by the question, Letha sat back in her chair. "What?"

"Well you live next door. He likes you — I can see it in his face whenever he talks about you."

"He talks…."

"He was here the other day and said he was worried about you. Besides, I remember you had a crush on him once."

"I was twelve years old, for goodness sake."

"Well, I thought he might be your type, given he isn't going to stay here. Heck, maybe he's the one that will take you away from all this." She waved her hand dramatically in the air and grinned. "Think about it. For all his faults — and as a sister I could name a few — he's not a bad guy."

Kristienne stood and began moving dishes off the table. Letha went to help her, but was so distracted she nearly dropped the platter of remaining meat. Disobey the elders — Spring knew, she wanted to do that. But Ty Hunt? His was a face she'd seen too often these days. And in her dreams.

Chapter 5

Over the next few weeks Letha couldn't get Kristienne's suggestion out of her mind, even as she fussed over the website development and dealt with Valley customers and made appropriate frames for Johnny Warner's paintings.

Somehow word had gotten to Williams Lake of the quirky crafts and art at the store, and Sunday traffic from the town found its way the thirty miles to her door. It left her with an ongoing anxiety to make sure the paintings were hung properly and the statues in the yard gleamed in the warming sun. Yesterday, a reporter from the Williams lake *Tribune* had said he was coming out to do a story, so it made it doubly important that everything be perfect.

She was just finishing hanging a collection of Johnny's smaller paintings in a display above the main window when she heard a truck drive up. She leapt down from the chair she was on, checked the evenness of the paintings' frames, scanned the room for things out of place, and scrambled to gather up her nails and hammer when she heard the clump of boots on the porch.

The bell tolled as Harry Zigheld walked in, a clump of mail in his hand. "Mornin', Letha. Thought I'd deliver these in person."

Letha felt herself sag. Not who she expected. Not who she wanted, either. He'd been doing this too often — bringing her mail to her personally.

"You know, you don't have to do that. You've got a long route, and the store has a perfectly good mailbox by the road." She hustled past him and behind the counter, wanting to keep something between them, because Harry Zigheld was something to be feared since Sylvia's news.

"Yeah, but coming in here is a bit of a break and I can get a cup of coffee and put my feet up for a bit after a morning of hard work." He grinned, his narrow gaze somehow reminding her of Tessa Roger's pet ferret — or one of those mongooses she'd seen on T.V. when it was catching a snake.

"Coffee? You want coffee?" She turned to the pot she kept ready. The locals liked to be able to come in and jaw a while — be neighborly — like her closest neighbor had pointed out to her. But when she poured it her hand shook and coffee slopped onto the kitchen counter. Damnation, Harry Zigheld shouldn't make her nervous, because there was no way the Valley elders could make her marry him. She handed him the full mug.

"You got another one o' those?"

She frowned, nodded.

"Then why don't you pour yourself a cup and join me on the porch. It's a fine day out — too nice to be cooped up inside a store."

Letha shook her head. "I've got things to do. Cleaning. Got other pictures to hang. Inventory stock. My horse needs to get out." She was talking too fast, darn it, and she couldn't quit shaking her head like the silly hockey bobble-head Harry had on the dash of his truck. "You go on and enjoy your coffee and I'll just get busy here."

She exhaled and gripped the counter edge to steady herself. Being around Harry Zigheld raised a whole other set of nerves than Ty Hunt did. She shook her head at the thought.

He sauntered over to the lone chair by the stack of books and slumped down. "Well then, I guess I'll set here a while instead, and enjoy the view. Git enough sun in my eyes driving all day. Time for some other brilliance, if you know what I mean."

She glanced at him, afraid of his flirting. He leaned back and sipped his coffee, his pale hair hanging over his pale eyes as he watched her. Then he absently picked up one of the books by the chair.

"*A Month in Prov-aance.* What the hell kinda title is that?"

"It's a book about living in France for a month." She bent to grab her inventory list and came around the counter to the shelves. Harry was someone who didn't read much more than the Farmer's Almanac, if that. "Some people like to read about places they've never been, places they'd like to go."

"Why the hell'd anyone want to go to France? Bunch of pansy frogs."

She ignored him and started counting off items. She'd planned to do this later this week and spend today getting the displays ship-shape before the reporter arrived tomorrow. Well, the displays would have to wait, because Harry's gaze never seemed to leave her and she couldn't think right now.

A little trickle of sweat ran down between her breasts. How many cans of beans was that? She'd forgotten already, swore at her own idiocy, and started again. Six. There were six. She scribbled it down and went to the next item. Five cans of peas. The vegetables weren't moving that well. Sylvia would be upset she'd ordered so many. It was the perishables the valley folks seemed to need when they came in. It would be the summer people who might shop here, but they came later, around Solstice. A lesson learned, but she'd need to do better. Sylvia would expect better.

"Letha, seems to me you and I got some jawing to do."

She almost jumped out of her skin. He was behind her, mug left precariously balanced on top of the books. A heavy floral cologne clogged her nostrils as he caught her arm and turned her.

Pull away! Her whole being demanded it, but she couldn't move, couldn't speak as he stepped in close to her and caught her arms, his fingers too hard on her skin. All her internal alarms went off.

"We got to look around us, Letha. We're both Valley folk. We're both not gettin' any younger, and we had fun once before, didn't we? We weren't too bad together, as I recall. Could be things'd be worse if we waited." He was stumbling over the words, but she knew what he was talking about. What he was hinting — however awkwardly.

Her stomach churned at the thought that she'd let this man touch her once. She was going to be sick, but she needed to deal with this. Needed to tell him no way in heck was she ever going to marry Harry Zigheld and be chained to the Valley for life — but his hand on her arm seemed to freeze her tongue. It was like the dream — her dream, and everything was dark and dying — but this time it was her hopes that were withering and she had to save them.

Then why couldn't she speak? She had choices, damn it!

She swallowed, parted her lips, just as Harry plunged in and planted a wet kiss on her mouth. Lips, rubbery like she remembered. Emotionless. Cold. Fish-kisses she'd called them when she was a teenager, giggling with Kristienne and Sylvia. His face blocked the light. His cologne reeked.

She yanked back, but his hands held her in place.

"Letha." Her name came out as a groan.

"Harry, cut it out.... We're just friends."

His lips caught hers again and she twisted away from the sickness they raised — from the darkness — yanked back so hard she fell against the shelves, knocking cans of tuna and salmon helter-skelter across the floor.

"Now look at what you've done," he growled. He grabbed for her arm, but she ducked away, slid past the shelves, and scrambled for the door. She was trapped inside. The cabin was darkness. Outside was sunlight. She wrenched the door open, the bell jangling with her fear, half-fell onto the porch.

Dark figure in the glare. She couldn't see. Didn't care. She stumbled down the stairs and was about to run — somewhere — anywhere.

"Letha? What's the matter?" The figure with Ty's voice jogged toward her and she didn't know whether that helped or not. All she could see was the black — even out here in the light — her head was filled with darkness. Something came — was coming. She could feel it in her soul.

Ty caught her hand and she jerked away. "I don't have time for this — for you."

"What the heck's got you so spooked?"

"I'm not spooked. Just leave me alone." She turned toward the barn.

"City boy bothering you, Letha?" She spun around as Harry came out onto the porch.

Her head pounded so hard she could barely see. She wanted — no, needed — to be alone, to steady herself before the reporter got here. Couldn't they just leave her alone, let her make her own choices for once?

"I'll ask you the same, Zigheld. What'd you do to her?" Ty didn't like the way all the color had gone from her face except for two bright spots on her cheeks. Her eyes were so black it was like there was no blue in them anymore, and her whole body shook with a radiating fear that brought a cold rage to his gut. He'd seen fear like this before — in sexual assault victims.

He left Letha and strode to the porch, controlling his need to clench his fists, to hit someone. Undercover work was good training for hiding his emotions.

"So, what did your ma need today?" He'd seen Harry at the store too often, and Letha had commented on how Harry was always picking up supplies for his mother.

"Came for m'self today. Had Letha's mail and thought I'd stop for coffee — not that it's any of yer damn bizness." Harry came to meet Ty at the top of the porch stair.

Harry looked down at Ty like a belligerent vulture, and that was the last straw. Ty's hands formed fists, even as he smelled the stink of cheap cologne. He knew what that meant, what Harry's real mission was. "What the hell'd you do to her?"

"None of your goddamn bizness what goes on between Letha and me."

"Well, I'm making it my business. She looks like a friggin' war victim. What'd you do, Harry? Hit her, like you beat on that colt? Or maybe you threw a little barbed wire into her life."

"I never beat that soddin' colt, and you know it. You and yer fuckin' nags. They're horses, not fuckin' children. Or women."

"So why's Letha afraid?"

"How the hell should I know? Woman's unstable. Always has been. Slut fucked anything that moved when she was a kid, but now she won't give a fella the time of day."

He couldn't stand it anymore — not that. Letha Rivers was many things, but never what Harry had named her. He looked to where she stood, still pale, blinking as if she walked some waking nightmare. "He touch you, Letha?"

"H…he kissed—" The words were so choked and unsteady Ty could barely understand, but he understood enough, and he cared, damn it, when everything told him he shouldn't get involved at all.

He swung back in one long, smooth motion and slammed his fist into Harry Zigheld's gut.

Air whooshed out of Harry's mouth and he caved over. Ty had him by the collar so fast, Harry didn't have a chance to recover as Ty dragged him down the stairs and across to Harry's truck. He slammed Harry against the fender and released him.

"Get the fuck out of here and be happy I don't wipe the floor with you."

"That so? You fuckin' city boys are all talk, always thinkin' yer better than the rest of us. You and yer stuck-up sister and yer drunk of a mother. You got your eye on Letha now? You figgerin' to get laid?"

Harry lunged forward, a round-house swing missing Ty by a mile. Ty's fist connected — this time with Harry's jaw. Letha blinked as Harry staggered back, as the two men eyed each other, as they circled. The darkness ran in waves over her eyes, constricted her breath, but she couldn't let this happen. Couldn't have these men fighting — not over her. It was her choice — not theirs.

That thought seemed to unfreeze her limbs.

"No! Stop it!" She ran at them, somehow imposed herself between them, so she was threatened by fists from both sides. "I don't need this! I don't want this! I don't want either of you. I don't need either of you. I want… myself!"

Damn it, she was crying, but she held her ground, and slowly the two men lowered their fists, even as their gazes flashed belligerence at each other. A truck ground down the gravel road toward them.

She looked from Ty to Harry. "You better hope that's not a William's Lake reporter, because if it is I might just sic him on you two idiots. Now get out of here, out of my sight."

"Fuckin' loon, if ya ask me," Harry muttered as he scrambled into his truck.

She turned to Ty. "What are you smiling at? I meant you, too."

"Letha. Don't." His hand came up to touch her, but she backed away.

She wasn't going to listen, even as her eyes overflowed with tears. All of these people, everyone who was involved with the Valley, they figured they made the decisions, that Letha Rivers wasn't able to make them. But she was learning, darn it. She was learning.

"Letha, please."

"Letha?" Sylvia's voice. "What's happened, honey?"

Letha shook her head. Sylvia had stolen her voice again.

"Ty, you better leave. Come on, honey, come on in the store."

Mortified, she let Sylvia tug her away. Ty looked at his fists and wondered when he'd started to care.

§

"It was like two cocks fighting, and I just couldn't stand it." She sat huddled in the store's chair and still couldn't stand it. Her whole body felt raw with what had happened, with Harry's touch and then Ty's proprietary actions. "I'm not something to be owned."

"Not words I'd expected to come out of Letha River's mouth." Sylvia pulled two cans of Coke out of the fridge, but Letha waved it away. Water was more her thing — not something sugary — but Sylvia popped the cap and took a long pull.

"Do I really look so helpless — like people can just walk over me?"

"Don't know how you look to other people," Sylvia said as she hefted herself onto the counter. "But you always seem to be waiting for someone to tell you what to do."

Letha closed her eyes and rubbed her arms. "I know." She'd acted like a fool — falling apart over a simple kiss. "Ever since I was eleven. Since the lake. Today, Harry came. He brought the mail, and he wanted to talk… about us. I can't explain it, Syl, but when he kissed me it was like something inside me started to die." She opened her eyes and stared out the window. "I acted like an idiot."

"Not like an idiot if he pushed himself on you."

Letha looked back at Sylvia. "It was just a kiss. I overreacted."

"Did you? Letha, why should you kiss someone who makes you feel like you're dying?"

"Because I'm the problem. I want something that the Valley can't allow me to have. You're the one who told me the Valley wants me to marry him. But I can't. I won't."

"So you know what you want." There was a question, and barely reserved judgment in Sylvia's voice.

Letha took a deep breath. She had to say something. It had gone on like this too long between Sylvia and her, with Sylvia setting both their courses and Letha resenting it but doing nothing about it.

"Do you remember when Mrs. Pratt arranged a field trip for the whole school into the Williams Lake fair, but you told me I couldn't go because I'd been chosen, and I had to be gracious and just say I didn't want to go? That was the first time you made a decision for me."

Sylvia took another long swig of her cola and pursed her lips. "I don't really remember."

There was a tightness in her voice, an unwillingness to remember, or take any responsibility for what their relationship had become. Letha looked away, feeling defeated even before she began, but she had to get this out. "It's been like that ever since, Syl. I want to do something, but you take the choice away. Even on the little things. You're a powerful woman, and I'm — not."

"That's laying a lot at my doorstep, Leth. You want me to own all your choices?"

"No, I want you to stop making them for me. I want to run the store my way, and not have you checking up on me and *tsk-tsking* your disapproval. I get enough of that from the Valley folk."

"So let you play with my money, with no questions asked. Do you know how ridiculous that sounds?"

"Yes. I'm asking for trust and faith — the same kind I've always had in you."

"In me?" Sylvia lifted a brow, a grim smile on her face. "Letha, you've gotta lot of nerve, you know."

"Syl, I'm sorry, but I need this — please, I feel like this whole Valley is smothering me in a vat of feathers, and Harry — well, he's just the final pillow on my face. Please…."

"Stop. Enough, already." Syl slid down off the counter.

"But I need you to understand. That's the one thing I don't think you've ever done. In the ceremony — the light in the lake — you wanted it to be you — you thought it *was* you. You wanted this so badly and I took it from you and you've — you've tried to hold onto your dream through me. Like my mother has. Oh, God, I'm sorry, Syl, but that's what I think."

Syl stood rigid by the counter, then jerked her head toward the door. "You seem okay, now, and I've got calls to make, but if you want to finish this discussion, come on up to my place. Maybe you've been working too hard at the store. I suggest you start taking a little time to relax every now and again. You're wound tight as a bad rope."

"Syl, please. I didn't mean to hurt your feelings. I know you've only tried to help me."

Syl already had the door open, but glanced back as the bell tolled. "Sure," she said.

§

Inca was acting skittish, like the darn-fool chestnut mare she was. Letha urged her through the groves of poplar, caught in the long dusk of the late May evening, into the dark closeness of the lodgepole pine. Here the trail narrowed and the trees sent out sharp broken branches to impale the unwary. The shadows under the haze of pine needles seemed to press into her, yet she knew it was okay for her to be here because it was her choice. Her choice to visit Sylvia or not. Sylvia hadn't told her to come, she'd invited as an equal. It left Letha a little breathless, in a good way. It had been a long time since she'd visited Sylvia's home.

Perhaps it was how the trees lifted up the slopes of the valley, more stunted in the rocky soil, or the fact Letha had been living by the lake for the last two months, but when she pushed through the last screen of trees she realized how poor the old Hill homestead was. The old clapboard house and its outbuildings stood in the shadows of the mountains, like small animals hunkered against attack. It sent a shiver up Letha's spine and Inca danced under her.

Sylvia's parents had been killed when she was eight, and Sylvia had spent most of her childhood and teen years being shifted from family to family around the Valley. She'd refused to leave — even when Social Services tried to place her in foster homes. She'd run away and come back, determined to be in the Valley.

Now she stood alone in her denim and work shirt, blonde hair bright as a candle, on the rickety front porch watching Letha down to the lone solid corral where the grey gelding loafed.

Letha unsaddled and set the mare loose in the corral with a slap on the rump and a flake of hay.

"Place is looking like it could use a little fixing, Syl. I thought you were planning repairs."

"And you rode all this way to insult me?"

Letha grinned and looked at the white wine bottle and two glasses Sylvia carried. "Nope. Came for the wine and your sparkling personality, of course."

When Sylvia burst out laughing, Letha climbed the tall flight of steps up to the porch and accepted her wine glass, then leaned against the porch rail that showed it had been recently repaired. "Been a long time since I've visited. Too long. You must get lonely."

Syl shrugged. "I never invited you. I rarely invite anyone. This place — it's not quite the kind of place you show off. Still a lot of things to do, and no time or money to do them."

Letha sipped her wine and glanced at the bottle. Okanagan Valley, Dark Horse Winery. Wines were another of the things Sylvia knew about. She knew so much about so much, but not about Letha. For some reason it was a blind spot.

"But I always feel safe here, where I was born. Say, you want to see my foundlings?"

"Sure." She went to set her wine glass down.

"Might as well bring it with you."

Letha followed behind as Sylvia went to the old barn. The gravel soil grated underfoot and the air smelled of evening dew on old wood, overcome with wild animal musk when they reached the sagging end of the barn. Under Sylvia's hand the door slid smoothly open onto darkness, illuminated only by a small nightlight.

Letha paused, her senses reaching. The scrabble of claws, a whisper of wings, a sense of horns and green eyes peered out of the gloom. A breeze caught her hair as it passed through the doorway, but she was uncertain whether it ran out or in, like breath.

"At least I've got this place modernized. It gets more use than the house. I seem to spend most of my waking hours out here."

Letha glanced at Sylvia, saw the determined pride and an edge of pain on her face. "You're doing more than ranch work, aren't you?"

"Yes." She shrugged. "It was needed. After Mom and Dad died, this place was left fallow. The bank took it back, but lucky for me no one wanted it. I bought it back when I started working — paid the back taxes — but then, you know all that."

She stepped into the barn. "I used to bring the occasional injured animal here when the rancher couldn't care for it himself. Lately, though — the past few years — I've been finding strays — animals coming down from the hills, injured. Some have been hurt naturally, some are young that have been abandoned, but lately a lot more have been shot."

She flicked on a set of lights next to the door to illuminate a set of immaculate cages and pens. "Took most of my money to do this, but it was worth it. They needed me. Seems no one else did."

Letha faltered, wondering for a moment how Sylvia had managed to buy the store, too. "We all need you, Syl."

"Sure. I'm so friggin' important to everyone." She lifted her chin. "Come meet the family."

Letha followed behind, drawn by the look of pure tenderness in Sylvia's eyes. It was a look Letha wished was turned on her.

"This is Max. He's been here the longest. I tried to set him free, but he kept coming around so I finally installed a dog door for him, and he comes and goes as he wants." She stood before a cage inhabited by a brindle-coated coyote, who looked up at them with contented golden eyes.

"No, I'm not going to feed you, you mooch. You filled up on squirrels, and more food will just make you sick." Sylvia slipped inside the cage and motioned Letha to follow as she ran her fingers through the thick fur of Max's coat. "He was shot when he came — not unusual for a young coyote. They're too cocky until they get some age on them. Now, well, he knows who to trust, and I swear he sees his job as guiding the injured ones back here." She caressed the base of Max's ears and left his cage, then introduced Letha to the inhabitants of each of the cages.

A saw-whet owl, tiny as a teacup, with a broken wing. Max had carried him home.

"What will you do if the wing doesn't heal right?" Letha asked, as she ran a finger over the soft russet feathers.

"Keep him, I guess. What else?"

A red fox kit with an injured paw nearly mended, but Sylvia was afraid to release him until he was older. A fawn suckling its mother, who was hung from the roof in a belly-sling, her leg shattered from a bullet. The fawn was speckled as a trout and peeked out at them from behind its mother. The poor mother keened heartbreakingly as she tried to crowd her baby to safety when Sylvia approached.

"Don't ask what's going to happen to them. The mother's in a bad way. I should put her down, but if she dies there's a good chance I'll lose them both — the fawn's that young. All I can do is keep the pain damped down a little." She shook her head helplessly. The entire scene brought Letha close to tears. She stepped closer, placed a hand on Sylvia's shoulder as she ran her hands over the mother deer's flanks and channeled calm so the deer stopped crying. *If only if would heal — if all hurt things could heal.*

"It'll be all right. It will. It has to be," Letha said, trying to sound positive but feeling exhaustion seep into her. How could Sylvia deal with this, day in and day out?

In the far corner of the hospital — for that was what Letha had come to think of it as — was a mesh-wire cage, and inside hunkered a lone animal. "Don't get too close. He's still pretty unpredictable."

Sylvia left Letha in the midst of the barn and entered the cage. The animal stood — wolf. Large, shaggy, and dusky black as the shadows under the trees. He turned feral eyes on her and bared his teeth, so Letha stepped back a pace, but not Sylvia, as she slipped inside the cage as smooth as a bit of wind.

"How you doin' tonight, Rhatha?" The name sounded rough in Letha's ears, as if Sylvia spoke another language. Perhaps she did, the way the wolf approached her, limping, nosing her hand, and settling only when Sylvia had placed both palms on the back of the large animal's neck.

"My god, Syl. Isn't he dangerous?"

"Probably. Usually. But not to me. He knows I'll help him. He knows I understand. He's very smart and very sick. Someone poisoned him — set out meat laced with arsenic. The ranchers hate the wolves in the area because they'll take a calf or two. Seems like a fair trade to me. We take most of the land and most of the game and the wolves take a small toll." She shrugged. "I'll be a minute here."

She closed her eyes, her head bent over the wolf, and slowly the animal lowered its head, closed its eyes, and began to sleep. "That's better. It eases the pain. I'm hoping with time he'll recover." She left the cage and stood gazing around her, that same look of tenderness on her face.

"You really aren't alone, are you?"

"They're my world." She sighed and led Letha back outside to the porch, leaving the animals with only the nightlight on. The sky faded to indigo and the evening star shone bright over the hills. Sylvia lit a candle on the porch rail, then settled into an antique glider and waited until Letha was seated, before setting them rocking with a contented push of her legs. "This is my world."

Letha leaned her head back and watched the stars blink on one by one in the sky as the last shades of blue were inked away. At times like these, feeling the breeze that came from somewhere beyond the valley, staring up at the stars, she always thought of how the skies must be different elsewhere. "We're quite the pair, aren't we. From the same place, but so totally different."

"Being unique is part of our charm." The sardonic cast of Sylvia's voice was clear, even in the darkness.

"You really do have the gift of talking to animals."

"And you really are the Consort of Spring."

"Who would have thunk it?"

"Valley folk, most like, though some like Kris don't want to believe." Sylvia drank back her wine and topped up their glasses, then kicked off her cowboy boots and curled her sock feet under her. "So tell me, do others think as little of me as you do?"

"Syl! I don't think 'little of you'!"

"You said this morning that I haven't got my own life, that I'm trying to steal yours."

Letha's gut clenched. She drew a deep breath. "Not steal — never steal — but you always seem to want to tell me what to do. You always take charge, and I feel like I never even have a chance to disagree —"

"Is this about the store? I've tried to leave you alone with the store." Sylvia's words were clipped. She uncurled her legs.

"Syl, don't. I love the store. That's one place you did know better, and I'm glad I listened to you."

Sylvia's brown eyes glittered, waiting, in the light from the guttering candle. The beeswax sizzled and sent up a thin thread of white smoke.

Letha caught her hand, wondering how it had come to this, that she was having to reassure Syl, who had always been the strongest of the three friends who had been caught in the lake's light so long ago.

"The store's good, Syl, as long as I can make it into my vision of a store. But you've let me do that. For once I get to make the choices." Sylvia wouldn't meet her gaze, and that sent a quiver of uncertainty down Letha's back. "What? What is it?"

"Nothing. Just thinking about what you're saying." But she'd pulled her hand away, was busy pouring them both more wine when it wasn't needed.

"Syl, I really need you to hear this. Ever since I was chosen, everyone has made all my choices for me. Think about it. Mom nearly pulled me from school — she thought I'd be better off at home, getting to know my duties — I was lucky the law was on my side."

"She was proud you were the Consort. She wanted you to be special. You were — are — special."

"Not special — different. Made different from everyone. Everyone else went with their folks to town for special nights out, for family events, for the Williams Lake Stampede. I've never seen any of those things since I was eleven. They're hazy memories from way, way back."

"Your parents love you, the Valley loves you. They want you safe."

"They hold me here because they're afraid."

Sylvia jerked and looked at her.

"That's the truth, isn't it?"

"There's a bond between you and the Valley — a covenant — that as long as you're here, there'll be Spring. Why wouldn't they be afraid of you leaving, of something happening to you?"

"I could fall under a tractor tomorrow."

Silence, as Orion lifted above the horizon, his sword belt gleaming amid the glimmer of the Milky Way. The universe was so vast and the Valley was so small. Letha sighed.

"They can't hold me here forever. I *will* get money from the store, even though it might not be breaking even right now. When I do, I'll go."

"You shouldn't say that too loud."

"What'd'you mean?"

"Just that others might not take that threat so kindly."

Sylvia turned back to her again. "Letha, you don't seem to under-stand, and I think it's because you've fought this thing for so long. You never accepted being chosen. Even during the ceremony, I was the one who wanted it — not you. I wanted to be Consort so badly my whole body ached for it. And I should have been the Consort. Look at what I can do with the animals — doesn't that tell you I have a bond with nature? It should have been me!"

"It should have been. So maybe I feel guilty, I don't know — because I was chosen and not you. And that's why I've let you run things — make my decisions — because it's the only way I can try to give it back to you. But I can't do that anymore." Letha closed her eyes. The darn years were choking her, tears caught at the edges of her eyes.

"Damn it, Letha, I'm tired of your poor-me attitudes." Sylvia was standing, a fierce expression on her candle-lit face. "You've got everything I ever wanted — a family, a place, a purpose, and you're special — not just to one person, not just to a family, but to a whole lot of people, and all you do is complain. I don't want your pity or your guilt. I want my own place in life and I'm prepared to work for it. What'd you ever do to work for yours?"

She turned away, looked out into the darkness, but Letha could still see the rapid rise and fall of her chest. Sylvia was as angry as Letha'd ever seen her. More angry than when she'd caught Tessa Roger's brother, Tad, whipping his horse because the animal had lost a race with Sammy Brewster. Worse, though, was the fact that in some ways she was right. What had Letha ever done? She'd been 'kept' like a prize Hereford all her life.

"What I'm saying is I want the chance to work for what I want, too. And that doesn't include marrying Harry Zigheld."

"The Valley wants you married, Leth."

"Are you suggesting I marry someone I don't love?"

"He's a Valley man. You'll stay here then. The elders will be happy."

"And no one gives a damn if I'm happy. Do you know what Harry Zigheld is like?"

"Not too good a kisser, from your reaction today."

"Damn it, Syl! Would you listen for a change, instead of sitting on your high horse with your mind made up already?"

Sylvia turned back to her. "So I'm closed-minded, too?" she asked sweetly.

"Not closed-minded. You just have your own thoughts and opinions, so you don't often hear mine." Letha picked up her wine glass and realized her hands were shaking. She didn't want this conversation to go like this, didn't want to chance ruining this precious friendship, but it had to be said; this thing between them had been growing into something ugly for too many years.

"Sylvia, there were things about Harry Zigheld I didn't tell you before. I was — too ashamed — too afraid."

"What does this have to do with anything?"

"It has to do with why I don't want any more to do with Harry than I have to." Her mouth suddenly dry, she took a sip of wine. "It wasn't a good time in my life after I was chosen. You'd told me that there were old tales that said a consort wasn't as bound to the lake if she was mated — I guess that's what you were talking about the other day, but I didn't understand it like that back then. I took it that I'd get my freedom if I could find the right sexual partner. You remember how I was. I guess I slept with most of the Valley boys at one time or another — and made a lot of enemies amongst the Valley girls at the same time — except for you and Kris.

"Harry — he was one of the guys — not the first, thank Spring, but one of the last ones I guess, because I always found him a little — off. We had sex a few times. In his parent's barn. In his truck. In the woods. It was always rough and fast and focused on him."

"What a surprise." Sylvia grinned down at her with an expression that said most men were that way.

"So you know. Well, I broke it off after just a few times, because Harry — he's hard. Hard to talk to and hard in his attitudes. He still is. Things had better obey him, when he demands it, or there'll be hell to pay." Letha closed her eyes, the memory coming back too swiftly and leaving her with a cramping stomach and feeling of filth that she had ever let that man touch her.

"He caught me riding home from school one day and asked for help understanding a homework assignment. I dismounted, and that was the worst decision I ever made. He said we had unfinished business, and I knew there was something wrong. He had this strange look in his eye, as if he was only half there. Then he grabbed me, had me on the ground so fast I couldn't believe it. He told me I had no right — I was sleeping with everyone and he wanted another piece. I... I... was going to fight, but... he was too strong... and I'd asked for it, hadn't I. I did what I was told."

She was shivering, and could still feel the way her back had ground into the dirt, the pine needles in her hair, his hands on her, and she was limp under him and he was laughing as he ground into her, and she was cold, cold as winter and so lost in the dark.

"Letha? Letha? Why didn't you tell me?" Sylvia was suddenly on the glider beside her, had caught Letha's cold hands in her warm ones. There were tears in Sylvia's eyes, just as Letha realized her own tears were running down her cheeks. Why was Sylvia crying?

"I… I deserved it, didn't I? I had been sleeping around. With anything in pants, he said. It made me realize what I was doing was wrong. That I would never get free that way. But doing what we did — I didn't think, I couldn't think. I… went home and told myself it was over, right?" And she'd showered and vainly tried to scrub herself clean until her mother yelled at her about her waste of water.

Sylvia caught Letha in her arms. "Damn. Damn him. I should have known, should have seen."

"You couldn't have known. I wasn't going to let anyone know, because it was my fault. I'd made choices. He just did what anyone would do."

Sylvia rocked her like a child.

"What am I going to do? No…" She wasn't going to let it be like that. She struggled free of her friend and swiped the tears off her face. "No. I don't want you to tell me. It's my problem. I'll figure it out."

Sylvia gave a slow nod and looked up at the sky. "It's late. Too late for you to ride the woods, what with all the animals coming down from the hills these days." Letha wasn't sure what she expected to see in Sylvia's eyes, but it wasn't the sorrow she saw there. There was no judgment or revulsion. "You can use the sofabed and ride back in the morning."

It was a prudent decision, given Letha's state. Once the tears had started, she could barely see clearly, let alone be aware of any dangers to her safety. She helped fold out the creaky couch and crawled between flannel sheets, wearing an ancient t-shirt of Sylvia's scrawled with *Williams Lake Stampeders*, the name of the town's hockey team. She fell asleep immediately, dreaming of the choosing and the green-gold flash that had surrounded them all, but stolen her life.

She awakened to the sound of a truck engine outside.

Letha lay frozen, bed springs digging into her back. She thought of Harry's mail truck and her breathing hitched. Had Sylvia betrayed her? Had she called Harry to come? *Don't be a fool, Sylvia wouldn't do that.* But she slid out of bed, her heart pounding like mad, and padded to the front window, twitched the curtain back to peer out.

The taillight glow of the truck's emergency brakes illuminated the yard. By the cab, in the glow of the dashboard, two people talked — Sylvia, her blonde hair glazed green in the light, and a man silhouetted black, who had his back to Letha.

Letha stepped closer to the window to listen, careful not to disturb the curtains. The voices were low and rushed with anger she could see in the quick hand-movements Sylvia made, the way she shook her head, the way the man's voice rose.

Still, she couldn't hear, and the smell of beef stew and onions — Sylvia's dinner — sat cloying in her nose. She pressed the latch of the window and pulled, fearing noise, but needing fresh air and to hear. Pine-scented wind rushed through the crack she made.

"...to hell with it, then," the man swore and climbed into his truck. The engine rumbled as he turned the wheel, as he flicked on the headlights and drove out of the yard, leaving Sylvia standing in the shadows cast by the quarter moon.

From the barn a sleek figure ran, Max lifting his head to fill Sylvia's waiting palm. Coyote — in local Native myth he was the trickster. For a moment they were like a statue, a single being waiting in the night, as the rumble of the truck faded into the darkness. Then came the sound of the wind in the pine boughs, the whoosh of bat wings, and fear cramped Letha's stomach as Sylvia turned, looked up at the house, directly at the window, and in the faded light of stars, Letha saw the tears on her face.

Chapter 6

Letha didn't wait for Sylvia to come back to the house. She'd scurried back to bed and feigned sleep when she heard her friend's heavy steps on the porch stairs, then huddled, wondering, through the rest of the night.

In the still, grey light of four a.m. Letha dressed, wrote a note of thanks — no mention of what's she'd seen — and went out to Inca. The wind had stopped, was waiting to see what the dawn would bring. Letha inhaled the familiar scent of horse, manure, and pine as the mare stomped her feet and complained at being asked to work before breakfast.

"Sorry, girl. I'll give you extra grain at home."

Then she was in the saddle and urging the mare into a canter among the trees on the long slope down toward the lake. She just needed to get free of this place where she had bared the dark places of her soul.

That story shouldn't have been told. It was one more piece of herself — a piece of history that just might be another binding to hold her in place.

She'd always sworn she wouldn't tell anyone about what had happened in high school; that the incident with Harry was no excuse for anything, was really all her fault because she was just filled with faulty choices. Then she'd tried to convince herself that his force, the bruises he'd left on her, and the sick, self-loathing she'd felt, had just been her imagination.

Just like the incident at the store yesterday. She thought of Ty's face — his concern and fury as he looked from her to Harry. She didn't need his help. She didn't need anyone's help. All she needed was a way out of the Valley.

Besides, it was all water under the bridge.

But Sylvia had done something with the information. That was as clear as the way Sylvia had looked at the house — as if she knew Letha were watching and was looking deep into her eyes. There had been ac-knowledgement and guilt in that sad gaze.

Sylvia had told. She'd stolen Letha's choices again, but for the first time in her life, Letha felt absolutely calm; she knew what she could do in her own defense. A coyote yipped as the sun rose and painted blood-red stains across the steel-surfaced lake as Letha and Inca reached home. She looked up at the hills and out at the lake.

"You're not going to do it to me again, friend. Never again."

§

By noon the day had warmed, and Johnny Warner came into the store dressed in a white Stetson, his best jeans, and a neatly ironed plaid cowboy shirt that was just a little too big across the shoulders and just a little droopy with heat.

"Hey, Letha. Any sign of that reporter, yet?" Johnny was growth-spurt thin, a gangly seventeen-year-old who was showing signs of growing into one of those lean ranchers who filled the pages of Marlborough ads.

Letha smoothed her navy cotton skirt and checked her watch, just as she had every few minutes for the past three hours, but the time dripped past as an-noyingly as a leaky faucet. She grinned at Johnny. "A might eager, are we? He's supposed to be here at one. Grab a chair, and you can help me stop biting my fingernails."

Slumping, as only a teenager could, into the store's comfortable chair, Johnny scanned the store. He nodded. "You been busy. Looks good. My paintings look good, too."

Letha released the breath she'd been holding. She'd spent all morn-ing putting the final touches on the painting displays and fussing over the other crafts. It kept her mind off other things, and the way her stomach flip-flopped with excitement. "You think so? God, I was so worried you wouldn't think it was right."

"Ya did good, Letha."

"You and Tessa — you did the paintings and the sculptures; all I had to do was display them. Easy, when you give me good stuff to work with. You want a Coke or something?"

When he hesitated, she went to the cooler and hauled them out. "Enjoy. It's on the house."

"But…"

"Leave your Valley pride at home today. I'm showing you off as one of my artists, and I plan on making some money from your paintings, so consider it fair trade."

She grabbed another Coke, cracked it open, and tapped the side of his bottle. "To a good session with the reporter and a gangbuster article coming out. Can't turn our noses up at free advertising."

An hour later and so promptly Letha wondered if the reporter had stopped along the side of the road to time his arrival, a blue compact car pulled into the yard and a tall, dark-haired man in jeans and navy polo shirt unfolded himself from the driver side door. Letha went down from the porch to great him.

"Martin Dietrich, right? I'm Letha Rivers. We spoke on the phone." She held out her hand, feeling strange and proud and almost giddy with excitement that *she* was doing this — was greeting a stranger *she* had invited to *her* store.

"So this is Letha's Store and Artwork." Martin Dietrich's grasp was firm. He was a long-time reporter with the Williams Lake *Tribune,* and the gray at his temples showed he'd been around. A bull neck and a little too much time in the Williams Lake pubs contributed to his sense of size: beer belly, swollen nose. "Been a while since I've been out to the Valley. Not much news here — not since that horse of the Hunts took the cutting horse world championship a few years back."

"Kristienne was really stoked," Johnny said.

Letha grinned at Johnny. "Stoked is one word for it. Mr. Dietrich, this is Johnny Warner, one of my artists." The words seemed sweet to her mouth. Her artist. She was in charge. What could she do in the world if she was given the chance to take control of her life?

Leading them inside, she showed Dietrich around the store, explaining how it was a partnership between Sylvia and herself and how she'd decided to make it more than a small country store. "It wasn't a decision between my partner and me — it was more of a chance thing." *More of a rebellion on my part, if I was going to tell the truth.* "Sylvia thought the Valley could benefit from a general store, but then I started thinking about the summer people who come to the lake. I always hear comments about how genuine it is here — the people, the log cabins, being close to nature, and so on. I thought people might like to be able to take something home that showed that genuineness. When I was visiting Johnny's place, I saw some of his sculpture and I knew what I had to do."

Dietrich turned to Johnny and had him show him around his art, allowing Letha to stand back and just watch. The reporter nodded encouragingly as Johnny nervously answered questions, but when Dietrich got him on the topic of how he chose his subjects, Johnny started to loosen up. Dietrich's gaze seemed drawn to the set of five small paintings Letha had hung over the window; scenes of the lake shore in all kinds of weather.

Letha smiled at the way Johnny's face lit up. He was trapped in the Valley, too, and just aching for a chance to express himself a new way. Well, she'd give him that chance.

When Johnny led the reporter outside to show him some of his favorite sculptures and point out some done by Tessa Rogers, Letha hauled out the pitcher of lemonade and a platter of cookies she'd made, then took them outside to the porch table.

Roscoe fluttered down onto the porch rail, tugged at one of the spirit catcher feathers to set the catcher bouncing against the store's wall.

"You behave yourself," Letha hissed.

The raven croaked and leapt from the railing to the table to peck at one of the cookies.

"Scat! These aren't for you!" She waved her arms and the raven fluttered up to the ridgepole of the store and croaked his displeasure. "If you're good, I might let you have a cookie. The operative word is 'might'."

"You've got some interesting customers."

Letha turned around to find Martin Dietrich looking up at her, camera in hand. He'd been clicking photos of the statues and of the front of the store. Behind him stood a smug Ty Hunt, Hauberk's reins in his hands, and she felt heat rush into her face. Was Dietrich talking about the bird or Ty? "Darn thing thinks he owns the place. He follows me all over and generally gets in the way."

"That'd be me, she's talking about — not the bird," Ty said, as he settled himself against the porch rail and far too close for comfort. The smug look on his face grew into a grin as if he thought the whole thing yesterday was a joke. He better not say anything to this reporter or she'd... she'd have his hide.

"You'd be over here a lot, then, would you? What do you think of the store?" Dietrich looked from one to the other of them and Letha found she couldn't breathe, was waiting for Ty's next answer.

"She's got the best peanut butter and jam in town." Ty's grin spread as he raised his brows at her. "Good bread, too, and a nice way about her. The art's not bad, either."

Chuckling, Dietrich snapped a few photos and scratched notes in on his paper. "So you're saying there are a variety of things to attract people to Letha's Store and Artwork."

Ty shrugged. "Could be. Yes. She runs a fine store and works hard to see that it brings in what people want and offers an opportunity to the artisans of the Valley. It's high time someone did that."

"Can I get your name — for the article?"

"Rather not. I'm a private man. Not much for the media. Just say 'a neighbor'." Ty turned back to Letha. "When you're done, I'd like to talk if you've got time. I'll be at home."

He mounted Hauberk in one smooth, athletic motion and then urged the horse into a slow trot out of the yard, but the way he moved in the saddle — the way his back narrowed down to slim hips that seemed to become one with Hauberk, brought Letha another small rush of heat.

"That is one hell of a big horse," Dietrich murmured.

"European Warmblood. He bought him in the States. Brought him up when he came for his visit."

"That so?" Dietrich looked at the lemonade pitcher sweating on the porch table. "That for me?"

She had to pull her gaze away from Ty and found she was smiling. "I thought you might like something after the drive."

"You this good to all your customers?"

Grinning, she poured him a tall glass. "Just to those who are going to write a glowing article on the store."

"Ah." He tested the lemonade after he sat down. "Pretty good. The real thing, right?" He took another long pull and emptied the glass. "This reporter-thing is thirsty work. Listen, Johnny, Letha. I really like this place and the art. You've got something unique here, and the art's quality — I know, 'cause I studied fine arts before falling into journalism to feed myself. You should do something with this place — advertise."

"Well, I'm doing a website — or I plan to, but I've never done one before."

Dietrich was nodding, his face florid in the heat as he drank back another glass of Letha's lemonade. When he was done his gaze held on Letha's face. "Tell you what. I've taken a bunch of photos here. I'll send 'em to you so you can use them on the website if you want. If you like, I'll even take a look at what you're thinking of putting on the site, but I really think you should think bigger. Maybe do a show or something. You've got quality stuff here, and Johnny says there's more where that came from."

The flutter in her stomach returned as a thrill. He was telling her he liked the place, the art, and her idea. He was suggesting she go bigger, when all her life people had made her feel like she had to retreat.

"I… don't…"

"Listen, to show you I'm not jerking you around, I'd like to know the price on that set of small paintings over the window. I've been looking for something. I'm redoing my place. My wife and I split a few years back. It's time I decorate my new place." He grinned. "Hey, maybe you could help me — I never did have much of an eye for decorating."

"And I've never decorated anything other than a store — so unless you want to look like you're selling canned peas, I'd say 'no'."

"All five?" Johnny asked, rocking back and forth on his heels so hard Letha was afraid he was going to fall off the porch.

Smoothing her skirt as she stood, she took her leave. "Let me go check." She ducked into the store and did a quick happy dance as the excitement ripped through her. She would whoop if it wouldn't have been unseemly. Almost exploding with excitement, she carefully took down the paintings and carried them outside, where the reporter was feeding cookies to a very cocky raven. Each painting had a price on the back of the frames she had so carefully made out of old barn boards she'd found in back of her shed. The weathered grey wood nicely set off the faded colors of the paintings and the feel of the landscapes.

Swiftly adding the prices and computing the tax, she told him the total and was amazed when he pulled out his check book. "Why don't you go wrap those up for me, while I write this out?"

Numbly she obeyed and accepted his check, then waved Dietrich out of the yard, his new paintings carefully wrapped in brown paper on the seat beside him. When he was gone, she inhaled and felt like she'd been holding her breath since he arrived.

She turned to Johnny and the two of them gave a huge whoop that sent Roscoe fluttering up from the cookies, back to the ridge pole, squawking all the way. Raven epithets rained down on them as they danced on the porch, but Letha didn't care. She wrote Johnny a check that covered everything but her commission, then sent him on his way.

There was money in her pocket. The day was shaping up pretty fine. And feeling as good as she felt, now was the time to meet with Ty Hunt.

It was quick work putting the last of the lemonade back in the fridge, breaking a cookie apart for Roscoe, and telling him that he might have charmed the reporter, but he was going to be one very chubby raven if he kept snacking like this. Then she closed the store up and left the 'back in 30 minutes' sign in the window.

She had money in her pocket. Well not money, yet, but she would when she deposited Martin Dietrich's check. The slim piece of paper seemed to place bulk in her pocket. She skipped along the overgrown gravel road that was the trail between the two cabins.

Even along the lake the air showed summer was coming. The sun beat down, had baked the green right out of the landscape except near the water. The green grass that had seemed to grow tall overnight, now rattled in the breeze and released grasshoppers wildly into the air as she passed. The air hummed with insect song, the gravel shimmered with heat, but Letha twirled — once, twice, again — her skirt belling around her, before stepping out of from between the silver-grey willows that hedged Ty's cabin.

That was how Ty saw her, a little breathless, her chin lifted and shoulders squared in that little defiant motion he knew so well from suspects he'd questioned. Letha Rivers wanted something, even if it was for him to leave her alone. Watching her sashay to his porch was enough to make him hope that wasn't the way she was feeling.

Lowering his feet from the porch rail, he set his beer down and stood to greet her. "Well howdy there, Ma'am. Yer looking mighty fine today. That smile o' yours is enough to plumb stir a man's blood."

She rolled her eyes and sat down on the top stair, letting her long legs catch some of the sun. "You got another of those beers? 'Cause I've got something to celebrate."

"Do ya now? And what would that be, Miss Letha?"

"Tell you what, you cut the accent and get me a beer, and I'll tell you."

He pulled a beer out of a bucket of ice beside his chair. "And I thought I was being all charming and old-fashioned."

"Actually, it was a little annoying." She grinned up at him as he feigned wounding to his heart.

"So tell me. This have anything to do with the reporter?" Ty shifted down beside her, the two beers in his hands, feeling a sharp pang slice across his lower back. It was supposed to be healing, damn it. He shook his head in impatience at the time it took to heal, and turned his attention to Letha. She took a sip of the beer, her long neck arching back prettily.

"It has everything to do with the reporter," she said. She told him what Dietrich had said. "I just can't believe it. Nothing has gone right for so long, and now suddenly this store — it gives me a chance. I've got money in my pocket — *my* money." She glanced sideways at him. "I suppose this makes no sense at all to you, 'cause you've been on your own for so long."

"Doing something important to you for the first time is one of the best feelings in the world."

She gave him a strange look, as if she were seeing him for the first time. "You know, you say things like that and I might actually like you."

"Well, isn't that nice to know." Her red curls were uncontrolled around her face. He couldn't help himself and gently pushed away a strand that had caught on her lips, but when he saw the way she stiffened, he pulled his hand away. "You were going to have it in your mouth in a minute."

She grinned. "It's just hair. After this many years I'm used to it misbehaving."

"Looks like your hair got all your willfulness."

She bit her lip in such a feminine gesture, Ty was tempted to kiss her right there, but he knew it was the wrong thing to do. With the wild ones, you step in, ease away, step closer, and ease back.

He stood up and looked out at the lake lying somnolent in the sun. "Hope I didn't cause any problems stopping by today. I just wanted to apologize if I caused a problem yesterday. I didn't want to. It was just that —" he took a deep breath. "I thought maybe he hurt you. I don't like to see women hurt."

"Is that why you have a horse like Hauberk? So you can be a knight and ride to the aid of damsels in distress? Is that why you're a cop?"

She said it softly, almost as if she said it to herself, but it spun him around as if he were on a string. He didn't like teasing about his choices in life. Yes, he'd left the Valley because he'd tried to rescue his mother from the exile his father had placed her in. After the final fight with his father, Ty had sworn he was never coming back. Well, he'd made the choice. He'd lived with it.

But she wasn't taunting him. No, her eyes were filled with thoughtful consideration as she studied him. He drew a deep breath and let his anger out with it.

"It's why I asked you to pop over. I didn't want my actions putting a strain on our… friendship."

She heard the hesitation in his voice and knew they were both struggling with the same thing — this tension between them, this thing that seemed to bell out around them whenever they touched. Well, now was the time to do something about it and deal with Harry Zigheld at the same time.

"Apology not accepted. It was my fault. You were just doing your thing." She took another swig of beer and set it down, then stood. Ty stood to face her and she realized again just how tall he was. "So. Now that we've dealt with that, I was going to ask you over for dinner to celebrate. Nothing fancy, you understand. Just ranch fare."

He held up a hand, stopping her, and for a moment she thought he was going to turn her down. Her whole stomach clenched. There was so much riding on him coming.

"I've got a better idea. This is a big deal and it deserves fancy fare — well, a big juicy steak, at least. How about I pick you up around six and we'll wander on into Williams Lake for dinner. The Stampede Grill's still around. Used to be the best steak in Cariboo country."

"Used to be…" Her voice all but failed her until she caught her breath. "Are you asking me on a date?"

"What else? You know what they are, right? You go get yourself dolled up and I put on something other than boots and breeches and we go somewhere to be served good food and be good company for each other. Sound okay?"

He wasn't making fun of her. He was treating her like any other woman that he might want to take on a date.

"Sounds okay," she agreed before her better sense could stop her. This *was* what she'd wanted. Ty to date her so the Valley would back off about Harry.

"Then this is the point where you head back to your place and start the dolling-up thing."

"Right. And you have to find something else to wear."

"Well, I could go like this, I imagine they'd let me in."

She looked him up and down appreciatively, gave a little hoot as if the idea tickled her, and started away.

"Hey, it's not that funny!"

"In this part of the world it sure 'nough is," she chortled as she headed back to the store feeling like all was right with the world.

§

At six o'clock she was sitting huddled on the edge of her bed, wondering what kind of darn fool she was. Ty Hunt wasn't the kind of man for her. He was too sure of himself, too different, and he sure as heck wasn't like any Valley man she'd ever met. Which, she supposed, was part of the thing that had set that little frisson of excitement in her belly.

That, and the fact he was taking her out of the Valley. The elders and Sylvia would have a fit, if they knew, but she sure as heck wasn't going to tell them. No, she was going to take her travel medicine, think positive thoughts that she *would* be able to leave the Valley, go out with Ty Hunt, and enjoy herself.

She was going to do more than enjoy herself, actually; she was going to encourage him enough that when he decided to head back to the city he'd take her with him. Hopefully that would be soon, because that would deal with her problem and get the darkness around him away from the Valley.

The Valley people couldn't say she wasn't trying to do her job of keeping the Valley safe.

From outside came the sound of a truck engine and she stood, looking down at herself and feeling hopelessly, inappropriately dressed. She hadn't been sure what to wear, and had looked at her clothes with despair. When you live on a ranch and the only family outing you take is to the little church in the Valley, you don't have much. So she'd chosen jeans that Kristienne had brought her from New York on a long-ago visit, because, Kris had said, they'd show off her long legs, and a deep blue, silk tunic she'd ordered years ago from a catalogue — much to her mother's consternation. The tunic was belted at the hip with an old belt complete with oversized silver rodeo buckle, and she wore large, silver, hoop earrings that tangled with her red curls.

But the jeans fit slimmer at the hips than she was used to and the blouse seemed to cling to her skin. There was no time to change, though, because the familiar clump of boots on the front stairs said Ty was here.

He knocked, and waited, looking out at the lake. At this time of day, the worst of the heat was starting to bleed away and the moist breath of the lake was starting to pull the dust out of the air. He loved this time, and the way it seemed to make every detail stand clear. Like the woman who opened the door at his knock.

"Whoa. Excuse me Ma'am. I'm looking for the girl next door — name's Letha Rivers." She was — stunning was the only word for it. Jeans, but not the faded riding clothes she usually wore — something about these made her legs look even longer and he swore he could see the long muscles of her thighs through the denim. The blue of her shirt showed the curve of her breasts, caught her eyes and made them blaze. With the tumble of her hair it was like she was afire, and he felt his own storm rising. Not a good sign when this was only a friendly dinner to celebrate her fortune.

"It's okay, right? I haven't gone to town much." The grin she had quirked up on one side, as if she was pleasantly pleased at his reaction.

"Letha, you'll blow 'em away." He closed the door behind her, and held the door of the truck as she entered, noting how she wasn't sure of his actions, or how to react. She really wasn't used to being treated as an attractive woman on a date. Well, he wasn't used to dealing with someone like Letha, either, so he guessed that made them even.

The long drive into town made his back ache, but it passed with light conversation and a burning awareness of the woman in the truck with him. How — *what was that?* — she held her breath and tensed as they passed Jed Hartley's cabin, how she finally relaxed into the truck seat and an excited joy seemed to radiate from her as she stared out the window, as she exclaimed over the way Williams Lake lay blue as a piece of sky removed from the heavens. He had to keep reminding himself he was driving, when all he really wanted to do was watch the clouds of emotion that passed over her face.

When he stopped the truck in the crowded parking lot beside the Stampede Grill, he turned to her. "Looks like we might have to wait a bit. Hope you don't mind."

She shook her head, but he saw the moment of hesitation, the little way her lips trembled and firmed. She was scared, damn it. This lovely woman was afraid of going into a restaurant with him.

"You ready?" A nod this time. He climbed out and rounded the truck, opened her door and she climbed down, then stood there with a dazed expression on her face. "Hey, Letha. You all right?"

His soft question brought her back to herself. Suddenly the world, her choices, what she was determined to do, all seemed overwhelming because she was out of the Valley and she was *well.* She looked up at him, all tall and handsome in indigo jeans and a brown cowboy-cut shirt that seemed to place shadows swimming in his eyes. She wanted to know what those shadows were. She wanted to understand a man who left the Valley and came back, but the task seemed totally daunting.

"You should know that the only time I've ever been in town since the ceremony was when Sylvia brought me to the bank. The trip made me sick. They'd told me leaving the Valley would. It always has."

"Are you okay now? If you're not feeling well we don't have to do this."

"No. I feel fine." She really did. It was strange — she'd been waiting for the nausea and headache to begin, she'd been waiting for that feeling of departure since they passed the dell where Jed Hartley's cabin lay, but it hadn't happened. It had been like — well it had been like she was too preoccupied with the heat she felt from Ty's side of the cab and with the energy she felt passing between them. She looked up at him, smiled. "I really am fine."

The inside of the restaurant held the hum of voices and the delicious scents of beef and seafood and baked potatoes. It was done up with memorabilia from the William's Lake Stampede rodeo — photos of cowboys on bucking horses and bulls, of calf ropers taking their calves, of barrel racers leaning hard into the turns around the barrels, and of rodeo queens sitting proudly on their horses. There were lariats and spurs and Stetsons on the walls, and even a section that made homage to rodeo clowns. The hostess's station Ty left his name at was made of Plexiglas with a silver-encrusted saddle inside.

They were assured it would only be a few minutes for a table, but Ty edged them into a corner and eased his back against the wall.

"As a kid I used to love this place and imagine I'd have my picture up there one day, just like Matt."

"Matt Kelly?" Somehow it didn't surprise her; Matt had always been a cut above in his ranch work.

"Yup, used to do some top-notch roping before he settled into buckarooing for my sister. Now I don't think he'll ever leave as long as she has the ranch. Following the rodeo circuit takes a man away from home way too much." There was a hint of regret in his voice.

"But you made a life outside the Valley."

His gaze flickered over her, assessing, as the hostess motioned for them to follow. When they were settled at a table in a corner with a view of the lake as the sky faded to evening blue, he looked at her. "Yeah, I guess you can say I had a life, but I'm not sure it was my own."

"You don't like to talk about it, do you?" She looked at him over the top of her menu, wondering how anyone who lived in the outside world could feel that their life wasn't their own.

"Letha, I know you feel you don't have a life. I remember when you were first chosen, how upset you were because you wanted to travel."

"You remember that?"

The softest of smiles flickered over his face. "How could I forget a pretty thirteen year old girl who promised to be my slave if I'd just steal her away with me when I went off to university? It kind of stays with you."

She felt her face color. She had been that desperate. Thing was, she still was. "It was a long time ago."

"And you still want to leave."

She nodded. "And this time I'm going to make it happen. I'm going to earn money so they can't stop me from going. If I have to, once I have the money, I'll walk into town."

He grinned. "You always were one stubborn kid."

"And I'm just as stubborn now." His grin infected her and she looked back at the menu. "So what's good here?"

"Steak. Steak and lobster, steak and crab, steak and prawns."

"I'm noticing a theme."

"Consider me a red meat kinda guy. Seafood — after being raised on a ranch, it's for whusses."

"Whusses, huh? Well, I've never had seafood — just trout and chicken and beef and pork, so what do you suggest I have?"

"Steak."

She rolled her eyes. "What a surprise. Steak it is."

When the waitress had taken their food order and brought them a bottle of California Merlot, she sat back, sipping the earthy-tasting wine. "You did it again, you know — avoided telling me about your life outside the Valley. Strange, given you offered to tell me about the outside world. That suggests there's something either unsavory or secret about your life."

"So you're a detective now?"

She waited, not allowing the subject to be changed.

Finally he shrugged. "Honey, you're a hard a woman. OK, I guess it was a little of both, really — unsavory and secret. I worked undercover, used my knowledge of horses to get into some pretty unsavory Mob dealings on the horse show circuits. It got pretty ugly toward the end."

He looked at her, waiting.

"Something happened, didn't it? That's why you're here." Her astuteness surprised him, and yet it didn't. She was brilliant in her own way, and there was something between them, he felt it every moment they were together.

Finally he nodded, shrugged. "They found out I was a Fed. I got shot. I came here to... recover."

"Ah. I saw the limp. Looks like you're on the mend."

"There's still numbness in my leg, but I'll get over it." He didn't bother mentioning the times the pain in his back was almost more than he could bear. No point. "Now, about that big world."

He launched into descriptions of Washington and New York, told from the perspective of someone who saw both the bright lights and the shadows they cast, but was interrupted by the arrival of dinner.

Thick fillet steaks wrapped in bacon, huge baked potatoes — fully decked out with sour cream, bacon, and chives — a sizzling pan of grilled mushrooms to split between them, and a salad on the side. The meat sliced with the slightest of pressure and Ty closed his eyes at his first bite.

"Ambrosia. I swear the Cariboo raises the best beef in the world." His eyes flicked open.

She gingerly sliced the steak, cringing a little at the pink in the middle because Ty had insisted she try it cooked no more than medium rare. She chewed tentatively. "Mom always cooked everything well done, but this is good."

"Almost better than my first sexual experience," he said around another bite, but his gaze was speculative, watching, and they both knew it.

"You were telling me about your travels."

She was fascinated, listening to his stories, watching the way his interest in his work, his commitment to truth and the protection of the innocent, played across his face. It was like those shadows lessened in his eyes as he opened the doors of his life to her, but always as he spoke it was of himself alone; other names were left carefully out of his tales and she began to sense his isolation. When he'd launched into a description of the island of Aruba visited on a vacation, she stopped him.

"There are no people in your stories. You're telling me about people you see, people you meet, but what about the people you know? What are people like out there, Ty? If I'm going to go out there, it would help me to know."

"People are — busy. That's the best way to put it. There's just no time to get involved with each other, unless it's a partner at work or a friend with a common interest, and even then the people I met on the job or through horses had their own lives to live. People come together and split apart. There's nothing like the way the Valley is — everyone knowing everyone and concerned about each other's lives. Outside, it's just too darn big. So when you go, be prepared." He smiled at her over a sip of wine.

"But I've talked too much. Tell me about your day. That's what we're here to celebrate."

He didn't want to talk about being alone, not when he was sitting here with a beautiful woman. He lifted his wineglass. "To new beginnings and old acquaintances rekindled."

Their glasses tinked together, but he saw the way her gaze dropped away. "Letha, why do I make you uncomfortable?"

She jerked upright. "You don't."

"Well that's good to hear, because I'm thinking that there's something interesting happening between us — something I intend to follow up on."

He was looking at her with such intensity she just knew this whole venture had been a mistake, but she'd gotten herself into this, so she was going to get through it.

"So today — the reporter — he was really complimentary on the store." She saw the amusement in his gaze at her sudden change of subject, but two could play that game of avoidance. The story of Martin Dietrich's visit spilled from her, gushing out so she was almost embarrassed at her excitement, at how he had said he would send her pictures for the web and she should do an actual show — not that she had any idea of how to go about that.

Through it all his gaze stayed on her, warming her face just as the wine warmed her limbs. She realized she was laughing with him about Roscoe, telling him her hopes for the store, for the Valley art, for herself if she could only get the money together.

"With your talent you'll get it all done, Letha."

"The artists' talents speak for themselves. Johnny Warner really deserves to have his work out there in the world."

"I said your talent, Letha. You have a talent, too."

"It's just the lake." She shrugged, and the way she did it made him a little angry.

"It's more than the lake. It was your decision to be more than a store. It was your decision to display things like you have. It was your recognition of Johnny Warner's talents and your ability to show them off for that reporter. And you look good enough any man would be a fool not to drive all the way to Shelter Lake just to visit Letha's Store and Artwork. How come you can't see that?"

"I'm just a shopkeeper."

"Letha, you need to see what I see, and what scares the heck out of the Valley elders."

She looked at him, her gaze frozen, afraid. "I think I need to visit the ladies room." She stood.

"Letha…" She shook her head, refusing to hear him. "I'll order dessert," he capitulated.

She had to stop herself from half-running through the maze of tables. If she was smart she'd just keep on going out the door, and out into the world, but she knew she wasn't ready yet. She needed the money to make it happen, unless she planned to be a street person, and that wasn't in her plans.

In the women's restroom she collapsed on a leather bench decorated with silver saddle-rosettes. "You okay?" asked an older woman replenishing her lipstick at the mirror. "Don't tell me that fine looking man's gone and upset you?"

"What? Who? No. If anything, I got myself upset."

"Well, don't be letting that one get away. You two make a fine-looking couple. I swear every head in the house turned when you two walked in. You up on vacation?"

"No. No vacation." She rubbed her forehead. It wasn't a headache like last time she'd come to town. This time it was a combination of wine and the knowledge she was too attracted to Ty when she had no business being. She just wanted him to help her out of the Valley. That was all.

"You have a nice evening, dear." The woman left Letha to run water over her face, try in vain to tug her hair into some type of order, then square her shoulders and head back to the table. Attraction couldn't hurt, darn it. It would make her task easier.

Ty had intended to keep things light, but he knew that he'd spooked her like a horse shying at something new. Now he stood to greet her, held her chair as she slipped into it to face the bowl set in the middle of the table. A look of dismay filled her face.

"Hope I didn't overstep, but I knew the serving sizes were huge so I ordered one to share. Help yourself," he said seating himself. "It's called tiramisu and is a concoction of coffee liqueur and whipping cream and something like cake. Happens to be my personal favorite."

He watched as she picked up a spoon, hesitated, then tasted, a look of surprised pleasure filling her face. That was one of the things he liked about her — the way her emotions played honestly across her face, like notes in a piece of music. She didn't have all the secrets, all the hard edges and thick skin that people in the larger world developed. It meant he had to take care. It meant he wanted to.

"You like it?"

"It's… different. Like coffee on a spoon with the freshest cream on the side." She dug in with spirit and he realized that was another thing he liked. She ate like a person — with gusto — not like women in the cities who were so concerned for their figures they never enjoyed their food.

Leaning his elbows on the table, he watched her enjoyment. "You know, I was thinking. My mom used to go to all the art shows in New York and she was pretty connected to that scene. Maybe I should ask her to talk to you about doing a show." He shrugged. "If nothing else, she might give you information that'll help you make up your mind if you want to do one or not."

She stopped eating and looked at him. "Kris mentioned she might know something, but your mom didn't seem interested. From you, though — that'd be great." She looked away to the bowl — woefully empty. "Arm wrestle you for the last spoonful." The grin on her face, the flush in her cheeks told him the liqueur had taken its toll.

She must have realized it, too, because she burst out laughing. "You should see your face. You look like you might almost be worried I *could* take you. I should warn you, I beat most of the boys in my school, and yes, if your mother would be willing to help, I know I've got questions."

He was tempted to take up her arm wrestling challenge — anything to touch her — but the quiet of the restaurant suddenly intruded. There were only a few patrons left, and outside, the hills were swathed in sunset, leaving a honey light that washed over Letha. He looked at his watch. Ten p.m.

"It always amazes me that the light still holds so late up here. Be Solstice soon."

He saw her cringe and he swore at himself for reminding her of that other Valley ceremony.

"I think we'll have to take that competition home. We should be heading out, given we've got an hour drive back." He paid the check, then held Letha's chair for her, and casually caught her elbow for the walk to the truck. There was that thrill again, the warmth of her skin through the slippery silk, the wild rose scent of her, and the way some of her hair brushed his chin. It made him hold his breath. It sent his blood surging, but like a gentleman he held her door, then only walked the miles around to the far side of the cab.

It was a long drive, with acres of cab between them, and all Ty could think of was how he'd like to get closer, pull over like a school kid and take her in his arms. But Letha Rivers was a challenge, a quest not so different than when he'd worked to insinuate himself into his underworld target's operations. He just had to make himself attractive to Letha, have skills she needed. When he pulled in, in front of the store, he was decided. Again he opened her door for her, helped her out, and knew he invaded her personal space when he saw her throat bob and the rapid rise and fall of her chest. At least he caused a reaction. That was hopeful.

"It's been a great evening, but I don't think I'm ready to call it a night yet," he said softly. He was standing so close she felt the heat of him, felt the way he almost leaned in, almost kissed her. Instead, he surprised her when he said, "Feel like going for a ride?"

He nodded up at the moon. "It's clear, there's enough light, and the breeze is great. Come on Leth, what do you say?"

She knew the liquor still buzzing in her blood set aside her natural caution, but he was so tall, his shoulders strong, and he had bought her dinner and been a friend and had taken her out of the Valley. What harm could it do? She nodded.

"Meet you back here in fifteen. Be ready."

He was back in the truck and gone, leaving her feeling giddy and slightly foolish as she dashed into the house to change into riding clothes, then ran out to saddle Inca and pray the mare wasn't too ornery at the disturbance.

She beat him by a minute, sat slumped in her saddle as she heard the heavy beat of Hauberk's hooves. "My God, you're slow. Inca and I have already been to the other end of the lake and back already."

"Like hell!"

"Who you calling a liar, Mister?"

"That mare's not fast enough."

"Wanna bet?" She squeezed Inca and the mare leapt forward. Another squeeze and they were into a gallop, whooping around the end of the lake and heading along the trail that edged the south side of the glimmering water.

The mare's hooves pounded in rhythm to her blood, but behind she heard the heavy fall of Hauberk's stride. Soon she heard more than that —

felt the blow of hot breath on her shoulder, peered over, and the stallion was there, ears pinned back as he ran.

She squealed and leaned forward, trying for the last ounce of speed from her mare, but Hauberk's longer stride ate the ground up between them, his head came even with her, with Inca's neck, he was nose to nose with Inca, and suddenly Ty was there beside her, had leaned down to catch her hand in his and bring them both to a halt. The two horses stood blowing, steam coming from their coats. Hauberk flipped his nose at Inca and the mare tried to bite. Ty shortened the stallion's reins, but his hand still held hers, warmth and strength enfolding her.

"Let's go for a swim," he said, his voice strangely rough. He didn't wait for her, just released her and urged Hauberk toward the lake. The big horse hesitated, half reared at the water's edge where reeds rustled in the night breeze. Ty called him a big goof. Then he was riding straight into the lake, splashing through the shallows to become a dark form caught in liquid silver, swimming out into the lake on great surges of the stallion's legs.

"You coming?" Ty's voice echoed back.

She pushed Inca down to the lake. She hadn't swum her horse in years, but the mare didn't hesitate, simply waded out into the water, and suddenly Letha was up to her waist, her chest in liquid that seemed to join with her body, flow with her blood. It was still cool from the long winter, but the layer closest to the surface had been warmed by the sun. The breeze swirled around her face, scented with mint and baby's breath, and the water plastered her clothes to her body, tingled on her skin. Inca plunged as she lost her footing, and the mare went under, taking Letha down too. She came up spluttering and laughing, blowing spray out her nose.

He'd watched her disappear, and fear had made him spur Hauberk through the water. When she came up laughing, he realized his heart was pounding too hard for this to only be his natural urge to rescue. It made him laugh at the ridiculousness of his situation. He was leaving soon, damn it. But then he was beside her in the warm water, his rumbling laughter mixing with her own, Hauberk blowing spray as Ty reached over, caught her hand as he forced their horses close, as his lips found hers, found her waiting, and his chest ached as if — please, no — he might be drowning.

Soft and then firm, his kiss, and she answered him back willingly, wantonly, warming at his touch as a soft bell-tone rose from the depth of the moonlit lake. She felt it in her bones, and the dark pulsing places of her body trembled. Letha parted her lips and knew that everything had changed.

Releasing her cost him, but Ty looked at her eyes, opened wide as the sky. Had he heard something?

"The moon's setting. We should get back." He turned Hauberk toward shore, rode onto the trail and waited until she joined him.

"Letha…," he started, but she sidled the mare over, caught his chin and kissed him lighter than a memory.

Again that sweet surge of desire through his body, but he wasn't going to do anything about it tonight. Approach and retreat was the only way this would work. He touched her face, her hair, groaning inwardly at the flare of arousal, and smiled as the night breeze ran fingers over his damp skin. "Come on. Let's get you home."

Chapter 7

Early sunshine blazing on her shoulders, Letha applied a little more saddle salve to the leather seat of the saddle and waited for it to absorb. Beyond, in the corral, Inca munched her way through a flake of first-cut Shelter Valley alfalfa. Letha shook her head at the saddle. She'd really done a number on the leather last night. Riding into the lake fully clothed and tacked up. Darn fool thing to do, but something had gotten into her. A wildness, a need, but it had finished the night unfulfilled.

So it still pulsed deep in her body, and she couldn't say she wasn't aware of it any more than she could say she wasn't aware of Ty's cabin just down the lake.

It had to be the wine. She'd never had as much to drink as she had last night. She grinned and rubbed salve into the tooled skirt of the saddle, careful not to leave anything to cake around the flowers and whorls that were shaped into the leather. Last night was a night of a lot of firsts. The sweet scent of the salve and the gleam of clean leather broadened her smile, just as it always did, but this time the smile felt bigger, like it was plastered on her face.

The mutual attraction with Ty was clear, something that would make her task so much easier. A relief, actually, as she wasn't a calculating person — just a little desperate. If whatever it was with Ty got her out of the Valley, then it was worth it. If it was just a fling, well then, they could go their separate ways, and no harm done.

But she could still feel his hands on hers, his lips. She touched fingers softened by saddle soap to her mouth.

The rumble of tires and the sight of Sylvia's truck forced her to tuck her thoughts away and square her shoulders to greet her partner in the store. Sylvia swung down from the cab and handed Letha a box of horse wormer. "It's the season. I got a shipment and knew you'd want to do Inca. I've got a case for Kristienne, too. Thought I might have a chance to check out her mother."

"And good morning to you, too."

Sylvia's gaze slipped from Letha's face to the saddle pads still dripping on the fence rails and the saddle and the bridle draped beside it. Her lips firmed into a line.

"Must be the air. Seems there's a lot of tack cleaning goin' on. I just dropped off a tube for that animal Ty calls a horse. He was busy as a bee, slicking expensive oils on that flat saddle of his." She looked at Letha speculatively. "Something I should know about?"

Shaking her head, Letha went back to her saddle. She left the saddle pads and hauled the saddle and bridle into the barn, Sylvia trailing behind. She plunked the saddle onto a stand.

"That reporter from the Williams Lake *Tribune* came by yesterday. He was very complimentary of the store."

"Complimentary, now. Jeeze, Letha. Next you'll be acting like all the summer people. You're already talking like them."

Letha glared at her, then caught herself. Just stay easy and natural and don't, for goodness sake, let Sylvia know what she had planned. "I'm not. I'm just stating a fact. He liked the store. He liked it enough he's sending me copies of his photos for the website."

She saw Sylvia stiffen. "And that's going to bring in customers in the winter."

Letha spun around. "Would you stop? Why are you so intent on putting my ideas down?" Darn it, why was she doing this? Just let things be. But she could feel the tears of frustration starting to fill her eyes.

The look on her face must have shocked Sylvia because she shook her head, her face softened, and she briefly touched Letha's shoulder, sending that comfortable little shimmer sensation that had always passed between the three friends. "I'm sorry. I'm not — or I don't mean to. It's just — where were you last night? I came by to drop off the wormer, but you weren't here."

It was Letha's turn to feel uncomfortable. "I went out. Ty and me. We — went out for a ride. It was a beautiful night, and we've been meaning to go for a ride together." Sylvia's appraising gaze weighed heavily on Letha. She grabbed a halter shank, stepped past the blonde woman and out to the corral. "Here. Give me a hand with Inca. Might as well get this done."

"So where'd you go?"

Letha glanced back at Sylvia, with guilt and that wild expression someone gets when they're quickly fabricating, and Sylvia knew something was going on. Something the elders would want to know about.

"Just along the lake. We swam the horses, thus the flurry of tack cleaning at this end of the lake."

"Ah. That explains it." She accepted the halter shank and held the mare while Letha grabbed Inca's tongue to hold the mare's mouth open and slipped the tube of paste in the side of the horse's mouth. When the plunger had pressed the right amount of paste into Inca, they released her. Inca tossed her head and trotted back to her hay. "She's looking good. Happy. Like her mistress."

Sylvia eyed Letha as she went — all business-like — back into the barn to carefully hang up the halter shank, then went to check the still-sodden saddle pad.

Something was up. Just what, wasn't clear, but there was a light in Letha's eyes she hadn't seen for a very long time. Not since Letha's first big crush when she was thirteen. And that had been over — Ty Hunt, no less.

"So'd he kiss you?"

Letha whirled around, her hands on her hips as if shocked at such a suggestion, but her face told the tale — all flushed excitement. Sylvia held up her hand.

"Don't bother denying it. It's on your face, clear as day. You don't have to keep it a secret from me. Wasn't I the one who suggested a little fling might brighten up your day? It has, I see."

"It's not like that. We — he — he took me out for dinner to celebrate."

"Dinner. You said you went for a ride. You eat at his place?" But she already knew, didn't she, because when she'd come by last night Inca was in her corral and Ty's truck was gone when she drove past. Letha was lying, and Sylvia felt her heart skip a beat. Letha didn't lie.

"We went into town — to the Stampede Grill — and had dinner. Steak. Ty was happy for me — unlike you. He even agreed with the reporter, and said he might get his mom to help me if I decide to do an art show."

Sylvia took one look at the defiance on Letha's face and had to walk away. It was the truth and she knew it. She stomped down to the lake. It was all too much. Letha leaving the Valley and being able to enjoy herself. Letha not only selling all this stupid art, but then doing a bloody website and now talking about a dammit-all-to-hell *art show*. Everything was falling apart and — how the hell had she left the Valley?

Sylvia stood among the willows, listening to the dry buzz of the grasshoppers and the hiss of the breeze over the lake. It was kissed by ripples today, but looked green and clear. Minnows darted in the amber-colored shallows and she remembered how they had danced in the water at the Ceremony. Today they felt cool-happy. Inca was content. Roscoe sat scheming on Letha's roof. But she couldn't get a good read on Letha, and Letha was the one that needed to be calm, settled, and content in the Valley. That she'd left it — even for dinner — was a very bad sign.

She turned around and saw Letha watching her, waiting, and — by her belligerent expression — ready to scrap. Since when had Letha gained the confidence to do that? Sylvia blew her hair back over her brow and marched back to her friend. She couldn't leave things as they were, and frankly, right now she was so darn mad, she could chew nails and spit rust.

"How could you be so stupid — leaving the Valley and going into town — and you were probably drinking, right? Ty was drinking too, right? What if there'd been an accident? What if you'd been killed? What would we do on the Solstice? Where would that leave the Valley?"

"Where it's always been. Right here. If I died, they'd choose another victim."

"So you'd rather be dead, than the Consort."

"Maybe."

That stopped Sylvia. It almost stole her breath away, and she could see the surprise in Letha's gaze as well.

"I'm still trying to decide, but I'm leaning more in that direction all the time."

"You can't be serious."

Letha nodded slowly and drew herself up. "A long time ago — when we were in school — Kristienne gave me a hard time about not being happy about being chosen. I mean, how bad could it be, right? You're special to everyone. You're different. It's every pre-teen girl's dream. I told her I'd show her what it was like. Every time she made a decision, or voiced an opinion, I questioned her. I asked her if she'd really thought about whatever it was, I pointed out all the reasons she was wrong and needed to do things my way — the old way. I talked to her like she was a child. I did it every time. It embarrassed her in front of our friends. At the end of a day she begged me to stop. She said she understood, then, because it made her feel small — like nothing she could do or say was ever right or good enough. That's how I grew up, Sylvia. Years of it. It makes me wonder what my life is worth."

She shook her head, her gaze dark blue steel, and then stalked back to the barn. It left Sylvia feeling empty, like there was nothing to do but leave. Wind lifted dust from her footsteps as she turned to her truck.

"Sylvia."

Sylvia turned back to her, hoping Letha would tell her it was all a joke. That things were fine, because feeling like she did, Kristienne's wormer could wait and she sure as heck wasn't going to try to read her mom..

Instead Letha said, "I should have done it to you."

§

Determined to show Sylvia she would do things her way, Letha made the decision to go ahead with the art show and chose the last weekend in August for the date. She had no idea what it would take, but she'd make it work, somehow. She'd make everything work, somehow. When Ty popped over for a beer, they sat on her porch together, talking, and she reminded him of his offer to ask Elizabeth Hunt if she would help. When she got up the courage, she invited him for dinner. It worked: he accepted, and she knew she was stronger than Sylvia.

When she received the photos from Martin Dietrich, she was blown away by their quality: Bright sculptures spinning among the willows. The spirit catcher with Roscoe catching at the feathers. The wooden windmills turning before the weathered face of the store. Blue bottles next to the red door, she and Ty talking, Hauberk's huge equine shadow at their feet. It was lovely. They were all lovely, including the individual photos of Johnny's paintings that seemed to capture the light in each canvas. She downloaded them to her computer, but found she couldn't decide what to include in the website.

She thought time would give her objectivity, but on the afternoon before the summer solstice she hadn't managed to make a decision, and time was ticking away. The quiet was interrupted by the sound of a truck, and she felt herself stiffen just as she did every time a vehicle approached.

She'd been waiting for the other shoe to drop after her confrontation with her sometime-friend. Would the elders come? If it was Sylvia again… but Sylvia hadn't shown her face here the past few weeks except to pick up a quart of milk, and that had been a weird, strained event where they'd both found nothing to talk about but the weather. They could use a little rain, Sylvia'd said, could use a little of Kristienne's old talents.

Letha stood up and stretched to peek outside. Ty's truck. She yanked open the store door and stepped from the cabin's cool to the dry heat of the day. She stopped. Ty was helping a woman out of the cab, and for a moment Letha felt a pang of jealousy until she realized the woman was Elizabeth Hunt.

Ty held his mother's elbow lightly as he led her around the truck. Her slight figure only emphasized the strength of Ty's torso, the trim line of his hips.

"Brought you company, Letha. I've been telling her about your project, but, well, today's the first day that things seemed right and Kris didn't need her at the house."

Letha stepped down the stairs to greet Ty's mom. She was so thin — still a beautiful woman, though — with huge, lustrous green eyes, and long blonde hair coiled up in a chignon that brought elegance even to the faded jeans and work-shirt she wore. Today — it looked like it might be one of her good days. "It's been a while, Mrs. H. I really appreciate you coming by."

"My boy tells me you've a project you'd like some help with." She looked fondly up at Ty and patted his hand, and Letha grinned at how this tall, strapping man was still 'my boy' to this woman. Her lips quirked as she met his slightly embarrassed gaze.

"It's an art show, Mrs. H. A reporter from the *Tribune* suggested it. He did an article you might have seen. It said the art's good enough it should be advertised, but aside from picking a date and trying to choose photos for a website — and not doing too well at that — I really don't have a clue."

"Well, an art show here can't be all that different from an art show in New York, except there'll be a little less black tie and tails and little more horse shit and country music." She stopped and covered her lips with her fingers, a faint shade of pink running up her neck. "Excuse me. Guess I've been hanging out with cowboys too long."

Easing her arm free of her son, Elizabeth Hunt mounted the steps of the store and entered, leaving Letha and Ty to enjoy a brief frisson of closeness, and then follow. Inside, Mrs. H. moved around the room, studying the paintings and carvings hung on display. When she had circled the room she came back to Letha.

"Well done. You've got a natural eye for display. I saw it outside when we drove up. In here, in these crowded surroundings, it shows even more. It's easy to make a good installation when you've got all the room in the world to play with, much harder in tight conditions."

"So, Ty, I believe we women have our work ahead of us and we don't need any distractions." She held up her hand to stem his protests. "I see you two looking at each other. Now leave us in peace. Kristienne said she'd be by to pick me up in a couple of hours."

Ty took his leave, with a quick, mouthed, "Later," and Mrs. H. turned back to Letha.

"You've really charmed him."

"I have?"

"I can see it in his eyes, though he doesn't say much."

"Ty and I are just friends."

Mrs. H. just raised a perfectly plucked brow that said just how bad a liar Letha was, and settled herself behind the computer. "Now, I don't know much about website thingies, but I do know good photos. Show me what you've got."

It was almost too fast. Mrs. H. didn't seem to need to be asked, it was like she'd already decided to help with the show and was charging full steam ahead, faster than Letha could follow. Better still, when Letha bent down to bring up the photos, there was only the soft scent of Chanel 22 that Letha had come to acquaint with Kristienne's mother years before. Mrs. H. was sober, or as near to as she had been in years.

The photos cascaded across the computer screen as Letha bought them up one by one. Mrs. H. studied them all, making small comments. "Too dark." "Too light." "Not sharp enough." "Doesn't show the piece well." "Good. Good."

She liked the individual shots of the paintings and a few others — the statue with the willows and the lake in the background, the windmill and the corral.

The shot of Letha and Ty stopped her. She touched the computer screen and smiled.

"This is your money shot, Letha. Look at the balance. Look at the color. The name of your store is there bold as day, you're in the picture, and the photo is good enough itself to be a piece of art on its own. This is your Homepage. You can have the pull down menu over here." She pointed to the right side of the screen.

"I thought you didn't know anything about websites."

"I've seen enough. I shop on line. I know what feels right. The menu would fit there without obscuring too much of the photo."

"You're sure?"

"Dear, I studied art along with music. Music was my life, but art was a passion as well. They go well together, I always thought." A sad expression crossed her face.

"You miss it, don't you?"

Mrs. H's luminous green eyes caught Letha's. "New York and the arts are like an addiction I developed years ago. I miss the gallery openings, opening nights. The excitement in the air. But that's all water under the bridge. I live here now."

There was such longing — quickly tucked away — in the older woman's voice, and Letha felt an answering ache in her heart. She placed her hand softly on Mrs. H.'s shoulder. "I'm glad you're here. We wouldn't have Ty and Kristienne if you hadn't come, and I wouldn't have your help now."

Mrs. H. looked up at her and an impish grin lit up her face. "And what doesn't kill us makes us stronger."

"You got it!" Letha guffawed and considered the photo of Ty and her again.

"Okay, then. I have a homepage." And the simple statement brought such a flutter of excitement to her stomach she leaned down and gave Mrs. H. a swift hug. "Thanks so much! I loved that photo, but I just wasn't sure it was the right thing to use. I feel like I've just been waiting for you to come."

"You should trust yourself, dear," Mrs. H. said, flipping through the photos again. "Like I said, you've got a good eye. Now I like this and this and this."

And so the hours swept past, with Letha in the midst of a cyclone that was Mrs. H. It wasn't that Mrs. H. bowled her over. It was more that the woman's enthusiasm and confidence — were infectious.

Kristienne found them at the table, heads together over pads of paper covered in long lists of things to do. Letha looked intent, her mother looked — well — like fifteen years and countless bottles of Grand Marnier and white wine had simply never been. Her face was alive with an excitement Kristienne hadn't seen for a very long time.

"Ha-hum," Kristienne cleared her throat and chuckled as the two women startled.

"Kris! Is it time already?" Her mother checked the slim diamond watch that was, along with her solitaire engagement ring and wedding band, the only piece of her jewelry she still wore.

"A little after four. I thought I'd rescue you from Letha's obsession."

"Rescue!?" Letha pouted.

"You push that lip out any farther you'll trip over it."

"I didn't need rescuing, Kristienne. This has been fun. As much fun as I've had in a long time."

"Thank you, Mrs. H. Your daughter — she comes into my house and she insults me. Mrs. H., I have to say, you failed with Kris. She has none of your social graces."

"Like you should talk." Kristienne scanned the room. "Mom, you've been here how long, and has she even offered you a drink?" Kristienne caught herself, but it was too late. Oh, God, what she'd said. She saw her mother's gaze flicker and the light in her eyes seemed to go out. Letha, on the other hand, colored brilliant red and her hand flew to her mouth.

"Ohmygawd! Mrs. H., I'm so sorry. You must think I'm a horrible hostess! It's just — we were so involved in planning — the time just flew — and, well. Ohmygawd I'm a horrible hostess, and after you've just given me all this time."

"Letha. Dear. Calm down. It's perfectly all right. I had a good lunch before I came over, and I was just as excited as you. I didn't need a drink."

Her mother cast a look in Kristienne's direction that said she wasn't going to forgive Kristienne's comment. "Besides, next time we'll plan better. Maybe you could come to the house."

"Maybe we could go one better than that." Letha and her mother looked at her and Kristienne shoved her hands in her pockets. "Tomorrow's solstice, right? Everyone'll be down to the lake to celebrate. How about afterward you come over, and you and Mom can plan until it's time for the big barbeque. Everyone'll be there. It'll be a combination business-and-pleasure day. What do you say, Mom?"

"I think it's a grand idea." She patted Letha's hand. "You'll come, won't you dear? We can pick up where my daughter so ungraciously interrupted us."

Kris gritted her teeth. Her mother was going to make her pay for that comment. The sound of another truck brought her around to the door, and she swore as Sylvia pulled in alongside her vehicle.

"Well, look who's here. Everyone's favorite pet psychic and Letha's favorite person."

Sylvia clumped onto the porch. "Nice day, Kristienne. Not that you had anything to do with it. Maybe you could call down some rain."

"You'd like that, wouldn't you — so the rest of us could be just as bitchy as you are."

"And you're sweetness and light?" Sylvia pushed past her into the store. "Letha. Mrs. H., nice to see you out and around."

"I'm helping Letha plan her art show."

Sylvia paused in opening the fridge door, and looked at the woman. All Spring she'd found excuses not to go visit Mrs. H. and do what Kristienne had requested. Truth was, the idea of using her ability on people had always creeped her out a little. Well, no time like the present. She opened herself to the room and then filtered the feel of Letha and Kristienne. Mrs. Hunt presence was a dark swirl of pain and longing, but a lovely glow of golden aura was eating away at the darkness. Hope. It was hope. Sylvia grabbed a bottled water and slammed the fridge door. "That so." She swung around to face them and considered Mrs. H. Something was – better – and it might even be this stupid art show was doing the helping. "So you're really going to go through with this."

"I said I would."

"And I said the Valley won't take this well."

"An Art Show, Dear? Why won't the Valley take it well? It's art."

"Mom, Sylvia's said a lot of things over the years. She's a regular doom-and-gloom maven — just ask Letha."

Letha stood and squared her shoulders. "Sylvia's welcome to her opinions, but I don't listen to them anymore. I listen to my own thoughts now."

Kristienne felt like clapping as Sylvia looked from face to face to face. She cracked open the bottle of water and took a long pull.

"Well. I can see when I'm unwelcome." She started for the door contemplating what she'd found in Mrs. H. Maybe there was something positive that could come out of all this. "Put this on my tab, would you, Letha. Kristienne, that thing you asked me to do? I can't tell you a damn thing." At the door she stopped. "I suppose I'll see you at Solstice tomorrow. Something to look forward to."

§

Solstice was one of the few times of the year that all the Valley folk came together. While the calling of Spring was a private matter between the Consort and the lake, the Solstice involved the dedication of the whole community to the seasons — and a heck of a lot of fun besides — at least for most of the Valley.

Before the sun rose, Letha scrambled out of bed to the rumble of trucks as families began to pour in from the outlying ranches. She packed the few things she needed: towels, a hair brush, and the notes from yesterday's meeting with Elizabeth Hunt, because she darn well was going to spend part of the day on the things that gave *her* joy.

Then she went out to the lake and plucked leaves from the willow and a sprig of juniper, and tacked them above the store's door and Inca's stall to bring fortune and good health to all who crossed that way. She wished that that was all the day entailed.

Across the lake, in the hayfields that sloped up to the old Stage Coach House, headlights illuminated people setting up awnings and building bonfires. Their voices carried their excitement across the water, stirring the predawn silences, and she wished she could share in their emotion.

Standing on her porch, her arms crossed against a chill that seemed to come both from the early misted air and from a place deep within, Letha missed the approach of the men until they stopped at the base of the porch stairs.

"Mornin' Letha. You ready for the day?"

In the grey predawn, Murphy Rogers looked up at her, his ruddy cheeks puffed into a smile. He was a kind man, she knew. That was probably why he was here, leading them, but behind him stood her father, a dour look on his narrow face and warning in his eyes. And Harry Zigheld.

"Yeah. I'm ready. Let's get this over with." She grabbed her bag, pulled the door closed, and shivered as Murphy Rogers caught her arm and the men surrounded her. It was like they thought she would run.

Mashed between Roger and her stick-man father, with Harry crouched in the bed of Roger's pickup, Letha's whole body tensed in the silence of the cab. Murphy Rogers drove them around the edge of the Lake and then bumped their way past the derelict Stage Coach House, following the truck-tracks in the newly mown field down toward the lake edge where the people had congregated.

"Here ya go." Murphy smiled his red-cheeked grin again. "You bring us in a good year, Letha. Just like always."

He patted her hand, easing her tension a little, then climbed out from behind the wheel. Her father, on the other hand, yanked her out of the truck and up to his chest. His eyes bore the familiar look of a man who brooked no nonsense. It brought a little tremor of fear, backed by a modicum of anger.

"You been causing trouble, girl. Yer mother's all upset about it. It's not good to upset yer Ma."

"Papa, no. I haven't done anything wrong." Across the slope, someone had left their truck doors open, sending a blast of Rolling Stones — 'Oh No!' — echoing her feelings as it thundered through the damp air.

"So yer sayin' that runnin' off to town and planning to bring strangers to the Valley ain't wrong?"

She yanked away from him. "I haven't done anything wrong. Now excuse me. There's a ceremony these people are waiting for."

Ignoring Harry Zigheld's leer, she went down among the people, joining Johnny Warner and Tessa Rogers and the other eligible young people as they picked wild flowers from along the lake. They were in the midst of bickering and trading blooms to try to build bouquets of the requisite seven or nine varieties. The right bouquet could give its bearer the ability to see their future and who they might marry — at least, so it was said.

"Look! Goldenrod, Queen Anne's Lace, daisy, and buttercup. I'm getting there." Tessa held up her bouquet of gold and white.

"You should have been out in the woods earlier. I was, and I got some coltsfoot." Johnny held up a pale cluster of white flowers amid the other purple blooms he'd found. "With this arnica and thistle, I've got a better bouquet started."

Letha held out her bouquet of brown-eyed Susans, yarrow, sage, purple skullcap, fireweed, and purple alfalfa. "If you like, you can split these up and you'll both have what you need."

"Really?" Blonde-haired Tessa's blue eyes gleamed with excitement. "It'll be the first time I've been able to get a nine-flower bouquet. Maybe this time I really will see the future."

"So they say, whoever *they* are."

"The elder's, silly." Tessa accepted Letha's bouquet and began splitting it up with Johnny.

Letha nodded solemnly, wishing she had such faith in what the elders said. Wishing she could feel the excitement these young people held. She watched the way they stood so close together, they way their hands lightly touched, then pulled away in a gentle shyness that spoke volumes. These two — the Solstice was for youngsters like them, not for jaded, angry, trapped women like herself. Someday, somewhere, she'd have a chance at her own life, at following her own path. She watched them wander along the shore as the crowd built.

Children scattered and ran screaming or caught minnows along the lake shore. Parents shared thermoses of coffee and the elders stood to one side like a dark cluster of crows, for all their voices sounded like the scolding of a murder of the black birds.

"Letha. See you're doing your duty here, at least."

Letha stiffened and turned to Sylvia, who stood holding two battered mugs of coffee. "Nice to see you, too. Here to gloat?"

"Here for Solstice, that's all. I never gloat, Letha. I just do my duty and take what small pleasures I can with the lake." She held out her hand, fingers spread, and considered. "Sometimes I even remember what it felt like — that brief hint of power before you were chosen. Do you think Kristienne remembers, too?"

Letha bit her lip, hearing the slight offering of peace in the sigh that followed Sylvia's words. "One of those for me?" She motioned to the coffee.

"If you like. I know you get pulled around on days like this. Never get time to have a cup."

Letha accepted the mug and the two women stood together, Letha not sure what to say. She was still angry because she knew darn well Sylvia was working for the elders. It made sense that the one person she had trusted beyond anyone else would be the one the elders used against her. And Sylvia would let them. In her need to be wanted, Sylvia had always done what was asked of her.

"You participating today?" Letha asked.

"Yeah. Though I can't for the life of me figure out why. There's no one out there for me."

"There's Harry Zigheld."

"Low blow, Letha. Really low."

"Hey, you'd wish it on me."

"No… No, I wouldn't do that. Others might, but not me." Her voice held the ring of sincerity.

"Good to hear — for a change."

Sylvia caught her arm. "Letha, please. Don't shut me out. I need you as my friend. What you said. I'm trying to understand."

"That so?"

Sylvia's gaze was earnest, pleading, and it would be nice to believe, but….

"Letha, it's time." Her father's harsh bark startled her. He marched up and caught her wrist in a vise grip, his breath already smelling of the beer that would be flowing like water all day. Papa never was a man of subtlety. "Elders are waiting."

He dragged her across the slope, leaving Sylvia behind as a dark-haired shadow joined her — Kristienne. So she had come as well, as all children of the Valley should. Matt wouldn't be far away, then.

The dark-clothed elders surrounded her, just as upslope the rock-and-roll song about being 'born in the USA' was cut short and someone with a set of bagpipes sent a mournful wail skirling through the air.

Then there were hands on her. Fingers tugging at her buttons, pulling off her shirt. She elbowed them away.

"Stop it! Stop it! I'm not eleven, for God's sake. I've done this before. I can disrobe myself."

They muttered as she swiftly pulled off her bra, peeled down her jeans and stepped free of them to stand naked. It took every ounce of inner strength to stare her defiance back at them. Finally, her mother stepped forward holding an empty wooden cup at chest height.

"Spring leads to Summer and on to harvest. Lead us to bounty." She paused. "You'll drink the summer cup with us?"

The ceremonial words, spoken by her mother, Pearl, who at fifty-eight looked much older. Her mass of red-gold hair was shorn into a nappy, graying carpet close to her skull, her fine features fractured into disapproval by disappointment and age.

"The Consort should be pregnant at her age. Set an example for the Valley. That would mean something — but this skinny girl…" It came as a whisper from amongst the elders. There was a stirring of nods, and for a moment Letha wondered what they'd do if she simply refused to cooperate — but her years of subjugation prevailed.

"I'll share the cup of summer, let the fruit spring forth." Letha grated out her answer. Let them grumble. They made her who she was. But she was going to grow above that. Let them watch.

Accepting the cup, she began her walk to the water's edge, ignoring the thistle and sharp edges of cut hay that sliced at her feet and ankles, ignoring the blood that started to flow because blood was also part of the life force.

In the grey light the elders parted around her, created a funnel down to the lake shore where the young people of the Valley waited in a long, barefoot line that snaked the edge of the water. Once, Sylvia had told her, the young people waited naked as the Consort, but the mores of North America had crept into the Valley until only the Consort disrobed.

And she was beyond embarrassment. There were too many years of this behind her, and her body was not her own on Solstice. It never would be hers as long as she lived here.

Water lapped at her toes, and she felt rather than saw the long line of young people step even with her, and the shiver run through them at the cool. They should try calling Spring. Behind her the first rays of the sun came through a crease in the landscape, warming her back in the first glow and laying her shadow across the width of the darkling water.

She held the cup up, out, stepped into the water. Cool on her toes, cool mud underfoot, and minnows came racing from around the lake as if they felt her presence. They nibbled at her instep as she waded out into the lake, the cup held out before her. The breeze lifted, went still, and the tone she'd heard that night on the lake belled up around her as she felt the earth fall away from her feet and she fell. But before she went under, across the lake amid the reeds she saw a dark form, like a horned stag impaled by the sun.

It wasn't there when she surfaced. When she came back to shore she bore the cup filled with wine-of-summer, the gift of the lake, and took it to the elders. They waited as she, still dripping and naked, took a draught from the cup and tasted the heady liquid like bees' nectar, transformed from lake water, she knew not how. It sent heat rushing through to her fingertips. If anything, it felt like her hair curled tighter.

Each of the elders touched their lips to the cup and then handed it back to her. Her task now was to take the cup of intoxication to the young people who had been with her in the lake.

She handed the chalice to the Bedard boy who stood closest, a dripping, leggy lad of sixteen who'd already had his way with a number of Valley girls, if the rumors were true. He accepted the cup, sipped.

"I give you the summer cup. Bring fruit to the Valley," Letha intoned.

"Do my best," he said, grinning as he passed the cup to the next lake-soaked young person in line. "Bring fruit to the Valley."

Letha watched as the cup passed down the line, as the young people melted away for their next part of the ceremony. They shifted down-lake, heading around the point by her store to circle the lake, as if the body of water was an ancient maypole that linked the earth and heaven. They would gather herbs as they went, because any herb gathered this day was more potent. And they would come together in secret couplings to bear fruit for next Spring. The Valley was one of the few places it was no shame for a girl to bear a March baby out of wedlock. Any Valley family would raise such a child as a gift.

She watched them go, sighing, then turned to reclaim her clothes. Her mother was waiting for her. "Nicely done, but you should be with them. Didn't you see Harry waiting for you? He'd be willing, Letha, you should consider it."

"Ma, don't. I don't want to discuss it." She hauled on her underwear and jeans.

"Ya got a place in this Valley, girl. You got responsibilities. You think it's good for a Consort to be barren? What do you think the land thinks? Yer not setting any example at all."

Letha settled her bra and yanked on her boots. Her mother still harangued her as she buttoned her shirt. Finally she turned. "Talk 'til you're blue in the face, Ma. I'm not marrying Harry, and you and the rest of the elders should get clear on that. You hear? If — mind, *if* — I decide I want to be bound to a man, it'll be a man of my choosing. You hear?"

"Yer a disgrace to the Valley. A disgrace to this family."

Letha suddenly felt tired, her defiance ebbing like moon-flow. "Yes, Ma. I'm sorry." She ran her fingers through her hair. "Sorry I'm alive to trouble you all."

She turned and fled, managing to find Kristienne in the clamor of adults and children jigging to the bagpipes as the sun rose higher into the sky. Kris was standing at the edge of the crowd, laughing as two toddlers got their feet tangled and took the legs out from under one of their fathers in the ensuing melee.

Feeling like she was in deep water, Letha grabbed Kris's arm. "Can we head to the ranch? I'll have no peace here. The elders and my mother are out for blood. Mine."

It was hard to hear in the crowd. Kris just nodded and caught her hand to lead her through the throngs to the trucks parked back from the water. A few small tailgate parties were already in full swing, and Kris snagged a bottle of beer for the road, then bumped out of the field and down the road toward Hunt Ranch.

"Every year I forget how loud it gets. Thank God this year I got smart and arranged our own celebration."

Letha rested her head against the back of the seat. "I'm surprised you even came. I wouldn't if I had a choice."

Kris glanced at her. "Sure you would. We're both Valley girls born and raised. Valley girls don't miss Solstice."

"What have you been smoking?"

"It's the truth, and you know it. It's like it's in the blood — a need to be close to the earth and what's living."

"You sound like Sylvia."

"That a problem?"

"Why?"

"I invited her." Letha felt the truck slow and opened her eyes to find Kris looking at her. "That a problem?" she repeated.

"No. No problem. I think she's trying to get back in my good graces."

"Hmm, there's possibilities there, then."

"Might say so." She opened one eye and saw Kris grinning back at her. Sylvia wanting something from one of them was always an opportunity to rebalance the scales of their relationship. It had gotten Kris a year's worth of free Vet work once. Who knew what it could get Letha, if she was strong enough to drive a bargain.

"And here we are." Kris pulled into the ranch yard, squeezing her truck in between two trucks with such pristine paint they obviously weren't from here. She grinned. "Summer people. Suddenly the old Ford looks a little worse for wear. Now you just relax and mingle and be surrogate host — maybe check that brother of mine isn't getting into trouble — and I'm going to check on Mom. You know, she hasn't quit talking about plans for your show. Was up early today to make salads and still nattering when I left." She slipped off to the house, leaving Letha to decide where one should go to play surrogate host.

Strains of a band just getting started came from around front, so she took that as her target, threading through the mass of vehicles — who knew there were that many summer people in the Valley already? — and around the house to the broad yard that ran on down to the lake. Near the water, a few of the Valley's Solstice youth were completing their circumambulation of the lake, but farther upslope a small platform stage had been erected on which a country band was just getting going with a couple of old Johnny Cash tunes. They had a long day ahead of them. A few youngsters were flashing their heels while the adults wandered around with the remains of a pancake breakfast on plastic plates. A long table set close to the house was just being cleaned off by Matt and a couple of the other ranch hands.

She grinned as she watched Matt juggling a couple of jugs of what must be maple syrup. Funny how men who looked perfectly in control in a saddle could look hopelessly lost doing kitchen duty.

"How was Solstice?" Billy Fitsch came up beside her, the ranch hand also watching the mini-disasters being averted at the table. "Thank God I dodged that bullet. I was low man on the totem, but Matt took my place."

"Lucky you."

"Not so lucky. Kristienne asked for volunteers, so of course he did. Gotta keep the Queen Bee happy. Course, then she left."

"That's what she is? Queen Bee?"

"Well, hell, that woman's got more balls than three guys put together — runnin' the ranch and all. Tell you, I wouldn't want to mess with her."

"Uh huh." She considered Billy. A nice enough guy, but like too many of the Valley men, they couldn't see a woman's strength as a skill developed out of necessity, like a hard shell to protect the soft underbelly. She thought of Kris's tears at her mother's drinking. But the men saw Kris's strength as a threat.

"So the Solstice — it go well?"

"You should have come."

"Couldn't. Kris had work for us to do and I wanted to be here. Heard the pipes, though. Jigged through the work on the stage. Wish I could have been. Solstice — it always leaves me feelin' a little bit lighter — if you know what I mean."

Letha smiled. "Then feel lighter today, as well. The earth and heavens have been joined — I'm sure of it." She nodded down toward the lake where a young couple came hand in hand along the water, their clothing looking a little askew and wildflowers in their hair.

"Gonna miss that," Billy mumbled.

"You're not too old, yet."

He flashed a grin. "Don't I know it. So you haven't heard. I'm kinda engaged."

"Engaged? Billy, congratulations! Who's the lucky girl? Your folks must be so pleased." Was that relief on his face, as if the fact she didn't know boded well?

Billy kicked the toe of a dusty boot into the soil. "You don't know her. Daughter of one of the summer people. I've known her three years. We haven't announced it yet, so don't tell, okay? Don't want no problems. But I'd like you to meet her when she arrives."

"Will do, Billy. I'd like that. But now I'd better do what Kris asked and go greet people." She walked away, pondering his news and looking for Ty. She hadn't seen him so far. It was clear that was why Billy had chosen not to attend Solstice. He'd be expected to join in the ceremony. The Fitschs were an original Valley family and they'd expect that of him — just like they probably wouldn't take kindly to the fact their son was stepping out with a Summer girl. A shudder ran up Letha's spine. There'd be trouble, and she knew it.

She greeted families of Summer people as they straggled in during the morning. Then at noon the band struck up in earnest, and one of the ranch hands brought out a passel of balloons, Frisbees, and kites for the kids. Families broke open picnic hampers and ate on blankets spread on the grass, drinking beer and pop provided by the ranch.

Kris caught up with her amid the music as a square dance caller started giving instructions to the adults standing around and the air filled with the roasting pig Kris had turning on a spit.

"Hey, hostess with the mostest, you seen Ty?" Kris handed her an open tin of soda.

"Not a glimpse. I was wondering if he was a figment of your imagination."

"Damn," Kris's mouth twisted in consideration. "He was going to ride over this morning. I can't imagine he'd just bugger off. Maybe check the arena. He's been itching to get that moose he rides in there."

Her insides did a little flutter at Kris's words. She'd been disappointed she hadn't found him. Maybe it showed in her face, because Kris's next words were: "Something's going on between you two, isn't it?"

"What makes you say that?"

"You should have seen the smile on your face when I told you where he probably was."

"Was it that obvious? I was kinda hoping to keep it to ourselves for a bit."

"Obvious is sometimes the way you have to work. Life isn't particularly full of knights on white chargers who whisk you away. A private life's a private life, even if it's kinda public. But hey, whaddaya think of that new guy I hired — Dwight Peters — kinda cute, isn't he?"

"The guy from dinner, right? I sat beside him." He'd been a typical kid, quiet, but solid-feeling. Animals would trust him. "Seems like the makings of a good hand. Kinda reminds me of Matt."

Kris snorted. "Matt. Right. I just wish he'd quit following me around. I was talking about Dwight's *other* qualities. Hell, today's Solstice and a party. Thought I might party, too. A little seduction never hurts." She winked and then looked up the hill where Matt and a couple of the other cowboys were putting a couple of huge grills up. "Listen, gotta run, but if you see Ty, tell him I'm getting ready to start the steak grills and I could use a hand."

"Sounds like you've got plenty of hands on your mind, woman."

"Don't rain on my parade."

"I believe it was you who affected the weather."

"Don't remind me of my childish ways." With that she dashed off, leaving Letha to survey the crowd around her. How was it possible to be among so many people and feel so alone? It reminded her of her dream — nightmare, more like — the feel of that city in her dream where people moved all around her, but no one knew her name. And here, at Kris's party with all the summer people, were a lot of people who didn't know who she was, who didn't think she was special. A man jostled her arm, nearly spilling her pop. Nope, not special at all — not even worthy of an apology.

She eased through the crowd, pausing to laugh at the stumbling square dancers doe-se-doeing their way across the stubble field. This'd give these folk something to tell tales about when they returned home to their cities — but as the husbands and wives fell into each other's arms at the end of the dance, she suddenly felt lonely and overwhelmed by all the noise.

She headed toward the ranch's outbuildings and the huge arena that sat back near the trees. Behind her the music rose again and more laughter followed as the caller harangued the couples through their promenades. By late afternoon he'd have them ship-shape. The smell of beef grilling told her that the hands had the barbeques going, but as she approached the barns, the scent of new hay, sawdust, and fresh manure became prominent.

She headed straight for the arena, feeling the beat of hoofs through her feet, but stopped when she got to the gate. Ty and Hauberk. Ty tall and easy in the English saddle, just like he'd been that night. She felt herself warm at the memory.

Hauberk flew — no, floated — across the arena at a trot, the beat of his steady hoofs belying her perception of him never touching down. At the corner he seemed to pause, then dance across the diagonal, his legs crossing at each stride, Ty unmoving in the saddle. At the next corner the stallion took up the canter, a slow, rocking-horse canter around the end of the arena, then a thundering gallop down the side that made her certain the horse would crash into the wall. Then suddenly he was cantering again, disaster averted. No hauling on the Hauberk's reins. He just — changed.

"How the heck do you do that?" She called as Ty rode by.

The horse came to an abrupt halt, all four legs squared, like it was planned. Ty grinned down at her.

"Well, aren't you a sight for sore eyes. Do what?"

"Whatever the heck it is you're doing. The horse just moves — like a dancer." From the direction of the house came a huge hoot of laughter and applause. "Well, better than any dancer in these parts. But you never look like you're doing anything."

"That's dressage. That's what he'd made for." He relaxed his reins so Hauberk could stretch, patted the stallion's neck, and swung down off the saddle. He led the horse through the gate. "We were just finishing. If I'd known you were here, I'd have cut the training short, but it took me a couple of hours to move all the cutting gates to the end of the arena. Kris is going to kill me." He grinned. "Come on. I've got to walk him out and then I'll put him in a stall."

"How come you weren't at Solstice?"

He looked down at her, his eyes dark, veiled. "Didn't think I'd be welcome, given I wasn't born here and have been away so long."

"I'd have welcomed you."

"Well now, Ma'am, that's mighty nice to know." She elbowed him in the side and his hand slipped around her shoulder, then warm down her back, so she felt her knees weaken.

That was how Sylvia first saw them, Ty leading his stallion, but his attention all for the woman beside him, his free hand resting lightly in the small of Letha's back with a tenderness Sylvia felt, even though she didn't use her other talents. It made her heart full — except she didn't feel Letha's emotions in return.

She followed them into the barn where Ty clipped a halter on his horse, then turned to Letha. Sylvia knew she should just turn and leave. This was their moment, something she shouldn't interrupt because there just weren't that many moments like this in any life, but ....

"Hey there, folks." She hefted her vet bag as they quickly pulled apart. "Got a colt to check on. Thought I might as well do it today, instead of making an extra trip." Her excuse sounded lame, even to her.

"Sylvia." Ty's voice held a certain reserve, and an edge that said he didn't appreciate being interrupted.

She squared her shoulders and marched up to him, patted his cheek. "Good to see you, too. How's the horse. Wounds healed?"

"Wounds? … Oh, his legs. Fine. Just fine."

"Good to hear," Sylvia said and thought about telling Ty what she'd found out about his mother. Then she thought better of it.

She turned to Letha. "Thought you'd still be over at Solstice."

"Nah. Kris rescued me from the hordes so I could help her out with hostess duty. Besides, I was hoping to spend some time with Mrs. H. More hordes here, though. Who knew?"

"So you came up here to escape, did you?" Sylvia motioned at their surroundings. "Off limits to the partiers."

"Yes. Sort of." But the way Ty looked at Letha told the real story. Solstice. Or something.

"Actually, your sister sent me up with a message, Ty," Letha said, lightly stroking his arm. "She's starting the grill. Asked if you might give her a hand with it."

"Lord save us all. That woman can't barbeque to save her life."

"Hey! You're speaking ill of my friend," Letha protested.

"Have you tried to eat one of her steaks?"

"Well, yes, but…"

"Then give me a hand with Hauberk. I've got beef to rescue." Sylvia stepped aside to let them unsaddle and hose the horse down.

When Hauberk was safely in a stall, Ty paused, looked down at Letha, and Sylvia looked away. He caught Letha's arms, his fingers running up and down them bringing a new heat to her body. "You'll be around later?"

"I'm co-hostess."

"Good, then." He turned to go.

"Ty?" He paused. She stood up on tiptoe and planted a big wet one on his lips. "There'll be more of those later."

Then he was gone, dashing down the slope to where smoke spiraled from the grills.

"Figure he'll rescue you, too, do you?"

Letha turned to Sylvia, standing in the shadows of the barn. "He likes to think he's a knight; that's what knights do." She answered softly, but her voice held a hint of guilt. "I better get back, too. See if Mrs. H. has some time."

Left behind, in the shadows, Sylvia watched her go. Her friend. "Tilting at windmills, then," she said, and wasn't quite sure whether it was herself or Ty or Letha she was referring to, but her clenched stomach told her something wasn't good.

Chapter 8

*Y*ou have to choose the right flowers, Danni. See here? It's got a long enough stem we can make it part of the chain and still be able to join other flowers." Letha sat on the stubbled grass, teaching the very young of the summer people how to make daisy chain crowns. With her was Tessa Rogers, but Tessa's concentration wasn't really all there. Her gaze rarely left Johnny Warner after the two of them came down the lake shore from the Solstice celebration, saying they wanted to be where it was more fun.

And closer to the forest, Letha thought. They could be together so easily today, the guilt they might feel other days forgotten. Because they had chosen each other.

Overhead the sky was showing the amber and apricot streaks of a long sunset, and the huge bonfire that had been stacked down close to the lake only awaited the first stars to leap into flame. It would mean the end of the day and she hadn't accomplished what she'd wanted.

She'd had so much to discuss with Mrs. H., but Elizabeth Hunt had been too busy with the day's events. Still, it was good to see the woman have the same spark Letha recalled from her childhood. Then, Mrs. H. had been the best mom in the Valley, always having time to play dress up with her daughter and her daughter's friends, and always full of stories of the bright lights of the big cities down south.

"Is this right?" Little, blonde-haired Danni held up a jumble of flowers in her four-year-old fist. Her large eyes held the fatigue lines at the edges that said her parents should be taking her home to bed soon.

"Let's see." Letha took them from the child's hand and straightened the bent stems. "I think you chose pretty darn good, Danni. Look here."

She split one stem with her thumb nail and inserted another flower through the hole. Danni giggled and clapped. "Now let me try another."

Swiftly Letha added Danni's flowers to the chain she'd already made and then joined the ends together, settling the crown of flowers onto Danni's head. "There. You see. I choose you to be the Solstice Queen."

Danni scrambled to her feet. "I want to show Mommy."

She scrambled off before Letha could stop her. The other children dispersed.

"If only all choices were as easy," Sylvia said, easing down onto the ground beside Letha. "It's not for any of us, you know — easy. Choices — we have to earn them and sometimes they get taken away from us and sometimes they're just plain hard."

Letha felt herself tense, expecting Sylvia to try guilting her again. "What would you know? You've been helping steal my choices for years."

"Have I? I didn't mean to, but I guess, when I think of things from your perspective, I have."

That brought Letha's gaze around, surprised. "That's the first time you've ever admitted it."

"I suppose it is. But in my defense I want to say that it wasn't to take your choices away. It was to protect everything I love. I haven't had a lot of choices in my life either, Letha. I want to make the right ones."

"A nice sentiment."

"Would you listen to yourself? And you say I won't hear! Neither of us asked to be born to the Valley. There was no choice there. Or what family we were born to."

"Everyone has that. But usually people get to make choices beyond that."

"Except you, is that what you're saying?"

Letha looked at her. How did Sylvia come off sounding so reasonable while she was sounding spoiled and whiney? She looked back at the crowd. Surely Ty must be done with the barbeque now. She didn't want to talk about this anymore.

Sylvia quietly plucked a few miniature daisies and began linking them together into a delicate chain. "Letha, you didn't choose to be Consort, that's true. But I didn't chose to be orphaned either — or to have this darn 'talent' of mine."

Sylvia met Letha's gaze, caught her hand, and slipped a perfect daisy bracelet around her wrist. Delighted and saddened, the gesture brought tears to Letha's eyes. Once, as children, they and Kris had sat for hours making flower jewelry and decorating each other until they had looked like fey children dashing around the meadows until their parents took them home for chores.

"Burdens. They're burdens we bear."

"They are. And there are consequences. For you, it means there are responsibilities to the lake. For me — it means my childhood was one of incurring a debt to all the people who took me in and helped me hold on to the family farm and get an education."

"You got scholarships. You made that choice yourself."

"Did I? Everyone thinks so, I guess. But I got told early on that I'd better become self-sufficient because I had a lot of debts to pay."

"People said that to you? You were a child."

Sylvia twined her fingers in Letha's and gave a small painful smile. "They showed me. When I talked about doing something else, the disapproval came through. When I needed things that cost money there were the heavy sighs. I learned. We all do. Choices — we're formed by them, just as your linkage to the land and my talent form us. The choice is what we do with it."

Letha was going to deny it, but memories surfaced: Of how Sylvia shifted from home to home around the Valley. Of how her own mother could stare disapproval better than any words. They made her squeeze Sylvia's fingers. Her life couldn't have been easy. She had had — no one, but Sylvia's life had changed. She'd taken charge of it....

"You can't equate your talent and being the Consort."

Sylvia's deep laughter cut through the square dancing music and the callers words. It reminded Letha of how, even among so many people, they could be alone. Sylvia shook her head, mirth in her eyes.

"You're one stubborn woman, you know? You are so hide-bound determined to be in more pain than anyone else — and look at you. You're beautiful. You're beloved. You've got Ty falling for you — just like you always dreamed as a kid." She held up her hand. "Don't deny it. You were always moony-eyed whenever you were around him."

"It's not all wonderful, you know," Letha replied archly. "You're not confined to a Valley caught in some time warp."

"And my talent isn't all friendly little animals romping in my lap."

"What do you mean?"

"I mean it's the sick and dying that come to me. That's what I feel. Veterinary work? Yeah, I may be there when mares foal or heifers calf, but I was there when that Belgian mare of the Zigheld's cast herself and broke her leg. I got to not only deal with the mare, I had to feel her fear, her horrific pain. I had to help her, I had to hold her, calm her, convince her that everything was going to be okay while old Mr. Zigheld got his deer rifle because he wasn't about to pay another vet bill. That's what my talent is about, Letha. That's what being the Valley's funny little 'pet psychic' is all about."

The bitterness of her words were matched by the tears that ran down her cheeks, and Letha caught Sylvia as she swayed, hugged her. "My God, Syl. I didn't know. My God."

Sylvia pushed loose, swiped at her eyes. "No one knows." She scrambled to her feet. "Because I deal with it and go on. That's the difference between the two of us, Letha. We might both be bound by choices or circumstances beyond our control, but we have choices how we deal with it and we have to take responsibility for our actions. You want to run. I've learned to deal."

"I do take responsibility."

"Do you? Do you think about what will happen to the Valley if you leave? Do you think about Ty and his feelings?"

Letha shook her head, confused at the mention of his name.

Sylvia crouched down in front of her, her face hard. "He's a good man. Always has been. I know he was always special to you, but if you're using him as a way to get out of here — that's wrong, Letha."

"Sylvia!" Letha couldn't meet her eyes. That Sylvia could figure it out — did that mean others knew? Did Ty? Besides, she was really attracted to Ty — more than she'd ever been to anyone. "I wouldn't do that." But her words came out unconvincing.

"Letha Rivers, I've known you since we were both in diapers together. You would, and we both know it, because you're getting desperate. But be warned, my friend. You don't use love that way — not without consequences."

§

Ty couldn't think of a better metaphor for the perfect undercover agent, than the piece of meat he was grilling. Good fillet steak, cut two inches thick: the flame could lick it, char it on the outside so it looked like one thing, but inside it was still succulent, red meat.

It had to be left on the flame a long time for that red meat to change, but then maybe that was what had happened to him. The years undercover had changed him inside, darkened and toughened him somehow so he no longer liked himself.

Coming to the Valley had brought that all home. So had reacquainting himself with Letha Rivers.

"That piece of meat done yet, son?"

Ty shook himself and pulled his thoughts back to the steak. He tested it with his tongs. "Rare, right?"

"Well, I don't want it mooing at me."

Ty looked out of the top of his eyes at the man holding out his plate. "You don't want to insult me, do you? You want it rare, right?"

The man grinned. "Rare'll do."

"Good choice." Ty plunked the steak down on the man's paper plate and motioned him toward the salads, then set his tongs down. It looked like that was going to be the last one. Good thing, too. His back was shot, his leg was aching like a sonofabitch, and the sky was turning that blue-black color of late evening. He checked his watch. Damn, almost nine thirty. He'd been at this six hours when he'd hoped to find some time for Letha.

"Hey, Matt. I think we're done here, finally. You want me to start taking the grill down?"

Matt looked over from his place by the barbeque spit where he'd been slicing pork all evening. The man's face was sweat- and smoke-covered. He swiped his hair back and set his Stetson back in place. Trust Matt. Never without his hat. Where the rest of his face was weathered and tanned, his forehead was pristine white, as if he had the purest thoughts.

"Don't bother. I'm going to cut the rest of the meat off this carcass. We can use the grill to keep it warm."

"I'll give it a scrub then."

"Leave it. I think you've got other things ta do." Matt lifted his chin toward the lake, and Ty followed his gaze. Letha was easing her way against the flow of party-goers who were all heading lake-ward for the lighting of the bonfire.

She stopped in front of him, hands in her pockets. "I'd say you were a sight for sore eyes, but, well — you've got stuff smudged right there." She pointed to the side of her nose.

Ty grinned and pulled a hanky out of his pocket, scrubbed at the spot.

"And right there." She pointed to his forehead now. He scrubbed.

Karen L. Abrahamson

"And right here." She touched her chin. He scrubbed and she pursed her lips. "And your t-shirt — well, it's not quite so white anymore."

Ty looked down at himself. Splatter covered the front of his chef's apron, but there were spatters around its edges, too. He untied his apron, wiped his face and hands on it, came around the grill to her, and held out his hands. "Better?"

"Good enough to eat."

"That's what they all say when they see me grill. You enjoy your steak?"

"Better than the Stampede Grill."

"It's all in the hands," he said, running his palms down her arms so she shivered. He caught her hands, held them up. "Good hands, but cold."

He leaned in for a kiss, but she stiffened as he grazed her soft lips. He paused, pulled back. There was something about this woman that made him question everything he had become, that made him want to be more than this thing hidden inside the charred skin of an undercover Bureau agent.

Her eyes — they carried such odd contradictions as vulnerability and strength — like a young willow that could be mowed down and contained, but still managed to throw out glorious new catkins every year. He would like to know how she did it — kept that strength to fight. He wanted to protect her from having to fight, too.

"Letha…," it came out half-strangled. "Let's go for a walk, find a quiet place to be."

Her gaze was a pool, dangerous to fall into, and yet he was willing to risk it. He could see the way she hesitated, the fear that skimmed across her features — but she'd kissed him earlier. She'd shown she felt something.

"Ty…." Her hand caught his arm.

"Ty! Ty! Phone!" His mother's voice, from the house. She stood silhouetted in the ranch house doorway.

"Wait right here," he told Letha, and didn't wait for her nod as he sprinted up to the doorway. His mother's hair had come loose, flowing over her shoulders like a fine silver cascade, but her eyes at least were still those of the woman he remembered. That was Letha's doing. Her art show had given his mother a purpose again.

"Mom, I told you to leave the phone. Just get some rest. You've been on your feet all day."

"It just rang and it rang and it rang and no one answered, so I thought I better. It might be important. Besides, it's high time I got back out with the people. I do love people." She held the phone out to him.

"Who's it for? Kris?"

"Ty," she rolled her eyes. "It's for you. Why else would I call you? Now be a dear and take this so I can get back outside. And don't be long. There's a bonfire to light and a certain young woman I think would like your company."

He looked after her, then down to the instrument in his hand, feeling like it was a bomb, armed and waiting to go off. No one knew he was here except Dave Buckley. He accepted it and strode into the house, into his father and Kris's den.

"Hello? Dave?"

The antiquated phone lines to the Valley crackled.

"Ty? That you?"

"In the flesh."

Not Dave. Samuels, once his partner, a man Ty had trusted. But that was before Ty was recruited for his latest assignment in the mafia-riddled horse world. He hadn't seen Samuels in what — four years?

"Thank God. I've been trying to find you for weeks. All hell's broken loose down here. I wanted to warn you, make sure you were safe."

Ty listened to the slight echo on the line as if Samuels' voice came not just across distance but across time. The Valley was that removed from Ty's past life. He didn't want it intruding.

"Why didn't Buckley call?"

"Shit. You haven't heard. Of course. You've been keeping your head down. Buckley's dead, Ty. Ran his car into a tree. We don't think it was an accident. The Federal Attorney has been frantic to know his star witness is safe."

The news sent Ty's old life sweeping over him in a single shudder through his skin. He was the charred man. The hard rind back in place that covered his soft spots, his wounds, because, at the end of the day, that was who he was, wasn't it? That was the life he'd chosen.

Ty relived the muggy heat of Smokey Mountain summer evenings, and his scars shot pain up his back. He'd been living in the small cabin for two months when Zochenko's men found him and shot him as he carried in wood for the woodstove, because the one old man he had befriended was probably going to drop by for dinner like he usually did. It was that same old man who'd found Ty, shot in the back and dying, and somehow managed to get to Buckley for help.

"Who's replacing Buckley?"

"Replacing… Ty, did you hear what I just said? Come in, and we can deal with this thing. Protect you. Out there — shit — in Canada we can't do a damn thing."

"No one knows I'm here. Only Buckley knew."

"Well, I know."

"And how did you come across that little piece of information?" He tried to make it light, conversational, but it was a worry, because if Buckley really was dead, then Ty was in a heap load of trouble.

After he'd stomped out on his Dad, he'd had virtually no contact at all with his family. When he'd applied to the Bureau he'd used his Uncle's Washington address as his own, because that was the address he'd used on his Law School application.

Someone would have had to dig hard and deep to find this contact information. Someone that maybe he'd mentioned something about Canada to in the past. But the devil you knew was better than the devil you didn't. Damn it, he didn't want to go in. He was finding things here that he'd forgotten he'd missed. Like peace. Like himself. Like Letha.

Samuels was rambling on about how he'd dug through Ty's records. He'd followed up with the Uncle and gotten this phone number. "It was easy as that. Besides, I knew you'd had something to do with Canada because every now and again you'd use some Britishism like 'bloody bastards' or you'd slip with an 'eh'." He chuckled. "Littlest thing can let things slip, can't they? But don't worry, I've got your back, and your Uncle and his family are under guard."

Ty listened absently, already considering his options. Leave and keep running. A moving target was harder to hit. Or should he stay here and hunker down? At least in the Valley he knew the rhythms of the place, who belonged here and who did not.

Stay then. If Samuels was telling the truth — and Ty had no reason to suspect otherwise — the chances of someone finding him here were still relatively small.

"So fill me in on what's happened. Then I'll decide how big a trouble I'm in — or if I need to relocate."

§

When Ty hung up the phone, he felt like one of those overdone steaks the German's preferred — wizened and overcooked and too hard to swallow. His whole life was too hard to swallow. He sank down in his father's old oxblood leather chair, for some reason seeking comfort there.

From outside came the reveler's cheers — the bonfire must have been lit — but all he could think of was the need to be alone, like always, when Letha was waiting for him outside.

"Relocate, Ty?"

Ty half-leapt ready for a fight, then realized it was Kris standing in the doorway. He grunted and sank back in the chair. Surely to God she could tell he didn't want company right now.

"You know, you look like Dad with that scowl on your face." She came into the room, took a seat at the desk, turning her chair to face him.

"Thanks. Just the cheerful thought I need right now."

"So what's going on? Was that Samuels?"

He nodded, not wanting to talk about it. He shouldn't have come here. He was putting the whole damn Valley at risk. He was better off running. The trouble was, he really didn't want to go. The certainty had been building in him for days. He met his sister's patient gaze. That she'd let him this far back into the family was a gift he hadn't thought he deserved. He was glad she had.

"There's trouble at work." He looked away.

"And just what work would that be, Ty? You never talk about it at all. Only the horses, which is kind of a surprise given all the bucks Dad paid for your law degree."

He jerked his gaze back to her.

She smiled and shook her head. "Poor Ty, always so mysterious. Did you really think Uncle Richard paid all those university expenses on his own?"

"I had scholarships," he protested lamely, not wanting to know what Kris was telling him.

"You and Dad might have had a fight, but Dad still wanted you to succeed. He was an autocrat and a tyrant, but he was still your father — our father. Uncle Richard sent him pictures of your graduation. Mom had one buried with him."

He slammed his feet on the floor and stood. "I don't need this right now, okay? I've got things to think about."

"Like relocation?"

"Damn it, Kris. You don't understand."

"So tell me, so I do." She had that all-knowing sister-look that had driven him nuts as a teenager having to deal with a precocious younger sibling.

"I work for the FBI, all right? A case I was on went bad, and now there are people who'd really like it if I was dead. That enough information?"

"Jeezus, Ty." She just stared at him. "What do I do with that?"

"How the hell do I know? You think this is easy?"

"If anything happens to you, it'll kill Mom."

"Don't you have somewhere else to be? Like playing hostess, maybe." He shook his head and, simmering, dropped back into his chair, swiping his anxiety off his face.

Kris tilted her chair back and stretched out her legs. "Not especially. You might, though, 'cause last I saw, Letha was waiting for you."

He groaned.

"Does she know about your career, your troubles?"

"She knows I'm in federal law enforcement and that I came here to convalesce."

Kris pursed her lips, as if rolling her tongue around this latest bit of news. "That's it?"

"Damn it, Kris. I didn't tell her because I wanted to keep her safe. I didn't want her to have to make a choice."

"And it's really working, isn't it." She boosted herself out of the chair to peer down at him. "Tell you what. I'll do you a big favor and take care of Letha — make sure she gets home and all, so you can take your time figuring out how the heck you're going to tell her and whatever the heck you're going to do."

She stepped toward the door, then stopped and came back to him to plant a kiss on his cheek. "Just remember, bro, I'm not doing this 'cause I love you or anything. This is just because I've always wanted to have my big brother so far in debt to me he'll never be able to pay himself out. I could use another ranch hand — even if he does ride a pansy saddle."

"That's usury! Not to mention against fair labor practices."

She smiled at him sweetly. "Damn straight. And just to put you further in debt — God in heaven, I love this — here's a piece of advice in the romance department: if there's one thing Letha Rivers doesn't need, it's someone else making her choices for her."

Chapter 9

The day after Solstice found Letha tired, but busy in the store. She hadn't slept well. Dreams had kept her thrashing until she woke. But sales were brisk, with new summer people coming in for the holidays and Valley folk replenishing supplies used in the Solstice celebration. Letha put off initializing her website to wait on Mrs. Warner and Mrs. Rogers and even the Zigheld's rolled up, though Harry kept himself outside the store.

"All in all, it was a good enough Solstice, I thought," said Nettie Zigheld as she compared prices with Maggie Rogers. "Enough of the young 'uns still believe. Unlike others."

She cast a glance in Letha's direction and Letha winced at the woman's disdain. She'd been like that ever since the incident between Ty and Harry at the store. If anything, it seemed worse this morning — probably as rumor swirled around the Valley of Ty and her at the Hunt party.

She supposed that had been the source of her dreams, because she woke up asking herself how she really felt about Ty.

"Well, I don't rightly care about *some* matches," Mrs. Zigheld continued, "But did you see the Betrix girl and the Fitsch's youngest boy? They went off together."

Maggie Rogers, Tessa's grandmother and the matriarch of the whole Rogers clan, no matter that her husband was a sweet man, nodded as she replaced one tin of peas and gathered up another. "You know, dear," she said to Letha. "These peas aren't the right kind. They're the more expensive brand, and Valley women are supposed to be thrifty. I'm just not sure I can shop here with these higher prices."

"I'll make a note of that, Mrs. Rogers. I'll do better when I order the next stock."

"Well, what about now? Can you give me a better price?"

"Let me check my records."

The two old women bent their heads together. "You know those two kids — they'd be a good match. We really should talk to their parents about it. Might make a nice summer wedding, don't you think? Then if there's fruit of the Solstice…."

Letha glanced in their direction. So — maybe if they were focused on Paul Betrix and Annie Fitsch they'd stop looking at her so much.

"Would be nice to see them all decked out in flowers and such. Girl has a nice way about her, I always said, but I hear she's making plans to go off to university or something." Mrs. Zigheld tsk-tsked her superior judgment as she turned her attention to the jars of jam. "Why would anyone buy jam when it's perfectly possible to make?" She shook her head in disdain.

"I hear those two have been spooning for a while," Maggie expounded. "Been riding their horses to school together for years, doing homework projects together, that sort of thing. It might even be a heart match."

Mrs. Zigheld snorted her opinion of that statement. "No such thing. No place for such a thing in the Valley. Since when do youngsters know best? I mean, I tell you, these new ideas — the Summer people are the reason our young folk are getting all these thoughts. Them, and that darned teacher at the school. I tell you, I'll be talking to the other elders about *that* position come time to choose a teacher for next year. Woman has no right filling our children's heads."

Letha felt herself cringe, and her fingers curled together at the strangled feeling in her chest. It was just too much. All the conniving and controlling by these old women and their husbands. Why couldn't people be allowed to make their own choices? But then she thought about her own actions, about Ty, and her stomach did a little flip flop.

"Poor babies don't even know what's best for them, and she just feeds into foolishness," Mrs. Zigheld expounded. Then she leaned in close to Maggie, but still spoke loudly enough anyone in the store could have heard. That was how the Valley kept confidences. "Seems to me, though, that Martha and Fred Fitsch should be looking at how they raise their children. Now, my Harry came home last night and he told me that Johnny told him that his older brother Seth said Billy Fitsch is courting a Summer girl. Can you believe it?!"

"No!" Maggie's voice was shocked.

"Yes! Some girl named something outlandish like Destiny or Tiffany or Amanda or something like that. Can you believe it? And the way I hear it, Martha and Fred don't even know, but it has been going on for a couple of summers now. I don't know if you noticed, but Billy didn't even come to Solstice. Probably because the girl wasn't there or something."

Maggie was shaking her head, her hand covering her mouth. "Shameful. Simply shameful. Martha is going to be devastated. Billy was always her darling. She spoiled the boy, if you ask me. We can't have our youngsters run off from the Valley or we'll have no one to carry on."

"Or we'll have troublemakers like that Hunt boy coming home, filled with all his new-fangled ideas. Love matches," Nettie Zigheld harrumphed, casting a scathing glance in Letha's direction as she brought up a tin of corn and a jar of peanut butter.

"Is that everything, Mrs. Zigheld?" Letha fought to keep her face smooth, her voice noncommittal. God, she wasn't sure, anymore, what she was doing.

"At these prices, I should say so." Nettie sniffed and turned to Maggie. "A good Valley child knows that what's from the Valley is best. They don't go looking too far afield, if you get my drift. Trouble only comes of that."

And change, Letha thought. Growth. Wasn't that what she, as Consort, was all about? Not according to these two old biddies and their nattering. They'd take away every young person's decision, just like they'd taken hers, and have them all living just the same as their great-grandparents had done a hundred years ago. She took a deep breath. "You know, the Valley does accept new ideas and new ways. Valley ranchers now like to have their cattle calve out earlier than the first folk in the Valley did."

She'd tried to make it sound simply conversational, but black-clad Mrs. Zigheld stopped, and she seemed to grow about six inches to loom up over Letha. "And so what are you saying? It only makes sense to fatten the calves for as long as possible over spring and summer, isn't that right, Maggie?"

"Of course, Nettie. Letha, you should mind the store and not try minding other people's business." She plunked a gallon of milk and three tins of peas on the counter. "Now, are you able to give me a reasonable price on these, or do I leave them behind?"

To Letha, the store felt like it was constricting around her, or maybe it was that the whole Valley just wasn't big enough to hold the three of them. She looked back at her notes. When she'd opened the store, she'd tried to put the price point on things like the peas so she'd make five cents profit.

"I can cut the price by five cents."

Maggie Rogers shook her head. "The other brand is ten cents less a tin in town."

"But these aren't in town. These had to come all the way out to the Valley, and there was a delivery cost."

The two old women sniffed, and Letha knew they were preparing a bartering tag-team that could go on for another hour, when she just desperately needed them to leave. Her chest tightened as she faced them. "Tell you what. I'll make a special deal for you. Just today, but don't tell anyone."

Of course they'd tell everyone, but anything to get some peace and time to think. Maggie Rogers nodded and Letha quickly rang up the bill and accepted the money.

The two women shuffled toward the door, Maggie Rogers pulling one of the tins triumphantly out of her bag.

"I always wanted to try these peas, but they were just never the right price. I hear they're much better than the others."

"Is that right?"

The door closed behind them and Letha sagged against the counter, her head pounding. The sound of another truck brought a groan to her lips, but it was only Kristienne who strolled in.

"Gads, Letha, you look like you had another party after I brought you home last night. Or survived a war."

"I didn't sleep well. Head too full, I guess. Too much stimulation. And there's been nothing but old women telling rumors in here all morning. All that disapproval and negative energy about people's choices."

"Uh huh," Kris went to the cooler and pulled out a quart of coffee cream. "This fresh?"

"Came in day before yesterday."

Kris sauntered over to the counter. "You know, this having a store nearby wasn't such a bad idea. I would have had to drink my fourth and fifth cups of lunch-time coffee without cream if you weren't here."

"Glad to know I'm needed." Letha rubbed her face.

"You okay?"

"I just need some air. That might clear my head."

"Ty talk to you?"

"No," Letha looked at her cautiously. "Should he have?"

Kris shrugged. "Said he was going to. About choices." She patted Letha's hand and grinned. The soft swirl of Kris's energy warmed Letha's palm. "One thing I will say, my brother's got lots of positive energy about you."

§

When Kris left, Letha finished the website, did an obligatory victory dance, and escaped the store, hoping fresh air and maybe a walk would rid her of the twisted confusion she felt. She placed the closed sign in the window and went back to Inca's corral, hoping the soothing presence of the mare would help, but Inca seemed to feel Letha's emotions and was bitchy and tried to bite.

"Typical chestnut mare. Ingrate," Letha swore, rubbing her nipped fingers. Probably indicative of all the good her choices were. Everyone had said the mare was a bitch and no good as a riding horse. Her folks had been going to sell her until Letha determined she was going to make it work.

She had made it work, too. But that was only a horse. She thought of Ty, who was the only person who had ever had positive things to say about Inca.

Horse ownership was simple compared to relationships. With a horse, you fed them, made sure they were healthy, and learned how to work around their idiosyncrasies. With humans, however, there were a whole lot of other things involved — like that tingling feeling you got in the pit of your stomach when the right man touched you.

Or the feeling of disgust at yourself you felt when you'd allowed the touch of a man who wasn't the right one.

If she could just get clear about what she felt about Ty, because she knew those tingly feelings were there, but Sylvia had pointed out a part of her that ached with disgust. Ty Hunt was a good man, and she shouldn't be using him.

She left Inca switching her tail irritably, and headed through the pine, around the back of the lake away from Ty's place. The trail was cut deeper today, the grass — brittle from the spring heat — now flattened by the passage of the Solstice revelers on their circumambulation.

The air smelled of juniper and roses and the lake mud drying along the shore. Grasshoppers leapt wildly away from her passage. The insect hum was like the single infuriating question in her head.

What the heck was the right thing to do?

The trouble was, Sylvia was right. Her damned talent must have told her what Letha was feeling, or else she just knew Letha far too well. Taking advantage of the attraction between Ty and herself had seemed the logical way to deal with two problems — getting free of Harry Zigheld and getting free of the Valley. Ty had even proved it when he took her out to dinner.

It was still a wonder. As a kid, every time she'd tried to leave the Valley that damned nausea had sent her home. As an adult, no one in the Valley would drive her out of the Valley until Sylvia's dirty trick with the store. She'd never really pushed it because the elders had done a darn good job at making her doubt all her choices — until now. The store had given her back a sense of herself, and now she wasn't sure why it was so important, but there was something — a feeling that if she didn't act soon she'd lose some very vital part of herself.

"The part that makes me, me," she muttered. She knew it sounded stupid, because she'd tried to explain it to Sylvia, and Sylvia just looked at her like she was a little crazy and a whole lot self-absorbed. But Sylvia hadn't lived her life with that heartbreaking emptiness that came every time she looked at the road heading beyond the Valley.

Was it so bad to use her relationship with Ty to try to deal with that ache? He was going to leave anyway. And it wasn't like she was pretending feelings for him. When he touched her —

A little shimmer of heat ran through her body at the thought of his hands on her arms, of his kiss yesterday in the barn, and of the deeper kiss in the lake. Maybe it was only Solstice, but she'd wanted more of those kisses and more of his touch. He was nothing like Harry Zigheld.

A little shudder ran through her. She shook her head. Thoughts of Ty Hunt actually got her heart beating hard enough she could hear it.

Then she realized it was hoofbeats she heard. A rider came through the trees behind her. Ty and Hauberk dappled with light and shadows, the horse floating along the trail in that spectacular trot, so immensely tall they could be gods coming for her.

The horse snorted and halted beside her and Ty looked down, his hair falling across his forehead, half-masking his eyes. The hum of the grasshoppers grew in the silence.

"Letha. I thought I might find you here," he said softly.

He dismounted easily, hauled riding gloves off, and gently caught a curl of her hair that had caught near her mouth. His knuckle lightly grazed her cheek, leaving her breathless. Such good hands, she thought, the fingers long and artistic, but with the strength of a rider.

He leaned in to kiss her, lightly, ever so lightly, but it stole her breath, made her think of long nights together and of touching him back. Until he yanked away.

"Damn. I shouldn't…. That wasn't why I came." He looked out at the lake. "Sorry I abandoned you last night. Something came up."

She swallowed, steadied herself. "Kris said you got a call. And that you wanted to talk to me." She looked at him, curious. "I need to talk to you, too."

He caught her hand before she could say anything, steered her onto the path, and walked beside her, Hauberk walking patiently behind. "There's something happening here, isn't there."

It wasn't a question, even though she said, "Yes." His hand squeezed hers.

"Letha, I told you I was in law enforcement, right? And that I was here to recover." His voice was so quiet it scared her, and he must have felt her stiffen because he let her hand go. She stopped dead in her tracks and Hauberk bumped her with his nose.

"From being shot," she said. "What is it Ty? What do you need to tell me?" The world narrowed until all she could see was Ty's face, the worry in his eyes, the way they couldn't quite meet hers.

"That was just part of it. I'm the star witness in a major case against a Russian mobster. His cartel was using international competition horses to smuggle drugs into the country. I got the goods on him when he used his wife, Marta's, horse — one of the horses I was training. It was enough to prosecute, and probably be successful at sending him away for a very long time — but his lawyers kept delaying the case until finally one of his men found where I was hiding out in a little Smokey Mountain town. I got shot — barely got out with my life, and my boss let everyone think I was dead.

"But last night it became very clear no one thinks that anymore. My boss is dead, and no one thinks it was an accident. My old partner tracked me down, and if he could do it — well — there's a chance the mob could, as well."

Letha felt cold in the afternoon sun. This man she cared about had come so close to dying. Worse, there was a chance someone might try to hurt him again. It made all her little problems seem so petty. Her plans to use Ty almost a sin. It made her insides hurt just thinking of it.

"Letha? What are you thinking? Have I scared you? —because if I have, well, I don't want that. I want Miss Letha to be safe and sound in her Valley, ya know?"

"Stop it. Just stop it." She placed her hand over his mouth. "This is no time for any of your awful cowboy impressions, Ty. This is serious." Her legs felt like they were going to give under her. All she could think of was Ty getting hurt. She looked up into his green-brown eyes and saw the waiting there, the concern there for her, and suddenly all she could think of was how much she cared about this man and wanted to be with him.

"If you're leaving, I'm going with you."

"Letha, you don't know what you're saying."

"Don't I? You said it yourself, that there's something happening between us. How could I let you leave me behind?"

"I'm not taking you out of here into danger."

"Then I'll follow you, somehow." What was she saying? No money, no ride, and she'd follow him? But somehow this was important. Ty was important to her.

He'd caught her hands, pulled her into him before she could move, and suddenly his lips were on hers, hard and urgent, and all she could think of was answering. Her arms came up around his neck as his hands pulled her into him, as his mouth devoured her lips, her neck.

"Oh, God, Letha," he groaned and pulled back. "I can't get you out of my head. I think I'm falling in love with you."

Was that what this was, she wondered, this ache for this man and his kisses, his touch. She stepped forward, conscious of what she was doing, of the choice she made, but this was Ty who made her ache inside. She pressed herself to him, kissed his chest where the buttons of his shirt stopped, and was astonished at her audacity and thrilled at the hard need of his response. When she looked up into his eyes, she knew what was about to happen.

"I think…" his voice was rough with emotion. "I think we should head back." He inhaled, looked at her and at Hauberk. "Because if we don't, I'm going to have you right here on the grass, and Hauberk's too young to see that kind of thing. It might stunt his growth."

"We wouldn't want that to happen."

"No. No, we wouldn't. Come on. I think we better get there in a hurry." He gave her a leg up onto Hauberk's saddle, that lovely tight bottom enticingly close, then climbed up behind her and gathered the reins, knowing he was in serious trouble because having Letha Rivers tucked tightly against his body was about the last stimulation his body needed right now.

"This is one time for you to prove your stuff, buddy. Softly and fast." He drove Hauberk forward and tried counting the number of strides to keep himself under control. It worked — barely.

The big horse broke into the smoothest trot Letha had ever felt. It was like — floating, with power — each stride of the stallion surging under her, carrying them home, and all the time Ty's arms were around her, holding her, his body pressed achingly, demandingly close.

They rounded the lake end, passed the store, to his cabin. He leapt down, lifted her down and caught her in his arms for another of those long, lingering kisses that only spoke of more to come. That demanded it.

"Sorry, bud. The hose-down comes later. Other priorities." He hauled Hauberk's saddle off, tossed a flake of hay into his stall, and shoved the horse in after. Then he turned to Letha. "You."

"I think we better hurry."

He caught her hand and jogged toward his cabin, up the steps and inside, barely slamming the door behind them before he had her in his arms again, was pulling her shirt tails out of her jeans, had slipped his hands under the plaid cotton shirt and found skin.

The shock of it sent ripples through her that turned all her strength to water. She reached for him, kissed him, tasted sweat and dust on his neck, felt the strength of his body under her hands. Yanked his shirt free and he had it pulled over his head so fast and was reaching for her, she barely had time to save the buttons on her shirt.

She faced him, saw the way his gaze roved over her and the slow smile that formed first in his eyes. "You're all I could have imagined."

Then his arms were around her again, lifting her, carrying her out of the front room, laying her back on the red quilt, lying down beside her. More kisses, softer, this time, but urgent, trailing down her neck, to the tops of her breasts, his long, spatulate fingers teasing her nipples though the cotton of her bra until his other hand slipped under her and unclasped it. She shrugged it off and he buried his head, his teeth bringing small gasps of pleasure to her throat as his hands lid down her belly, flicked open her jeans.

"I think we need to get rid of these."

"Yes." She knelt on the bed, pulled her jeans down, and then lay back and kicked them off. He stripped off her panties, then tried to rid himself of his boots and breeches. The boots didn't want to be rid of.

"Hold that thought." He scrambled for the door of the cabin and the boot jack outside. A crash came from the main room and then he was back, swiftly divesting himself of his breeches and his underwear, freeing his erection.

He lay down beside her, stroking her sides, her belly, her breasts. God, he wanted to lose himself in this woman, could lose himself, he thought, as her pale hide pressed up into his with the same urgency he felt. Breasts pale as peaches, he wanted to feast — on her mouth, her neck, her shoulders. Sliding his body down hers, tasting, tasting, sweetness, salt, a hint of mint like what grew in the sinkholes found in the forest, lower down she tasted like the clean soil of the Valley, the moisture of the lake. He spread her legs apart and she whimpered, and the small cry of need ignited him more. His tongue, his fingers stroked, satisfaction washing over him as she cried out and shudders ran through her.

He paused long enough to roll a condom on, then lifted himself above her and she saw awe in his gaze, wonder that this was happening, but there was so much more to come. She reached for him, pulled his mouth to hers, kissed him as they rolled. She rose above him and he lifted to suckle her breast; she felt his erection press upward and she caught it in her hand, lowered herself down as he caught her hips. She arched her back, he bucked upward — and then they were one and the room disappeared in a bright explosion of light.

§

In his arms she dreamed of choices like shadows, but they were shadows under trees, dappling her nakedness. The alfalfa and clover were in bloom in the grass, and the red winged blackbird sang from his nest in the reeds. The air reeked of the scent of dry heat and sweat as she turned to Ty, to tell him she loved him. But a deeper shadow swathed his face, loomed over them and filled his eyes. When he leaned down to kiss her there was only darkness, filling her.

Darkness and cold that crackled all around. That seared the earth, the sky above, and her lungs. There were only white billows of snow, the bone-chilling cold, and the frozen lake as, terrified, she fled. More terrifying still was the certainty that she had left herself with nowhere to run.

Chapter 10

Ty's heart still beat a wilder pulse as he lay in the half light in his bedroom. The afternoon had faded. Now sunset sent a gilded gleam around the plain white blinds he'd hung over the windows. He'd lain this way, with Letha pulled into his chest, for hours, since their love-play had lapsed to slumber. Unable to sleep himself, listening to her soft breathing had held him mesmerized.

How long had it been since he'd held someone like this, since he'd felt this way? *Ever?* It didn't seem so, and so his mind had turned over and over like a penny spinning in air. What the hell was he doing — doing this at a time when he should be packing up and running, not laying here caught between slumber and the ache of arousal?

Perhaps this was just an interlude until he could get his thoughts clear, but he already knew he was fooling himself.

He knew when Letha woke by the way she stiffened and the slight gasp of breath. His arms tightened around her, his hand cupping her breast — gently, so gently, wanting her to wake remembering desire and the pleasure of fulfilling it. His own flesh trembled and betrayed him; he eased himself up on his elbows to face her.

Large, grey eyes that made his heart stutter. They looked at him with — was that fear?

"Hey," he said softly. "I think we've used up most of the day." He stroked her face and smiled down at her, wishing he could see the same joy on her face that had appeared when he was inside her. What are you so afraid of, he wanted to ask. Instead he said, "Was high time we did that, Ma'am. We bin trying to avoid it fer long enough a man could hurt hisself."

He leaned down to caress her cheek with his, felt her tremble and then her arms came up around his neck, her mouth found his ear. "It were high time, Mister, and now I'm afeard my heart's so full it could break at the littlest sorrow."

There was dampness on his cheek when he pulled back to gaze down at her. "Then we'll make sure there are no little sorrows, won't we." And he couldn't stop himself then. He leaned down and caught her lower lip in his, nibbled the edge of her jaw until she threw her head back and curved her body up to his.

"Ty," she cried as he found her again, and he knew she was seeking that joy again, too.

When they finally rested, Letha was too breathless to do aught but stroke Ty's body and feel the stirrings of desire all over again. It was like something pulsed in her, a hunger, a power, a desire that could not be quenched, and when she looked at him, she saw it matched in his eyes.

This — this was something she'd never felt before, like a deep ache that could only be filled by this man. No. She was wrong. She had lived with an ache like this all her life. She thought of the road out of the Valley and shook her head.

"Penny for your thoughts."

His voice was rough with emotions as she suddenly sat up. She smiled down at him. "How you make me feel. How Inca is going to buck me off and stomp me to a pulp for being late for her evening feed."

"Damnation. Hauberk."

He sat up and grabbed her. "So what have you done? Bewitched me so that I forget all my other responsibilities? Stolen my mind so I have no choice but to stay with you?"

The words were out of his mouth before he realized what he'd said. He saw the horror on her face as she scrambled up and away. He barely managed to catch her before she reached the door.

"Letha, no. I was joking, okay. Being with you is a choice — my choice." Again he stroked her cheek, and called himself a hundred kinds of fool. He shouldn't have done this. It was too fast, too soon — if it should have been done at all. Judging by the look on her face, it probably shouldn't have been. Letha Rivers had her own baggage to deal with. Too much.

"I never want you to stay against your will. I never would," she intoned. She pulled loose to gather up her clothes. "But I have to go. I've left Inca. And the store. She checked her watch. "Oh, God, how many people have waited for me and I just never came back." She looked at him as if she were going to cry. "I put up a sign that said back in five minutes and that was how many hours ago."

It must have been the look on her face — he couldn't help himself. He laughed. "Well, I darn well better have kept you longer than five minutes, or it wouldn't have been worth it all, would it?"

Her worried expression didn't change, and finally he clutched his chest and looked heavenward. "Kill me now! The woman can't even show some enthusiasm."

She boxed his arm, then stood on her toes to plant a long slow kiss on his mouth and press her nakedness into his. "Enough enthusiasm?"

He shook his head, tickled her, and she shrieked, tugging her clothes on as he corralled her for another kiss and began hauling her shirt off her, and her off to his bed, so his kisses could wander.

"Ty, come on." She shrugged her way loose. "We have to do something — show some responsibility for our animals."

"Another race? Fifteen minutes, and we're back here to do more of what comes natural?"

She hauled on her boots and raked his nakedness with a playful leer. "You're on, Mister." Then she grabbed his supply of boots and shoes from the doorway before he could protest and ran — leaving him to wonder who was this woman, who held the wounded heart of a child and yet was so clearly the woman he wanted in his bed.

§

A golden glow lay over the lake and Letha's mad dash slowed. The air smelled like honeyed clover, felt like syrup on her skin. She inhaled. It was almost hard to breathe her chest was so full — but not like she had felt in the cabin or when Harry Zigheld looked at her. This was the heaviness of satiation or power, of being full after a lifetime of starving, and it seemed to run through the air and the earth to her blood.

She looked out over the lake — could feel every ripple and stirring of wind, every dance of a water strider across the surface. It reminded her of Ty and his touches. Ty and his kisses. Her body ached with the feel of Ty. And her heart…

She was being silly and she knew it. She'd slept with the man — that was all. She'd done it with other men. It was lust, pure and simple. But the way her arms goose-pimpled at the thought of him said differently. And there were his words to her, the look in his eye, and this weird feeling as if the air crackled when they were together.

It could still be simple lust, couldn't it? He was a man, and he'd been here alone for a while. She had been without a lover for a long time. She held that thought as she resumed her dash to her cabin, fed Inca, who wouldn't even come up to Letha until she bribed her with grain. The mare looked at her reproachfully and pulled her head away when Letha tried to pat her.

"Fine, then. Be like that, but just remember that I always had sympathy for you when you were in heat." The mare tossed her head. Letha left her and ran back to Ty's.

The last of the sun's rays caught him as he hobbled back from the barn, his chest and feet bare, low-slung, faded jeans hiding what she knew lay in between. She swallowed at how his skin was amber in the sun, and striated with light and shadow. She stopped to watch him move and felt her body quicken.

Damn it, she shouldn't be here.

But she was, and she wanted him, and maybe even — certainly even, at this moment — it was more. Looking at Ty Hunt made her chest hurt with an emotion that she was afraid to name.

"Brat," he said, scooping up his foot apparel from where she dumped them in the centre of the yard, and then catching her around the waist, so his touch sent a bright flash across her vision. "You made me brave a very pissed off stallion in bare feet. I could have been badly hurt. There I'd be, maimed and lamed. Wouldn't that have made you feel bad?" He nuzzled her hair.

It did, actually. The comment brought back the dream she'd had and the sense of darkness welling around him. She pulled free and found herself gasping for breath, her heart pounding.

"What is it, Leth?" She caught his hand, fighting back the welling darkness that was blinding her, and shook her head.

"Nothing —," She saw he wasn't going to accept that. "It — I was just thinking about what you told me yesterday. About you being hurt." Her gaze trailed down the breadth of his chest. He'd already been hurt, and badly, by the look of the scars on him. She'd explored them today in the interludes between their love-making: the long puckered lines across his forearms and chest, the puckered buttonhole scar just inside of his lower left hip, the incision on his lower back, the crater on his upper left thigh.

The darkness — she knew it was coming and it flowed through this man, but she wouldn't see him injured again, or possibly killed. She had to encourage him to leave, to hide.

And she would go with him.

That thought made her pull back because she wasn't going to do what Sylvia suspected and try to seduce Ty Hunt into taking her. Whatever he felt, that was his business. She wanted him safe. "You should leave the Valley. There's too much chance of you being found here."

He tried to touch her again and she stepped back, ignoring the brief look of consternation on his face. She shook her head and he caught her wrist in a move so fast she missed it.

"Letha, I know you don't like other people making your choices, but neither do I. We're both adults. We both have our own choices to make, and right now my choice is to be with you."

His nearness made it hard to move, and the air seemed to thicken with that sensation of something around them, something rising from them. He smelled of the musk of their love-making; and all the sounds of the evening — the bat wings, the loon on the water, and the chorus of frogs from the lake edge — seemed to crescendo and then die away so she was caught in a still, crystal moment where there was only the two of them. Only the feel of her heart, yammering in her chest, and surely to goodness it was loud enough for him to hear it as he looked down at her with all good things promised in his eyes, and kissed her again.

"There. That's my choice, Letha. For now. You and me, getting to know each other better."

"But maybe it's only lust — just an animal attraction. We're two healthy adults, but we don't know a thing about each other."

"So you're telling me I'm just like — like Hauberk — just drawn when a mare in heat comes around? That's all this is. I'm just a slave to instinct." He twined his fingers in hers, holding her hand to his heart in a gesture so intimate she found herself holding her breath.

Then he released her and stepped away, and the frogs were still singing mightily and a cricket buzzed and the loon sent a long, haunting cry across the water that made Letha shiver where she stood, because his absence was like suddenly being dashed in cold water.

"We know things about each other Letha. We both grew up here. I remember a wild-eyed, whimsical girl who was my sister's friend, and so damned appealing I had to watch myself whenever I was around her. I remember a girl just becoming a young woman who came to me and asked me to take her away with me when I was going off to college, and I remember the hurt and betrayal in her eyes when I told her 'no'. I remember that *too* well."

He nodded to the cabin. "Let me show you how much I remember — and what I think of the woman you've become. I'm used to making choices, Letha. Right now, I'm thinking the best thing to do is grab a bite, and then — if your choice coincides with mine — spend the night making up for these past ten years."

The soft yearning in his voice, the way his hair fell across his forehead and his gaze held on her, told her whatever it was that was happening, it was something more than she'd suggested. Even the fulsomeness of the sunset suggested it in the way the whole sky throbbed with glorious light, the way the breeze sent a heavy shimmer across her skin.

She took a step toward him. Another. Just like, he thought, a cautious animal lured by food.

At the doorway to the cabin she looked up at Ty, then out at the lake, and thought she saw — briefly — a deep, green-gold stirring in the heart of the lake.

Chapter 11

The next morning she untangled herself from Ty's embraces and ran home as dawn stirred mist from the lake. Birds chirped sleepily in the trees. On the wild rose petals the bees still slumbered in the cool, but overhead the sky was a clear blue cauldron. It was going to be one of those scorcher summer days when all you wanted to do was make like one of the ranch cattle and doze in the shadows of the silver-leaved poplar trees.

Not Letha. She had planning to do.

At the store, tucked into the crimson doorframe, a sheet of paper gleamed whitely. She stopped, the sight of its crisp edges sent a cold chill down her back. She plucked it free and unfolded it.

Kris's crisp handwriting filled the page. She'd brought her mom over to work on the show planning last evening. They'd waited thirty minutes, and where the heck *was* she? P.S. Inca had been upset in the corral, so Kris had fed her another flake of hay.

Stuffing the note in her pocket, she went back to feed the mare and tell her that there was no way she was going to keep her filly-ish figure if she kept eating like a hog, and Letha was no longer going to believe the hang-dog looks the mare gave her. But Kris's question kept running through her head. Just where was she? If God knew, he sure as heck wasn't telling.

Sure, she'd had plans to use Ty, but no more. She'd never use someone she cared about like that, even though the rest of the Valley folk seemed able to do it easier than breathing. What she felt for Ty was more than simple physical attraction. She'd known it in her flesh even before she knew it in her head — that was why touching him was a flashpoint. That glimpse of something in the lake last night had only confirmed it. It seemed to run in her blood. She held out her hand, half expecting to see a shimmer running over her fingers. There was nothing there, but there was something like an electric feeling in the air, even though there wasn't the faintest sign of storm clouds.

Ty had caused that — or at least, whatever had happened between them had caused it — there simply was no other explanation. And she wanted Ty — her lover — safe. She'd have to encourage him to leave, and do it in such a way that he thought it was his idea.

How was the question, because Ty Hunt seemed to see into her and know the motivation behind her words even before she did. She went inside and made a pot of coffee, tidied the store while it brewed, and then went outside with a piece of toast and a steaming mug to watch the day begin. Roscoe fluttered down beside her to peck at the spirit catcher's string webbing. The dangling feathers hung limp and tattered as the spirit catcher bumped, bumped, bumped against the side of the building.

"You did that, didn't you, you pesky bird. Look at those feathers. You set a horrible example, you know. Always refusing to do as you're told. You've been a bad influence on Inca." Of course, that could be the other way around, because Inca was a chestnut mare and they were notoriously difficult. Roscoe simply stopped pecking for a moment and stared at her out of one black eye.

She finished the coffee and fed half the toast to Roscoe, then went in to refill her cup. She really should ride over to Kris's to apologize for not being here. Maybe after this cup. Maybe the ride would help her figure out what to do. Or Kris might have some ideas how to get Ty to leave. Heck, maybe she'd help.

From outside, the rhythm of the spirit catcher changed, increased. Damn that bird. If he kept that up she was going to have to take the beautiful hanging down, because she wouldn't have Roscoe totally ruin it. As it was, she was probably going to have to replace the eagle feathers soon.

She paused to grab a piece of paper to jot down ideas she'd had for the art show so she'd be ready, then shushed Roscoe up to the roof and headed for the barn. With the mare quickly saddled, she headed around the lake, enjoying the spring in Inca's gait even though the mare tried to bog her head and buck once or twice, the sound of the wind in the trees, the scent of new grass growing near the lake edge. It was a scent she normally associated with spring.

Inca splashed into the river at the end of lake, the spray soaking Letha, then the mare bounded up the slope where the grass was still beaten down from the party two days before. It was like the mare had all the un-tapped energy of a barely-broke colt.

At the house, Letha slid off the saddle and patted the mare's side as she tied her to a hitching post in the shade. "What's gotten into you today?"

Inca simply flipped her head and snorted grass-stained saliva as if to say, what do you think, on such a fine day?

The ranch house back door was open as Letha clumped up the steps. She called 'hellooo' and entered at the kitchen.

Through the mud room, the kitchen sat filled with the bright morn-ing light and a scent of cinnamon buns that sent Letha's stomach growling. A tray of them sat cooling on top of the stove, and Mrs. H. was just pull-ing another tray out of the oven. The bright, city-scape painting gleamed in the light.

"Morning, Letha," she said. "Fine morning, isn't it? I thought the boys would like a treat when they come up for coffee in a few hours."

"You spoil 'em, Mrs. H."

"They're a good crew," Kris said from where she sipped a cup of coffee at the large kitchen table. Spread in front of her were pages and pages of official-looking documents, but right now her slightly stressed gaze felt stuck on Letha. "What brings you by?"

Letha poured herself a cup of coffee and settled herself on another chair. "I was hoping to catch some time with Mrs. H. if she has it. Maybe work on the art show, because I need to get those invitations out."

"Just let me get finished with these, and I'm all yours, dear." Mrs. H. slid another two pans of cinnamon buns into the oven. "Feeding this crew is like feeding an army, I think sometimes. Who knew I'd spend my older years up to my elbows in flour and yeast." She joined them at the table, her nose dusted with flour so she looked like a young woman again. "Once these hands were manicured weekly, and all my food basically came from restaurants. Funny the rolls life spins us, isn't it?"

Kris was still studying Letha and it was becoming downright uncom-fortable. "Have I got a zit on my nose, or something?" Letha asked.

"No. No." Kris looked away, then looked speculatively back at Letha. Her gaze narrowed. "There's something about you today…."

Letha felt the color spread up her neck, because she knew darn well what it was that Kris was seeing — the look of a woman who hadn't slept all that much last night and whose body had been well and truly used up.

Well, not so truly used up that thoughts of Ty didn't bring a little zing up through her body.

"So just where were you yesterday?" The sharpness of Kris's tone brought Letha back from the little quiver of pleasure, in time to see the dawning of suspicion in Kris's gaze. "Your mare was there, circling her corral like some wild thing, but you weren't anywhere to be found, and we waited a good long time."

Letha couldn't meet Kris's gaze, because she just knew if she did Kris would know.

"She was with Ty. Didn't I tell you that?"

Letha's gaze jerked to Mrs. H., who sat with her coffee cup cradled in her hands. Her clear eyes smiled. "You know, I went out for a walk last night and I swear it smelled like Spring again along the lake shore. There were new grass shoots, and I found a new crop of baby's breath blooming down by the grove of poplar by the barns. I brought some home for the house — can't you smell it?"

Letha could, even through the cinnamon. The soft, sweet scent of clean growth and new beginnings the flower always brought to mind. But how do you respond to a mother, that you're sleeping with her son?

"Ty and I had dinner at his place last night." She knew it was lame, even when she said it, and it sent Kris choking on her coffee.

"Letha Rivers," she sputtered, blowing coffee spray across her papers. She pulled them into a stack in front of her as she fought to control her guffawing. "That's the weakest euphemism for sleeping with someone I've ever heard."

The grin on Kris's face, the patience on Mrs. H.'s — there were too many eyes on Letha and she felt the burning on her face. "Oh, God, does everyone know how I spent my night?"

"Well, there won't be too many surprised faces around this place. When I went out to the barns this morning, Matt said he thought we were having a second Spring and the other guys were making jokes about the smoke rising at the other end of the lake. Let's face it, Letha. It was only a matter of time. It was written all over both of your faces, even though neither of you wanted to admit it."

"I'm that obvious."

"I'm sorry, Letha, dear, but lying has never been your forte. You wear your emotions on your sleeve, so to speak."

"Oh, God." She covered her face in her hands, absolutely mortified. "If the crew knows, then the Valley's going to know in short order."

"I'd think they'd already suspect, Letha," Mrs. H. said. "If I can feel the change in the air, well, then, someone who was born here surely would. I'm right aren't I, Kristienne?"

"It's like my skin tingles with anticipation. Everyone feels it. I suppose this is what happens when Spring falls in love. The old man — he was bucking and snorting this morning like he was two again." Kris shook her head and grinned, as if the memory of the eighteen-year-old stallion that was the Hunt Ranch champion stud bucking around his paddock was a particular delight. "Do you know how long it's been since we've seen that? Hell, we've been having a hard time even getting him to cover mares anymore. Matt's going nuts because all the brood mares have gone in heat all at once, and the old man's acting like he's going to leap the fence."

Letha covered her face with her hands. How the heck did you have a private life in this sort of situation? She and Ty would just have to cool it. It might be better that way, anyway, given she needed to encourage him to leave. She'd be a friend — not a lover.

Who was she kidding? She groaned.

Kris reached across the table and caught Letha's hands, and the familiar warm flow of friendship passed through her. "It's all right, you know. You're allowed to be happy. You're allowed to fall in love. This — it's to be expected. And you and Ty…."

"I know, I know. I mooned over him when I was a kid. But it's not love. It can't be. I'm sorry if I offend you Mrs. H., but this was simply lust, okay? That's all it was and now I really shouldn't be here all day given I was so lax yesterday at the store. Mrs. H., maybe I should leave and come back later when you have time."

"Don't let me stop you two from your planning. I'll just take off for my office. Got accounts to do, and so on." Kris pushed her chair back and stood, looking down at Letha like a stern schoolteacher. "Letha, don't go getting all uptight about this. It's good, okay? It's good for you, if you'll just relax. I can see it in your face. As for the Valley, to heck with 'em."

Oh, God, Kris needed to understand. It wasn't just the Valley's reaction, though there'd be hell to pay. It was Ty, and the need for him to leave.

"I need to talk to you, too," Letha said, glancing at Mrs. H. She knew it wouldn't be good for Ty's mother to know about his situation. "I'll pop into the office when your mom and I are done, okay?"

Kris agreed, and made her exit.

That left Letha with a strong sense of embarrassment in Mrs. H.'s presence. Just how did you deal with a mother whose son you had just spent a long, glorious night of very active sex with? Again that zing through her body, and she pulled her thoughts back. She found Mrs. H.'s gaze on her, and that just brought the embarrassment to the fore again.

"It's all right, dear. About Ty. I was young once, you know. Jackson and I…." She got a faraway look in her eyes. "Besides, I've known for years there was something special about you two."

Letha frowned at this. How could Mrs. H. have known, when she didn't know herself?

"When you were kids, there were times he'd be ready to scream at Kristienne, and then you'd arrive and do exactly the same thing as Kristienne, and he'd interrupt whatever he was doing to take the time for you. I could never figure out why, but it was there. Affection, I thought. Like a big brother."

Letha's thoughts ran to Ty's hard body, the way he moved inside her, and another wave of heat swept color to her face. Nothing brotherly there. She tore herself away from the image. "Let's not talk about this. I was thinking about the opening. I suddenly realized we've got to get the invitations out right away."

"I was thinking the same thing. The New York art world is gone on holidays through much of August. They've got to receive invitations well before then so they can book this into their calendars — maybe even make this show part of their holiday plans."

Mrs. H. set her cup down and tapped her chipped fingernail on the table top. Letha noticed the cuticles were chewed and torn, the skin stained dark. Nerves, she thought. From not drinking, perhaps.

"I have to say we've left this very late, dear. Normally I'd suggest we set the show to November." She raised her hand to quell the argument that coalesced in Letha's gut. "I've lived here long enough to know November's not an option. So we need an angle that will make turning down our invitation even harder."

The firm line of her lips said she'd made a hard decision. Mrs. H. stood. "Come with me."

She led Letha through the house and up the stairs, into a part of the house Letha had never been before — Mr. and Mrs. H's part of the house. It was one end of the upstairs, a house-length apart from the rooms that Kris and Ty had occupied as kids.

The room they stepped into stopped Letha in her tracks. It was nothing she had ever seen before — a second living room, with silk-covered, curved-leg couch and chairs, another fireplace, and books. Books everywhere, strewn across the floor, across the furniture. Some looked like they'd been thrown against the wall. Askew on the wall hung whimsical, brightly-colored paintings that caught and held Letha's gaze. They reminded her of the one in the kitchen.

"What is it, dear?"

"Nothing — well — what is this place?"

Mrs. H. smiled, looking around her. "My home. My real home. My little bit of New York." She caught Letha's hand. "This is my sitting room. I wanted a place that was just mine and Jackson's."

Letha scanned the furniture again, finding it hard to imagine Ty's father's large frame on the delicate furniture.

"Follow me."

Mrs. H. led her across the room to where two doors stood. One, open, gave onto a large, disheveled bedroom that filled the end of the house. The other, closed, was where Mrs. H. paused, as if uncertain about her actions. She glanced at Letha, inhaled, and opened the door.

The room was small, but filled with light and the smell of turpentine: that was Letha's first impression. Early sunlight poured through the dormer windows that gave a wide view of the lake. The floor of the room was ancient vinyl, stained and spattered with rainbows of colors — colors reflected in the bright paintings hung and leaning against the walls.

"Welcome to my garret."

"Your what?" Letha stepped farther into the room, a slow understanding forming. "You painted that picture in the kitchen. And those ones in your sitting room." She turned to Mrs. H. "I never knew you painted."

Mrs. H. looked away, and wandered the room around the various easels standing like skeletons in the room. Her fingers trailed across the tops of paintings. Then she stopped and examined her fingertips for dust. "I haven't. Not for years. I did, before I was married and before my career took off. I was actually quite good — or so I'm told. I had one or two shows of my own in small galleries."

She colored sweetly as she said it, as if she couldn't believe what she'd been told.

Letha looked at the paintings stacked against the wall. There must be at least fifty. More, probably. Those she could see were beautiful: a woman's face shadowed under a wide-brimmed gardening hat — again with that sense of whimsy in her smile. A scene of a family picnicking in a field bright with flowers, the foreground larger in perspective so the family appeared lost in a jungle of blooms. Silver-spangled ranch hands and russet cattle lost in a sea of grass and forest, a coyote peering out at them. Others. So many others.

"Mrs. H. these are great. I mean, I don't know much about art, but… wow! Why are you hiding them away like this?"

Mrs. H. shook her head, the chignon she wore gently nodding with the motion. "Kristienne isn't really partial to them. Neither was Jackson. It made the whole thing, the time painting, seem rather pointless."

"They didn't like them?" Letha rounded on her. "My God, these should be out there for the world to see."

Seemingly avoiding Letha's gaze, Mrs. H. looked back out the window. A flight of ducks came in for a splashy landing on the lake, and Letha saw Mrs. H.'s lips curve in a smile.

"After I was well-known as a singer — and quit my career to come here — well, a couple of the larger galleries wanted to show my stuff. Oddities, I thought — like the Sinatra paintings, or Joni Mitchell's. I was odd enough out here. I didn't need more of it in my life."

Her voice had gone soft and sad as she spoke, and the sound of it almost broke Letha's heart. She'd known Mrs. H. must have given things up to come to the Valley. She'd known, as well, that Mrs. H. had always carried a faint scent of sadness, even though she must have chosen to come here, but this room — it showed the huge open wound that still oozed in this woman. Suddenly Letha was angry.

"It's this damned Valley. It does this to people. It stole your choices, just like it stole mine."

"No." Mrs. H.'s calm voice startled Letha. "That's not the way it was. I made the decision to come here. I made the decision to stop painting. I won't lay that responsibility on anyone or anything."

"But you quit painting, and look at these — they're wonderful." She couldn't believe Mrs. H. could be an apologist for the Valley. Not after everything she'd lost by coming here.

"Do you really think so? Because I was thinking. I've kept in touch with some of the gallery people — most are old friends I visit when I go to New York. I thought, well, maybe I could show my stuff at your store, too. It might be a draw for the gallery owners."

She seemed embarrassed to even suggest it, stiffened when Letha crossed the room to catch her in a hug. "Yes and yes. Your paintings are marvelous. We're going to knock 'em dead with your and Johnny's paintings. Oh, my God, we're going to do this!"

Maybe it was Letha's own excitement that caught Mrs. H., or maybe it was the thought of the show, but a long, true smile spread across Mrs. H.'s face and into her eyes. She held Letha away.

"Then can I show you something else?" Vulnerability there.

"There's more?" Letha's hand rose to her throat. "I don't know if I can take more."

Mrs. H. went over to one corner, turned the easel there. It was a painting of square dancers, two little children collapsed, sleeping at one corner of the dance area. All the adult partners were caught in various awkward positions, and beyond lay a lake shore reflecting a sky heavy with stars.

"The Solstice," Letha breathed. "This is new."

"I haven't painted in years, but yesterday afternoon I came in here again. It was like I had all this energy. This painting finished so fast I couldn't believe it. The next one — well it's not quite finished, but it's close."

She showed another canvas, this one of a traditional Solstice, the people ringing the lake, a single white figure bathing in the waters. The figure looked so lonely it sent a shiver up Letha's spine.

"What do you think?"

"I'm beyond words. Yes, we'll include your work in the show. This is a gift, Mrs. H. Almost too big a one."

Mrs. H. shook her head and caught Letha's hand. "You've given me a bigger gift, Letha. You helped me remember myself."

Letha almost argued, but Mrs. H. turned to mundane matters like the list of names, like the design of the invitations. The next two hours were spent pouring over Mrs. H.'s ideas and making phone calls to printers. When they were done, Letha felt like she'd been through a whirlwind, and wondered if this was what the old Mrs. H. had been like. Letha seemed to remember something like that from her childhood.

After excusing herself, Letha wanted to just head home; but her need to talk to Kris sent her down the hall to the office while Mrs. H. started to the long process of preparing afternoon and evening meals for the ranch hands.

Collapsing in the red leather chair, she met Kris's eyes. "Your mother's amazing."

Kris just raised her brows.

"I didn't know she was a painter. Have you seen all her stuff upstairs?"

"I've seen some of it. That thing in the kitchen, for example." Kris shook her head. "Not exactly ranch focused."

"Well it's fabulous, and I'm going to include it in the art show."

"You sound like one of Mom's old New York friends. Fabulous." She snorted and glanced back at her books. "Darn art, just costs money for supplies."

"Kris, give her a break. Her work is good."

"Fine. So you tell me. Art's always subjective. But you should think hard about including it. I thought this was an art show about Valley art — not some transplanted New Yorker's art."

The bitterness on Kris's face took the wind out of Letha's sails. "It is good," she softly. "And I'm going to include it."

"Fine. What do I know? Just don't get her all excited about it, because if her art work flops, I can just see her going to go into another bottle funk. I need that like I need a hole in my head."

It didn't make sense, this attitude of Kris's. She should be happy that her mother was happy. Mrs. H. seemed alive again. "What's going on, Kris?"

She took a deep breath. "Nothing that you need to be concerned with. Nothing at all." She closed the file in front of her. "You wanted to talk to me, didn't you?"

Letha got up and closed the office door, then sank back in her chair.

"It's about Ty. On Solstice you said he needed to talk to me. That's what I need to talk to you about."

"So?"

"Kris, did he tell you the danger he's in? He was doing undercover work against some mobster. He got found out. They nearly killed him — you should see the scars —" her voice faded out as she colored again. Damn it, this was Ty she was talking about — not just a sexual partner. "They thought he was dead, but somehow they've found out he's alive and they're looking for him."

Kris just looked at her, but her hands were pressed flat on the desk and her knuckles were white.

"Kris, we have to get him to leave, run for cover."

"Or we have to make sure he stay's hidden here."

"He won't be safe. The Valley's too small. Everyone knows Ty here."

"And so everyone will help."

"Not everyone, and you know it. Kris, we have to figure out a way to get him to move quickly, before they pick up his trail. Before they succeed in — heaven forbid — killing him."

Kris met her gaze, shook her head. "You and Ty. I always thought it might happen, but then he went away."

"What are you talking about?"

"You're in love with him. I can see it all over your face."

"You cannot, because I'm not. I'm just concerned for him. For your brother." But her protests sounded flat. "All right, I'll give you that I care a lot about him. Enough to sleep with him. But that doesn't mean anything. How did it go with Dwight on Solstice?"

"Don't try changing the subject, Letha. You're about as good at that as you are at hiding your real feelings. Dwight and I — well, I was going to try for a little tryst in the grass, but it seems Matt has infected all these ranch hands with that damned buckaroo honor of his." She shook her head in disgust.

"Bummer."

"You don't know the half of it — do you know how *long* it has been?"

"Long enough you're in an evil temper a lot of the time. We were talking about Ty and how to keep him safe."

Kris grinned. "Not bad, Letha. You're getting better at that changing-the-subject thing. I'm going to have to watch out for it." She tapped her fingers on the desk. "Tell you what. I'll talk to Matt, 'cause for all his damned honor, he does have a hell of a lot of common sense. I'll see what he says and what we can come up with, okay?"

"He needs to go soon, Kris." Her whole body vibrated with the need to move on and take action. Waiting for another opinion wasn't what she needed.

Kris's steady gaze caught her attention.

"What? What is it?"

"Hard question for you. Is it Ty who needs to leave, or is it you?"

It shouldn't have, but the question knocked the wind out of Letha as fully as when Inca bucked her off. The trouble was, she wasn't sure of the answer.

Chapter 12

An impatient whinny woke Ty with a start. He opened his eyes, and for a moment thought he was in the spacious apartment above the even more spacious barn that the Zochenko's operated, and Marta Zochenko was once more using her pale, ice-colored eyes and her pouting, sultry lips to let him know just how available she was — if he'd only take advantage of the offer.

Where the hell had that come from?

Ty rolled over, seeking Letha, and found the empty side of the bed. He sat up, his head still wrapping itself around the fact that he wasn't at the Zochenko farm, where Marta Zochenko had decorated his apartment with her collection of brightly colored 'primitive' art. He was at the Valley in the snug back bedroom in the log-walled cabin by the lake. But the dream — if that's what it was — had been so damned real it made his whole body tighten with alarm.

Not what he wanted. He'd rather curl up in bed and spend another day playing hooky — or whatever else came to mind — with a certain red-haired shopkeeper and sometime keeper of Spring. The sheets, his skin, his nostrils seemed filled with her faint scent of roses, mint, and promises.

Another impatient whinny, followed — this time — by the alarming sound of metal-shod hoofs crashing against a barn wall. Hauberk was not happy, and that meant Ty's idea of a lazy morning was shot right out the window.

He got up, hauled on cut-offs, a t-shirt, and a pair of runners, before heading for the barn. There'd be time for a shower and breakfast later. Horses came first — well, almost first.

The small barn rang with another resounding thud just as Ty entered. The stall door shuddered against its lock. Hauberk heard him coming and turned in his stall, sticking his head out over the top of his stall door, his impatience just as evident in his snort and his flared nostrils.

"Sorry, old man. I guess I shouldn't have locked you in like that, but I didn't want you getting chilled after I hosed you down yesterday."

Looking at the stallion's chest, still patterned with dried sweat, he hadn't done a very good job of it, either. Contrite, now, Ty scratched his horse's face and the stallion leaned into him.

"Okay. I get it. I've neglected you big time, and for what — a woman. Not nearly as good as horse, I know, but I gotta tell you, buddy, this is one heck of a woman. She's giving you a heck of a run for your money."

He fed the horse his grain and a new flake of hay, then stood leaning on the stall door until Hauberk had finished his grain. "Let's get you cleaned up proper, shall we?"

Leading Hauberk outside, Ty tied him to the corral beside the barn, then turned on the water and, scraper in hand, began the process of hosing and soaping and scraping the old sweat off the stallion's coat. When he was finished, Hauberk stood there looking like a massive mahogany statue. Then he ducked his head, swept his tail around, and caught Ty smack dab across the face and chest.

Ty sputtered and fell back a step. Damn, it stung like a bitch, Hauberk's thick tail like a lashing cat-o-nine-tails and made only harsher by the water in the heavy strands.

"Okay, okay. I beg forgiveness and plead infatuation as my excuse. It won't happen again… I promise… hopefully."

When Hauberk was loose in his corral and had promptly dropped to a roll in the dust, Ty just shook his head and turned back to the cabin. Horses. As bad as women, and just as impossible to live without.

It was a fine day — blue and hot, but with just enough breeze across the lake not to be insufferable. The feel of the air on his skin reminded him of Letha. Hell, he could still feel her under him, around him. A shimmy of arousal ran through him and he stopped at the stairs to the porch. A cold shower would help.

He looked back at the lake, then down at his horse-splattered shirt. Why waste the water? He toed off his shoes and went down to the water, splashed in up to his hips, then made a clean dive toward the centre of the lake.

Cool water across his skin. He came up and hauled off his shirt, tying it around his waist, then began swimming. The powerful pull of his shoulder muscles reminded him that as a kid he'd done this every morning. He hadn't for years now, but it felt like home. Right.

Just like everything was right. Letha was like coming home, too. She might be a bit of work right now, but that was just skittishness on her part.

When they were together there was no one who'd ever even come as close as a friend, a confidant, and now as a lover.

He pulled up in the water, bobbing almost in the center of the lake. "And you wake up thinking of Marta Zochenko, no less."

But the feeling the memory had evoked was one of misgiving, as if he'd done — or not done — something important, like the time he'd neglected to bring Marta's favorite saddle pad to a competition and had had to deal with the woman's tantrum.

A far cry from Letha. He closed his eyes and lay back, letting the water lift up his legs and torso so the sunlight flooded his eyelids with red. God, he loved it here. He could imagine doing just what he had been doing for the past few days, for the rest of his life.

Water gurgled in his ears as he rolled over and felt something tickle his leg; a school of tiny fishes surrounded him. He swept his arm through them and they parted around his motion, briefly glowing in the green-gold depths. The sight of them brought a smile to his lips, a full feeling to his heart that reminded him of Letha as he stroked toward shore.

Back on the beach, he half-dried himself off with the sodden t-shirt and climbed the porch, only to sink down into one of his Cape Cod chairs and peer out over the lake. The only thing that would make this better was if Letha were here. He smiled to himself. She'd be back. She couldn't help herself any more than he could.

§

But she wasn't back by noon, and Ty had to shake his head at how he felt just a tad put out by that fact. To keep himself busy he readied Hauberk for a ride. He'd go see what Letha was doing and see if he could talk her into going for a ride with him. He looked up at the hills and thought of some of the quiet glades he'd known as a boy. Perhaps in the plush growth of one of the mint sinks....

His mind went over the gentle ministrations of getting her laid down in the grass, the way she got that shocked, excited look in her eyes and the way her cautious shyness disappeared into passion.

"You've really got it bad, man," he swore as he hauled up on the girth strap and Hauberk grunted. Then he swung up into the saddle and rode down the lake.

The mare was gone and the sign in the store window simply said 'closed', with no time set for opening again. He frowned. Darn woman had run off without him, and for a moment it bothered him, then he was pleased that she had. She'd had far too few choices. If she didn't want to spend today with him, then so be it. He was a big boy.

"Guess we guys are on our own." He patted the big horse's neck, then turned him back toward the road. Might as well go exploring a little and then head over and bother Kris. She'd be pleased he'd told Letha. He might even let on what had happened.

His explorations showed him new summer cabins that sat back from the road on ten acre parcels of land that used to be part of Hunt Ranch. It reminded him of the land he'd seen for sale along the road. It was some of the best of the ranchland, including part of one of the best producing hay fields, and Ty saw red. What the hell was Kristienne doing? Dad would have died before he ever sold part of this ranch. He'd loved this place with a passion equaled only by his love for horses. That, at least, was something he and Ty had shared.

Of course, his father never really had time for his wife or his son or his daughter. They weren't his passions.

Well, his son was damned well going to get to the bottom of this. He turned Hauberk down the road toward the ranch and urged the big horse into a ground-devouring trot.

By the time he reached the ranch house he was fit to be tied. He was about to swing down off Hauberk when his mother came out the door with a big enough grin on her face it almost set him back. She looked — herself, for a change. "Ty! You looking for Letha? She left about a half hour ago."

"Where's Kris?"

"Ty? Is something wrong?"

"Damn right. Now where is she?"

"Last I heard, she was going to talk to Matt about something." His mother lifted her chin toward the arena. "Probably there, if I know Matt."

He reined Hauberk past her and cantered the stallion up the hill. Matt, Kris, and Billy Fitsch were shifting the cattle pens back into position.

"I want to talk to you."

When Kris saw him he looked like a demon. His face had gone dark, and sitting on that huge moose of a horse with its flaring nostrils — she could almost be afraid if it wasn't Ty.

"Sure, Ty. You're just in time to help us put back everything you screwed up. What's up?" She wiped her hands on her jeans and motioned at Matt and Billy to keep shifting the damned gates.

"I screwed up?" He side-passed Hauberk up to the gate, unlocked it, and came inside, almost as good as a reining horse could. Then he headed Hauberk straight at her fast enough she had to leap aside.

"Jeezus, Ty! What the hell's going on?" He wheeled the horse so fast he seemed to canter in place. Then the stallion was galloping at her again. Who knew a big animal like this could move so fast, so smooth. You had to give the big lummox credit. She ducked away again. And again. And again, but somehow she found herself herded into a corner, until she was standing with her back to the arena walls with a huge dark horse snorting in front of her. The horse's rider could have almost been snorting as well — his look was that angry.

Ty slipped off the horse's back and stepped up to her, seeming somehow taller — and definitely angrier — than she had seen him before. And that was going some.

"What the hell are you doing with the ranch," he growled, low-voiced enough that Matt and Billy probably wouldn't hear the words, but they sure as hell heard the tone.

Matt had stopped what he was doing and was sauntering toward them, motioning Billy to stay back. Kris swallowed as she looked back at her brother. She'd hoped she'd have things sorted before he ever found out about the problems they were in.

"We got in some money problems, Ty. We're working our way out of them."

"By selling Dad's land? The ranch?"

She couldn't deny it. It was clear as day, by the summer cabins and the 'for sale' signs.

"Let me guess. I wasn't meant to see it until the deed was done."

She lifted her chin to face him. "That's right. You relinquished your say in what happens here when you left and didn't return for ten years."

She saw his face tighten and she knew that hit him hard, because Ty had always loved the ranch. His hands made fists. He inhaled as if to calm himself, and Kristienne had the sudden thought that she didn't know this man anymore. This man knew violence and showed it.

"All right," he said slowly. "I'll give you that one. What I want to know is what's happened."

"It's no business of yours. You're not from here anymore."

"Who says?"

"You're the one who said you were here for a short time. You're the one who was talking about relocation the other night."

"I talk about a lot of things. That doesn't mean I'll do them. But you — you don't talk about things."

"Talking doesn't fix things, Ty. At least, not here. Maybe it does in the big city. Isn't that what Mom used to talk about — how words are the currency of the city?"

"And out here a man's word is his bond."

"Well Dad's bond got us in some trouble, all right? I'm trying to dig us out."

"So tell me."

Suddenly she was so tired she didn't want to argue anymore. How long had she been carrying this around, fighting to be cheerful in the face of the possibility of the loss of everything she held dear.

"Dad made an agreement with a major Quarter Horse breeder in Arizona. It was a big deal, where they paid a premium to have the old man sent down so they could breed their mares and get a crop of foals with our blood lines. Dad agreed because we all know the Hunt horses are tops, but we're too far away to have a lot of mares brought for covering."

"So? That doesn't explain why you're selling off our land."

"So when we sent Peppy's Blood Red Brother down to them, he couldn't perform. He only got three mares in foal, and one of the mares aborted. They demanded their money back, but Dad had already used it to put up this arena. They filed a lawsuit and they won. They placed a lien against everything we've got. When we got the old man back, he wasn't producing foals like he used to here, either. Let's face it: Peppy's Blood Red Brother is eighteen — an old man now — and we haven't got a prospect we've shown enough to get the same kind of stud fees and be a draw to reining and cutting horse breeders. Selling a few lots of land was the only way I could come up with to pay off the lien."

She sagged back against the wall. It was out. It was all out, and all she wanted was for someone to take the load off her shoulders. "I'm sorry, Ty. I really tried to hold it all together, but Dad got sick right in the middle of the court action and I've been playing catch-up ever since."

"If you'd talked to me, maybe I could have helped. We could have worked it out together. But you don't talk."

The offer surprised her. So did the trying-to-find-patience look on his face, but that didn't mean he meant it. It hadn't with Dad. "But you left here like you couldn't wait to get away."

"From Dad. Kris, I could have helped you. I've got money saved. Hell, I've got no life, and this ranch — the Valley — they were the best parts of my life, I realize now."

"And Letha," Matt said coming up beside Kris.

"And Letha." Ty stopped. "Did she tell you something?" he asked, looking from face to face.

"Didn't have to, did she?" Matt drawled. "Flowers are in a second bloom. Hay seems to have thickened in the field overnight, and the horses are all acting like youngsters. Even the old man's frisky today. Actually managed to breed, and the look on that old stallion's face has me thinkin' that mare's going to catch." He bumped Ty on the shoulder with his fist. "Lookin' good on ya, fella."

Ty didn't like the turn the conversation had taken, nor the way Matt and Kris had matching cat-that-ate-the-canary smiles on their faces. "I didn't come here to talk about my sex life. I came to sort out what's happening to the ranch, and to make sure whatever it is doesn't continue."

"Then maybe we better take this conversation down to the house, Ty. Matt can take care of your horse."

Matt eased the leather reins out of Ty's hand and patted Hauberk on the shoulder. "You're a pretty good horse, fella. Might even make a decent reining horse if you weren't so hellish big. Who woulda thought you could move like that?"

"I did," Ty muttered as he followed his blasted sister out of the arena.

§

When Ty rode home that afternoon he was exhausted and sick at heart. How things had gotten so bad at the ranch was something he could barely comprehend. His father had made some very bad business decisions toward the end of his life. Kris had worked hard to make things right, but some things were just too — well — big, to be fixed easily.

Looking at the books and all of Kris's facts and figures, she hadn't had much option other than to sell small parcels of land. So far she'd resisted selling lake shore lots because she knew it was wrong to do so, and the Valley folk would rise up in protest if she did. At least he'd been able to offer some help. He had money saved — his paycheck for the past five years simply banked while he worked undercover — and some investments that had done well, but Kris resisted the help. She wanted to survive this thing herself and had made it obvious she hated the fact that her brother offered to bale her out. She didn't take charity, she'd said.

So they hadn't been able to reach an agreement — yet. Kris and he both had been too angry to deal with each other calmly, and they had left it that they needed to think about their positions and then talk again.

Hauberk sauntered the south lake shore trail through the trees, enjoying the loose rein Ty allowed him. Insects buzzed in the trees and grasshoppers bounded away from Hauberk's hooves. The sun lay heavily on Ty's shoulders and head, and ignited flashes of light off the lake. Red-winged blackbirds whistled among the reeds where their nests were hidden. A male mallard duck dabbled in the lake mud. Another swim would be good. Cool among the fishes. Better than these high boots and breeches, his shirt sticking to his chest.

Damn Kris. She should just take his money and fix things, but her damnable Hunt pride wouldn't let her. It was damned Hunt pride that had led her to go even further in debt to host that stupid Solstice party. The grand gesture — just like their father — and she couldn't see it. She was stubborn as a mule and as difficult as — Letha.

Who had left him this morning after their time together. Was that a symbol of her feelings, too? The memory of her skin under his palm made him shiver with want. Right now, right now when he was feeling like Kris, his father, the whole damned Hunt Ranch thing, had kicked him in the belly, he really needed someone to make him feel whole. He wanted to feel that skin again, even if it was just holding her hand. He wanted someone to talk to.

He shortened his reins and urged the stallion into a trot. Each great surge of Hauberk's strides seemed to increase his need. Desire, yes. There would always be desire where Letha was concerned — that was something he just knew at his core. But more than desire, as well.

Friendship, companionship, humor and — love. Damn it, they were right, and it had happened so quickly it had even slipped out of his mouth.

He drove Hauberk into a canter and rode like a demon along the lake shore, the wind in his hair cooling his sweat but not his heat.

At the store he reined in, leapt down. By that time the door to the cabin had opened. Letha stood there barefoot, desirable beyond words in cut-offs that showed her long, slim legs, and the ubiquitous plaid shirt over a plain white t-shirt.

"Ty?" Letha saw the stricken look of him. Crisis in his eyes, so the green was almost lost in darkness, and need that made sweat dapple the front of his polo shirt.

She was in his arms, felt them envelope her and heard his groan as he pulled her close, as he ducked his face to her hair. Kisses on her forehead, her eyes, her cheeks, her mouth. His entire body seemed to vibrate with tension. "You left this morning."

Keep it light, she thought. Something had happened, she could see. This was no time to talk about her fears or her feelings. "I had work to do. Some of us have to — we aren't on a government-bank-rolled holiday."

"I thought you'd pop by."

"And I did, but you weren't there. I guess we missed each other when you went out for your ride." She pulled back and smiled up at him, placed her palm against his cheek. "I was hoping maybe we'd run into each other today, though."

He saw the playful leer in her eye. "Run into each other — is that what they're calling it these days?"

She shrugged. "Don't know. Don't care." She stood on tiptoe and placed a slow, passionate kiss on his lips that set his blood racing as if he'd suddenly been revived from the dead.

"Oh, God, I needed you." He pulled her close, wanted to lift her up and carry her inside the store, but he still held Hauberk's reins. He set her away, his arm slipping down around her waist. "I need to put Hauberk away. Walk with me?"

She looked at him, nodded, then went back to the store. She put the 'back in fifteen minutes' sign in her window, then came to the door, took one look at him, and replaced the sign with 'Closed'.

When she pulled the door shut behind her, he nodded at the signs. "What gives?"

She grinned. "I didn't want to hurt your feelings — or set unrealistic expectations."

"Are you giving me a hard time? Because I really don't need someone else to give me a hard time." He asked as he pulled her into his side and began leading Hauberk down the trail.

"It's a compliment," she said, as she matched his stride. "Fifteen minutes just didn't seem fair — to my customers."

"Ah. Your customers come first. Of course." He looked down at her, feeling the tight cords of anxiety gradually loosen at the banter.

"Of course it's my customers. What else would I be referring to?" Again that little leer that set his pulse racing.

He stopped and Hauberk bumped him with his nose, then dumped his head down to grab a mouthful of the new grass near the lake. How the heck it stayed green under this sun, was a wonder — but then there were a lot of wonders in this Valley, the biggest one right beside him.

"Letha. You are a godsend."

"Me?"

"You make me smile."

Her mouth quirked. "I hope I do a little more than that."

"Actually, you make me want to do whatever it takes to make you smile."

"Ah, a slave. I never had a slave before." She stepped back to study him, her leg cocked, her bare toe tapping in the dust, and the sight of that long, smooth, inner-thigh made him swallow. "That could work," she said after a moment.

"I could show you," he said, his voice suddenly rough.

"Yes… you could."

He grabbed her hand and led her to the cabin. "Wait here," he said and ran Hauberk around to the barn, conscious he was doing it again, leaving his horse ill-cared for. He could ask himself what the hell he was thinking, but right now, with that woman waiting for him, he didn't care. She was the source and the centre of desire and relief.

When he returned to where he'd left her, she wasn't there. Instead, there was a pile of clothing and the sound of splashing from down by the lake.

Ty followed the sound and swallowed when he saw her. Letha stood naked, up to the swell of her hips in the water, facing out into the lake.

"Swim with me, slave," she said and dove, splitting the water like a silver-skinned fish.

Ty looked down the lake shore and down at his clothes. It was broad daylight, dammit, but he knew he'd obey. He wanted this woman. He wanted her now. His blood beat with that need and the knowledge that with her he'd find peace — if only for a little while.

He fought his boots off and stripped down, then splashed into the water, conscious of the white butt he bared to the sky. If Matt saw him, he'd laugh, but right now it didn't matter. What mattered was that wisp of red hair that floated on the lake, the white curve of arm and buttock.

He dove in and stroked toward her. She lay back on the water, her breasts bared luxuriously to the sun, until he grabbed her foot.

She squealed and pulled away, splashing water in his face. Then she swam away. She was fast, a mermaid without the tail, and he had to work to catch up. Long strokes and there were her flashing feet in front of him. He grabbed, but she eluded him. Long strokes and he was beside her, had her waist, had pulled them both under as he pulled her to him, as he kissed her and hardened, as her legs came up around him.

Dammit, he didn't have a condom, but the need was too much. This woman was too much. The lake pressed around him. He thrust into her, holding her hips as they bobbed to the surface, as he gasped for breath, as she cried out and clutched his shoulders. Her head fell back and he bit her neck, thrust again, and her legs tightened to meet him as they went under again.

Thrust, as the breath left his lungs, but Letha was all. Letha was his world and everything was green-gold light, and bubbles frothing around them. The water pressed around them, cupped them together.

Thrust, and he could feel her trembling, feel the spasms inside her.

Thrust, and he was drowning in the lake, in the deepness of Letha, and it didn't matter he would die, didn't matter the ranch would be lost, and he thrust and her legs tightened around him, her body thrust back, her breasts mashed against him, and his world reduced to the tight sheath around him, the body under his hands, and he thrust.

The world exploded in a green-gold flash and an explosion of reverberating sound.

Chapter 13

They clung to each other, unable to speak; their sobbing breath communicated everything between them, all Letha wanted between them. Then Ty caught her hand and they began the long swim back to shore, only to collapse once more in the weedy shallows, their limbs entwined, bodies glistening.

"What. The hell. Was that?" Ty panted, his fingers still twined in hers. His dark gaze felt like it raised steam on her skin, the green of his eyes almost the same as the lake.

Letha shivered and looked away at the sound of tires spraying gravel from the road. She scrambled up, away, but the chill that ran through her, the flash of sunlight on chrome, and the glimpse of white told her it was far too late. She looked back at Ty, now sitting up, the water not quite covering the fact he was aroused again. Far too late.

"Who was it?"

"White truck. Sylvia, I think. To hell with her. So she got an eyeful. It's not a sin."

"Well, that's good news." He caught her hand and pulled her down into the warm shallows. God, the feel of their skin when they touched. His, hard with muscle, the calluses of a rider she felt as his hands rounded on her breasts, her fanny, found the soft spots that brought a stuttering gasp from her.

"Ty. We're just inviting trouble — more voyeurs — if we stay here."

"And that's bad how?" His voice was muffled as he laid her back, as he nipped at her breast and an oh-so-skilled hand parted her legs to allow him entry.

"Ty! I'm not just a sex toy, you know." She jerked away, and her words came out crosser than she'd intended. Ty opened his palms.

"Far be it from me to force myself on a woman." She heard the bit of ice there, and knew she'd erred. Something had him on edge today. She'd known it as soon as he came to her door.

"I'm sorry. It's just — well — there's going to be trouble enough about you and me. We don't need to flaunt it in their faces."

"So what would you have us do, Letha? Pretend we barely know each other, but sneak into each other's bed after dark?" He shook his head and stood, his hair shaggy around his ears, his body magnificent with the water streaming off him and oh-God-she-wanted-him. "Because if that's what you're after, let me fill you in. I've lived my life that way for too long. I'm tired of not doing what I want and of secrets and dishonesty. I'm not sneaking around anymore. I want you in my life. I don't care who knows it. Understand?"

He offered a hand and she accepted, stood before him not knowing what to do until he suddenly closed his eyes and pulled her to him, covering her mouth with his, his body cool, his arousal hot and pulsing between them, urging her up, up, on her toes to find some way to take him inside.

"Come," she said, and realized she was panting, realized she wanted the hard scrape of his chest pressed against the sensitivity of her nipples. She reached down to cup him, smiled up at him. "Slave," she whispered and Ty burst out laughing, tweaked her breast, and before she could protest had her up over his shoulder and was carrying her buck-assed naked across the yard like he was some Neanderthal man taking his catch back to the cave.

Inside, he threw her on the bed and tickled her until she could barely breathe, then took her until all breath was gone. They lay in a tangle, smelling of lake water and lovemaking, touching each other. Letha still was unable to get enough of this man.

"Come on, my mistress." Afterward Ty finally hauled her up, shushed her into the shower, and busied himself finding food to fuel them after all the hard work they'd done. Good work. It left him with a lazy sense of rightness. Had eased the tightness in his chest until he realized what the answer was to all his problems, and that made the tightness go away completely.

When Letha came out of the shower, she found Ty in his cutoffs, sprawled in one of his Cape Cod chairs, drinking a beer and eating crackers and cheese. He handed her a beer and hauled her down into his lap, his hands running proprietarily over her bare thighs.

"So, you didn't answer my question."

She looked at him blankly, but she knew what he asked. "I don't know what you mean."

"The lake. What happened in the lake?"

She looked out to the water; it seemed more ruffled than it should be under such a light breeze. "We made love," she said softly. "That's all."

"Look at me and tell me that."

She looked back at him and repeated herself, but couldn't meet his eyes.

"Letha." A light touch on her chin turned her face to his, demanded her attention. "It was more than that. I heard — music, under water. It filled me and made me deaf. There was light and I was blind. All there was, was you and me and whatever it was we'd become."

She shivered and knew it was inevitable he would feel it, because the appearance of Sylvia's truck had brought the blonde woman's words back to her and had reminded her of the tales of the lake and of the horned god of the old ceremonies.

She scrambled out of his arms and looked down at him. "I really need to get back to the store, but I'll come back later." Then she lit out down the stairs before he could grab her or say anything to stop her. She hit the trail still running, because she needed to think. She needed Ty away from here, darn it. But she and Ty had made love in the lake, and somehow she was certain that act had wakened something very old.

Whatever it was, it was now very aware of Letha Rivers and Ty Hunt.

§

He watched her go, jogging off down the trail in a flash of long legs and tangled red hair, her stride working the fabric of her cutoffs very nicely over her very delectable ass.

"Scared her again, idiot. When're you gonna learn that you don't push this one too hard?"

It was true. Letha Rivers was worse — more suspicious and capricious — than any of the suspects he'd sidled up to over his years of work. He grinned. But, oh, was she worth it.

He stared out at the lake. It felt like home here. Truly like home. A place to raise a family, to have quiet winters by a fireplace, to have sleigh rides and go out on horseback to find the perfect Christmas tree and drag it back wrapped in a horse blanket. They'd done those things when he was a kid. He wanted to pass that on to his children.

Shit, where was all this coming from? He'd said goodbye to the Valley years ago and grown into a man in the outside world. He didn't need all the woo-woo stuff of the Valley and everybody knowing his business as well as he did and people feeling like they could just drop in anytime.

He grinned at that thought. He'd certainly made a point of dropping in on Letha. And there was no way he'd have been able to skinny dip in broad daylight and make out with his girl in any bigger town. So maybe this way wasn't all bad.

Oh hell, who was he kidding? The friggin' place and Letha were working a sort of magic on him. He felt whole — more than whole — alive and — dammit — happy! He didn't really know if he could leave again or wanted to. Hell, he didn't want to, and he could already see how his life would play out if he stayed.

"Shee-it," he muttered. What the hell was he going to do with that?

The first thing, was make contact with Samuels and arrange help to move his money, because whether Kris wanted his help or not, she was going to get it. Kristienne Hunt might think she was stubborn, but she had absolutely nothing on her brother when it came to protecting his own.

§

Letha held the edge of her computer table trying in vain to make her body stop trembling. It had been like this since she left Ty. Any bit of breeze sent her shaking. She felt like a leaf in the wind or a wave on the water — tossed wherever the stronger force wanted her to go and she-was-not-going-to-stand-for-it.

"Damn it, you can't do this to me!" she shouted at no one. Her words were far too loud for the small cabin. All they did was hurt her ears. Just like everything hurt right now. Her skin was so sensitive it hurt to wear clothes. It hurt to breathe, to drink, to see, to hear, even to inhale the scent of the cinnamon toast she'd had as a snack when she first got home.

She'd ask what was happening but she bloody well knew already. It was the damned lake doing its magic. It was Ty and her and the water and that bloody great tone of music that had left her teeth chattering near as bad as Ty's touch left her knees shaking.

It meant the two of them were bound together, she was sure of it. But she couldn't very well tell Ty, or it might make him think twice about leaving the Valley, and he had to leave. The more she'd thought about it, the more she thought about the darkness of her dreams, the more she was sure of it. She just needed to figure out how to make it happen.

Sylvia found Letha there, still seated at the table, her face pale, her fingers drumming syncopated rhythms on the wood. The bell tolled as Sylvia entered and she settled herself in the store's reading chair, idly examining the titles.

"French for Beginners. Book of the Seven Seas. Nice." Letha looked over and met her gaze. "So just how're you gonna do the traveling now, Letha?"

She saw the rise and fall of Letha's throat as she swallowed. She was scared, by the look of her. Truly scared and not sure what to do — not even where to look. She certainly couldn't meet Sylvia's gaze for any period of time. "Well?"

"I'll still leave. We both will."

"Uh-huh. Just like you planned it. And here I thought you didn't have it in you to set the poor guy up."

Letha was on her feet so fast, it surprised Sylvia. "I didn't set him up. I had no plans for this to happen. None of it. He pursued me. He came after me in the lake. It happened."

"And of course he had to tear your clothes off and overpower you," Sylvia said dryly. "Course, that must have happened before I drove up."

"Damn it, Sylvia. It's not like that and you know it. I... like him. He's a good guy."

"Sure." Sylvia pushed herself to her feet, and went to face Letha. "Ty Hunt is a good guy. A great guy, and he deserves better than to be tricked in to taking you away. I've said it before. I just thought maybe you should hear it again before the elders come for you."

"The elders?"

"You think they wouldn't? Jeeze, Letha, what happened today, well, heck, we felt the Spring return the other day, but this — hell I know I've never felt anything like it, but I sure as hell know where it came from — the lake, because you and Ty were in it, making like a two-headed waterbaby or whatever. You've called up a heap of power, Letha. Question the elders'll have is what are you going to do with it."

She waited a beat, and Letha finally sagged back into her chair, leaving Sylvia with a small feeling of gratification that she'd gotten Letha to back down again. She knelt in front of the chair. "So?"

"I've got to get him out of here, Sylvia. He has to go and I've been trying for the life of me to think of a way to get him to leave, but every time I go near him, I never get a chance to get it out. We end up — like you saw."

Letha shook her head like her situation was really very sad, and Sylvia ground her teeth. Like having a hot guy was such a hardship.

"Does he know why you're trying to get him to leave?"

"N…no. I don't feel comfortable talking about it." *With you.* Letha's eyes spoke of her distrust, and Sylvia had to look away from the pain of it. So it had come down to this. Letha didn't trust her, even though Sylvia had gone out of her way to mend fences, to give good advice. What Letha was planning to do went against all the things Sylvia had once thought of her friend. It was dishonest and cruel to use someone like that. As bad as anything the Valley elders had planned. Perhaps Letha deserved it.

"All right. If you won't talk to me, I'd best be going. I shouldn't be caught here or the elders will think I'm helping you." Sylvia could still hear her own bitterness. It would be a rainy day in hell before she ever thought of helping Letha Rivers again.

She clumped out the door and down the steps, kicking a stone with the toe of her boot so it clattered off the nearest metal statue. Damn art. Damn Letha Rivers. Damn Valley. There really wasn't much here to love.

Chapter 14

July passed in a flurry of activity for Letha. She sent the invitations out on heavy paper the color of clotted cream. With them went letters of introduction Mrs. H. had composed in lovely flowing script, and brochures prepared with the assistance of Martin Dietrich. The store was busy with the influx of summer people — children wanting ice cream and popsicles, so Letha had had to bring in a freezer; mothers who had run out of milk and bread — so the cash register kept ringing up.

Late in the month she'd received a few enquiries from the distant galleries, asking about the number of art pieces available in the show and whether they might be able to view the art before the actual date. Mrs. H. had advised her to decline the request and leave the viewings for the date of the show. It would be better to build some competition between the dealers.

Best of all was the way a few of the smaller paintings had started to sell, and she could tell by the way Billy Fitsch's girlfriend's mother kept eyeing a summer piece of Mrs. H.'s, that that painting would probably be gone before the summer was over. Letha had a few dollars in her pocket and that made her feel like she had finally become a real person, not a figment of the Valley's constantly fermenting rumors.

But the rumors were there. Sylvia had alluded to the fact everyone knew something had happened. Valley trucks slowed when they passed her store and Ty's cabin. The Valley folk, when they came into the store, dropped small hints, questions really. Had she seen Ty? How was her neighbor doing? She felt like she was waiting for the other shoe to drop, but that couldn't stop her happiness.

She was busy enough she managed to cool the torrid heat of her relationship with Ty and make it manageable. It was better that way; it would allow Ty to make his decision to leave, because he did seem to be thinking about something. She found him watching her whenever he thought she wasn't looking — that quiet assessing look that sent a tremor of guilt through her. She wasn't trying to get him to leave for her! At times she almost believed it.

Most nights they took the horses out together, or sat on his porch, then came together with such passion her body ached for him whenever they weren't together.

But she'd avoided the lake, even though Ty had tried to lure her in for a swim. The look in his eyes and the throb of her body told her what would happen, and there was already enough power in the lake. On those nights she wasn't with Ty that power left her so nervous she felt like she could jump right out of her too-sensitive skin. She didn't sleep those nights, as if it was the lake's punishment for not being with Ty. And there were the dreams.

The sensitivity of her skin was enough to send her back to Ty, but her feelings for him — the ones that went right back to her adolescence — were the main reason she smiled whenever she thought of him.

On an early August morning, with her coffee mug in hand, Letha settled at her computer table, intent on updating the website. With all the store traffic and her nights playing hooky — amongst other things — with Ty, she hadn't found the time to add photos of Mrs. H.'s paintings to the gallery on the site.

Luckily, Martin Dietrich had again sent her copies of his photos. When he'd come out to see Mrs. H.'s work and to give them a hand with the brochure, he'd immediately had to purchase one of her paintings. It hadn't been expected, nor had Mrs. H.'s insistence that Letha receive her commission.

Letha opened the digital files of the photos. Mrs. H. had told her which ones were her favorite paintings, but she'd left the selection for the website to Letha. God bless that woman. Her confidence in Letha helped Letha believe she could do this. Heck, she'd proved she could do just about anything — including taking a lover and defying the elders.

Best thing was, they didn't seem to know what to do about it.

The rest of the artwork on the site were mainly pieces depicting rural Valley life. She should keep with that theme, she supposed. She began making her selections — the cattle drive piece, the picnic painting, a collection of small pieces of wild flower forests, with cowboys lost among their roots. Mrs. H.'s perspectives were what gave her work its uniqueness.

She began the careful work of uploading the painting photos into the site, then added another pull-down menu that gave the names of the pieces and a short bio of the artist.

Mrs. H. as artist. It was wonderful to see how she'd changed. She was back painting again — much to Kris's thinly veiled disdain.

Letha sat back to assess the addition to the website. It didn't quite work, and she wasn't sure why. She brought up Mrs. H.'s paintings one by one, and then knew. The pieces she'd chosen might capture the essence of the Valley, but they didn't capture the essence of Mrs. H. or of this whole art show.

It took only a moment, and Letha added the photo of her favorite painting. The bright colors of umbrellas on a New York street popped out at her. It would shock the viewers. It was a picture she'd be part of someday.

§

Sitting within the aesthetic white walls of New York's Mythorpe Gallery Marta Zochenko could feel the shock like a mask on her face. It had nothing to do with the too-lifelike Shona sculptures in the centre of the room, nor the almost violent black and white African paintings on the walls that were the latest gallery exposition.

"Marta, darling, what is it?" Susan Klepper asked. She was thirty-five or so and slim, and with her honey-blonde hair and California-girl tan, just slightly less beautiful than Marta. It made her an acceptable friend. The gallery director quickly swiveled her chair around in her spaciously appointed office at one end of the gallery and pulled a bottle of Evian from the small fridge. "Water?"

Typical Susan. She thought water was the cure for everything. Marta shook her head, sleeking her long black hair off her face. She tapped her long, tapered finger on the offending piece of paper on Susan's desk.

"What it this, Susan?"

"This? Oh a funny little invitation from a woman who used to live in New York. She's a friend of the owner, and he asked me to look at it and decide if it was worth the trouble to send someone. Apparently, he once showed some of the woman's paintings." She shrugged, the single coil of her pony tail bobbing on her shoulders as she shoved the brochure in Marta's direction.

There it was again — the feeling that she'd just seen a ghost. The brochure — it was laid out in a rather amateurish fashion, and the paper wasn't the thickest nor the glossiest — but she supposed that should be expected when the photo on the front was of *cowboys*. Well not quite cow-boys. Ranchers, perhaps. A grubby dress on the woman standing in front of what looked like a log cabin, the man in a western-style shirt that cer-tainly didn't hide the breadth of his shoulders. Not folk you'd expect to see displayed on a brochure in one of the finest New York galleries to promote primitive art.

"Yum. Yum." Susan looked over Marta's shoulder. "A good looking guy. Sexy. Looks like he might have a thing for the woman, too."

It was as if those words allowed Marta to shift her gaze to the man's face. Dark hair falling across the forehead. She couldn't see the color of the eyes, but she knew they were green-brown, and even though his face was in silhouette she knew how his smile would quirk up in the corners.

"Ty Hunt. Dammit, it's Ty Hunt."

"Who's Ty Hunt?"

Marta smiled a slow smile as she remembered the man who'd been the best dressage trainer she'd ever ridden with, and whom she'd been de-termined to have train her in other athletic pursuits. But this. If this were Ty, then it was a complete slap in the face — something she damn well wouldn't stand for.

"My trainer — or I should say ex-trainer. He disappeared one day and I haven't seen him since. I'd heard he'd run off to Tennessee and there'd been accident." Her mind ticking over with a million possibilities, she looked up at Susan. "Can I borrow this?" she asked, waving the bro-chure.

Susan shrugged. "Sure. I'd just decided it wasn't worth the trip. Only two main artists from the look of it, and a darn long trip. He important to you?"

Marta picked up her Prada purse and stood, feeling the coldness of her jilted anger. Instead she said, "Darling, he was the best lay I never had — but then he went and got himself dead. I want to understand how a dead man has his picture taken. And maybe finally jump his bones."

She stalked out of the gallery, her mind already ticking over. Some-one was going to pay for this, and she already knew who. Her husband had been making a perfect ass of himself trying to keep her from the men she fancied, while it was fine for him to keep his little chippies on the side. This time he'd gone too far. She glanced at the brochure. When she'd dealt with Victor, she'd need to make plans to travel to some place with the ridiculous name of William's Lake.

§

Ty had never thought that paper was caustic until now, when this damned letter was virtually burning a hole in his pocket. It had taken over a month, but he had done it, and now the fruits of all his labors sat in one, crisply folded, 8½ by 11 piece of paper.

He looked down at himself: the ironed western shirt, the pressed jeans and — wonder of wonders — the gleaming new western boots on his feet. If Hauberk saw him, he likely wouldn't recognize him.

The fact he was dressed this way — what Ty would do for a woman — showed just how much this whole thing meant to him. He climbed up into the truck cab and headed out for the ranch knowing, even if no one else did, that this was make-or-break-it time.

He pulled the truck in next to Kris's truck and sat for a moment, calming the yammering of his heart. How to do this, he wasn't sure. Blurt it out, most likely, and then try to cajole Kris in to liking the idea.

He went up to the house and in the main door. As usual, since this whole thing with the art show, the house smelled of paint, even though his mom confined her art to her apartments upstairs.

Kris must really love this and the turpentine-rag chaser. He grinned. Not making this any easier.

"Anyone home?" he called.

No answer. He wandered into the kitchen and down the hall. The door to the office was closed. He opened it, and Kris glanced crossly up at him. "For God's sake, if you're coming in, get in and close the door."

He did. "Paint's getting to you, huh?"

"Paint. Paint brushes. Drops of paint. Canvas for paint. Paint itself. And then there're the lectures about paint, the discussions about painting, and the truly dramatic question of 'what shall I paint'." She sighed and raked her fingers back through her hair, in a gesture that told just how tired and frustrated his sister was.

"Sounds like Mom's got her old passion back."

She shook her head and worked her neck left and right. "And then some."

"Hard to live with."

"You don't know the half of it."

"I'd like to." There. Easier than he'd thought it was going to be.

Across the desk, Kris had gone still as a deer watching for danger. Ty grinned at her, aware of the growing alarm in Kris's face as she registered his get-up. He shrugged and got up and came around the desk to knead her shoulders. "You look like you could use some help around here. Maybe have someone to take some of the load."

She jerked out of his hands. "You sound like Dad used to — that I need a husband. I don't."

"Not talking about a husband. Your shoulders are like one massive muscle spasm. Now just shut up and let me work. I used it to do this when my riders were too tense before a show."

"Bet the women loved it." Her taunt didn't get to him.

"Bet they did," he agreed affably and tweaked her trapezius muscles so she groaned. "I've got good hands, they tell me."

"That's too much information." She pulled away from him again. "So what's this all about, Ty?"

"The same thing I've been trying to talk to you about for the last month. The same thing you've been avoiding me about."

"I haven't been avoiding you."

"That right?" He relinquished her muscles and sank into his father's chair and studied his sister. There were way too many lines around her eyes these days, and dark circles that spoke of not enough sleep. He'd seen the way she worked hard every day and the way she looked at the ranch. It was her heart and he loved that about her. The only question was whether she had a big enough heart to share.

He hauled out the paper in his pocket and handed it to her.

"What's this?" Suspicion on her face as she gingerly accepted what he held. He shrugged and waited as she cautiously unfolded the document. Read it. "I repeat. What the hell is this?"

"What? You can't read? The document confirms I've got a Canadian fund bank account at a bank in Williams Lake. It sets out the balance. I believe there's enough there for me to buy out the lien."

"No." She'd been shaking her head the whole time he spoke. Now she shook it once more, with feeling.

"Just 'no'. You expect me to accept that? I'm a Hunt, for God's sake. We're stubborn, remember?"

"Well, I don't need my older brother riding in for the rescue, thank you very much. We'll manage. We have up to now." She shoved the letter back across the desk at him so hard it fluttered to the floor before he could catch it, and all of his excitement turned into a cold, childish, determination that his ruddy sister was not going to win.

"You're being an idiot."

"Name calling won't get you what you want."

"I'm part owner of the ranch already."

"But you left, right? For ten friggin' years. And now you figure you can just waltz back in here and turn all our lives upside down and everyone will be so thrilled and thankful because the prodigal son has returned." Her words came out in a gush of bitterness and venom that almost took his breath away. How do you combat resentment that's been held under wraps for years? Ty took a deep breath.

"Kris, don't do this. I'm sorry I left you holding the bag, but I had to go and you know it."

"Had to? Had to?" Her voice rose in volume and her hands pushed her up from her desk. "Sure. You had to leave. You had to be free to live your life. You ran away and left Mom and me with Dad."

She was around the desk now; she stood over him, spittle on her lips as she lectured him, and Ty sank a little lower in his chair, knowing she needed to get this out, that his offer of money, of himself as a partner in the ranch, was like the lancing of a boil.

"You left and I chose to stay, like a good daughter. And you know the sick thing of it was that the whole time I stayed all I ever heard from Dad was how I could never be as good as you. I wasn't Ty the magnificent who could ride better, train better, swim farther, plan better. But I stayed!" She was shouting now, and the words were coming out hard, just like the tears that poured down her cheeks. She swiped at them, then groaned and turned away to the window that looked onto the system of corrals and paddocks.

"Damn you, Ty. You made me cry."

"It's a talent that comes from years of practice. When we were kids it was almost a game."

"Thanks a bunch. So I'm that easy."

"Not easy. Just predictable." He came to her and put an arm around her shoulders. "I'm sorry I left. I had to get out from under. We were going to kill each other if I stayed. But I'm sorry. It sounds like all that — whatever it was he used on me — he turned it on you twice as hard when I was gone. I should have realized." He squeezed her and felt the hitch of pain in her breathing.

"God, he wasn't an easy man."

"Nope."

"You're a lot like him."

"Hell, I am." He rounded on her, but her grin brought him up short. "Gotcha."

"Brat."

"Ah, the intelligent conversation of siblings."

"Kris, I was serious. I want to come back. I want to come home and be part of something real, something that's honest and living — not death. Not subterfuge."

She went back to the desk, the chair squealing as she sat down heavily. She blew her hair back off her face and faced him. "All right. Tell me what you've got in mind and I'll listen."

She held up her hand as he leapt in talking. "Whoa, there, bro." It stopped him cold. "I said I'd listen. It doesn't mean I'll agree to anything. Got that? I've got to do what I think it best for the ranch, and frankly, you're going to have to have one hell of an argument to make me think that having two owners can be good for this place."

He started talking, and right away Kris could see the passion on his face, the way his eyes glittered as he spoke and he leaned forward in his chair. He told her how he thought the ranch could branch out. Yes, they'd still keep producing the top cutting and reining horses, once they found a replacement for Peppy's Blood Red Brother, but there was another market to tap — the sport horse market — and he had just the commodity that that market sought. Hauberk. Kris couldn't contain her snort.

"You're so caught in your biases you can't even recognize a good horse when you see one, can you?"

The crossness in his voice came through, and she was a little sorry she'd shown what she thought. But a horse like Hauberk had no place on a working ranch. He was the kind of animal that you found in tanbark arenas, or with perfectly attired riders quaffing martinis or gin and tonic at the end of 'tiring' one-hour rides.

She hadn't realized she said it out loud until she saw Ty's face. He grabbed her wrist and stood. "You're going to eat your words."

He dragged her out to his truck and into the cab, then spun out of the driveway and down the road to the cabin. There he hauled her out and to the barn. "Wait here."

She didn't of course, following him into the barn where he put Hauberk into cross ties, brushed him, and threw a flat saddle on his back and a bridle into his face. At least the horse was mannered — unusually so, for a stud.

Ty unclipped the cross ties and spun around, then handed the reins to Kris. "Get on."

She looked up at the horse and back at Ty, frowning. "Why would I want to ride something like this? If I want to ride a tyro's horse, I'll go rent one at Spring Lake Guest Ranch."

He grabbed her and half threw her up onto the saddle until she hauled herself up and over. "My God, he's tall."

"I know. Every inch increases his value."

"You don't say." Kris said, struggling to find the stirrups. Shit, where were the stirrups? These little silver doo-ma-hickies just flopped around at the end of thin leather straps — not like the solid flaps of her reining saddle. Hell, the whole thing felt like nothing more than a kidney pad. She might as well ride bareback.

Ty took pity on her and helped her insert her boots into the stirrups. He caught Hauberk's reins and began to lead the horse at a walk, something that set Kris's pride on edge.

"I can ride, dammit! I'm not a kid at the pony rides."

"Oh? Show me." Ty released the stallion's reins.

Kris shortened them until she had contact with the horse's mouth, gave the light squeeze that would urge her horse, Strata, forward. The frigging horse leapt into a canter.

"Holy shit!" She half-jerked the reins, flopped in the saddle, caught her balance, and managed to get the horse back to a stop. This pansy saddle was less than useless at giving support. She had to use her legs more than she ever had before, and her bloody brother was laughing at her!

"He's pretty light in his commands. Just sort of 'think' canter and he'll go." He could barely get it out and Kris ground her teeth at his mirth. Smart ass.

But she tried what he'd said. She thought trot and the huge horse leapt forward. This time she was ready as the stallion lowered his head into a ground-eating trot, where each stride felt like it went on forever compared to the stride of the shorter-legged Quarter Horses she was used to.

She caught herself enjoying the feel, thought canter, and the horse rose under her, began to roll along the trail beside the lake. She thought flying change and Hauberk did. Kris brought the stallion back to a walk, tried a little side pass, then let the reins dangle.

It was still a hell of a long way off the ground. The horse was too big, but she had to give him marks for smoothness and responsive ride.

Maybe there was a market for this kind of horse. It did feel kind of like being king of the world, sitting so high off the ground. She arrived back at Ty.

"So?"

"So what?"

"So what did you think of my 'moose,' as you call him?"

She slid down to the ground and patted Hauberk's shoulder, glancing sideways at Ty to see his reaction. "Not bad. Not as light as some of the reining horses, but not bad."

It was his turn to snort and he did, reacting just as her brother always did when his favorite piece of horseflesh had been maligned. He started to argue, and that in itself gave a certain sense of satisfaction after him embarrassing her like that. He took way too much pleasure in it.

"Whoa, there, cowboy. I get what you're talking about. He's a good horse, aren't you, Hauberk?" Hauberk chewed his snaffle bit and snorted.

"So what do you think? If I bought in, I'd want to buy some mares that could pass the Warmblood inspection, or that are already licensed for breeding. Then I'd advertise Hauberk's services. When I bought him, I was looking for top bloodlines; he's passed his stallion tests. When they see what he can do, he'll be popular. I'll focus on getting that part of the business going. The other horses are yours. The cattle, well, we can work that part of the ranch together if you want. If that doesn't make sense, then propose something different. Bottom line is I want in, Kris. I want to come home. To stay."

Ty felt like a school boy coming up with excuses. Kris was silent, considering, and it was the hardest thing he'd ever done just to wait. When she finally looked at him, there was a small hint of mischief in her eyes, just like when she was a girl.

"This could really be to my advantage, you know. Especially given you owe me and all."

He looked heavenward — he owed far too many women these days. "The woman will never forget."

"No. I won't. Ty, you left once before and I thought I'd never forgive you. I'm putting myself way out on a limb with everything I hold dear. If you pull out again and expect your money back — well, it's just not going to happen. I mean, you can walk away, but the ranch — you know it's never a business that gives you big bucks in the bank."

"So if I buy in, it's for life. I get it."

"But what if we don't get along?"

"We will."

"Dammit, Ty. Don't be so cavalier with this. This is our lives, the ranch here. What's to keep you — me — us — from blowing up and never speaking to each other again?"

"The Valley. The ranch. Because both of us want this almost more than anything. Because everything we love is here, and we won't risk it."

Kristienne looked away to the lake. This was her world. It was the place she felt safe, because it was home. She hadn't wanted to admit it, but somehow, having Ty around made the place feel even more like home — even when they were bickering. She liked that, but it wasn't going to sway her totally.

"You said almost more than anything. What do you want more?"

"Letha."

A little tingle of ill-ease ran up Kris's back. "So this is about her. Does she know?"

"I've been waiting to get this sorted before I surprise her."

She faced him, knowing she should warn him, but damn it all, he was trying to be all big brotherly and come to her rescue, when he hadn't thought everything through. Somehow that made him a little more endearing, even though he had to pay the price for that mistake.

It was him that wanted the perfect life in the Valley, and him that was too blind to see how all the pieces didn't quite fit together. So the big strong cop in him wasn't infallible, and that was a bit of a comfort after the way their dad had always thrown Ty in her face. He had to grow up and see that not everything or everyone worked exactly like Ty Hunt expected. Hauberk tugged at the reins as he munched green grass from the verge of the drive.

"Tell you what. You tell Letha what you've got planned, and if everything works out, then you've got a deal. But you can't have the house. The ranch house is mine and Mom's."

He stuck out his hand. "Deal."

She nodded and looked back at the lake, letting a satisfied grin bloom across her lips. There was only one way Letha could react. Be interesting to see how her big brother coped with that.

Chapter 15

It took a week of preparations before Ty felt ready, and the Valley rested in a haze of long days of lingering summer. The mornings already came later, and showed the first signs of mist and dew that came with the early fall. He'd forgotten how swiftly the seasons changed here. The wild roses — so sweet — were now swelling rose hips that had the Valley children harvesting the crop for winter teas and jellies.

But Ty's focus wasn't on endings, it was on a single night and the life that would begin beyond. First he had to plan how to break the news. Not just on the porch, or out for a ride. It deserved something special because Letha was special, because this whole change of his life was special.

Each morning he woke and he felt alive. There was none of the sick dread that came with his old life. Cocooned in the red quilt, he lay with a woman in his arms whom he knew he honestly loved. There was the slow beat of their hearts and the slow pulse of life in the Valley. That was honest, too.

Whatever magic the Lake gave to this place, he was caught in it and he was happy.

He drove into Williams Lake and spent a day shopping, coming home with the makings for a special dinner. He'd bought a table cloth and wine glasses and serving plates for the meal he planned, and spent more than he'd intended for the propane barbeque that he knew was going to be too big for the cabin porch. Might as well show Letha his repertoire went beyond peanut butter and jam.

But most of his time in the town had been spent poking around the few jewelry stores. A ring was what he'd really wanted to buy, but he knew something like that would send Letha running for the hills. He'd contented himself with a gold chain and a single small diamond that was held in the petals of a wild rose.

Now he just had to pull this off.

It was the fifteenth of August. When he woke with Letha that morning he casually told he had something special planned for that evening. Letha, in her typical whimsical manner, had tried to pry the secret out of him, but he'd held her off, shushed her out the door, and set to work on his meal.

Beef, of course. A beautiful tenderloin he'd cajoled out of Kris, to much eyebrow raising and gentle teasing from Matt. He prepped it with garlic cloves set into the skin, added a pepper coating, then set it aside as he fought to make tiramisu, won the battle, and set it to chill.

Then there was the cabin to scrub and the table and chairs to drag out into the yard, so that they could be surrounded by everything he loved as he told her what he had planned. At six o'clock, with the food cooking and a flowered towel tied as an apron, he chuckled thinking what all his Bureau co-workers would think.

Yeah, he had it bad.

When Letha saw him, all she could think of was the way the darned towel showed off his slim hips and the breadth of his shoulders, and how, if anything, the flowers only emphasized his masculinity. And how he had to leave.

She stood at the end of the trail that, between Ty and herself, had been well worn into hard-packed earth. The sun had lowered toward the hills and sent long slanting shadows across the cabin's yard. It painted the white table cloth amber, and silhouetted the tall candles sitting in the middle of perfectly set dinnerware.

A nervous twinge ran through her and she considered just leaving, but as usual, Ty Hunt was like honey to a bee, and she stepped out into the clearing wanting to touch him. She was dressed in a calf-length, Indian cotton dress. The blue fabric set off her eyes, she knew, but somehow it seemed drab and unfitting for such a fine setting. Such a fine man.

Ty checked his watch. "Right on time, as usual."

She knew she was early, but the lake's pulse had been buzzing in her so hard all day, she'd had a hard time leaving this morning and a harder time not coming back, even though Ty had made her promise she wouldn't.

"You've gone to a lot of trouble," her mouth was dry and she felt sweat between her breasts. "What gives?"

Ty caught her hands and pulled her to him. "Only a dinner for my favorite Consort of Spring. I thought it was time to feed you again, but I didn't want to have to drive all the way into town to do it."

"Don't like driving?"

"Don't like making out in a truck with a gear box between the seats. It can be dangerous, and you know me — avoid danger like the plague."

"Ah." She loosed herself to survey the table, and Ty felt the loss of her in his arms. "This looks really nice. I didn't know you *had* a table cloth."

God, she was lovely with the apricot light on her skin, the delicate features. He loved the way her mouth quirked as if she's accidentally swallowed a joke, and the way her soft hair was an omnipresent halo around her face. Most of all, he loved the way she thought long and hard about things and was learning that her opinions had value. The combination left him feeling helpless in the face of his feelings. He had to touch her.

"There's lots you don't know about me. Did you know I've taken up studying magic?" He turned her to face him and saw the quick rise of her brow.

"Really?"

"Yup. Had to. Self-defense in the face of a woman who's bewitching me." He leaned down, and the sweet scent of mint and roses filled his nostrils as she answered his kiss. It took his breath away, and really all he wanted to do was sweep her into the cabin and bed, but this wasn't the time. He pulled back.

She looked up at him, fighting the full feeling in her chest, and managed to pull herself back together in the face of the heat he raised in her. "You are one quick study, mister. Or should I call you the great Hunter?"

"Am I really?"

She gave him an assessing leer. "Really."

"Aw, shucks, Ma'am, now you've gone and got me all excited. How do you expect me to do my tricks like this?"

"I thought you did your best work then."

"Well I do, but I wanted to show you my other magic." He nodded at the grill, where the heavenly odor of searing juices escaped the barbecue top. "May I offer you a glass of wine, Ma'am?"

He poured them both a glass, then tinked glasses together. "To a memorable evening."

When he held her chair for her, she felt like a lady, sat and looked at the table settings, at his back as he checked the grill. The air still carried the heat of the day, and a breeze brushed it soft across her skin.

She could love this man. Did love him, and the fact he would do this for her. No one ever had before. Since the Ceremony so many years before, she had had to deal with others' expectations and the tasks they set her. This attention to her needs was sort of overwhelming.

He came out of the cabin with two plates and set one before her. Salad shapes she'd never seen before. Sliced strawberries — and shouldn't they be in dessert, not a salad? Nuts — were those pecans?

Ty settled himself across from her and picked up his wine glass again, with a look of desire in his eyes so strong it almost left her weak. "To you."

"To the cook." She looked down at her plate. "I've never seen salad like this before."

"You'll like it. It's baby greens in a light apple dressing, and the pecans are smoked." He poked a forkful of lettuce and a strawberry and held it out for her to try. It should have felt childish — she could eat her own food — but with the want in Ty's eyes, it was one of the most sensual things she'd ever experienced. The way his fork slipped into her mouth, the closing of her lips, the slip of the tines away from her, and his gaze on her — it was enough to make her forget to even taste the food.

But she did, and nodded. "Good. Different, but good." She picked up her own fork. "That's sort of how I figure the outside world is. Yeah, there are hard things, but mostly it's different, but good. Right?"

Ty nodded around the food. She had his attention. Now was the time to remind him he had to go. To get him to set a date so the darkness wouldn't come.

"So you look like the summer has been good for you."

He smiled at her. "The summer and you."

She felt the color slide up her neck and knew he saw it, smiled. "I was talking about your back and leg. It doesn't seem to be bothering you as much as it did. You're almost all healed."

"Surprising what the right exercise will do. I've realized that was what I needed. I think it's something a man could get used to."

She nodded and fished around for a strawberry. "I'm worried about you, Ty. I don't want anything to happen. Have you heard any more from your job?"

"My job?" He set his fork down, and a small frown creased his forehead. As if to cover confusion, he got up and took their salad plates away, came back with a platter of baby potatoes smothered in butter and fresh chives, and another of asparagus in home-made hollandaise. Then he busied himself at the barbecue, pulling the tenderloin from the grill and placing it on a wooden board to slice.

Damn, he hadn't realized he'd be so nervous about this, and her asking about his job just made it harder. He'd put off phoning Samuels since the banking process went through, and hadn't come clean with Samuels about his intentions. Better to just get it out, and then he and Letha could discuss what it really meant — the commitment he was ready to make.

He touched the necklace box in his pocket, then brought the meat to the table, carved, and frowned at the color; the meat wasn't as rare as he preferred. "How much would you like?" He made his voice casual.

In truth, her stomach felt so tied up in knots she didn't know if she could keep anything down. There was something about him. A softness under the hard surface of him. All this attention to a perfect, romantic evening, the whole white-table-cloth-and-candles thing of it. It made her feel special and especially nervous.

"Just a slice, please."

"Just a slice?! After I've labored all day?"

"Two, then." How she was going to eat all that was beyond her, but she'd give it a try. She forced a smile on her face as she placed a few potatoes and asparagus on her plate. "It looks great."

"So do you. Good enough to eat." The wink of promise he gave her sent a rush of heat through her. "Try it." He motioned with his fork at her meal.

She did, and nodded her appreciation at the flood of flavor from the meat. "Really good."

"I was afraid I'd overdone it."

"It's perfect."

"Spoken like a confirmed well-done fan." OK. Make it light, but get it done. His stomach did a little flip flop, because this was just about the most dangerous thing he'd ever done in his life. "So I did something momentous this summer."

"Really? I thought you lay around, played with that horse, and distracted me from my work."

He took his cue from her light banter. If that was what made her feel comfortable, than that was how he would do this. "Well, those and other things. Pretty momentous, then — I mean the fact that I've fallen in love."

She lowered her fork, the piece of meat untouched, and her gaze flickered like she was seeking cover. OK. Slower then. Light and slow and loving, like the way they moved together until they were both overcome.

"I can't believe I left you behind all those years ago."

"I was thirteen, Ty."

"Well then, I can't understand why I didn't come back sooner."

She looked so uncertain, pale skin — if anything, paler.

"Letha?"

She looked up at him, and her eyes were filled with tears so the candlelight seemed to fill them with a golden light. "But you came back and… and… it terrifies me how I feel, Ty. Like I'm going to burst. I didn't want this to happen."

He caught her hand — cold, cold fingers. "But it did, and it's wonderful, and there's so much more." He came around the table to place a soft kiss on her cheek. "Sometimes life just gives gifts. Unexpected ones."

She nodded and he returned to his seat. "I had a meeting with Kris the other day. We were talking about the ranch."

Letha felt the lump in her chest relax at the change in topic. How he felt for her was one thing, but when he told her he'd fallen in love she'd nearly blurted out how she'd go with him if he'd just leave — run and be safe. She nodded, only half following what he was saying.

Then something he said caught her attention. "So I made her an offer. I told her that I'd be prepared to get the ranch out of financial hock if she'd let me stay and be part of it. I thought we could stand Hauberk at stud, and maybe start a small breeding program. We could stay here in the cabin and eventually build a larger house. Kris suggested I talk it over with you." *We.* He said 'we,' and she knew it wasn't Kris and him he was talking about.

Letha put her fork down and realized the sun had fallen below the hills. The wind off the lake was cold, and carried a promise of fall.

She wanted to ask him to repeat what he'd said, but she knew she hadn't misheard. No! a part of her screamed. This can't be happening. It's not fair! Then, suddenly she felt wooden, empty, as she looked at this man she thought she loved. His eyes might say he loved her, but there was darkness there — the same darkness she'd seen in far too many dreams, and she had to get away.

Ty Hunt hadn't fallen in love with her — he'd been seduced by the Valley. He'd turned into one of the Valley elders, intent on trapping her here.

§

Sylvia sat at the back of the room in the Valley's Council of Elders meeting and tried to deal with the chalk dust that was tickling her throat.

She regretted again that she'd ever become part of this. She was a friggin' flunky — a minion, no less, and she didn't enjoy it, but there were some things that just had to be done, didn't they.

For the elders, she was the go-to girl, and that kept her in their favor. At least that was something.

The student desks in the Valley's one room school house had been pushed into a ragged circle around the walls, decorated with out-of-date maps of the world and student art projects. A small library and student cubbyholes for belongings filled the back of the room. The air stank of student's peanut butter sandwiches left in the garbage from lunch and that damned chalk dust.

The elders themselves looked silly, mushed into the children's desks discussing the fate of the woman who was Consort to Spring. Murphy Rogers had his legs stuck a mile out, trying to ease the pressure on his knees from the too-small desk. Mrs. Zigheld looked like a dumpling pressed into the small space between the chair back and the desk proper. Served her right, given what she was suggesting.

"I tell you, we've let this go on too long. We oughta do somethin'. Make her marry one of our own," Mrs. Zigheld said, her voice carrying over the others. At Mrs. Zigheld's back, Harry Zigheld nodded.

The room had become a bit of bedlam after the initial structured discussions. No one had a clear idea what to do, when the lake had clearly reacted to the Consort's relationship with a man. It hadn't happened like this before—at least not within living memory. And it sure as hell hadn't happened with a man who wasn't Valley.

That was the kicker. Everyone had suspected it when the Spring prolonged, but everyone hoped it was simply a fling. It was the cumulative knowledge over the past month that had shown this was damned serious and required action. But now the question was what.

"We cannot allow Letha Rivers to be taken. Fine that she's fallen for a man. About time, if you ask me. If she gets pregnant, all the better for us. But the main issue is, he's not from here, and we can't risk her leaving. We need to keep her secure until Ty Hunt leaves."

Sylvia stirred, and the image of a bee to honey came to mind. Actually, it was more like the frantic need of birds to mate — they were both drawn to each other. Given the way Ty had seemed around Letha, she wasn't sure he was going to leave anytime soon.

"I agree we need to make sure she doesn't leave, but I think we've got a larger question here. What the heck has happened? Yeah, I knew something had happened the way the animals were acting, but I don't know about you, but this last thing — whatever it was — was like a shot to the heart. It was like everything stopped for a moment that day," Maggie Rogers said, looking around to the others who nodded.

It had felt like that. Sylvia could tell them exactly when that tremor had run through her and all the air had seemed sucked from her lungs — when two naked bodies had come together like a prayer in the midst of Shelter Lake.

She'd sat there feeling jealous when she saw them swimming together. It had turned to anger when the tremor stopped. Not that Ty was the man of her dreams, but it should have been her, dammit. She should have been the Consort.

"Has anyone gone through the old books to see if this has happened before?" She knew by the silence that her question was considered inappropriate, but she didn't really care. She wanted to know, even if they didn't. She wanted access to those books, and the only way to get the elders to unlock them was to pose a question that needed answering.

The elders looked at each other. Mrs. Rivers shook her head. "I'm sorry. Truly I am. I thought I had my daughter under control."

Mrs. Zigheld harrumphed. "Under control. So under control we finally had to do what Sylvia said, and finance that store so we could keep her tied down. And look how well *that's* worked out." She sent a glare in Sylvia's direction. Spending the money for the store had been a serious point of contention in the Valley. It had been a problem getting the elders to agree that they would not spill the beans to Letha. The old busy-bodies would have just loved to lord it over the Consort, but finally they'd agreed.

"Sylvia's right. We need to understand what's going on with the lake," Murphy Rogers said.

"Fine. Have her do her research, but that doesn't deal with the fact that Letha Rivers could up and leave any time."

And they didn't know the half of it. Sylvia hadn't told them about Letha's dinner in town. She'd found, growing up in Valley life, that there were some things that were just better kept to one's self. A bit of power in information.

"So what do we do? Make her go home? Close the store, and then hold her in her room, where she should still be?" Maggie, this time. Her round face looked from face to face. There was a lot of nodding.

"That's not the best way to deal with this. The store — it has actually been a success. Believe it or not, it's started to make money, and I suspect this art thing might not have been as bad an idea as we all thought." Sylvia held up her hand at the objections muttered around the room. Sometimes she could just scream at the old-fashioned ideas represented by these people. They'd swat a fly with an elephant to keep things the same — even if the elephant would eventually trample them. She waited until the murmurs had quieted down, then waited for Murphy Rogers' nod to continue.

"Sometimes there are simpler ways of dealing with a problem. You're all focused on controlling Letha, and I agree that she's out of control right now. So how to fix this. Not by confronting Letha, I think. You take her prisoner and you watch — Ty'll try to rescue her. Then try and tear them apart. No, the better way is to deal with Ty. You all remember him."

"Beat up my boy," Mrs. Zigheld muttered. Harry's frown reminded Sylvia of a weasel.

"He's an outsider, just like all the Hunts."

"He came here as a baby and grew up here."

"He went away."

"He came back, and he's involved with the Consort," Sylvia cut in, amazed at how they could focus on bickering about facts that everyone knew. She had their attention, and it gave her a sense of satisfaction that was enough to quell the hard core of guilt she felt at what she was going to do. "Now, I wouldn't have any problem if he was going to just have a fling, or if he was going to stay, but that's not the way it is. He cares about Letha, and there's something about him and Letha that's caused the lake's reaction. Again, I wouldn't have a problem with that if he was going to stay. But he's not. So the question is, 'how do we convince Ty Hunt that our Consort is not for him'." She looked around the room and realized for once they were really listening to her. Because she made sense, of course — instead of pointless bickering.

And the nice thing was, she held the key to this whole thing.

"How?" Maggie Rogers asked.

"Yes, how?" Mrs. Zigheld's voice snapped.

Sylvia couldn't help but have a slow smile as she answered the question in all their eyes.

"Ty Hunt's an honest man, and he values honesty above all else. So we use that. We tell Ty the truth. We tell him that Letha planned their whole courtship — she only seduced him so he'd take her away."

§

Letha couldn't move from her place by the candle-lit table. She felt like she was going to be sick at the sight of the excitement in Ty's eyes. He wanted to stay. He somehow didn't know her well enough, and thought that was what they should do. All the love she felt for this man clenched up like a tight fist in her belly and it hurt her — bad.

"You're awfully quiet, Leth. What do you say? A good idea, me staying? We can see where this whole thing takes us." He rubbed her fingers, as if trying to bring heat to them.

She swallowed down bile as the breeze made the candles gutter and spit. "You'll be a sitting duck." The words were out of her mouth before she could think.

All of his pride and pleasure leached out of him. Not the response he'd been expecting, and the food he'd eaten sat, a hard lump, in his belly. "I'll be with you."

"Ty, you told me they nearly killed you once. That there was danger of them finding you here. You can't stay here. You can't." Letha shook her head, and all her fear coalesced. She had to make him understand. She stood, went around to him, and kissed him. "Ty, for me. You have to go! We'll both go."

"Baby, I'm sorry." He stood, and his strong, warm arms crushed her to his chest. "I know you're concerned, but if a man can't have a home to fight for — well, what else is there? I've pushed this too far, too fast, but I had to strike while the iron was hot with Kris, you know?"

He looked down at her with a gentle concern on his face that was just too darn similar to all the condescending looks she'd received in the Valley over the years. It made her angry, but more than anything it left her with a feeling of defeat. She'd thought Ty was different. Instead, he was just going to trap her in a different way, and that thought broke her heart.

She did love him, but this decision — it went against everything she'd had planned, and it made the darkness of her dreams somehow much clearer. It wasn't darkness to the Valley. She'd been wrong there. It was a long winter for herself. She had fallen for a man who would bring *her* only coldness and death. She had to pull away and protect herself.

But in the warm circle of his arms, she couldn't move.

"Ty, I'm sorry I can't be excited, when I know you are. But this — it only makes me afraid — for you."

Her voice sounded so faint, and the pools of her eyes had only deepened as if the light that was Letha had sunk deep within. It didn't make sense, the way she shivered in his arms, when all he wanted to do was love her, live with her, protect her.

"Letha, sweetheart, I'm sorry I sprang this on you like this." He kissed her hair, smoothed it back from her face.

"I guess I wasn't thinking straight. I didn't know you were so afraid." Kissed her forehead and felt her tremble. Damn it, he was an idiot. How could he have missed this?

"You tried to tell me you were afraid, didn't you? A bunch of times, and I just plumb didn't notice. Ah, babe, I'm so sorry." His lips slid down her face, tasting the first tear as it slid down her cheek. "Ah, God, Letha, I'm a damn fool. We don't need to talk about this now. There are so many better things to do."

He scanned the ruins of his dinner and contained his sigh. So much for good intentions. Letha Rivers, the woman he might never fully understand, but he seriously wanted to try.

"Look, let's get this mess put away so we don't attract bears, and then let's just enjoy the evening — take a walk, be with each other, do what comes naturally. We can have dessert later." He winked at her and saw her struggle to smile in return.

So they carried the platters and their half-full plates into the cabin, blew out the candles, and Ty caught her hand. He twined her fingers in his and led her along the lake shore. Maybe he should toss her in and let the lake do its magic, but the pained look on her face held him back.

The crickets hummed a steady rhythm in dry grass back from the lake. Small things rustled there. The water rippled along the shore, and the mint-scented breeze caught in the willow leaves and reeds. It was a small night song, but it didn't fill the silence that seemed to rest between them.

"I love the nights here."

"Yes."

"It's peaceful."

She glanced up at him as if to ask what peace he was talking of, when he'd somehow blown a serious hole in their relationship. "I suppose it is. Aren't there places like this outside?"

"Letha, I don't think we should talk about this now. I think we should just be." She nodded, but the breeze caught her hair and she freed her hand to brush it from her face, then crossed her arms, effectively cutting him off from her. He tried not to dwell on it, kept walking beside her with a canyon of space between them. When she shivered, he put his arm around her.

"You're freezing. Let's head back."

"I'm okay. Really." She tried to shrug him off, but dammit, he wasn't going to let her go. Not this easily. He'd caused the wound. He'd fix it. *Keep it light*, he admonished.

"That tiramisu of mine — I'm going to need you to tell me whether it's as good as what we had at the Stampede Grill."

It was like coming out of a daze, when she looked at him, tried to focus on his words. "It was good, yes."

"Well I slaved over making one today, so hopefully I matched it."

"Uh huh."

"So you'll be the judge."

She was swimming in deep water, and it felt like drowning. She knew he was trying to give her time, space to get used to his idea, but all she'd felt since he told her was cold. Freezing, and she knew it was part fear for him, but also for her, and she hated that fact.

"I'll try," she managed to answer. "But the Stampede Grill's was pretty good."

"So I noticed."

"What's that supposed to mean?" Play along. Keep it light. This she could do.

"I mean you ate most of it, greedy girl."

"Greedy! We both helped ourselves."

"So you say. But all that tiramisu, I think it settled on all my favorite parts of you — like here." He patted her butt. "And here." His fingers slid up her side, tickling, and she squealed, sprang away, and he was after her in a flash, catching her by the cabin in a long deep kiss.

Then he was hauling her after him into the cabin, jostling each other to get free of their clothes. Falling on the bed and reaching for each other, but it wasn't the same, wasn't the same. There wasn't the ardor in her eyes; instead there was sorrow, and Letha sinking away. Her hands knew what he liked, but there was none of the keen inventiveness or the sensitivity to his feelings. She didn't react in the same ways to his touch, and the knowledge tore at him, made the act of loving this woman so much more important.

"Don't pull away," he said as he moved inside her, as their eyes met, but didn't hold. Her little gasps said she still felt him, was with him in the act, but she was distant, wooden.

He'd missed something — something deep and wrong, and he had to find a way to fix it.

He wanted to ask her, to understand, because her hurt drove a deep pain into his heart that he didn't think he could deal with. He slowed, but

Letha caught his hips in her hands, pulled him into her, thrust up to meet him, even as she turned her head away.

The movement caught his breath. Just be now, be in this moment. He somehow knew there might never be another. He thrust deeper and heard her moan. Deeper, and perhaps things would heal. Deeper, and at least he might find forgetfulness for a while.

Chapter 16

According to the sayings of Victor Zochenko, the trouble with women was that they were too predictable. A woman, like Marta, for instance, was driven by the need to keep seeking what behavioral anthropologists called 'the best provider'. She wanted to sample other possible providers, and it was his job to keep reminding her that he was, and would continue to be, 'the best' she would find. Blasted woman might be a whore, but she was hell on wheels between the sheets, and for that he'd keep her around.

Of course, it didn't stop him from taking his latest model, Freddi, to the Cayman's with him and boffing her until he was almost sore. A man's prerogative was to spread his seed around. Survival of the fittest and all that — like the Discovery Channel said.

Dressed in his Armani trousers and leather jacket, he swept into the foyer of his Central Park townhouse, leaving the door open for the staff to bring in his bags.

"Marta, I'm home!" The staircase swept upward, empty. She should be down here waiting for him. So should the staff, with a martini in hand, but the stillness of the house was almost unnerving. "Marta!"

"In here."

A stiff voice from the library that set the little hairs on his neck on end. It was Marta's fighting voice, and damn-it-all-to-hell, he was in no mood to fight, because he'd just spent the last five days fighting with his investors in the Caymans in order to protect his business interests. Seemed someone had gotten wind of the Federal case against him and now everyone was nervous. Of course, that was until he assured them that witnesses had been taken care of.

Let Marta stew in whatever juices had her angry. It would make her even hotter when he wanted her tonight. He headed up the stairs for his bedroom, focused on getting a shower and some clean clothes, and maybe wiping Freddi's last kisses off his neck.

He'd barely sluiced off the herb-scented soap in the green, Italian-tiled shower and wrapped a towel around his waist when Marta pushed open the bathroom door. He ignored her as he finished toweling off and combed his graying black hair back from his brow and sculpted features. Yes, there might be a few more wrinkles around the eyes, but he'd traded youth for power.

Besides, he had been a powerfully built man to start with. Years of heavy lifting in the old country had given him well-developed shoulders and torso, and he wasn't going to let that go. Let the body go and it was a sure sign to competitors that he was ready to be pushed aside. But no one was going to try anything like that any time soon. His enemies were swiftly eliminated.

"You look like you swallowed a lemon," he said to Marta's reflection in the mirror as he studied his features. Not bad. Still a Slavic warrior women flocked to.

She leaned her tall frame against the door, her high cheekbones seeming even higher with her brows arched in disapproval. Her lips — once her main selling feature as a model — were pressed in a hard line.

"You've been meddling again." She pushed off from the door and came to him, placed her long narrow palm on his bare chest in a gesture he could choose to think was suggestive — but not with that look in her eyes. "I don't appreciate it."

"Meddling?"

She leaned against the edge of the counter and crossed her arms. "You know damn well what I'm talking about. Those pet veterinarians of yours got to my new mare."

Victor's brain ticked over, clicked into what she was talking about — one more little operation in the world of Victor Zochenko's endeavors. He ran his electric razor over his chin and knew the noise grated on Marta by the way she stiffened. Usually it chased her away. This time it didn't work. So she was really pissed.

When he was done, he wiped his face, patted on the light aftershave with the ridiculous name of 'SNOW' that he knew turned her on, and glanced at his wife. "So what were you saying?"

"Damn it, Victor. You did it again — used one of my horses as a mule."

Well, aside from the fact that he considered most anything of the equine species as a mule in one way or another — regardless of how much the animal cost him — now at least he knew what she was pissed about. Not Freddi, at least.

"Is that what's got your ass in a knot? Sure, I used the mare. It was too good an opportunity to get the diamonds brought over from Antwerp. The Europeans had to pay me somehow." He shrugged and walked past her to his closet.

"Well, the mare fucking near died, Victor. Aborted the fetus, too. As it is, my vets tell me she's probably sterile from the infection. That's a quarter of a million dollar animal good for nothing but riding."

"So we write it off. A tax loss." He pulled on a silk shirt and jeans, shrugged.

"Write it off…." He heard the hiss in her voice. She stepped up to him, slapped him, and pushed something at his face before he could react. Usually any act of aggression on Marta's part was a cue that she really needed to get laid. "So was Ty Hunt another something you just wrote off?"

The question stopped him. Ty Hunt. A name he hadn't thought of since the hit in Tennessee erased the State Attorney's main witness and made a big problem go away. "Ty Hunt was killed in an unfortunate hunting accident."

"Well that's fucking interesting Victor, because for a dead man, he's looking remarkably well."

Again she waved something in his face, and anger snapped in his belly. He grabbed her wrist. "What the hell are you ranting about?"

"It's him. Ty Hunt. In some stupid little art brochure. What the hell's your game, Victor? Was his 'death' just a way to get him out of my sight? Was I so infatuated you'd finally noticed you might have to pay attention to me, other than fucking me once a month?"

He grabbed the piece of paper from her, stared at the brochure cover, and suddenly the house seemed inordinately cold. *Letha's Store and Artwork Offers The Finest in Primitive Art.* The photo, though muddied in reproduction, was clear. A woman — probably this 'Letha' — and Ty Hunt.

A shiver of apprehension went up Victor's spine. All his smoothing in the Caymans had just been blown away — like Ty Hunt should have been.

§

The morning after the disastrous dinner, Letha slipped away at dawn. She suspected Ty had been awake because his breathing had changed, but he hadn't tried to stop her. That in itself spoke of just how deeply their problem ran.

Back at the safety of her cabin, she made coffee and collapsed on the porch with a huge mug for company. It really wasn't wise to drink so much caffeine without eating, but her belly felt tender and unready for food. Actually, being away from Ty, her whole body felt tender and wanting.

The morning sun rose, bringing mist from the lake and turning it golden. The vapors spun onto shore in the breeze so that she sat in a mystical land, could almost feel the melody of the lake. Without Ty around, it set her teeth on edge and her fingers tap-tap-tapping at the arm of her chair. Roscoe fluttered down and grabbed the spirit catcher, releasing it to tap on the cabin wall in a syncopated rhythm.

It made her head hurt, but she was too tired and distraught to deal with it.

It had all gone bad, and it was her fault. Ty had been excited, happy, loving, and she — she'd ruined it by pushing him too hard to leave and then reacting so strongly to the news he'd decided to stay. *But he'd decided to stay.*

Just thinking it made her stomach cramp. He'd fallen to the magic of the Lake. All the summer people said it was there. They loved the hints of something more than normal about the lake and that there was someone who was tied to the land. *They* figured it was romantic and old-fashioned. The new-agers even liked to boast they 'felt' something special about the place.

She snorted, disturbing Roscoe's pecking. "Let them try living with it."

But Ty — he'd decided to stay for her, damn him. He'd just assumed she would want to stay with him, and that was the end of the story. Had he completely forgotten how she felt? All the times as a kid he'd caught her crying about being trapped. She shook her head.

He'd said he'd fallen in love with her, and yet he couldn't remember the most fundamental thing about her. That hurt most of all, because she knew she'd fallen for him too. It was more than a crush. More than lust or the fling Sylvia had suggested. She'd fallen lock, stock, and barrel over the guy.

She leaned forward and placed her head in her hands. "What am I going to do, buddy?" she asked the raven. Roscoe cocked a coal black eye at her and croaked, like two rocks cracked together. She knew what that felt like.

Her heart hurt with it. Her body ached with it.

"Well, ain't this a fine kettle of fish."

She had to do something. Move. Run, ride, scream — something. She stood and looked toward the lake. A quartet of Canada geese floated past in the mist, like black and white ghosts.

Feed Inca. She did. She went into the store, but the place was spotless from work the day before to keep her mind from straying to her pending dinner with Ty. How much she'd looked forward to it.

Again that hurt, like a punch to the gut.

She couldn't stay inside. It was like a prison cell. The whole Valley was a prison cell, and Ty Hunt had volunteered to be her keeper.

Slamming out the front door and down the stairs, she started running down the trail southward along the lake front. Away from the cabin, away from Ty, if she just kept going she could be on the road shortly and thumb a ride with a logging truck. They knew her. They'd stop.

She should have done it before, shouldn't she, but she was too bloody timid. Angry, but unable to focus her anger to get herself out of this darned Valley.

Well, she'd learned how to put plans to action. Just turn right at the next tree and cut through the woods. There were logging trucks and summer people coming all the time. She could do this.

She came to the tree and her legs stopped.

It's just a short run, and she'd be gone. Listening, she could hear the down-gear of engine brakes needed by a truck hauling a load of logs.

Just go. Just leave.

But Ty.

Damn it, why did she feel like she was breaking in two? It wasn't fair. It wasn't fair.

But Sylvia had said no life was fair and all lives were made of choices. Stay or run, she had to choose.

How do you choose between the two parts of your dream? Letha spun on her heel and plunged into the lake.

She was strangling with the choice, strangling in her dress. She tore it off, kicked off her shoes and didn't care if they floated away. Just... do something.

She dove deep and swam out into the golden mist. It was soft on her face, seemed to rime her arms with a soft glow. The water slicked her skin, and the feel of it was like a lover's hands, Ty's hands.

She swam faster, fighting to outrun the feeling, fighting to be free, fighting to find exhaustion so her turmoil would cease. In the middle of the lake she stopped, hung in the water. It wasn't working. Would never work.

"Take it back," she whispered futilely into the mist, and she realized she was crying because she knew her confusion and her love were wholly hers — not the lake's fault — just as surely as she knew she could never wholly leave the Valley as long as Ty was in it.

§

Hauberk snorted when the woman came to the barn door, and for a moment Ty was heartened by the feminine shadow on the wall. The necklace was still in his pocket and he hoped maybe the right moment to give it would present itself today. Then he glanced over his shoulder from brushing the stallion's legs and realized who had come.

"Sylvia, hi." For a moment he resented her and the fact she wasn't Letha.

"You riding out today?" Sylvia quirked her trademark ironic grin and stepped into the barn, her blonde hair askew on her head as if she had slept badly on it. There were shadows under her eyes, though she looked at him appraisingly.

"That's the plan." Ty straightened and eased his back. Contrary to Letha's assessment it was still not totally healed, but a darn sight better. Working with Hauberk had been a balm he needed after last night and after Letha snuck out this morning. Something had kept him from speaking to her, even though every part of him had wanted to pull her into his arms and kiss her until things were right between them again. But the kisses hadn't worked last night.

Nope. Letha needed to work things out in her own way, and then maybe they could talk about it and reach some sort of agreement. She needed space and he had rushed in and filled it last night. He'd just been too intense. This time he'd give her space.

"There something I can do for you?" Ty asked, realizing he'd been lost in his thoughts too long again. It was a cycle that had recurred all morning.

He slipped the English saddle off the block of wood on the wall and lifted it onto Hauberk's back. Sylvia stood there, looking like she was waiting for something — or deciding.

She stepped up to Hauberk, patted his neck, and the stallion nosed her hand. "He's a fine animal, Ty. Just like you're a fine man."

That was an odd statement coming from Sylvia. He'd hardly spoken with her since he'd come back to the Valley and they'd never been that close. Since his return she'd been tending to her business, he supposed, and he'd — well, he'd been busy with Letha. He glanced sideways at her as he reached under Hauberk for the girth strap and buckled it tight. And waited, wondering where Sylvia was heading.

"Warmblood, right?"

"Yeah. Top European bloodlines. Bought him as a colt and took him through the stallion approval tests. He scored as high as any stud in Europe — much to the tester's surprise."

"He must be worth a mint."

"More than I could afford on my wages."

"You going to stand him at stud?"

"That's the plan — if everything works out." He grabbed his bridle, but then paused. "Syl, I don't mean to be rude, but is there a reason you dropped by?"

He saw the brief look of consternation at his bluntness, and then her features went smooth. She inhaled and he saw all the tell-tales — the squaring shoulders, the resolve in her eyes — that whatever she'd come to say was about to come out.

"I wanted to talk about Letha."

His stomach did a nose dive. He should have expected it, given the day he was having and the fact that Letha Rivers was the one person he didn't want to talk about right now. Still…. "What about her?"

Sylvia settled a hip on the lip of a grain bin as if she were planning on being here a while, and Ty sighed inwardly, knowing his planned escape to the hills was going to, at best, be delayed.

"Ty, I know you've spent a lot of time with her over the summer. The rumor is you've fallen for her pretty hard."

He was about to protest that this was none of her business, but she stopped him with a raised hand. "Just let me finish, all right. I know this is your business, but I'm here because I don't like to see people make choices without all the facts. Right? People need to make informed decisions. Like having all the evidence before you make an arrest, right?"

Her words set his teeth on edge. His law enforcement days were soon to be over. He'd be what he'd always wanted to be — a horseman. He hung the bridle back on its peg and settled his back to Hauberk. "What're you talking about?"

"About Letha." Her gaze dropped from him, but then she met his eyes. "Now I'm telling you this because I don't want to see anyone get hurt. As I said, from what I hear, you're serious about Letha, and in a relationship, honesty is important. I think that's fair, don't you?"

Okay, now she was starting to make him nervous. He needed to move, not stand here in the barn. He went to the barn door and looked out at the lake. "So what are you worried about. I haven't lied to Letha. I wouldn't. And she's the most honest person I've ever met."

Her sigh made his shoulders tense like he was expecting a blow.

"I would have agreed with you at the start of the summer. Letha's always worn her emotions on her sleeve."

Ty thought of the pain on Letha's face last night, the tears in her eyes. Those were honest. He could read honest. "She still does."

"But she doesn't, Ty."

That spun him around, his throat clogged with protests waiting to come out, but she waved him off again.

"That's what I came to talk to you about. Before you came to the Valley all Letha could think about was running away from here. You remember how she was after the ceremony. Well, she's no better now. She doesn't know it, but the elders financed her store to keep her occupied until they could get her married off and settled. It was planned for this summer. But then you came. All Letha could talk about was you and how you weren't from here, but it wasn't about love or anything. It was about how, if you fell for her, then you'd take her with you when you left. You need to know this — so you don't get strung along and hurt."

It was like the earth lurched under him. He reached for the barn door to steady himself. Shook his head. It couldn't be true. He'd seen Letha's love in her eyes….

"Oh, God, Ty, I'm sorry. I can see how she's affected you. How this affects you. I wanted to tell you sooner — to warn you — but I wanted Letha to deal with it first. It wasn't my business. I told her. I did. I told her to come clean."

Sylvia watched the war of emotions on Ty's face, and it was worse than she'd expected. He didn't want to believe, but a part of him knew truth when he heard it. The worst of it was, he really did love Letha. That was clear as day.

"Ty? Are you all right?"

He turned around and walked away, out into the yard, and she strode after him and caught his arm. When he turned on her, his hands were fists and she fell back a pace at the raw emotion in his eyes.

Even with the compassion in Sylvia's gaze, Ty knew he couldn't stay where he was. If he did, he'd lash out. He'd hurt something, like he was hurting. He wanted to run to the ends of the earth and find a new place to be, because what she said made too much sense in light of what had happened last night. Letha hadn't been upset because she wanted him to be safe. The woman had seen her plans go up in smoke. He had to fight back his anger at the news, and at Sylvia, who had ruined his foolish little fantasy.

Sylvia raised her hand again, as if to console him.

"Don't touch me," he snarled. "Letha thinks you're her friend. Some friend. Is everything in the Valley as false?" He thought of Kris' smile when she suggested he tell Letha of his plans, and thought he knew the answer — and it sickened him. "Just get the hell out of here."

He stalked off to the barn. There was no way he could ride Hauberk in the state he was in. This angry, there was too much potential for him to take it out on the horse. This… there was only one way he could think of to deal, aside from hurting something.

He went up to the cabin and opened a beer.

At noon, Letha found him slouched in his Cape Cod chair, his booted feet on the porch rail, staring out at the lake that gleamed silver in the hot August sun. At his side stood eight empties, lined up like soldiers — unlike him to be drinking so early in the day. His hair was tousled, the green of his eyes eaten by an ugly darkness so they were two black pits that watched her approach. She shivered.

"Ty?" She wasn't certain how to begin to apologize, to explain everything and that, yes, she wanted to be with him as he built his dream in the Valley. Even if it meant the end of her dream.

"You bring any beer?" he muttered.

"No… I… Ty, I wanted to talk. About last night."

"I don't. It's better we don't talk. I don't think I could stomach anymore lies."

He looked over her head toward the lake, but still he was too aware of her and her scent of mint and roses. Damn her, for her ability to look confused and so damned vulnerable he still wanted to take her in his arms and tell her everything was all right.

Letha shook her head, not sure what she had done to bring about Ty's anger. She had no plans to lie. She wanted to tell him the truest thing she'd ever known — that she loved him. Loved him enough to stay. It brought an anxious shiver up her back.

"Ty… what's the matter? You said last night we both needed to think and to decide what we wanted. I've done that." He looked at her then, the disgust in his gaze curdling all her excitement. What had changed so drastically since this morning?

He chuckled, and it was a sick sound even to his ears. He looked at her, thinking of their times together, forced himself to see how it had all been a lie, a trap this woman had set for him. "It's over Letha. Cat's out of the bag. I gotta give you credit though, you played me like a pro. Innocence, thy name is Letha."

He took a long swig on his beer, wiped his lips with the back of his hand, and Letha knew there'd be no way to talk to him. Ty might not be drunk, but he was working his way there.

"Damn. Empty, and that was the last. You got more at the store?"

"Ty, don't you think you've had enough?"

"Don't. Just don't, Letha. Your buddy, Sylvia. She was here earlier. Thought she and I should have a little talk because she was concerned. She told me about your plan. You know — where you seduce me in to taking you out of the Valley. You get free and I get laid — isn't that how it goes? When the time comes, you bugger off." He picked up the beer bottle, tried to drink, and swore even though he knew Letha probably was right — he was as numb as he'd ever been. Unfortunately, it still didn't stop the pain that ate his heart.

"That's not true!" Letha could barely breathe. Her legs — she couldn't feel her legs except that they wanted to give under her.

"Don't lie to me!" He came half out of his seat, grabbed hold of the porch rail, and hauled himself to his feet. "You're still lying — I can read it in your eyes. I was just too blinded by your tricks to see it before. The sick thing is I wanted to believe. Even bought you something to show you how much I wanted this to work."

He picked up a long, slim box that had been perched on the railing beside his booted feet. He snapped the box open and something glittering fell into his hand. "I wanted to buy you a ring, but I was afraid I'd scare you. Idiot me."

"Ty, I *was* scared. That's what the problem was last night." Please, let him understand. Please. But the tight feeling in her stomach, the guilt that she bore, said she deserved this.

"Scared of me staying in the Valley, more like." He looked at what he held in his hand, then threw it at her so it bounced off her chest, fell to the ground. "You might as well have it. Sell it. Use it to finance your escape, because it's the only thing you'll ever get from me now."

He turned from her, lurched through the cabin door, and slammed it behind him.

Alone, the lake's silence ached around her. Finally a song sparrow trilled and Letha found a way to breathe. She looked down at her feet. They were still there. In front of them lay a gold chain and diamond pendant that glittered in its setting of rose petals. Somehow she had the strength to retrieve them. Looking at it broke her heart again. She slipped it in her pocket.

It took all her resolve to turn back to her cabin, and somehow she found her way along the trail. A mist seemed to fill her eyes, and this near to the lake her skin was on fire with need that she knew could only be fulfilled in one way. A way that was cut off to her now.

Ty. She wanted to go back to him. She wanted to plead his forgiveness, but the look on his face said there was no room for forgiveness in his heart. Oh, God, what had she done? How had she done it?

But it was clear, wasn't it, in the pin-prickles that burned her skin, in the way each breath hurt. When her feelings had shifted from self-interest to love, why hadn't she addressed it? Why hadn't she come clean — even with herself?

Because she *had* hoped Ty'd take her from here. That admission brought a strangled moan from her. It was her fault, because she had been so intent on getting her own needs met, she'd set aside truth and honesty and the importance of allowing people to make their own choices.

Someone was seated on the store's porch.

She stopped, blinked, and swiped away her tears, saw it was Sylvia, slumped in a chair. Come to gloat most likely, and the thought of dealing with her left Letha exhausted even as the need ignited by the lake throbbed in her. The look on Sylvia's face was grim.

"Not a good day, all round," Sylvia said softly as Letha reached the porch. Something black lay in Sylvia's lap under her hands. Beside her, the spirit catcher swayed in the breeze.

And Letha knew the day had gotten worse.

"No!" She leapt up the stairs, yanked Sylvia's hands away. "Roscoe!"

The Raven lay twisted in Sylvia's lap, one wing bent unnaturally back. The bird's chest rose and fell rapidly, its bright eyes glazed and unseeing.

"I came to see how you were, and Roscoe was hung up in the spirit catcher. I thought he was dead. I managed to get him free without wrecking the damn thing."

"Oh, God, what can you do? What does he need?" Letha smoothed the ruffled feathers, felt the light tremor of the bird's heart. Oh, God, she'd ruined everything with her store and her art and with Ty.

"Letha. There's nothing anybody can do. He's dying."

There was pity in Sylvia's voice, and that ignited Letha's anger. She didn't want pity — she wanted someone to take action. To fix things. She grabbed Roscoe's body and hugged him to her chest.

"Roscoe, you can't die, you silly bird. You make me smile." Ty had made her smile, too. "Roscoe, you're my darned familiar, remember? You have to stay around to make trouble. Even if you don't make trouble, you have to stay around. You belong here."

Her pleas sounded so damned childlike and empty when every part of her ached with hurt and the need to make the bird whole. There was a tingling in her palms and the bird's large black beak moved. A soft croak.

"Letha, it's too late. Let him go."

"What do you know?" she spat at Sylvia. "You're no better a vet than you are a friend. You helped make this happen — all of it. You and the store and your suggestion I have a fling with Ty. And then you go and destroy the most precious relationship I've ever had. If it's forgiveness you want, forget it. Just leave, and don't bother ever coming back."

All her focus on Roscoe, Letha turned away, strode down to the lake. He had to live, he would live — but not through any ministrations of Sylvia's. She kicked off her shoes and stepped into the lake, not really knowing why. Cool on her feet, her toes sinking in mud, but there was warmth up her legs. Heat filling her body, her hands, in a sensation she remembered from the night Hauberk was injured.

She hadn't quite believed it then, but she had to now. It had to be true. She had to make it happen.

Rough feathers under her fingers as she stroked Roscoe's head; her hand gently ran down the twisted wing, easing it back against his body. Be whole, she thought. Be free and wild. Heat and a shimmer and flow in her hands that seemed to move into Roscoe, began to move with his heart.

Roscoe croaked. Croaked again, louder, as she fed the flow into him. He struggled in her hands until she released him and he leapt away, flapped up to the sky. He croaked once more, then swooped across the lake as her legs gave under her.

Pain in her hands. Pain in her heart, and she was just so damned tired it took everything she had to look after Roscoe.

He wouldn't be coming back — not after the hurt he'd experienced. Just as Ty wouldn't.

There would be no more spirit catcher knocking on her wall and no more interludes with Ty. The knowledge hurt, her chest ached with a strangling need to cry.

But she wouldn't. Instead she stood up. She would go on alone. And find the strength to breathe through her exhaustion and the pain.

Chapter 17

Victor Zochenko slammed down his office phone and swore. He'd been fucking blind. He'd been an idiot to leave killing Ty Hunt to his men, and an even bigger fool when he hadn't demanded proof of the agent's death. But then, he wasn't medieval enough to demand a finger be brought to him, even though he came from a country that hadn't raised itself much beyond serfs and lords.

The fact his men had thought Hunt was dead just proved how much of a mess this operation had been, right from the moment he discovered just what Ty Hunt really was.

Victor had hired Ty to keep his wife happy — she was always looking for a new wonder-kind trainer — and to help with Victor's smuggling operations that involved the horses. Ty had been known in the horse world, and had a good rep with the beasts, but a bad reputation with the law — or at least, that was what Victor's enquiries had yielded. Then Ty had proved to have a real talent for smuggling; that led Victor to take the man deeper into his trust.

Damn Ty Hunt. Victor's index finger tapped out his anger on his rosewood desk as he stared out the window to the city spread below his office. Everything had been fine until the cameras he'd installed in the trainer's apartment to catch Marta's little indiscretions also caught Ty making a compromising phone call on a cell phone he shouldn't have. Stupid move on his part.

And then Ty Hunt had had the gall to escape and somehow survive the hit Victor had sent. The phone call confirmed it. Samuels, his 'friend' in the FBI now said no one had known except Hunt's supervisor, but Hunt had been hospitalized under an alias while being treated for serious wounds, and then kept under wraps until he turned up in Williams Lake. No one had known, until said supervisor turned up dead.

Victor smiled.

Knowing Marta's proclivity for meddling, against her objections he'd bundled her off to their estate in the Caribbean, so she wouldn't get in the way. His men were already moving across the Canadian border. And this time he'd be there to supervise.

"We're going to make things right, my friend. This time we will." He slid the brochure toward him, pointed his finger at the man on the cover and pulled an imaginary trigger.

§

Ty knew his feelings for Letha were all a figment of his imagination. They had to be, because a man in his line of work would never leave himself so vulnerable. He'd totally misread her because he'd been taken in by her looks and her apparent aloofness. Hell, she'd used his own trick of step in, step away on him and he'd fallen for it. If nothing else, he supposed the one good thing out of the whole debacle was he'd realized he'd lost his edge for undercover work. He was well shed of her.

That was what he kept telling himself as he drove onto Hunt Ranch. It had taken three days to calm down enough he thought he could deal with Kris, but he wasn't going to let his sister get away with this.

The ranch house siding shone weathered grey-gold in the sunlight. The field down to the lake was a parched gold and the air through his open window smelled of dust and a hint of autumn. The poplars already had the hint of gold they got before they changed for the fall. Here, summer began to fade before September. You could taste it in the cool morning mist off the lake, and it made him feel like things were ending when he should be thinking about beginnings.

Squaring his shoulders, he stomped into the house. Kris wasn't going to like what he had to say, but to hell with her. He'd made a hard decision for all the right reasons. Letha Rivers couldn't change that.

He went down the hall to the kitchen. His mother was there, sketch pad in front of her on the table. She looked up with a smile when he entered.

"Morning, Mom." He leaned down to place a kiss on her cheek and inhaled her baby-powder scent. "Whatcha working on?"

"Just ideas for the show displays." She smoothed the drawing she was working on.

He glanced over her shoulder. He'd forgotten how she loved her art when he was a child. She'd take him and Kris, when Kris was a baby, out into the woods and stop for picnics while she'd sketch wild flowers or leaves. Funny how, as a child, you don't see those things as important.

It was important. Art had given his mother back herself. She might still drink, but it wasn't like when he first arrived in the Valley.

Letha and her store had helped with that.

"Looks good," he said studying his mother's design to distract himself. The drawing showed staggered display stands that would allow the best light to fall on the maximum number of paintings.

"Matt and the boys are going to come over and help build them. Kris said it was okay. Letha talk to you about helping?"

"No. She didn't." The words felt tight in his chest.

"Would you let her know that I'll be bringing Matt over this afternoon to dig the post holes for the stands."

"I probably won't be seeing her, Mom. I'm pretty busy."

There must have been something in his voice, he realized, because his mother put down her pencil and looked up at him with a concerned frown on her face. "Is everything all right, Ty?"

"Everything's fine. I just need to talk to Kris."

"She's in the office, I think. Are you sure you're all right? You have that little line between your brows that always used to tell me when you had a mad on when you were a kid."

"I said I'm fine." His voice snapped before he could stop himself, and the open brightness of his mother seemed to collapse in on itself like a drug bust gone bad. He'd sounded just like his father, damn it.

"Okay, Ty." His mother looked down at her sketches and closed the book. "I've got better things to do. Hands to feed. Time I got to it."

"Mom, don't. I'm sorry."

But she pulled away and went to the stove, pulling out pots and pans, her shoulders a cowed slope for his words to roll off of. Just like so many times when he was a kid and his father had spoken. His selfish, immoveable, sonofabitch father.

Hating himself for what he had done and for being unable to take it back, he left the kitchen. Sure enough, Kris was immersed in a stack of papers in the office. She sat, her hands holding back stray bits of her hair from her face. She'd looked that way as a kid doing homework and he'd always teased her about it.

"Still too vain for a hair-band, I see." He sagged down into his father's chair, then stood and sat on its arm. His father always hated it when he did that.

"And I need you to come busting in here, why?"

"Because I'm your favorite indentured brother and we have business to discuss."

"Sorry Ty. Hate to break it to you, but you're my only brother. That means you're also my least favorite brother."

"And that you have to accept the good and bad." He grinned. "You're at it early. Mom was telling me you've freed up Matt to help with Mom's art show."

"Mom's and Letha's. Yes."

He couldn't even say the name, could he? *You're really something, Hunt. Might as well get straight to the point.*

"So I want to pick up on our discussions about the ranch — the little business deal."

"Little business…." Kris sat back and stretched. She'd wondered whether he'd come back to this. Frankly, she'd thought he'd probably come to his senses. The horse business was a losing proposition most of the time. The proverbial hole in the ground to through money into. "Ty, this isn't something you should jump into quickly. You should think about it."

He rolled his eyes and she saw him stiffen.

"Would everyone just quit treating me like a kid! I'm a grown man, for God's sake. I can make a decision in my own best interest."

"Yes, the petulance is very manly," she said, letting her sarcasm cut where it would.

Kris pushed the stack of papers away from her. She studied her brother. She didn't like the way there were dark circles under his eyes and a haunted look in the way his hair was uncombed and his eyes had flooded with brown.

"Everything all right, Ty?" She said it quietly, but Ty exploded up off the chair arm.

"Damn it, would you just back off? I came here to talk business, not to talk about feelings, or whether I'm all right. I'm fine. Just fine, and I've made a decision. I still want to go into partnership in the ranch. I'd like to get the paperwork done in the next few weeks. I've got the money in a local account. We could have that lien dealt with ASAP and then get on with things."

Kris took a deep breath and nodded back to the chair. "You should take a seat, Ty. I don't do business with men who stand over me like a storm cloud." She said it easily, but she could see the gathering darkness in his gaze. Ty was a lightening bolt looking for a place to flash.

He hauled a straight-backed chair from against the wall and sat. He'd be damned if he was going to act like his father, or look like him, though he knew he had his father's height and breadth of shoulder. He looked back at Kris.

"Well? Is it a deal?"

She placed her hands flat on the desk in a motion he knew was how she settled herself to answer. He felt the little surge of anger that came with the knowledge she was trying to manage him.

"You know, I remember when we were kids, there were times Mom said to let you just be by yourself. She'd take me into the house and make me a peanut butter and jelly sandwich to keep me busy, because you were in a foul mood and she was afraid I'd just make it worse. I have this feeling — right now — that I really need a PB and J sandwich and that I'm not sure I want to have to tiptoe around a business partner." She cocked her head. "Not much good at it, I guess. The tiptoeing, I mean."

She stood up and Ty was on his feet in an instant. He didn't want to admit it, but he knew she was right. He was acting like an ass, and he couldn't seem to control it. "I'm sorry, all right. I don't know what the hell's gotten into me. But I came here to talk. Can we do that?"

She heard the plea in his voice and she knew that request came hard. Her brother was a proud man who — aside from his hormone-laden puberty — was always self-contained. Only something serious could have rattled his composure like this.

"So what's going on?" She settled back into her chair and then reached for the coffeepot. "Coffee? A few hours old, but livable."

He nodded and she poured, allowing him the time to figure out what he wanted to say. He liked that about Kris — from the little bratty sister she'd been, she'd grown into a woman he could admire. He took a sip of the coffee.

"All right. I'm pissed."

"Geeze, what a surprise. Let me guess — something to do with Letha."

Just hearing her name made Ty wince. Damn it, she shouldn't have such an effect on him. She wasn't in his life anymore. She could do anything she damn well wanted and it meant nothing to him.

"Well, that's a clear answer. What little crisis has arisen in lover-land, now?"

"Dammit, Kris. Stop. I'm barely holding together as it is, and one more taunt from you is going to blow the few controls I've got all over the room."

He didn't like to admit how close to the edge he was, but trying to hold a conversation was harder than it ever should be. It was like his thoughts were iron and the only magnet in his head was Letha.

"You set me up," he finally managed to get it out, and saw a frown form on Kris's face. "When we talked the other day. You told me I should discuss my decision with — her. You knew what would happen, didn't you."

He was gripping the edge of his seat so hard he could feel the wood give under his fingers.

"Heck, yeah. I knew it would cause one heck of a row."

The fact she admitted it so easily took him by surprise. "And you thought that would help me?"

Kris's grin spread across her face and she winked. "I thought you'd have one hell of a time making up."

Breathless, Ty stood, but he didn't know where to go. He went to the bookshelves, filled with his father's books on stock horses and Quarter Horse bloodlines and first editions of Louie L'Amour westerns. He'd read all the novels as a kid, and sometimes he credited them for his choice of law enforcement as a profession. As a kid, he'd always wanted to play sheriff.

"Well we didn't." He glanced at his sister. "It was bad. Not a fight. That came later. But she wanted me to leave and I had just told her I was staying. We spent the night together but things weren't good. I found out why the next day. Sylvia came by and spilled the beans. Told me Letha had planned to use me as a way out of the Valley. She didn't deny it when I called her on it."

"Oh, Ty." Kris was shaking her head as if she didn't believe him, and that curled his fists. He slapped the wall to try to rid himself of the emotion — he didn't need to fight with Kris, too — and all it did was knock a stack of papers onto the floor.

"Kris, I'm going to roast a couple of chickens for lunch. That sound okay?" Ty's mom poked her head around the door, looked at the two of them and the papers on the floor, and stepped into the office. "Everything okay?"

Ty groaned. He didn't want his business spread around. It was bad enough Kris knew, but he had to talk to someone, and this whole business deal had brought it up, even though he'd have rather talked to Matt. "Fine, Mom. Just fine."

His mother looked at Kris as if she chose not to believe him, and that set his teeth on edge even more.

"Ty was just telling me that things aren't going so well with Letha, and I was just about to remind him that Letha may have messed up, but she'd been crazy about him since she was a kid."

"Sure. She used that as a way to lure me in."

Kris rolled her eyes and her mother came in and sank into the leather chair. "We women are such lurers. Heck, I know I am. Not that many are attracted — not the right feathers or something. How about you, Mom? Did you lure men into your clutches?"

"Well, luring men wasn't really how I was raised, dear. I mean, a proper woman waited for the man to make the first move."

"Dammit, stop! Stop it, both of you! Letha Rivers and I are over." His hands were shaking and he didn't need to listen to this. He knew what he knew, and they had no right to make him feel like an idiot.

"Ty, before you go off on a rampage again, let me just point out to you that when we were kids and me and Sylvia and Letha were under your feet all the time — well, it wasn't me that was always chasing after you."

"That was years ago. We're adults now." He would not let them change his mind. They might be his sister and his mother, but they had no idea of the betrayal he was feeling.

"You're being a fool, dear. Letha loves you."

Ty turned to Kris. "Fine. I hear you. I'll decide myself whether I believe you. And now I'm outta here. Kris, can I assume we've got a deal, because regardless of this — other thing — I'm staying."

Slowly Kris nodded, and Ty stepped up to her and shook her hand. "Partners."

Then he left, before either of the women could resume the attack. They were wrong and he knew it. Besides, as an agent you learned from your mistakes. He wasn't going to allow himself to be vulnerable to anyone again.

§

Letha fought the emptiness by trying to fill up her days. The first thing she did was take down the spirit catcher so no other bird could meet the fate that Roscoe had so narrowly avoided. She sadly slid the large frame under her bed and felt alone and vulnerable whenever she sat on the porch.

Thankfully the art show was coming up fast, so she cleaned and readied the store, working with Mrs. H. on the details.

In the snug horse stall behind the store, Letha ran her brush over Inca's coat and the chestnut mare ducked her back and stomped her feet.

"What? You don't like brushing now?" Letha stepped back and considered the mare. To keep herself busy, every morning Letha had given Inca an extra brushing. It had brought the oils to the horse's coat so that, even sunburned, the mare gleamed like a new copper penny in the dusty sunlight. "You've always like brushing." Letha stepped up and began combing through the mare's long mane, and Inca turned and snapped at Letha.

"What's gotten into you? You used to love this." Letha considered her horse. The mare was acting just as bitchy as Letha felt, but Inca didn't have the excuse of feeling like your insides had been scooped as clean as a soft-boiled egg.

The sound of tires over gravel brought Letha around. She checked her watch and was surprised to find that it was nearly eleven o'clock — when Kris was going to drop off her mother.

Letha sighed. She'd lost track of time — again. No wonder Inca was fretting. She'd had the mare in cross ties for what — two hours? Sure as anything she was losing it, because she had intended to go for a ride. She had to get the heck out of this Valley just as soon as the show was over. She'd wait that long because she couldn't let Mrs. H. and Johnny and Tessa down.

She patted the irritable mare and released her into the corral. The mare immediately dropped and rolled, giving Letha a reproachful glare. Inca didn't understand that the attention was Letha's way of saying goodbye, but Letha knew. She'd lingered in the Valley too long, lost in a haze of infatuation. She'd wasted the summer when she could have been on the road.

Infatuation. That was all her feelings for Ty could ever be, and she should have realized it. She told herself that every time she thought of him.

So far even she didn't believe it, but if she kept saying it, eventually she would. Believing otherwise just hurt too much.

The RSVPs had been coming in — not a flood, but a nice steady trickle that gave her something to be excited about whenever she saw one of the creamy vellum envelopes in her mailbox. She'd actually started going out to the road to wait for Harry Zigheld's delivery, though she'd stand back in the trees until Harry was gone. This morning there were five more envelopes and she was excited to show Mrs. H. who had said 'yes'.

Heck, she was excited just to have company. What with the summer people leaving, her falling out with Sylvia, and Kris probably not wanting to talk to her because she'd hurt Ty — well, she was feeling pretty alone.

She put the brushes away and headed for the store, finding Mrs. H seated on the porch, looking out at the lake like a queen surveying her domain. Kris and the truck were gone — no surprise.

"Hi," Letha found herself a little bit shy. "You know, I really appreciate you being a friend through all this."

Mrs. H. turned her smile toward Letha. "You've got lots of friends, dear. Kris is still your friend, though she doesn't want to get in the middle of this. She thinks like I do, that you two will work this out."

The sick laugh escaped before Letha could stop it. "Not too likely, when Ty avoids me like the plague. He won't even look at the store when he passes. I actually tried putting up a funny apology sign to try to get him to at least loosen up. No luck." She shook her head, and the memory of Hauberk's hoof beats never even changing a beat brought more tightness to her chest.

"But hey, five more RSVPs came in today. I think you'll be pleased." She climbed the stairs and went into the store for the envelopes and their list of names. "This means we'll need extra food, don't you think?" she asked as she sank down onto the other porch chair.

"Probably. I'll make some more mini quiches and some more sausage rolls. I've asked Tessa to come and give me a hand, and even Kris has offered."

"Are you sure that will be okay for food? These people are coming from New York and San Francisco and Vancouver."

"The food is part of the whole effect. We're selling Primitives. Let's give them the whole experience. Trout pate, venison sausage rolls, moose skewers. You wait. We'll be a hit."

It seemed odd that Mrs. H. was the one brimming with confidence now. Her infectious enthusiasm and that of Tessa and Johnny was what got Letha out of bed each morning. She caught Mrs. H.'s hand.

"Have I told you 'thank you?' I mean, really thanked you for what you're doing for me and the artists of the Valley?"

Mrs. H. stopped her reading of the RSVPs and turned a mild eye on Letha. "It's me that should be thanking you, dear. You're the one who had this idea. I should have seen it years ago, but it took you — always looking out for others — to see the value of what was here in the Valley."

Letha was already shaking her head, knowing that Mrs. H. was seriously off base. "You've got it all wrong. All I did was see the talent."

"That's a talent in itself — and finding a way to give people a chance to grow. That's another talent, too."

"Well — it's kind of you to say, but I think I've got you buffaloed or something because I really don't have any talents at all. Maybe — maybe we both just needed each other to make this happen."

From along the southern lake shore trail came the steady, metronome beat of Hauberk's hooves heading home. Letha had seen them head out early this morning, like an apparition in the mist. At the sight of the huge dark horse moving through the brush, Letha's hand rose to the necklace under her t-shirt. She'd put it on after their fight — still didn't know why, but it was probably just a childish hope on her part.

She should just go inside and save herself the embarrassment of Ty ignoring her, but she couldn't very well leave Mrs. H. on the porch alone, nor could she ask Mrs. H. to avoid her son. In a word, Letha was stuck, so she sat back in her chair and tried to make herself unobtrusive.

As Hauberk came into the parking area, Mrs. H. stood up. "Ty! Fine morning for a ride, I'll bet."

The big horse halted in the space of one stride and Ty's gaze fixed on his mother. He looked tired, as if he weren't sleeping well at night — just as Letha wasn't. Always dark dreams seemed to settle over her in the night, and she woke sweating and wishing for strong arms around her. She missed his teasing and his frequent, annoying visits to the store.

"Mom. Wasn't expecting to see you here."

"Letha and I had business. The show's in less than a week."

"Ah. I forgot." But he hadn't forgotten, had he. It was like a burn in his brain, and seemed to hold far more importance to him than it should — given he had nothing to do with the show. But somehow the date held significance — as if it were D-day or something.

He held his gaze on his mother, fighting the way his gaze wanted to pull to her left, to the red-haired woman who was trying to remain unnoticed. Not that she could ever go unnoticed. There was too much about Letha Rivers that demanded notice — the wild hair, the eyes of mist, the pale skin and the hint of….

He shook his head and looked back at his mother. "So'd you get those stands framed up yet?"

"No, actually, I just popped over to show them to Letha and make our final decision, and then I was going to have Kris send Matt go into town for the wood."

"You know, I've got time on my hands this afternoon. I could go pick the wood up, if you like. Matt's got the whole ranch to keep running. Maybe I can give a hand putting them up, too." *Now why the hell did you go and offer something as stupid as that?*

"Would you? That would help Letha and me a lot, wouldn't it Letha?"

Letha couldn't force herself to meet Mrs. H.'s gaze. She felt color stream into her face as she managed a nod, and was certain that Ty's face held a certain smug satisfaction at her discomfort. She inhaled and finally managed to look at Mrs. H. "Anything that will help this event run smoothly will be much appreciated."

She knew she sounded as prissy as if she had something poked up her back, but she couldn't help herself. *What do you say, when the man you love wants to be a stranger to you?* You try and meet his frost as if you don't care. It was the only way to survive.

"So bring the list over when you're done, okay?" Speak to his mother, not Letha. Make it clear who he was invited by. "Maybe you can drop it off on your way home."

His mother nodded, and Ty nodded goodbye and urged Hauberk out of there at as fast a canter as he could do without it looking like he was running for the hills. Damn her, Letha sitting there looking powerful and aloof and beautiful as hell and like she really didn't give a damn about what had happened between them.

When the hoofbeats faded away, Letha realized she'd been holding her breath. She sagged back in her chair and found Mrs. H. gazing at her kindly. Finally Mrs. H. shook her head.

"You really don't believe it, do you?"

"Believe what?"

"That he loves you."

"How can he love me when I've hurt him so badly?"

"That's just it. He's hurt. He's proud. Eventually, he'll realize you didn't mean to hurt him."

"But…" She looked at Mrs. H. Tell her the truth, that she had planned to use Ty, but love had gotten in the way?

"We all make mistakes, dear," Mrs. H. said, catching Letha's hand. "We think we want one thing only to discover we want another, and by then it's too late. Or at least it seems so. When you're young, the days seem so black and white."

"He has a right to be angry. I was going to use him, and I shouldn't have."

"But you didn't." Mrs. H. pulled out her sketch book and flipped it open to a page of painting display racks. "I'm not going to belabor this, but I know my son. He loves you. He'll come around."

"No. He won't. And before you suggest it, I've already tried to apologize." Letha fought back the clenching feeling of tears the discussion raised in her. Instead she focused on Mrs. H.'s drawings. Wood and nails and display angles was so much easier than the vagaries of human hearts and honesty.

Chapter 18

Even answering all her veterinary calls and caring for the animals in her hospital barn didn't seem to fill up all of Sylvia's time. Nor did it solve her problems.

Instead, her problems seemed to multiply. The elders weren't happy. Yes, her plan had broken up Letha's burgeoning relationship, that was clear, but it left them with only a tenuous hold on the Consort at best, and a need to keep her under close watch. They'd wanted Sylvia to do it, but she was persona non grata with Letha. That still hurt. She hadn't realized the cost of her actions. At the time, she'd thought that things would just be like always — Letha would forgive her after they talked. This time, though, Sylvia had crossed a line that left her with the status 'enemy'.

So she couldn't do her job, and worse, she had begun having nightmares that left her exhausted. They began with an image of the Ceremony, so long ago, and the green-gold light of the lake surrounding her and Kris and Letha. It circled them, and she could feel the power, yearned for the power. She reached, and the green-gold touched her, just as it touched Letha and Kris. For one glorious moment it filled her, and then flashed away. Its passing left indeterminate darkness and cold that could only be the Valley after Letha's departure. That was worst of all; Sylvia had lost a dear friend.

She shivered from more than the cool, late August evening as she filled the animals' water pans in the barn and measured out the feed for each of her patients. Rhatha growled at her when she placed the bowl of scraps in his cage. He still wasn't doing well. His dark coat looked mangy. The poison had damaged his internal organs so that he still suffered from diarrhea and had difficulty keeping food down.

Rhatha wasn't alone in not doing well. Amongst her animal patients in the Valley, there seemed to be a general malaise and irritability that was affecting all of their behaviors. Cattle were off their feed. Mares weren't producing milk. Favorite dogs and cats were fading away or had bitten owners when once the animals had been totally gentle.

It didn't make sense, and it left Sylvia feeling jumpy as a hare when she was out on house calls. Unfortunately, at home things weren't much better. Sure, the mother deer had actually healed — far better than Sylvia had ever thought possible, and that was a puzzle indeed, but otherwise there was Rhatha, and everything else seemed just — off. That was the best she could put it.

She went back to Max, who had bolted his food and clearly was caging for more. His brindled fur was thick and warm, something she appreciated in the cool of the late summer evening.

"So just what is it that's going on, fella? I can tell we're all restless, but I don't know why."

In truth, there was something in the air. Maybe it was the change of the seasons, or maybe it was her other sense, but something — just didn't feel right. It was like something was watching, waiting.

As she left the barn for the yard with its long, angled shadows, she heard Max's animal door flap and then the coyote loped across the yard to her. He followed her up to the house, but she stopped him there. She was not allowing a wild animal to get too familiar with human habitats, that would only get Max killed. But he butted her leg with his head until she plunked down on the bottom porch stair and gave his ears a serious scratch.

"I hope you know you're spoiled," she said, and looked affectionately into the coyote's yellow eyes. Max simply pushed at her hand for more pats. She grinned. "You *do* know how to make a girl feel wanted. Or used," she said, burying her hands in the soft fur behind the ears and scratching.

A glare of light through the trees stiffened both of them. "Better go, Max. Go on."

He hesitated, and she shushed him away from the house until he disappeared into the brush beyond the yard. Sylvia stood to meet whoever came. She could guess.

A crew-cab pickup jounced over the potholes and into her yard, stopping in front of her. Murphy Rogers stepped out and was joined by Kurt Zigheld, Harry's father, and Paul Rivers, Letha's dad. All were clad in go-to-meetin' clothes. Not good, not good at all, because this was clearly a planned show of force by the elders. The three were the most influential men in the Valley.

"Evening, Sylvia. Catching your breath at the end of the day?" Murphy nodded at her. He always was smoother than the other two, probably why they let him take the lead.

"End of the summer, more like."

"There's still Indian Summer. Not winter yet."

She shrugged. "What can I do for you gentlemen tonight?"

"A chair would be good," Kurt Zigheld snapped.

"Of course." Sylvia motioned them to the stairs, resenting that she had to invite them up. In chairs they were likely to stay longer — and to want more. She caught Paul Rivers and Kurt Zigheld's glances at each other; they wanted something big this time. Her stomach clenched.

Kurt Rivers slumped down on the glider, and Paul perched himself on the edge of the railing — not a good idea, given the age of the rail, even with the repairs she'd done, but his choice. Murphy hauled over an old wooden chair and sank down like an old friend just come to jaw a spell.

"Syl, we know you've been real helpful in all these dealings with the Consort. You're a good girl. Always have been."

"Ya understand the way o' the lake," Kurt interrupted. "That's what matters. The way o' the lake."

"What matters," Paul Rivers intoned, his head bobbing like one of Harry Zigheld's hockey figurines.

They were like three witches, surrounding her with their machinations, and Sylvia's apprehension grew. Whatever they wanted, she knew she wasn't going to like it, but then she'd managed to stomach a lot from these men and their families over the years.

"So what do you need? You know if the Valley calls, I'll be there."

"Good words, Syl. You've always done your part, no questions." Murphy, ever the smoother. Tonight, though, his words didn't sit quite properly in her ears. They were too smooth — as if he knew she wasn't going to agree to what they would ask.

The three men went quiet, then: "It's been quite a summer, ain't it, Syl." Paul Rivers said. "Long. Good hay crop. Alfalfa of a quality we ain't seen in a generation, at least."

Sylvia looked him in the eye. The fact they were talking around things made her apprehension bloom into all-around fear. How many times would she have to ask it?

"So what is it this time?"

None of the men could hold her gaze.

"Well? You drove over here to do more than sit on my porch and jaw at me about what a good Valley girl I've been. Haven't I always done what you asked?"

"If ya'd done yer job right, we wouldn't be in this fix," Karl blurted.

"What the heck are you talking about?" Sylvia rounded on him.

"Just what I said." Ever the bully, he stood up from the glider so he could use his height against her. "Ya messed up with the store and with yer sabotage of the Consort and Ty Hunt."

"How did I mess up? It wasn't me making the decisions. You — all of you — made them."

"It was yer idea to break up that relationship, and rumor has it the Hunt boy's planning on stayin' in-Valley. All the problems woulda just gone away."

That stopped Sylvia. Ty Hunt deciding to stay was the most unexpected news she'd heard in a while. Oh, God, what had she done to Letha? She looked from face to face. Karl and Paul had belligerent looks on their faces and Murphy Rogers still couldn't look her in the eye. She took a deep breath.

"So this is all my fault, then. You and the other elders had nothing to do with it." The fear had coalesced into anger at these hulking examples of the worst part of life in the Valley. "You never take responsibility, do you? You get me to do your dirty work for you. You get me to plot against my friend. You get me to do things that ruin my friend's life, and ruin a friendship that's been more precious than breathing."

"Couldn't be that precious, given what you did," Paul Rivers murmured.

"What?" But his comment cut deep because it was true. That she could do what she had done to Letha spoke volumes of her priorities. The Valley had always come first. It had to. And if she was to keep the Valley as her home, she had to do as she was told. That was the way of things. She owed the Valley, these men and their families, everything. But Letha....

She sighed and slumped down onto the glider, knowing that if actions speak louder than words she'd done the equivalent of screaming at the top of her lungs how little Letha mattered. "Letha and me — we were babies together. Grew up together. What I did, I did for you."

"We know that, Sylvia. We do. But we got a problem now — a big one that we all helped create. Letha's going to go and we all know it. Nothing to hold her here, now that she and her young man come apart."

Come apart. Such a nice phrasing for what had been out and out sabotage of a love affair that had existed since they were kids. A lot had come apart at Sylvia's words. Letha's face when she'd come back from Ty's had been enough to tell the tale. She loved Ty Hunt. Without him, she'd hurt for a very long time.

Sylvia nodded. "So?"

"So we need to follow through on what we planned earlier. Harry's willing. We got to marry her off…"

Their faces hung over her, mouths moving, but Sylvia couldn't believe her ears. Not *that* again. Not to Harry. Most certainly not to Harry. She'd seen Letha's face. The woman had put up with so much in her life. She was imprisoned in the Valley — it was too much to think of her imprisoned with Harry Zigheld as well.

Not Letha. Because regardless of what Letha might think, they *were* friends.

"She's not some brood mare to be sent off to whatever stud you pick for her." She saw their momentary surprise at her argument and took that as her opening. "She's a woman, for God's sake. We don't force women to marry. They might do that in other parts of the world, but not here."

"Sylvia, we understand this is upsetting, but what choice do we have? The Valley will be mortally harmed if she leaves. I don't know if you recall — it was before your time — but the bad winter of '67 was caused just by the Consort having to be hospitalized in Williams Lake after she was in a car accident. Led to the ruling that Consorts can't drive. You know that."

"That's history. What I know now is I've meddled too much. I'm not doing it again."

"Ya were prepared to help marry her off before," Kurt Zigheld said.

"And I was wrong. I know who Letha loves, and it sure as hell isn't your son. I swear he makes her physically ill." She swung around to Letha's father. "Is that what you want? Your daughter in an abusive marriage?"

"Abusive? What the hell are ya talking about? My Harry's a good boy."

Sylvia stood up. She'd found her strength in the memory of Letha's face. Her friend. Letha was alone — as alone or more so than Sylvia had ever been. With Ty at her side, Letha'd stood a chance at a full life. What, or who, did she have now?

"Do your own dirty work. I won't help. But let me say this — all our meddling to make Letha's decisions for her — they've backfired every time. Letha deserves her own choices, and they were good ones that were good for the Valley, too. We're the ones who ruined everything. Maybe it's time we stopped and gave the Valley and Letha a chance to make things right again."

She looked out at her barn, the weathered wood gilded in the last of the evening light. Dusk came earlier now.

She'd probably just thrown away her business and any chance she had of maintaining her life in the Valley. She'd probably have to sell, and leave these animals behind. It made her sad, but she knew she was making this choice for the right reason — for Letha.

Turning back to the men, she lifted her chin stubbornly. "I'm not changing my mind, so you might as well leave."

Karl muttered under his breath. Paul shook his head. Roger Murphy gave her a long, last look. There was a hint of a smile on his face as he nodded and started down the stairs.

Sylvia stayed where she was, watching them out of her yard and then slumping back onto the glider.

"Well, that's that, then," she said to no one in particular. Life as she knew it was over and she felt cut loose, like a seed in the wind. But lighter, with a little less guilt.

The flutter of wings brought her head up. In the dusk a familiar, dark bird settled on the railing. It croaked, and the sound brought a chill to her bones and a sense of impending doom.

"Roscoe?" she whispered. "How?"

But she knew, and it shot a shiver of yearning through her at all that she had lost.

§

"Thanks for bringing the mail, Harry, but I really can walk to the mailbox. It's good exercise and an excuse to get out of the store."

Letha knew she was talking too much, but Harry always made her nervous and he had hung around much too long on this August morning. "Don't you have a route to finish?"

"Yeah, but those folks at the far end of the Valley are used to waitin' fer their mail." He settled back in the reading chair and glanced at the books again. "Now 'at winter's comin' ya can get rid of all this stuff and get some real books in. Or maybe ya should just ferget it. Not too many of the Valley folk are big readers."

Letha cast a glance in Harry's direction and could see he was readying to set for a while. He'd been doing it ever since word got out that she and Ty had broken up, and frankly, today she just couldn't stomach it anymore.

"Harry, I'm sorry, but I can't let you get comfortable today. I've got the art show tomorrow and I have way too many things to do to get ready. Do you mind? I'm planning to shift all the furniture around."

"I could give ya a hand with it."

"No! No." She scrambled for an excuse. "I haven't quite decided what I want to do, but I know I need to shift things and wash floors and set up the tables and so on. I've got Mrs. H. and the Hunt Ranch crew coming over to help later."

Looking at him, she prayed he'd take the hint and leave. Finally he shrugged and stood.

"Don't want no one saying Harry Zigheld keeps a woman from her work." He took his bottle of cherry cola out onto the porch and settled into one of the chairs there, his feet up on the rail.

At least she could breathe again, because being in Harry Zigheld's presence always left her feeling like she was tied and trussed, and when she was feeling like that she couldn't think, and consequently things didn't get done. Let him have his cola and leave. She got busy.

Much of her store's stock she had put back in boxes, leaving just enough of a sampling of her wares on the shelves to give the sense that this was a functioning store. Now was the time to finish her cleaning and putting up the displays, so that tomorrow morning all that was left to do was hang the paintings on the outdoor displays.

So far the weather reports said everything was going to be good tomorrow, but she still wished that Kris had the weather control power she'd pretended to as a child; because if it rained tomorrow, they were in trouble. She had nowhere but outside to show the paintings.

She pushed furniture around and began scrubbing the floors, dealing with summer people who came in for supplies and with Billy Fitsch who rode over from Hunt Ranch for his last meeting with his fiancée, Amanda. The young couple had just broken the news of their engagement to Amanda's parents, and they were just about as pleased at the match as the Valley was.

Amanda drove up in her parent's Range Rover, and the two young people stopped in to say hello to Letha, then went for a walk along the lake shore. Harry still nursed his pop on the porch, and the mail truck still sat in the driveway. If anything, the fact he stayed made Letha more nervous. When he stomped back into the store for another cola, putting tracks on her newly washed floor, she realized what bothered her.

Harry was starting to act like he owned the place. She had to get rid of him, but subtle tactics just weren't working and, given Harry's status as favored Zigheld son, she couldn't very well just ask him to leave.

She kept working inside when she really needed to be outside raking out the driveway before the displays stands were put up this afternoon. The sound of more tires on the gravel made her sigh. Another interruption was about the last thing she needed. She needed to focus, and all these minor annoyances just made it harder to, when her body still beat with the needs of the lake and her pain over the loss of Ty.

Someone had once said to her that after a relationship ended, healing took the equivalent of half the length of the relationship. Well, she and Ty had been involved only a few months and it had been almost a month since the blow up. It didn't feel like she was going to heal any time soon.

Footsteps — more than one set — on the porch, and she looked up at the voices. Not Valley folk. She knew the summer people pretty well, as well. Strangers.

§

To Victor Zochenko, Williams Lake was bad enough — a town back of beyond — not even worth mentioning on any map of his. Hell, Vancouver barely warranted a mention, except for the skiing and the harbor that was pretty damn fine for bringing in his special kinds of imports.

He wiped his head of sweat, looked down in disgust at the dust on his Italian leather shoes, and out at the lake that fronted Letha's Art and Store. Pretty enough, but really, in this heat, this was the asshole of the earth, and the fellow lounging on the porch of the store looked only one evolutionary step up from something that walked with the help of its hands.

All in the name of getting the job done.

"This where the art show is going to be?"

The cretin on the porch nodded and took a swig of whatever pink concoction he was swilling.

"You the owner?"

"That'd be Letha. She's inside."

"Ah." All the idiot needed was a banjo. Victor motioned his men after him and stepped inside to a surprising cool. The wood walls and floor glowed, and a surprisingly pretty red-haired woman looked up from her place by the counter. She might be missing the refinements of a New York model, but there were definite curves there and a sensuality about the mouth Victor liked.

"Welcome to Letha's Store and Artwork. I'm Letha. What can I do for you?" Letha came around the counter, wiping her hands from scrubbing the floor behind the counter, but she felt like she was moving through deep water. Something about these men — especially the man in the lead. He was tall — as tall as Ty, certainly — and had almost-black hair slicked back from his angular face, and the coldest eyes she'd ever seen set in tanned skin. They were hard eyes, and with his thin lips, they hinted at a cruelty of nature.

"The very person I wanted to see." He stepped up to her, caught her hand. "My name is Victor Zochenko. I'm sorry, I'm not on your guest list, but my wife and I are collectors of primitive art and I heard about your show. I was hoping to wrangle an invitation to attend, or to be able to arrange a private viewing before the gallery owners swoop in and take it all."

Darkness. There was only darkness flooding into the Valley, and cold. Letha swayed where she stood, barely able to register his words, she was so overwhelmed by his touch. She managed to pull her hand away and stood rooted, looking up at him.

She needed to say something, when all she wanted was to run past him out of the store and to safety. Even Harry's presence was better than this.

"Well… I suppose… I should thank you for coming all this way… for our little show." Dammit, put a coherent sentence together. Just because she didn't know this man didn't mean she should be afraid of him. Was that how she was going to react to men in the outside world?

"You've come all the way from New York?" she managed.

"Yes. Via Vancouver and Williams Lake. It's a lovely part of the world you've got here. I didn't know it existed."

She heard the lie in his voice. He didn't think much of the Valley, but then she supposed she should be prepared for that reaction from the New Yorkers coming to the show.

"Well, it's our little bit of paradise. So how did you hear about the show?"

He smiled down at her like a wolf at its prey, and she crossed her arms to hide her shiver.

"I was talking to the owner of my favorite gallery. I saw this." He hauled out a much-handled copy of the brochure, then sauntered over to the cooler and pulled out one of Letha's few bottles of Evian, brought in at special request of one of the summer people — who then promptly left the Valley. "I couldn't resist. Even more so when I saw the paintings."

He came back to her and fished a worn American five dollar bill from his pocket. "Keep the change. First thing that caught my eye, though, was you and your friend. He tapped the photo of Ty and herself on the front. When I saw the photo, I said that has got to be Ty Hunt. It is Ty Hunt, isn't it?"

Letha found herself nodding despite herself as the guy kept rambling on.

"Seeing him reminded me of college days. Ty and I were roommates. Did everything together back then, but we lost touch after school. I've always regretted it. When I saw the photo and the quality of the art, I thought maybe I could kill two birds with one stone, so to speak."

His brilliant smile almost stunned her, and Letha knew he'd used this charming weapon before. And it was a weapon. She tore her gaze away and looked down at the shine on Victor's shoes. Even through the patina of dust, she'd never seen such a shine. It was almost unnatural.

This whole meeting was somehow unnatural. She sought her voice, found it. "As far as the art show, Victor, let me extend a personal invitation to you to attend. Letha's Store and Artwork would be honored at your presence." She glanced up at him, hoping that was enough, but his gaze locked on hers and she found she couldn't look away.

"Thanks. We'll be here. Now about Ty. Where can I surprise the old man?"

The two men with him looked at her expectantly, while Victor himself held her pinned in place. It was like she was ordered to speak, to tell, but everything inside her, everything she'd seen of this New Yorker, told her to hold her tongue. She managed a smile. "It's such a shame. Ty Hunt was here earlier in the summer, but you missed him by about a week. All these summer people — they come, then they leave, like the Canada geese when the nights get longer."

She saw disappointment form on his face and a flicker of something else that made her feel like she wanted to hide, even though he smiled.

"Such a shame. And here I've come all this way." He nodded his head to her. "Until tomorrow then." And he was gone, the red door thunking home nicely behind him as Letha collapsed back against the counter.

Zochenko and his men paused on the porch, Victor considering the man on the chair. "Hot here," he said.

"Always pretty much hot this time of year. Brown rocks and brown grass — that'd be all ya get in the Valley in August if it weren't fer the lake."

"Well, it is warm, Mr… ah, what did you say your name was?"

"Zigheld, Harry. From one of the oldest Valley families."

"Is that right?" Victor eyed the cretin. It made sense — a bunch of inbred hillbillies. "So I'll bet you know everyone in the area."

The Harry creature hitched himself up importantly. "Ya got that right. I deliver the mail. Got to know everyone."

"The right man for the job, I'm sure. So tell me. You ever heard of someone named Ty Hunt? I believe he's from this area."

The cretin hawked and spat — a habit that Victor had always found particularly loathsome, but he smoothed the distaste from his face and waited.

"Sure I know Ty. *Everyone* knows the *great* Ty Hunt."

The dislike in the man's words was surely something to be used. Victor motioned his men toward the limousine they'd rented for the drive to Letha's Store and Artwork. Some things were better done mano-a-mano. Victor turned back to Harry and leaned casually against the porch rail.

"So tell me, you have any idea where I might find Mr. Hunt? The kind proprietress tells me he's left the Valley." The Harry creature put down his bottle of pop and eyed Victor up and down, as if assessing the value of his information and Victor's intent. Then he glanced at the store.

"Who's askin'?"

"Let's just say an old friend with a debt to repay."

"That so? You come all this way, it's got to be a hell of a debt."

"You could say that."

Harry took a long pull on his pop and drained the bottle, then stood. "Well Ty and I, we haven't always been the best of friends, but, well, fer an' old friend and all — ya might try lookin' next cabin down the lake. Far as I know, he hasn't left yet."

The cretin, his shirt ripe from sweating in the sun, went down to his truck, climbed in, and waved. Victor watched him go, then glanced back at the store. So Ty had his protectors here, as well. Not that it would do the man any good.

Chapter 19

The darkness of Letha's dream swallowed her whole. Caught in the darkness and cold she floundered through snow, knowing they were hunting her and Ty and everyone else she loved. The wind whistled around her and there were whispers caught in its folds. Whispers of death, with a soft, cultured accent.

The end was coming on a wind that smelled only of astringent winter, coming on fast. Through the darkness, a cold white light shone from two matching fonts — pale eyes in the darkness.

She knew those eyes — or ones almost like them. Had heard the smooth voice that went with them. Cold. Bitter. She had betrayed, and the danger came on with a pounding like hooves. Pounding in her head. Pounding that settled into her blood and pulsed fear through her body for...

Ty!

Letha sat up in a drenched tangle of sheets and with the certainty that something was horribly wrong. Her heart pounded in rhythm with the pounding in her head. Pounding that came from somewhere in her cabin.

What? Who? She scrambled off the bed and grabbed a shirt to throw over her pajamas. Darkness all around. Cold. So cold that gooseflesh covered her body. The scent of snow, bitter in her lungs, gagging her.

Still, the pounding beat at her like a hammer on her head. Words. Someone calling her name.

Staggering out to the main room of the store, she bumped her shin on the table she'd shifted to hold snacks at the show. She tripped over a low display of local pottery, barely able to stop a teapot from toppling, then stumbled against the door.

Her breath sounded loud in her ears. The door rattled in its frame with whatever was pounding. Just get her head clear. Just get free of the darkness.

Ty was in the darkness.

That thought brought her upright as she grabbed for her shotgun. The voice, she recognized. Sylvia was softly calling her name through the door.

Letha unbolted the door and yanked it open. "For God's sake, Syl, you'll wake the dead."

Sylvia grabbed her arm and shoved her inside the store, slamming the door behind them. "I almost thought you *were* dead. Took you long enough to answer."

Letha rubbed her eyes, still fighting the grogginess, and wondering at Sylvia Hill coming in the middle of the night. "What time is it? You shouldn't be here. I told you, I don't want you as a friend anymore."

Sylvia grabbed her arm and Letha shook her off, but Syl had that stubborn look on her face that said she wasn't backing off. "It's only midnight, and regardless of what you think, I'm your friend. Something's happening, Leth. I know it. Something's got my animals in a stir like you wouldn't believe. Roscoe pecked at my bedroom window and wouldn't let me sleep. Then Max got started. He and Rhatha are howling like the moon is full. The deer are actually trying to jump out of their stall, and the birds are throwing themselves at their cage doors. Listen." She pointed down at the lake. The sound of geese squawking pierced what should be silence.

"What does that have to do with me?" She was awake now, and had remembered what Sylvia Hill had done to her and her life.

"Letha, I was wrong, seriously wrong, to do what I did. I had no right. I know you would have told Ty, and everything would have been all right, but I thought — I thought like an elder. I thought I knew better — that my way was better. I was wrong." She stood there, pleading in her eyes, but Letha still didn't know if she could find forgiveness. Out on the lake, the clamor was getting worse.

"You ruined everything, Syl. Everything."

"You think I don't know? I ruined it for you and for Ty and for me, because I need you, Letha. I need your friendship more than anything. You show me there's just plain goodness in the world."

There were tears in Sylvia's eyes. So much pain in her voice, it broke Letha's heart. She didn't want anything, anyone to have such pain.

"I'm not so good, either. I did what you said. It took what you did to make me realize I was wrong, too." She caught Sylvia's hand, squeezed. "Truce, then?"

And Sylvia caught her in a hug so hard Letha finally had to pound her friend's back so she could catch her breath. "Friends forever, Leth. Truly. But something's wrong. Really wrong. Like I said, the animals are freaking out and I — well, I had dreams. I fell asleep watching a stupid movie and had this dream of...."

"Ty!"

Syl gave her a weird look. "How...." She stopped herself. "Don't tell me — the same way you healed Roscoe."

"Oh, God, Ty!" Letha was already throwing on jeans and hauling on boots because she knew — just knew — that something bad had happened to the man she loved.

§

Ty sat in the darkness, the single light above his stove the only illumination in his cabin. Not enough to read with. Not enough to do anything — which was just fine, given he'd been sitting here staring into the darkness for the past three hours and imagining a better life with Letha.

Dammit, he had to get the woman out of his system, but everywhere he turned there were reminders of her. Thus the darkness, where he couldn't see the place where she usually sat on his counter, or the chair she used at his table, or the place he'd almost taken her on the floor.

Of course, the darkness wasn't a help in itself, because he kept thinking of the glimpses of her cream flesh as they moved with each other.

Ty groaned. There was no question he wanted the woman, her voice, her temper, her whimsy, and her heart. The issue was whether he could trust her.

His mother had called him six kinds of fool more than once over the past month, and worse than that when he avoided Letha when he helped with building the display frames. Kris's evaluation of his performance wasn't much better, and Matt just knew to stay out of the whole damned mess.

How did you ever know if you could trust someone? Simple answer was, you trusted until the other person proved they couldn't be trusted. Well, Letha had crossed that boundary. He'd confronted her on it, and she'd as much as admitted it.

He frowned and stood, thinking once again of the feel of her with him. Dammit, she'd succeeded far too well in her seduction, too! He didn't know if he'd ever get the feel of her off of his skin.

"Then do something about it, would you? Because this sitting-in-the-dark is getting friggin' boring."

Maybe if he went to her. Maybe if he gave her a chance, she could prove herself one way or another. He would either trust her or be able to let her go.

"Shee-it. And you call yourself a man of action."

He hauled on his boots, ran his fingers through his hair, and stepped out into the night air. It didn't matter what time it was: it was time for him and Letha to talk this out.

He leapt down the three porch steps and had headed for the lake trail but an ungodly squawking came from out on the water. What the heck had the geese so riled up? At night, the air was usually filled with crickets and other 'cheepers' as he called them, but not this.

Slowly he turreted around. The barn. Hauberk. Not that there was any sign of anything, but…. He closed his eyes. Would Harry Zigheld never learn?

Dammit all to hell, fixing things with Letha would have to wait — again.

Thankfully, his jeans and dark t-shirt blended into the night as he followed the edge of the willow brush back around the cabin toward the small barn. Silence rested over the building. Then Hauberk snorted and stomped.

Ty realized he'd been holding his breath. If anything had happened to Hauberk…. He scanned the brush by the door to the barn. Nothing that looked like a person.

Better not go in the front way. That was what Harry'd expect. He bent low and ducked into the brush, intent on circling the barn and coming in the back through Hauberk's corral.

At the corner of the barn he stopped and waited. The night felt too still around him. Even the breeze off the lake had stopped. There were no bats whistling overhead — only the stars glistening. The air smelled of the manure pile and fresh hay and shavings. All as it should be, except for the darned cacophony of geese, and yet every hair on his body stood on end.

He was up and over the rails in one fluid movement and then shifted along the shadowed rear of the barn to the door to Hauberk's stall.

"Hey, buddy," he said softly. Usually the horse would be out to meet him, nosing around for the treats that Ty carried in his pockets, but Hauberk didn't show.

Concerned, Ty stepped into the darkness.

It was Hauberk's snort that saved his life. Ty looked to the noise and caught a flash of something slashing toward him.

Knife. Harry Zigheld had taken their grudge to a whole new level.

He stepped sideways, into the weapon, slamming down on his attacker's wrist. Knuckles — find the knuckles and twist down — but the man was too fast. He twisted and lunged. Ty met him but was driven out into the corral as he grappled for the knife.

The man who stepped out after him was vaguely familiar, but not Harry. Big. Long arms that gave him a good range for knife fighting. Moved like a dancer — light on the balls of his feet even as he moved low, feet wide in a street-fighters stance.

Ty managed to catch the darting snake of a knife hand. He twisted down. His opponent grunted, half went to his knees, then turned and used his greater bulk to toss Ty away.

He hit the fence rail as the man came up and at him again. Just get out.

Ty threw himself at the top rail, swung himself up. The man with the knife was on him, grabbing at his leg, plunging the knife into his pant leg, slicing into flesh so the roll became a plunge to the ground.

The fall sent a sudden rip of pain up his back. He couldn't breathe as he scrambled to his feet. Just get to the cabin. Get to his gun. He turned and plowed into the chest of a man standing beside Victor Zochenko. Shock slowed Ty a split second too long.

The bullish man with Victor slammed Ty back against the fence. The knife wielder grabbed Ty's neck from behind. Squeezed as Ty dug his fingers into sensitive spots near the man's elbow.

"Well, well. Ty Hunt, alive and well. Temporarily, at least." Victor Zochenko stepped forward, 9 mm pistol ready in his hand.

Ty froze. It was hard to concentrate on the dark-haired man, because his back sent a firestorm of pain through his body. His legs burned, and the effort to stand almost took his breath away.

All he knew was he'd been a fool to stay. All his judgment thrown out the window — not because of a woman, though she was part of it — but because he truly was tired of his life in the outside world. A part of him had always longed to return to the Valley. So much so that even common sense and Letha's pleas to leave had not been enough. *So get yourself out of this one, Hunt.*

"What do you want?" he managed. Just get Zochenko talking. If he was talking, he wasn't shooting.

"What I've wanted since I heard your little phone call in D.C. You, dead. Imagine my surprise when darling Marta points out your picture on a brochure for some hick art show. So I came to make sure the job was done right this time." The barrel of the gun lowered slightly.

"I've left sworn statements with the Federal Prosecutor. They don't need me."

"Documents have a bad habit of going missing, Ty. Especially when your friend Agent Samuels works for me. No, you're the last serious threat I need to take care of." Zochenko's pistol steadied.

"Let him go. Now." Letha's quiet voice cut through the night and spun Zochenko and his men to face her. Ty gulped at the sudden influx of air. Letha stood there, her shotgun aimed directly at Zochenko, belying the fear on her face. Sylvia stood at her side, with her rifle trained on Zochenko's helper.

"You think those weapons can stop us? We've got pistols. We can take you out before you can shoot and reload."

"You'd still have enough holes in you to slow you down, and we've got friends on the way. Now get the hell away from Ty."

Ty stepped away from the fence. Zochenko looked locked in place. His man stood beyond him, Glock in his hand.

Ty took another step. The slice in his leg and the pain in his back sent a shimmer of darkness through him. Where was the knife wielder? He glanced over his shoulder. The corral was empty.

Where?

The night slowed as Ty's senses assumed combat mode. A movement from the front of the barn. Not leaves in wind. Not bats in flight. All the night noises filtered away one by one.

Rough breathing.

There, in the shadows behind Letha. A figure, gun drawn and trained on the women. He had to do something.

Take the head and the snake quits moving. Take Zochenko and his men wouldn't dare a shot. Ignoring the pain, Ty leapt.

Something betrayed him. Maybe it was the shift of gravel under his feet. Maybe it was the way Letha jerked toward him. Zochenko spun as Ty hung in the air.

A flash from Zochenko's pistol and a thin trail of smoke. A flash from the gun in the knife-wielder's hand. Then two fists slammed into Ty's chest. They hurled him backward to the ground.

"Nooooo!" Letha's scream telescoped, and the whole night seemed to stretch forever.

Hard to breathe. Pain somewhere beyond numbing. Cricket sounds slid away and so did the geese, the stars overhead shimmied and were gone, the low, harsh, cannon-sound of gunfire, and all Ty could think of in the long tunnel of darkness was Letha, and how he had wrecked things, and how he could never make it work with her if he couldn't even get off the damn ground.

§

It happened so fast Letha barely got her shot off. The shotgun blast sent Ty's shooter careening. He dropped his pistol, but the shotgun only carried bird shot. It didn't kill him, only created black blooms over his face and neck and chest as he staggered back.

Sylvia, on the other hand, had shot one man through his shoulder and spun so her rifle was trained on the other man.

"Move and you get it, too."

Headlights flooded the driveway, but Letha was already running, already on her knees at Ty's side. Ty, her beloved. Ty, who she'd betrayed through her lies.

She grabbed his hand, touched his face. So cold. His skin was so cold, and there was blood — oh, God, so much blood. Blood everywhere, soaking his clothes, and the most horrible sucking sound came from the holes in his chest.

"Ty! Ty, can you hear me?"

He stared straight up to heaven, and Letha started to panic. He couldn't be dead. He couldn't be dead!

His chest rose and fell. She had to stop the bleeding. She placed her hands over the wound, pressed, and felt the suction of the wound on her palm.

"Get a doctor. Someone get a doctor!"

Voices above her, voices beside her. Kris across from her. "We've called, Letha. They're coming as fast as they can."

But Williams Lake was an hour away. Even at top speed, they'd be too late. Ty was dying, and she knew it. She could feel it, like her own blood was flowing away, like her life was flowing away. Light, against the darkness of death.

She had to stop it. There was no one else. Just as there was no one else for her but Ty. Hadn't she healed Roscoe?

She closed her eyes and felt the heat of her body, felt it flow down her arms to her hands that pressed so hard on Ty's chest.

"Heal," she whispered. "Heal."

She felt the tears on her cheeks, but they didn't matter. Just heal him. Heal Ty. Her hands tingled, burned as she poured herself into Ty, as her energy flowed out of her and she braced herself to stay upright. Did he move under her hands? A groan.

Ty's eyelids fluttered. His gaze locked on her. The green was gone. Only darkness abounded.

"Leth — a." It was only a lip movement. A faint smile. Then his eyes closed.

"No! It has to work. It has to work!" But she didn't have much more to give. Still, she poured herself like a torrent of light, but the night, the darkness, was too strong. It was sucking her dry.

"What has to work, Letha? What has to work?"

Kris's voice. Her face across Ty's body.

"Healing. I have to heal."

Sylvia was beside her then, Kris across from her. "He's not a crow, Leth. He's a man. He's badly hurt."

"You think I don't know?" Letha tore one hand away and nearly collapsed onto Ty. She steadied herself, brushed her hair from her face, and knew she'd painted herself with Ty's blood. It didn't matter. Nothing mattered except Ty, and saving him.

"Letha, you can't do this. Not alone. He needs doctors."

"He needs me! Us! His home!" Couldn't they see, couldn't they understand?

Letha collapsed across him and Sylvia caught her shoulders, tried to lift her away, and a surge of energy flashed through Letha. Flashed like a green-gold lightening bolt that Letha remembered all too well. Sylvia froze.

Struggling to understand, Letha pushed herself upright and met Sylvia's gaze. There was shock there, and eagerness, hope even. She nodded, and Letha turned back to Ty, new energy running through her, carrying the familiar taste of old friendship and threads of pain Letha never knew existed. The new force of energy pulsed into his body. Her hands throbbed with new heat. *Heal, damn you. Heal.* She thought of bones knitting, of flesh mending, and tore energy from her friend.

Sylvia gasped, sagged. Slumped, as Letha stole strength for the task. It still wasn't enough. There still wasn't enough power. Letha looked up at Kris, knowing that she was the last hope. "Help me," Letha whispered.

Kristienne shook her head, fear in her eyes. "What can I do?"

"Put your hands over mine."

Kris hesitated, then laid her ranch-callused hands over Letha's, and the night froze. It was like a geyser surging. Like a searchlight in the sky.

Like the sum was greater than all the parts.

At Kris's touch, energy poured into Letha. Not just from Kris. It came from her friends, it came from the earth, the lake, the Valley, the sky, in a huge stream of power that slammed into her, exploded her, lifted her up until she hung over the Valley, hung over the pathetic little scene of a woman frantic for her lover, until she could place her hands across them all and say, "HEAL!"

A single musical note gonged up from the lake, so pure and sweet she knew it had always been meant to be like this. Not just her as Consort. The three of them were, somehow, for the lake. And with the lake, they could do wonders.

Like heal, she thought, as she collapsed back into herself, and over the body of the living man she so desperately loved.

Chapter 20

The sun burst too brightly through the store window and sent Letha stumbling out of bed. She'd hardly slept; she was still so hyped with adrenaline that seemed to flow through her like a fountain, so terrified that saving Ty had all been a dream.

Ty'd been awake when the ambulance took him away. That she knew was true. But the power, the music, the healing — it had all been like a wonderful dream against darkness. And yet she felt empty.

Something had changed.

Shaking her hair out after her shower, after the coffee was brewed and she stepped out to the porch to welcome the day, she still could not understand what. Yet with the sun gilding the morning mists over the lake, she began to suspect.

"Thank you," she whispered, reaching out with her mind. "Thank you for saving him."

In the quiet of the morning with its robin chirrup, the soft lap of water at the lake shore, and the scent of dew-dampened grass, it was hard to remember the noises of the night before. Her sobs. The scream of the sirens. The rumbling voice of the police, and Matt and the ranch hands and Valley elders who had come at the call of danger to their Consort. Even Harry had come.

They had helped her and Kris and Sylvia up and to the store, traipsing all over the floors Letha had cleaned the day before, and would clean again this morning for THE DAY.

At least they had come and they had prayed Ty was well, their voices lifting out over the lake like wings on the wind. Letha had known something was listening. Something great and caring, that she had never fully acknowledged before. And now it was gone.

At least from her.

She left her coffee on the porch and went down to the shore, stripping off her boots to stand in the water. Minnows darted in around her toes and away, just like the fish in any lake.

"I see you. I know you. I'm yours for all time."

But there was no sweet tingling power up her legs. No soft gong in the lake. The power was there — she felt it like a heartbeat in a beloved chest — but it wasn't for her anymore. A slight breeze brought the scent of mint and wild roses that were no longer in bloom.

The magic had moved on.

"Friends, then? Yes?" She bowed to the lake and stepped back to shore, to find Sylvia behind her, the reins of her gelding in her hands. Letha felt herself color at the strange look in Sylvia's eyes. "How long have you been there?"

"Long enough to know things have changed." She cocked her head, her gaze one of enquiry that would have sent Letha's teeth on edge a few months before. Now it only made her smile, and feel concern at the shadows under Sylvia's eyes. They shouldn't be there.

"I'd say things have changed for you, too." Letha held out her hand, watched Sylvia hesitate, then meet her palm to palm. There *was* a tingle there — like what she'd felt last night, and this time it made sense. The same tingle they'd felt all their lives, running out to them from the lake. "It wasn't just me that day when we were eleven. It was all of us — you — Kris — me."

Sylvia's nod was slow as she looked out at the lake. "I couldn't sleep last night. Instead, I looked through a bunch of the old books the elders gave me, trying to find something to explain what's happened. All I found were hints this has happened before, but I can't find anything certain — only references to the women of the lake. I'll need to look deeper to understand more."

Letha sighed at her friend's devotion to the Valley ways.

"The magic's moved on, Syl. Or most of it. From me. I'm not Consort anymore. Spring has set me free." She grinned, and a frisson of excitement ran through her again. "Do you know what that means?"

Sylvia's shocked gaze said everything. So — the lake hadn't chosen her — again. The shock turned to hurt and a tad of anger. "What do you mean?"

"I mean, when I woke up this morning, something had changed. I knew the lake was there, but it wasn't the same. I couldn't hear the grass grow, or feel my dad's diabetes. You caught me checking. My connection to the lake's gone. Or it's changed. It knows I'm there, but the fish don't swim to me like before."

She caught Sylvia's arm and led her up to the store. "A small price to pay, I suppose. For our survival. For Ty's."

Sylvia's silence brought fear stabbing her gut and she jerked around to Sylvia. "Is there news? Is that why you're here?"

Sylvia caught her arm as Letha swayed. "No news, Leth. Not a word. I just wanted to be here to help. This is your day. I keep telling myself maybe I had a small bit to do with it." Her voice was thoughtful. "You're really not the Consort anymore?"

"It's gone."

"Then there'll be a choosing, I suppose." Grief in her voice.

Letha's arms went around her shoulders as a Hunt Ranch truck trundled down the gravel lane and disgorged Kris and Mrs. H. and a crew of ranch hands.

"My wonderful friends. This is more than my day, this is the Valley's day to celebrate," Letha said, as she pulled Kris to her and the three of them hugged. The tingle was there — greater this time — under the warm, girlish friendship they had for the first in a very long time. But when Kris pulled away, there was something strange in her gaze. A little surprise — a little panic, perhaps. Letha kept an eye on her as they got to work.

By three o'clock the place was a beehive of activity, as Mrs. H. directed the ranch hands and Johnny Warner in hanging the paintings, and Tessa Rogers helped Letha set out the food and pop and white wine and Evian on a long table covered in white damask that Mrs. H. said brought a little class to the occasion.

"Are you okay?" Letha asked Kris in a quiet moment.

Kris shook her head. "I'm fine. Just a headache. I've had it since this morning. Nothing to worry about. Just have your day."

She left Letha to help Mrs. H sort out a problem with the displays, but seemed to avoid Letha the rest of the afternoon. Strange, but the pending event took all Letha's attention.

At four o'clock the rumble of engines came from the road toward town, and gleaming town cars and Hummers and Suburbans began to arrive, parking along the driveway next to the dusty and dented vehicles of the Valley. The strange vehicles released groups of elegantly clad people into the afternoon. More strange were the Valley families, dressed in their best bib and tucker, trailing between the displays of art.

"It's our friends' art," explained Maggie Rogers as she dragged past a very uncomfortable looking Murphy Rogers in a suit and tie that probably hadn't been worn since their wedding day. "How could we not come and support them, eh?"

And so the strange day continued, with Valley folk trickling in amongst the people from outside. In the cities they came from, they might have looked like they dressed down, Letha figured, but for the Valley, the high-heeled boots and the designer jeans and sleek silk shirts looked just a tad too tony. Still, the men and women who studied the art were gracious to their hosts. They talked to Letha and to Mrs. H., and Mrs. H. was like a queen, clad in a pale grey pantsuit of flowing cotton, with her silver hair rolled up in a chignon.

The people — even though she'd seen the RSVPs, Letha hadn't imagined there would be so many who would come. She stood aside, catching her breath and sipping a glass of water, as Martin Dietrich came up beside her.

"Quite the event, Letha. Valley's never seen the like. And people are saying great things about the artists, too."

"Thanks, Martin. You know, I never would have done it without your encouragement." She was going to say more, but a shadow at the far side of the cabin coalesced into Ty. Letha stopped breathing. "Excuse me, please."

He stood at the crowd's edge, dressed in a simple western shirt and jeans, his brown hair shadowing his eyes. His form was half-hidden in the store's shadow as he sipped from a glass much like hers, but the way he leaned against the logs, the way his lips curved in a half-smile, she knew he was well; and that made this strangest of days more right.

When their eyes met, he raised his glass and the crowd disappeared. The noise and energy and her excitement at the event were all gone. There was only Ty, and telling him what had burned in her heart for the past month.

She pushed through the crowd, never losing his gaze, ignoring the people congratulating her.

She reached Ty, looked up at him.

"You're all right?" She was afraid to touch him. Afraid he might be an illusion, or might tell her he still felt the same way, even though the look in his eyes told her all she needed to know.

"Right as rain. Whatever you did worked wonders. I don't even limp." He caught her hand and he was real. Really, truly, real. Whole.

"How'd you get here?"

"Matt," he said, lifting his chin toward the crowd where the ranch hand casually shadowed Kristienne.

"Letha Rivers, I have to thank you for sending me that invitation." The insistence of the New York accent brought Letha around to face the speaker. Woman, tall, blonde, in black jeans and an almost-see-through silk blouse. "Signe Rhimes," the woman said as if she could see the blankness of Letha's mind. "I buy for the Fifth Avenue Gallery. Truly, the work you've got here is unique. Quaint, but lovely. Like a visit to a younger day when we weren't all so — shall we say — jaded?" She laughed a throaty, drinker's laugh when Letha could barely find the focus to smile.

Ty. She wanted to be alone with Ty.

"Signe, dear. I think poor Letha is a trifle overcome with the heat and all the excitement. Why don't you tell me what you're thinking as we walk through the displays?" Mrs. H. slid smoothly between Letha and the New Yorker, tossing a smile over her shoulder. "Just go, you two. Kris and Sylvia and I can take care of this."

And then Letha and Ty were alone in the shadows. He captured her other hand, looked down at her long fingers, and thought how empty they looked. He pulled Letha deeper into the shadows and tugged her into him, burying his face in her rose-scented hair, his arms around her body. He'd missed her even more than he'd known.

When he pulled back he smiled down at her, then bent to nibble her ear. "Well howdy there, Ma'am," he murmured. "I was wonderin' if you'd accept an apology and a thank you from a mighty stupid man?"

Letha pulled back from him and screwed up her face. "Would this be a man who had a preference for large brown horses and swimming in the nude?"

"Might be, if the right person is asking."

"And if it was a foolish, stubborn woman, who's too blind to see that the best thing in her life is right in front of her?"

"Might be worth it if that woman wielded magic to save some sod's life." He pressed her hands to his heart and then to his lips, and she felt a sudden concern that he might not be as accepting if he knew the magic was gone. But there would only be truth between them.

"It wasn't my magic. It was the lake's. And the magic's gone Ty. From me. The man should be thankin' the lake."

Ty frowned, then began hauling her through the brush, laughing as branches caught in her hair until they reached Hauberk's barn.

The stallion didn't protest when Ty barely brushed him, nor when he had to stand overlong in the crossties as Ty pressed Letha against the wall, as their hands sought flesh through their clothing.

"Oh, God," she said, panting, as they pulled apart from each other. "Maybe we should do it right here."

"Nope," Ty said, hauling Hauberk's bridle over his head and Letha into his chest one more time for a deep, love-drunk kiss. "There's a principle here. After last night, when you say the lake did this, then it's the lake to be thanked, but we better be damned quick about it."

He swung up on the stallion and hauled Letha up into his lap, then heeled Hauberk around. "Sorry old boy, this is an emergency." He squeezed his legs and Hauberk half-reared.

And then they were galloping. Down the trail, almost running over art show guests, then plunging along the shore of the lake, plunging through tall grass, through lodgepole pine, through the reeds at the lake shore, sending mallards and Canada geese scattering into the sky.

Water plumed around Hauberk's legs, and then the stallion was swimming and Ty let himself loose from the saddle, loose from his clothes, loose into Letha's naked arms as Hauberk towed them out into the lake. Letha's laughter echoed out over the water and Ty turned her, pulled her wild wet body to him, her hair like lake weeds in his eyes, her flesh cool against him just as her mouth was hot.

"Ty! Ty I have to tell you," she said, disentangling herself. There were tears in her eyes and they had to be magic the way they seemed to catch in his chest. "I love you. I'll go or stay, wherever you are."

"And I'll keep you safe, but show you the world. Now, come here."

He grabbed her, and the two of them went under in a cascade of laugher and silver bubbles as Ty loosed Hauberk's reins, as the two of them joined in the lake that had brought them together. Green-gold liquid embraced their union and they knew, no matter what else happened, they had both found their answers in each other.

About the Author

Karen L. Abrahamson once lived in a community very much like Spring Lake that waited overlong for Spring. She is a well-traveled writer who has explored numerous cultures and countries. She is the author of literary, erotic and fantasy fiction and lives on the west coast of Canada with two Bengal cats that aren't quite as well traveled as she is.

If you'd like to learn more about her, visit her at: *www.karenlabrahamson.com*.

If you enjoyed *"Second Spring"* please let me know. Drop me a note at my website or send me a note on Twitter @kabrhamson, or friend me on Facebook at Karen L. Abrahamson.

Books By the Author

Romance
Ashes and Light
Shades of Moonlight
Judas Kiss
Second Spring
Mutable Things
A Different Nightmusic
Shadow Play
Surviving Safe Harbor

Fantasy

***The Cartographer Universe* series:**
The Cartographer's Daughter

Afterburn
Aftershock

Terra Incognita
Terra Infirma
Terra Nueva

KAREN L. ABRAHAMSON
Writing as Karen L. McKee
SHADES
of
MOONLIGHT
Paranormal Romantic Suspense

Spirit Light

**Pagan, ancient capital of Burma
Central Myanmar, Modern day**

Kalla plunged through tall grass and thorn brush, the ornate wooden puppet clutched to her breast. Spirit light glinted like fool's gold in the stone underfoot. It shimmered pale blue from empty, parched fields and set beacon candles of azure and indigo from the tops of the huge step-pyramid temples that loomed out of the darkness. The rising wind scoured her chilled skin with dust, and the air smelled of ozone and lung-clinging jasmine.

And her fevered fear.

She had to get there. She had to protect.

She stumbled across a dirt road. Through a hedge of cactus, she ripped the red longyi that wrapped her legs and half-fell into a fallow field. Spirit light glinted on her skin.

"No." It came out as a whimper, but too loud in the night as she tried to wipe the shimmering dust away. Already too late. It glowed on her skin—seemed to run *into* her damp flesh. Flickering blue light flashed up her arm, even as she lurched up and kept on. Even as the spirit light seemed to stab into her brain.

And then there was the laughter.

She whirled, her midnight hair sweeping around her shoulders and the puppet. No. Her imagination. They couldn't know where she was. Keep going. Keep going.

The longyi's fabric restricted her panicked stride as she staggered on. The spirit light flashed tingling sparks across her skin, across the puppet, as her palm smoothed the antique figure's fine hair and protected the delicate Votaress' features, from the scour of the wind.

The puppet moved in her grasp.

Insanity, the scientist part of her said. Madness to be out here. Madness to be running like this, into the night and the darkness.

It was darkness that had killed her before.

She squeezed her eyes shut and almost fell across a heap of bricks. Small, collapsed temple. Her breath rang in her ears as she picked her way through, remembering how it had been before, whose temple this had been and the fine teak house that had stood here. A memory of pickled tea and garlic, but the air now smelled of sage and slow-moving river water. From the road came the sound of a jeep.

Military?

Cold sweat in her eyes, but ahead the spirit light shone bright blue flame from Dhammayangyi temple. A mountain with eyes, a yawning mouth. A mountain that would devour her; a mountain that was part of her.

Panting, she stopped, listening to the dying leaves chatter in the rising wind and the bats whoosh through the sky. Towering clouds blocked the moon.

She shivered with need, but the fear held her in place. Her mouth tasted of copper and bile.

To go in that place would mean—*ending? Beginning?* Insanity. She was going mad. The fever raged her thoughts into a whirlwind, impossible to comprehend. But she knew what waited. What had to be done. And that others would try to stop her.

But no one could follow her to the place she would go.

She staggered through the gate, the wind skirling wild Burmese music through the crumbling stone. Darkness, a void waited, but she swallowed her fear.

Do this thing.

And she would save them.

Do this thing.

The night seemed to hold its breath.

Do this thing.

The scent of musk and incense reached her on a fresh gust of wind and she froze, knowing the rough breathing she heard was not her own.

If she moved they would see her, but she had to get past. Get free.

A cautious step.

Then heated hands found her shoulders. Spirit fire swept through her and she knew she was lost.

Meet the Darkness

Ten days earlier
Somewhere in central Myanmar:
4 a.m.

Who knew three hundred miles would take over twelve hours and just about every ounce of strength Kalla Jervis had and *still* leave her in the middle of nowhere?

The pitted road lifted under the bucking jeep as she peered ahead through the darkness. The air through her window carried the welcome scents of moisture and life after hours of acrid scrub desert. Cook fires and curry. The strange smells of animal dung and incense. But a whiff of jasmine spurred Kalla's headache to life big time.

She fought the sick feeling as the mutinous jeep slewed around a corner. Damn. She was driving too fast given she had no headlights, but she didn't dare stop for fear this bucket of bolts would never start again.

She tapped the brakes as buildings materialized out of the darkness. A cream-colored bullock too solid to be a ghost lifted its head to stare at her with luminous eyes. Black-stained bougainvillea draped across low wooden buildings, spindly papaya trees, and thick foliage of jack fruit trees and teak. To the northeast, a deeper darkness showed where a lone mountain blocked part of the sky that might, just might, show a hope of fading into dawn.

Kyaukpadaung. Or else she was hopelessly lost. It had to be, by the map she'd studied the last time she'd had light. It meant she was getting close to Pagan and the archaeological project.

She breathed a sigh of relief—the first one since Alex and the others had failed to meet her delayed flight into Yangon.

Soon she could rest and refocus on what she knew—not navigate the problems at home or a desolate country that had far too few street lights and far too many miles of rough roads that had just added insult to her already aching head.

Relaxing, she steered the jeep around a curve that brought her into the centre of town.

Sudden headlights flared into her eyes. Blind, she slammed on the brakes, shielded her sight. The jeep careened to a stop, stalled when she forgot the clutch.

Lights all around—headlights and half-seen figures running and voices yelling—at her.

She fumbled the keys, cranked the protesting engine to get the hell out of there. Her door was yanked open. A hand dragged her out.

"Hey!"

The lights kept her blind. Male voices set off earthquakes in her head. Rice and curry and sweat stung her nose. Hands on her shoulders, her arms.

"Let me go, dammit!" Years of Seattle self-defense classes kicked in and she slammed her heel down on the foot of whoever held her. Jabbed her elbow into his gut. She yanked loose and turned in a fighter's stance as her vision cleared, ready to defend against wild men and bandits.

Not bandits.

Men in tattered green fatigues.

Soldiers, her mind registered. Myanmar soldiers. All with rifles aimed directly at her.

All the heat suddenly left her.

She straightened. Slowly.

Raised her hands. Slowly.

Damnitalltohell, she should have assessed the situation before she reacted. She was always in control, wasn't she?

Unbidden laughter bubbled up to catch in her throat. The whole damn tableau was ridiculous–like a clichéd drawing for a fairy tale or folk story—damsel in distress surrounded by a band of demons. All the picture needed was the handsome prince coming over the rise of the next hill.

Alex would do. Flare of trumpets, please.

At this particular moment she wouldn't mind Alex striding out of the darkness to her rescue. It would be a little proof that she was doing the right thing joining him and the linguist, Simon Renault, on the project.

One of the soldiers barked an order she didn't understand.

"Listen, I'm sorry, okay? You surprised me. I was blinded by your headlights. I didn't realize you were military."

She tried lowering open hands, but the jerk of the soldiers' rifles was pretty international.

So much gun-metal grey, all pointed in her direction. Did they have the safeties on? Heck, did they even *have* safeties?

She could die here and no one would ever know. No one would even come looking for her. No—Dad would look–if he lived long enough. He'd probably get his psychics right on it. Right. Like that'd work.

The strangled feeling too close to hysteria swelled in her throat.

And Alex might look, too, if he knew she'd actually arrived.

The leader of the soldiers nattered at her again. Two men stepped into the circle of weapons and grabbed her arms. They hauled her, resisting, from the safety of the jeep, while another soldier grabbed her keys.

Her stomach plummeted farther. This didn't look like they were going to let her go. What you going to do now, Kalla?

More men went to the jeep's rear and removed her extra-large black roller suitcase and the small trunk that contained her books and precious equipment.

"Hey! That's my stuff!" Because maybe they *were* bandits. The government couldn't be paying soldiers much, by the look of them. She'd heard soldiers on the coast had stolen supplies meant for the typhoon victims. These could be augmenting their wages by robbing unsuspecting travelers.

They unzipped her bag.

"Stop it, damn you!" She jerked in the men's hold. Tried to pull free, and a rifle butt jabbed into her belly.

Her knees gave. There was only pain and indignation. Come on, Kalla, you got to be the careful, methodical, cultural anthropologist you are if you're going to get through this with your skin intact. But....

How are all those fairy tales gonna get you out of this one? She could almost hear her sister's taunting voice.

She opened teary eyes, and the idiotic factoid that these soldiers wore tattered, green-canvas runners on their feet—not boots—struck her as overwhelmingly funny. She was friggin' Alice falling down that rabbit hole, and what nobody had told her was it was really a bottomless pit.

Biting back the hysteria, she struggled to her feet, the grips of the soldiers still too-hot, too-hard on her arms. Others hauled her belongings from her suitcase one by one.

Jeans. T-shirts. Oh god, her diaphragm, brought in anticipation of the reconciliation with Alex that her father had urged. They were holding it up, examining it with their flashlights. The fact they didn't seem to know what it was didn't stop her face from flaming.

"Perhaps, mademoiselle, I may be of some assistance?"

Well thank god, it was English. She twisted in her captors' grasp, but the not-quite French accent didn't prepare her for the man who coalesced out of the darkness.

She froze.

His blue-black hair fell across his forehead in a rough forelock that accentuated black eyes that seemed to drink in everything at once-and find a humor in her situation she just couldn't match. Darkness seemed to cling to him and set all her alarm bells klaxoning. He didn't look French. He was too tall, too athletic, and almost American in the confident way he moved. The fact his high, almost Asian cheekbones and full lips held her gaze just made it worse. This guy was a babe magnet and knew it, and she hated that kind.

The neatly pressed khakis he wore and the khaki shirt rolled up to expose the dark hair of his forearms just reinforced the mess she was: jeans with red earth soiling the knees, sweat-sodden t-shirt from the long drive, her long black hair falling out of its pony tail.

His predatory saunter across the square and sardonic smile set Kalla's teeth on edge. It didn't help that his gaze settled briefly on what the soldiers were examining. One look said this was a man who knew what they held.

His smirk deepened, but he didn't seem to even notice the weapons trained on him. He just waded into the scene with a graceful panther-stride, then stopped and spoke in a long string of fluid Burmese—or was that Myanmarese?-that made the soldiers lower their rifles.

Damn it, if she'd ever been good with languages she'd have dealt with the soldiers just as calmly. Wouldn't she? She shook her hair out of her face.

"I don't need your help." It was a stupid thing to say, but she didn't want to be in debt to this man.

"Pardon?" He said it the French way and motioned around her. "It seems you do, Mademoiselle…" He paused waiting for her to fill in her name, but she'd be damned if she wanted this guy—this Frenchman—helping her. She was dealing with things—or was going to. She tried to shrug loose from her captors, but no dice.

Nearby a car door thunked and she half-turned as a short, barrel-chested man approached. He wore a uniform and one of those over-large military hats that always seemed to go with despotic generals and too many medals on the chest, but....

He barked something and the soldiers released her arms. That was something, even if she didn't want to give the Frenchman credit. She rubbed her biceps, knowing there'd be bruises there later, but all her attention turned back to the too-handsome stranger.

His Burmese flowed like a river; natural. Was it as seductively accented as his English? How had he learned it? Burmese wasn't exactly the kind of thing they'd teach in school, even in France. *All a ridiculous number of questions about a man you're not remotely interested in, Kalla.*

The round-faced officer looked the Frenchman up and down and his frown deepened. He snapped a question, and then held out his hand.

The Frenchman fished in his pocket. Pulled out a packet of documents and handed them to the officer, all the time speaking another of those long strings of Burmese. There was a reason the language was written in its beautiful round script, because that was how it sounded. But this time she caught something. Western words she understood.

The worst kind of news, because they meant this stranger wasn't someone she could just kiss off. The recognition sent her headache jackhammering harder and her vision dimmed, red and black at the edges.

"*You're* Simon Renault?"

Find *Shades of Moonlight* wherever books and e-books are sold.

Romance and Adventure
from Karen L. Abrahamson

If you enjoyed this book, you might enjoy other
titles available from Karen L. Abrahamson at your
favorite bookstore or wherever e-books are sold.
www.karenlabrahamson.com